# Prologue

They both arrived in Pasadena with enough baggage to submerge an average human. He came from a war in Korea that killed a million people. He returned to Los Angeles a hero on the outside, completely changed on the inside—a person his mother barely recognized.

She came from Cornwall, Ontario, by way of Dallas, sixteen, and fleeing a rape she was forced to bottle up. She dreamed of becoming a fashion designer and sang in a quartet back home. But in the United States she left her unwanted baby in Texas and fled to California.

They met at a Catholic Church dance. She hid her baby weight with a loose blouse. Shell-shocked, he jumped under a table when a car backfired. Her mother said they were a handsome couple. His parents asked how old she was. She conceived on the second date. They were married without discussion. They had five children in six years. She was seventeen when Grace was born.

# 1

Amber and Paul played Barbies in Grace's room upstairs. From Grace's window you could see the Magnolia blossoms, white like doves, dancing beyond the pane. Magnolia Street was named for the trees. They lined the sidewalk on both sides. In Winter time the boys wrenched the pods from the boughs and lobbed them in mock battles. But in Summer, when the light shined brightest, the white blossoms waved, oblivious it seemed to the horrors of Winter. The old Craftsman house was too small for five kids. Steve and Bryan stayed outdoors until the last touch of light. Amber and Paul had the upstairs all to themselves. Grandma D would let them dress up in her gowns, put on her makeup and earrings, prance in front of the mirror. That was before she went back to Canada. It was always Amber's idea. Neither of them minded the light jabs from Steve and Bryan because they were the youngest and everyone thought it was cute. "I hope you never grow up," Grandma D said. It sounded like a curse, one she repeated a little too often. Amber and Paul had each other, and Grace. Grace was the oldest. She kept them safe, in those days, away from the drinking, and the violence.

"There was a sister, Amber..." Grace started every story this way. And it never failed to bring Amber to tears; laughter tears, the kind that come out under pressure, not sadness. "...she grew up to be a princess, and lived happily ever after."

Mom and Dad fought constantly. It was a rambunctious house, everyone, adult and child, running downhill, breakneck, and destined. Dad was a bachelor, moonlighting as a father. Mom was a diva, shedding children.

It was 1968, the Age of Aquarius. The tectonic plates of society were shifting in America. The rumbling could be felt on every block. In California, the rising voice of youth and counter culture heralded the dawn of a new era where anything goes.

Dad was a brick mason, who got caught cheating on his taxes. He chose a job in Vietnam with Mortsen Knudsen over jail time. The Rentano family shattered when he left. Mom was left with five young children and an open invitation to pandemonium.

#####

Grace lost her virginity at Dad's going away party. He was leaving for Vietnam the next day. His foreman cornered her in the bathroom off the kitchen, her chin on the sill with her skirt hiked up. She kept still and stared out the window. Steve and Bryan sat on plum branches, shooting buds with rubber band and tire tube sling shots. They waved at the face in the window, she looked away, so did they. The foreman left his sticky mess on the back of her dress. He thanked her, and not until she was much older did she understand why a man so old, so strong, would thank a slight twelve-year-old for that brief yet indelible moment. She rushed to the children's bathroom upstairs, frantically working the stain with her toothbrush and Ivory liquid.

Later, in the kitchen, Mom asked, "Why aren't you wearing the dress Grandma D made you?"

"Amber had an accident," she lied, afraid of what Mom would do if she knew the truth.

When Grace grew breasts, Mom stopped seeing her as her daughter. Grace became the competition. The going away party was an end and a beginning. Dad was gone the next day. When he left, *Family* died. Now they were a single mother and five children and instead of running downhill, they plummeted.

Within the week, Mom returned home from the grocery store one day, and Gloria was with her. Mom needed an accomplice. Gloria bragged how she'd killed her husband in Mexico. It was the sixties. Everyone under thirty was suddenly "anti-establishment". Mom "dropped out".

That first night Mom and Gloria ran down the porch steps and didn't come home until noon the next day. From then on, until the day the family moved, Mom and Gloria were inseparable, feeding off one another, living the Dionysian dream. Grace, the oldest, saw it coming before the other children. The Rentano children had never come first, but now, they were shuffled into the shadows. Pandemonium settled over the Magnolia house: an endless supply of alcohol, open door sex, incense and herb, an unfettered 24/7 bacchanal. They were now on a psychedelic wave that was turning darker by the day.

#####

It felt like the safest place in the house. The upstairs bathroom. Grace, Amber and Paul sat on the edge of the claw foot tub. Grace hadn't spoken with Mom all day. Amber and Paul waited in the dry tub patiently, watching Grace's every move. Grace poured in bubble bath, and turned on the faucet. Amber and Paul faced each other, toes wiggling as the water level rose. Grace took off her bathrobe and slid in with her younger siblings. Grace began to scrub Amber and Paul while they made beards with the suds. Grace worked their brown edges with a tattered pink wash cloth. She reached into the opaque water and gripped Amber's foot. Pink cheeked Amber squealed, inhaled a mouthful of suds and spat. Grace examined Amber's pink stump. "Do you remember how you lost your toe?"

"Yes, Nana. The bike chain got it." Amber's eyes lit up. She pursed her lips, making an "oooooo" sound.

Grace ran the cloth over her tiny toes, slowing around the stump. She leaned forward, searching the tub for the other foot. Amber squirmed playfully. As if seeing for the first time that her older sister was changing, Amber exclaimed joyfully, "Boobies!" She reached for them wildly, delighted at this budding mystery. Paul squeezed in next to Amber and suddenly they were knee to knee with Grace.

Grace played along. Pointing to each breast she sang, "Chocolate, strawberry," and pointing to the water, "and vanilla."

Paul leaned forward and latched onto Grace's breast. "I want chocolate," he said, suckling her breast.

Grace froze. It was a pleasant sensation. She gently nudged Paul away, but Amber did the same to the other breast. It was too much. Grace tickled Amber to break the connection. They both reached for her breasts, giggling wildly, as Grace batted their wrinkly hands away, and covered their bare teeth with the soapy wash cloth. Amber, beside herself, took the ivory soap and pretended to take a large bite. She pantomimed sharing the tasty soap with Paul, who played along. Amber took it a little too far, put the soap on her tongue. She blinked and spat into the murky water. Grace kissed her forehead, started on Paul's feet.

As the tub drained, Amber stared at the droplets streaking down the steamy window. Paul, a year older, followed her gaze. Suddenly, Amber looked at Grace. They all listened for a moment to the music rising up from the kitchen.

"Is Mommy drunk again?"

Grace sighed. "I don't know." Her mouth tightened into a line as she swung her long black hair over her shoulder. She pulled her shivering siblings out of the tub, and buffed them dry. Amber always required more attention. She still cried and laughed easily.

Amber was Mom's last pregnancy. Mom drank the entire nine months. Grace had been in the waiting room when she was born. Amber was so small and red, it was a miracle she'd survived. When Grace looked at Amber, she saw someone who wasn't born with the right stuff. She wondered if she'd ever make it on her own.

"Grace!" Mom yelled. She and Gloria had been in the kitchen all afternoon, drinking and smoking.

Grace quickly helped Amber and Paul dress. They tumbled down the stairs in their natty pajamas and joined Steve and Bryan in the living room. The room was a musty, dark place with age-old drapes, threadbare rugs and dusty portraits of elegant dead people in their prime. A blocked up red brick fireplace loomed behind the small black and white TV sagging on an orange crate.

Grace set Amber and Paul in front of the TV and twisted the clothes hanger antenna. Steve and Bryan lounged on the large tattered sofa behind them.

"Grace!"

Grace rushed into the kitchen and came out red-faced, with a tray of plates. She passed the plates to the boys on the couch, then to Amber and Paul. When she was finished Grace sat with her plate next to Amber on the floor. Steve got off the couch and started switching the channels. Images and faces clicked by. He paused on the CBS news with Harry Reasoner, "Today in Vietnam..." before flipping to *The Twilight Zone*, "You unlock this door with the key of imagination..." and the stoic Rod Serling.

Amber pointed up at the screen. "Daddy!"

Gloria came in from the kitchen drying her stained hands on a ghastly red dish towel. As the door swung wide, Grace spied Mom leaning over the kitchen sink, her hair dripping blood red. "That's not your Daddy. He's dead by now." Gloria turned the volume down and returned to the kitchen. Everyone stopped eating.

"Is Daddy dead?" Amber asked. She was ready to blow, lips quivering, eyes glazed. Grace shoved a spoonful of food in

Amber's mouth. Amber chewed slowly, blank faced, eyes back on the screen.

Later upstairs, Grace slid in next to Amber. Paul was already asleep in his little bed against the wall. Grace listened to their slow breaths rising and falling. Mom was downstairs ranting. She wondered if she still loved them, if she ever had.

#####

Grace didn't like the new color of Mom's hair. And she didn't like being housebound. Even if she had friends, she could no longer trust Mom and Gloria to watch Amber and Paul. She watched from the shadows as Mom spent less and less time with her children, and in those infrequent moments she was impatient and harsh. Starting on Friday night the kitchen door was locked. Come Saturday morning the kids were herded out the front door—banished for the day.

The family was adrift, headless and fractured.

One Saturday Grace, Amber and Paul grazed the dandelion lawn for Skippers; Grace taught them how to catch the little butterflies without hurting them, to house them in a Ragu spaghetti sauce jar. Amber limped on the stiff brown grass; the nub on her lost toe was still raw. Paul showed Grace the wing dust on his thumb and forefinger. Presently, Mom called them into the house.

All the kids crammed onto the couch. Mom strutted in front of them, waving her cigarette. "This place is a mess," she declared. They'd never seen her in shorts, let alone red, white and blue hot pants. They were struck by the purple web of varicose veins and her shocking pale thighs. Gloria hovered behind her, sipping from a frosty glass.

"You don't get dinner until it's all cleaned up," Mom slurred. "Boys, you clean up the front yard. Girls, you're inside. Dust, vacuum and make sure everything is picked up." She lit another cigarette on the butt of the last. The children waited for her next volley.

"I've got special friends coming over tonight. If you make it look real nice, you can have pizza for dinner." The kids looked at one another. Had she forgotten? They'd had pizza every day that week. Mom stormed back to the kitchen. Steve and Bryan ran outside.

Gloria stood on the porch scratching a rash on her neck. Steve and Bryan chased each other across the knee high lawn, kicking the downy afros off of Dandelions. "Get busy, you two!" she yelled.

Grace, Amber and Paul got right to work picking up. They started upstairs in the boys' room. "Put the dirty clothes in the hamper," Grace instructed. They weren't much help, but it was better to keep them busy. Grace opened the drapes, a cloud of dust was caught in the sunlight. Amber and Paul were awestruck by the slow motion cloud. Amber jumped off the bed and swatted the moving light. To her delight, the floating dust scattered in the current. Paul joined her. He tried to write his name in the cloud, tracing it over and over. Amber blew the floating dust toward the window. Paul joined her until they lay dizzy and out of breath on Bryan's bed. Grace watched them, amused at first. Spurred by fear, of a beating or worse, she opened the window. The soft morning breeze cleared the dust away. "Let's get this done so we can get some pizza," she said.

Amber and Paul dragged the hamper out of the closet and began filling it with clothes. They held up each article, giggling at the size of their brothers' pants. They spent a half hour in the boys' room, before moving on to their room, and then the bathroom. The work was slow. Grace kept them close, double duty, they were so young and disinclined to work. After an hour they took a break in the living room.

Amber and Paul waited on the couch while Grace went into the kitchen to get them water. When she was out of earshot Paul pulled something out of his pocket.

"Grace!" Amber yelled, grimacing at the matches.

"Shush! They're mine!" he said proudly.

Grace walked through the door with three glasses of water. Paul tucked the matches back in his pocket. They drank their water and after a few minutes went back to work.

Grace handed Amber and Paul damp rags and directed them to dust the living room.

Grace didn't see Paul sneak into the closet, but soon, she saw smoke gathering at the bottom of the front door. Flames licked at the bottom of the closet door. Grace gathered up Amber and scanned the room for Paul. She ran into the kitchen. Mom and Gloria recoiled. "Fire!" Grace screamed. They all rushed out to the back yard.

"Where's Paul?" Mom asked, running up the driveway.

Smoke billowed out the front window over the porch. Flames pummeled the window overlooking the porch. Grace and Mom ran up the steps, covering their faces. Inside, the closet was a wall of flame. Grace banged the flashing next to the window. "Paul, come on!" The heat forced them off the porch. The fire truck arrived as the window by the front door shattered.

"Is everyone out of the house?' the Chief asked. The rest of the firemen kicked in the front door, and sprayed down the closet. The red hibiscus bush by the porch was singed and sagging.

"Paul is missing," Mom said, her hands on her waist. "He's got..."

Her voice trailed off as she focused on something over the Chief's shoulder.

She pointed. "There he is!"

Paul walked up the street staring at his shoes. Grace ran to him, knelt in front of him and hugged him. "Where were you?" She tensed, knowing her Mom's eyes were on her back. She shielded Paul as they returned to the sidewalk where everyone was standing.

The firemen in the house rumbled down the steps. "We caught it just in time," one said, winking at the kids. Everyone waited. Paul looked from Grace to the Chief, and then back to

Mom. His chin dropped to his chest. He reached into his pocket and held out the matches.

Mom grabbed the matches. "Where did you get these?" she screamed.

Even the Chief took a step back.

Mom lunged toward Paul. "Where did you get these?"

"I found them," he mumbled, beginning to shake.

The Fire Chief stepped between them. "What happened, son?" He was a white-haired gentlemen with a brush mustache.

Paul took a deep breath. He wiped his nose on his t-shirt. "I was making a rocket ship."

Paul looked up at Mom and Gloria. He shook so hard Grace thought he might wet himself. She wanted to run away with Paul, just then. She could take Amber and Paul, and live with Grandma D in Canada. Amber took Paul's hand. She put her free thumb in her mouth.

The Chief turned to Mom, who was still glaring at Paul. "Ma'am, Please come with me. I have some questions."

Gloria scowled at the fire chief. She shadowed them for a few steps, then retreated to the porch. She turned at the top of the steps, surveying the damage. In a moment she marched around the side of the house. "Come on! In the kitchen...now!"

The children followed Gloria, shoulders sagging for what was about to come. They filed in the back door, dazed. The smoke was still thick. A kidney shaped puddle filled the entryway. Gloria herded them into the living room and turned on the TV. When the pizza came Mom didn't say a word. She dropped the pizzas on the rug, stomped back to the kitchen. They ate pizza in silence. The smell of soggy char was so strong, they kept all the windows open. It was dark out, and the fresh evening breeze brought in moths and made them shiver.

Mom and Gloria stayed in the kitchen. Grace thought it frightful that, for the first time since her Dad left, there were no guests over, no music, and not the slightest murmur. All she could hear was the sound of chewing. It was the worst pizza she'd ever had. At that moment the warmth of Amber and Paul leaning close seemed like an aberration, the calm before the storm.

Then it happened.

Gloria burst into the room making a beeline for Paul. She grabbed his arm roughly and pulled him to his feet. Steve jumped off the couch and lunged at Gloria. It was a long time coming. He struck Gloria in the small of her back with all his might. She turned, twice his size, and slapped him across the room. Grace jumped to her feet. Amber was upended; she began to wail at an ear-piercing pitch. Paul shook his head. "I'm sorry, I'm sorry!" he repeated over and over, dragging his feet. At the kitchen door, he grabbed for the jamb but missed. Gloria kicked him in the rump, propelling him through the doorway in one motion.

Paul whimpered when he saw Mom sitting at the kitchen table. Her foot jiggled wildly as she blew smoke up into the kitchen light overhead. Gloria dragged Paul to the stove. He fell to his knees, trying to lay flat, to root into the linoleum floor. It was hopeless. Gloria was too strong. She yanked him off the floor, and now he was inches from the stove. She turned on the burner. The flaming blue ring hissed. Grace and Steve rushed toward them. Gloria picked up a pan on the stove and hurled it inches above their heads. The pan bounced off the kitchen door, leaving a massive dent. Paul looked at his Mom one last time. Mom was a statue now, avoiding his eyes. A slow rising feral cry escaped Paul. Gloria placed his hand over the flame. He began to dance as his eyes grew wild.

Grace leaped forward, clutching air, inches from Paul now. Gloria picked up the iron skillet from the back burner. She swung it toward Grace, grazing her forehead.

Gloria screamed in Paul's face, "Are you going to play with fire?"

Grace brushed her hand across her face, it was painted in blood. She rushed toward Mom.

A cat-like scream froze them. All eyes turned to the kitchen door, where Amber stood wide-eyed—a trickle running down her leg.

#####

The word *Divorce* was new to them. Grace heard it for the first time when she was in the kitchen putting margarine on Paul's blistered fingers. She stayed home from school now to watch Paul and Amber. They stayed upstairs mostly. Hungover, Mom and Gloria ignored them; *his* injuries were *her* business now. Grace stole glances at them while Paul licked the excess margarine off his wrist. They were in an adult orbit she found suffocating.

Later, Grace and Steve met in his room, away from the other kids. Last night was an especially raucous affair: wine and liquor bottles, overflowing ashtrays and a shredded Doors album cover were all scattered about the living room. The room reeked of sulfur, the origin of which was a mystery. She hadn't noticed it last night.

They met to confirm what they'd both heard, fragments of conversation, up through the floor.

"We're moving," Grace said.

"I know. Where?"

"Highland Park," she replied.

"Why?"

"To get away from Dad."

"What's a divorce?" Steve asked.

"It's when families are separated."

"Oh."

They sat there in silence, facing one another like adults they'd seen on TV. The house was eerily quiet. Grace wondered if he knew. He seemed so impassive, never a word about what Mom was doing, or if he missed Dad. Grace wanted to tell him about last night, how Mom had awakened her hours after all the other children were asleep, when the party was peaking, and the living room was wall-to-wall people. How Mom had taken her by the arm

—still in her nightgown—and guided her to the master bedroom next to the living room, and how Mom's friends took turns lying on her, while Mom stood in the doorway drinking and dancing. Steve was the man of the house, he helped keep the kids in line. *There was nothing he could do*, she thought. Yet, it was the way he *didn't* look at her, instead staring off her shoulder to the Magnolia trees out by the curb. He knew. When he did look her in the eye Grace looked away. She stood up and stretched her back. Her limbs ached, her pubis a screaming bruise. They separated without a plan.

Downstairs, they skirted the mess and headed out the front door on their way to the backyard, where the rest of the kids were messing around. They didn't tell Bryan, Paul or Amber what was about to happen. They sat still on the porch watching the other kids —too engrossed in their play to see the change whirling about them.

Mom and Gloria came home on the backs of a pair of Harleys. The children watched as they stumbled by on the arms of two leather-vested behemoths. When the stereo kicked in, Grace and Steve's eyes met. They jumped off the porch and the others followed. The children spent the rest of the day walking along the Rose Bowl parade route, noticing things they hadn't before— stopping at the slightest whim, marveling at the rose bushes the residents nurtured for the once-a-year event. On a perfectly manicured lawn, they lay on their backs as Grace told a story of the time they'd walked to the parade, together as a family. She found herself talking incessantly. Amber held her hand so tight, it felt like they'd fused together.

At one point, near Magnolia Street, she walked in silence, listening to the pitter-patter of Amber's imbalanced feet. She longed to be young and innocent and oblivious. Lost in thought, she walked past their house, stopping only when she realized everyone had gone in, and she was down the block alone.

When she came in the front door the kids were all sitting still on the couch. Mom stood over them, just about to light a Viceroy. She motioned with the unlit cigarette for Grace to sit down.

"We're moving to Highland Park. We're only taking what we can fit in the Pontiac. We're leaving tonight." Mom threw her cigarette into the fireplace and returned to the party in the kitchen. A volley of laughter boomed from the cloistered adults. The children sat in the still smog of Mom's words as if their next breath would stop the world from turning. Finally, they stirred, the older ones first, the younger ones in tow.

After hearing the news the children let loose a torrent on the house. It was not a planned assault. Steve stampeded them to the shed, where they found their father's scaffolding pipes. Next, he led them upstairs to the boys' room. They took turns ramrodding the poles into the wall until they made a jagged passage to the girls' room. Grace, Amber, and Paul ramrodded from the other side. It took them ten minutes to break through. From there it was only a matter of widening the opening, until, in less than fifteen minutes, the entire family stepped, one by one, giggling and coughing, through to the other side. At one point Amber went to the window to watch the Magnolia blossoms wave. Their white petals seemed to be saying goodbye.

Gloria yelled up the stairs and the mood shifted back to the job at hand. They packed their clothes in trash bags, stepping over piles of wood slat and sheetrock.

Within the hour, they were all waiting on the porch steps, ready for transport to Highland Park, a house, and place they'd never seen. All they'd known was Magnolia Street: the trees, the alleys, the sidewalks, the railroad tracks and the penny candy store. After herding Amber and Paul onto the porch Grace crept into her parents' room.

The bed loomed like a sacrificial slab, and her legs felt weak, as she edged into the musty space. In spite of her fear, Grace was compelled to find something, but she couldn't quite grasp what it was; some proof that they'd been there, been a family. Mom and

Gloria's laundry mixed together on the bed. A plastic gallon of vodka sat on the bedside. The curtains were drawn, and an extra blanket was pinned to them, keeping the light out. She spied herself in the mirror of the bureau, saw a pretty young woman she didn't feel like.

She went to the closet. The doors were offtrack, but she was able to wrench one free. There were boxes stacked in the back behind old, musty coats. She pulled out a box marked "albums". One album was labeled "Mama and Papa Rentano" She turned the leather bound cover and went from page to page, touching some old photos of her father's parents when they still had dark hair. She liked how she resembled her grandmother. She heard the Pontiac's horn and frantically flipped the thick pages. At last, she found a photo of her grandparents with a toddler. She recognized the sweater. SHE was in her grandfather's arms. The expression on his face was one of pride, and in his massive palm, her doll-like hand lay. She had a sudden flash of playing with those strong hands, their permanence and the aroma of pipe tobacco.

Grace turned the photograph over. *Grace Anne, 2yrs.* Only Mama and Papa called her that. Grace turned suddenly at the sound of Mom's voice on the porch. She returned the photograph to its plastic sleeve. She emptied a box of old ribbons and bows and placed the albums inside. A silver-framed picture lodged between two albums caught her eye. It was a new photo, obscured intentionally, it seemed. It was their family, all dressed up in Christmas clothes, and she suddenly remembered the day they'd spent making the memory. It was a dream day because it was Christmas in February. Paul sat with his legs crossed in the front row, she was in the back row with Amber on one side and Steve on the other. Bryan, in suspenders, knelt next to Paul. She remembered holding onto Amber's dress from behind to keep her from squirming. Even so, Amber's face was blurred and upturned to her. Paul wasn't smiling.

When she lumbered across the porch, Mom was in the driver's seat of the old Pontiac station wagon. The rest of the kids watched Grace cross the lawn. Grace loaded the box into the back and closed the tailgate. She pulled some of Mom's old coats over the box. As they pulled away from the curb, Amber sat on her lap. Paul cried next to her. She took one last look at the house on Magnolia Street.

# 2

In Highland Park, Mom left Grace to settle the kids into the house on the hill. She'd found a biker gang at a local bar, and the kids watched her complete her transformation. No more *Leave it to Beaver*, she was full tilt *Easy Rider*. She pulled off on the back of a Harley, clutching the midriff of a bear named Jimmy. She was going to a rock concert at the Santa Clara Fairgrounds. Grace and Steve went food shopping with some money Mom left on the counter. Grace made the meals she knew: beans, spaghetti, chili, cheese and peanut butter sandwiches, cold cereal. The creaky house was quiet, and after the first nights alone without adults, they settled in to explore their new surroundings. It was a dilapidated old Victorian, with a subterranean garage, and a large bricked patio in the backyard. There was a big avocado tree for the boys to climb, and it didn't take long for Steve to hang some ropes for a swing. They had their squabbles, but on the whole, life without adults was tenable. Sadly, Grace knew their world without adults would not last—Mom and her new lifestyle would return.

After a month at the Highland Park house, Mom gave up the boys. While the girls were popular pets at the revolving parties, the boys were out of place, mugging the guests, hackles up their backs.

Mom wrote Dad in Vietnam that he needed to come get them. She would keep the girls. The die was set.

When Dad returned from Vietnam he seemed different, prone to violent outbursts, quick to strike. He'd escaped capture in Saigon, it was told, and now with the divorce final, and the boys in his grasp, he set forth to do-the-right-thing.

On the day the boys were taken away few words passed between them. Dad was a long-haul trucker now and showed up in a shiny new diesel truck. It was a massive spectacle on their quiet street. The neighbors gawked from doorways. The boys were seduced by the thirty tons of mobile steel, rubber and chrome. They climbed into the cab, giddy and unsuspecting.

Grace and Amber stood on the curb holding hands. *Divorce.* It's when families are separated. Grace smiled up at Paul, who was now sitting on Steve's lap. He'd never sat on Steve's lap before and was squirming uncomfortably. Her face twisted uncontrollably. He was smiling, but she knew him too well, enough to see that his eyes did not match his smile. His lower lip quivered, but he was smiling and tears were running down his cheeks. She let go of Amber's hand, stepped onto the ladder step, and wiped his face with the sleeve of her sweater. She descended and retrieved Amber's hand. Dad blew the air horn, frightening a murder of crows to flight from the pepper tree in the yard. At the bottom of the hill, the truck veered toward the freeway. Grace stared at the asphalt. Amber was strangely silent beside her. The boys were out of sight, but she could still hear the diesel shifting gears, diminishing, as solitude and their new life began to fuse.

#####

Grace *was* alone without the boys. Mom and her friends did their own thing. Amber teetered between them. Grace watched Mom dangle Amber before her guests like candy. For the first few days after the boys left, they had dinner at the table in the kitchen. Mom wore an apron over her daisy patched bellbottoms and made boxed macaroni and cheese with ketchup. Jimmy joined them, smiling lustily at Mom, and winking at Grace. Those were the last family meals they shared. Jimmy lasted a week until Mom caught him going into the bathroom when Grace was taking a shower. Mom went on a bender. "You little whore!" Mom screamed, drunk again. So Grace and Amber spent the night in the musty garage. It was a cycle that would repeat until the day Grace left.

Grace was embarrassed by her mother: halter tops, hot pants, and tight paisley stretch pants. She acted with a peculiar amnesia toward the last thirteen years of family life. And Grace hated the way her boyfriends looked at her.

It was New Years and the buzz of a party vibrated around them. Grace lived in the garage now. Amber waddled between the house and the garage. Large swarthy men accessorized with women, leather and fur-clad, with more skin than she'd ever seen, traipsed up the walkway, and filled the house to a breaking point. The Sixties glow was now a toxic haze. Mom sent Amber down to the garage. Amber called it "the fort". Grace loved how Amber made things fun for herself. While the party raged all around her, Amber built a tent in the middle of the garage out of stained bed sheets. She pulled the old black and white TV they'd brought from Magnolia Street in with her and stayed there for hours, arranging her Barbies and the little snacks she'd stockpiled—Pop Tarts, Fig Newtons, and her favorite cup. As Grace escaped down the back steps to check on Amber, Mom stopped her.

"Gracie. Amber can take care of herself," she said, flicking ash into a beer can. Grace hesitated. The hairs on the back of her neck lit up. She nodded and pointed toward Amber and the garage. "Don't be long." Mom smiled. Grace's senses heightened. Mom was being too nice and her eyes were glassed over. She had an instant flashback of the night she'd been pulled into Mom's room, sleepy and pliable. She would be ready this time.

Down in the garage, Grace checked on Amber before returning to the party. Amber seemed so plump and happy in her own little world. She envied her.

Walking up the path to the house, Grace passed a group of leathery men in the backyard. She felt their eyes plaster her backside as she ascended the steps. The kitchen was full of thick, painted women, laughing loudly at nothing in particular, and everything, all at once. Grace looked around. No one her age.

"That's Marie's daughter. Isn't she cute?" a platinum blonde announced as she slid by.

Grace rushed through the kitchen. Before she could get out of reach the blonde handed her a bottle of wine. "Here, honey. Let your hair down."

Grace obediently took the bottle. She carried it into the living room, where Mom was squeezed onto the couch with another couple. The man of the pair had a long blond ponytail, and his face was disturbingly pocked. Mom waved for her to sit next to him.

The room was hazy and wall-to-wall people packed together, some making out, most smoking joints. A big tray of green dope sat on the coffee table for the taking. The lusty ladies from the kitchen migrated into the living room, and their momentum pushed Grace toward the couch. Mom was making out with the woman of the couple, to the delight of a nearby group of men. When Grace neared the couch, Pocked Face grabbed her hand and pulled her onto his lap. He was hard. Grace reached for her mother's arm, but all she got was a flaccid breast. Mom moaned and threw her leg over the woman's thigh. Pocked Face grabbed the wine bottle, twisted the lid off with his teeth and held it to her mouth. He stroked her hair. "You hot, baby," he slurred into her neck. Grace grabbed the bottle, pretended to take a sip, put the bottle on the table with the dope. Grace looked at the faces around her. Some were watching, others held up the walls, already obliterated. Pocked Face ground his crotch into her. Bile rose in her throat, paired with a jittery impulse to flee. She nudged her Mom with more force than intended. Mom turned, annoyed. Her red lipstick was smeared across her chin.

"What?" she said, harshly. Her eyes lit up when she saw what Pocked Face was doing. "Well?" she slurred. Pocked Face took a large clump of Grace's long black hair in his grasp. He tugged her head back to kiss her, and in the struggle Grace kicked out, knocking the tray of dope and the wine bottle onto the carpet.

In the chaos, Grace rushed toward the bathroom, eyes darting around the room. She squeezed through a gauntlet of meshed adults. Everyone was with everyone, it seemed. Finally, in the bathroom, she closed the door and locked it. The bathroom never seemed smaller. The walls knocked around her. She sat on the toilet seat rocking and trying to catch her breath. She wanted to scream, but drawing attention to herself was the last thing she needed. She clutched her knees to keep them from shaking. The next emotion surprised her, but she welcomed it. Her hands clenched in rage, her eyes seeing only Mom's impassive face. *Well?* She jumped up and kicked the bathroom door. The truth was all around her, pressing in. She was alone. She would need to be there for Amber. Mom was lost, forever. *I will never do this to my...*

Someone knocked on the door. Grace held her breath and waited. Finally, the knock came again. "Hey, baby. You cool?" *Pocked Face.*

Grace didn't wait. She opened the window and slipped out onto the roof. She edged along the house, aware of the group of men in the yard below. She worked her way toward the corner, slid down on her bottom to the gutter, turned onto her belly, shimmied over the side, suspended by her fingertips. She dropped onto the soft grass near the side gate. Heart pounding, she crept along the side of the garage and disappeared through the door.

The garage was an empty shell compared to the house. Her heart leaped out of her chest at her next thought. *She's gone,* or worse yet, they took her! Grace dove under the sheet. Amber smiled up at her. Amber had found a tube of airplane glue and had gotten the cap off. A glistening gob of glue was stuck on her upper lip. Amber's glazed stare confirmed her fear.

"Give me that. Amber!" Grace resisted the impulse to slap her. Instead, she took Amber in her arms. Amber was limp at first, then slowly wrapped her arms around Grace. They sat entwined in the frosty glow of the little TV. The assault of noise from upstairs, the stereo and an unsettling melange of adults' voices and lurid whispers rained down on them.

"I feel funny," Amber whispered into Grace's chest.

Grace sighed. "Me too."

Grace turned up the black and white TV. They lay together on the floor watching *My Favorite Martian* Grace watched Amber doze next to her. Her face was so calm; how could she be so remote when everything was falling apart? Grace wanted so badly to join that world. At the sound of loud voices on the street, Grace got up and relocked the door. It was another one of those nights.

#####

Highland Park was an overhang in a rising storm. During the next party, all the talk was of the Manson Family and Helter Skelter. A charged sense of danger filled the air; the word was that a few of their guests had been in the Family, and the closeness of the murders put the guests on edge. Mom was in peak form, parading her latest boyfriend Largo through every room, letting everyone know it would be their last party. "We're going to live at the beach," she announced. A week later they left in the middle of the night, hopping from seedy motel to seedy motel, edging closer to the Pacific. It took them three weeks to land in a one bedroom apartment less than a mile from the beach, in Venice, California. Grace kept Amber by her side in those days. They were surrounded by wolves, wherever they turned.

Early on in Venice, Grace learned to adapt. There was a filament of permanence in their existence there; Mom and Largo settled into routines, so Grace was able to navigate around them, and with Amber in tow, they were often able to avoid the violence that bonded Mom and Largo. Their parties continued nightly, which included sex on display and a parade of motley strangers looking for a good time.

Grace got out of the house by enrolling in Junior High School. She brought Mom the paperwork, and she signed it, happy to get Grace out of the house.  She did the same for Amber, who was now too old for Kindergarten. Grace walked Amber to her first day of school, First Grade.  Grace watched her on the carpet with her classmates. They appeared much larger than Amber, she thought, but innocent and carefree—while Amber looked so serious and grown up in her best dress and best shiny shoes. It had been Amber's idea to dress up for her first day.

After school, Grace picked Amber up and on the way home they hailed the ice cream truck and got orange pushups. It was a routine they both enjoyed, and kept them out of the house during the "busy time" in the apartment. Grace found out from one of her friends at school that HER house was a good place to get drugs.

The first time Grace smoked pot was alone in the bathroom of their little apartment. She'd found half a joint in one of Mom's ashtrays. She'd been curious for some time. Afterward, she walked Amber to school and spent the rest of the day in a wondrous cloud. After school, it was as if she'd never had an orange pushup. Amber squinted at her sideways, as she devoured the sloppy orange ice cream. That was before she caught Amber smoking cigarettes in the basement with the kids next door.

Amber changed when she was seven, after Largo started giving her baths. She missed school that same day, complaining of a sore stomach. She was growing out of her clothes and was spending more and more time in the basement with the kids next door. She stopped holding Grace's hand when they walked to and from school.

Grace objected to Amber being alone and nude with Largo. She said as much, and Mom slapped her. "What do you know? You think just because you've got tits, you can tell me how to raise MY girl?" Amber started going between Mom and Grace at that point. Good, bad, right or wrong did not register—she listed toward the strongest voice. Soon, the baths were a daily occurrence. Nothing was so black and white to anyone then. Grace watched Amber closely. Amber needed so much. She never smiled the same after that. The light went out of her eyes.

##### 

It was before school, bath time. Grace followed Largo and Amber into the bathroom. Largo usually just ignored her hovering. Mom was passed out in the bedroom. On this occasion, Largo shoved her back out and locked the door. Grace knocked on the door. "Amber, tell me if he hurts you!" The tub was filling and it was impossible to tell what they were doing. When the water stopped Grace could hear the sound of splashing and what she imagined were Largo's knees knocking the side of the tub. She knocked again as if her presence could prevent the abuse. Amber didn't make a sound from the other side, but Grace did hear Largo's dulcet tone above the splashing water. When they were finished Largo opened the door. His face was a ruddy blank slate. His thick beard had droplets in it. He stepped by Grace on his way to the kitchen. Amber sat on the toilet wrapped in a towel, shivering, her eyes locked on the towel rack. Grace knelt in front of her. Amber had always loved bath time. "What's the matter, Amber?"

Amber stared past her absently, her lips tight over her chattering teeth.

Grace looked into the living room. Largo was on the couch sipping a beer— watching *Leave it to Beaver*, with the slightest hint of a smile.

"Are you okay?" Grace asked, placing a hand on Amber's leg. Amber jumped off the toilet and ran to the closet by the front door. Grace followed her. She'd been dressing her since Amber was born. Amber grabbed underwear and began putting it on. Grace glanced at Largo on the couch. He was chuckling now, brazenly staring at them. Amber grabbed a pair of dirty pants from the pile on the floor. "Why don't you wear the clean pants I washed for you?" Grace asked.

Amber threw the pants on the floor and stamped her feet. "Let me do it myself!" Amber had never yelled at her. Grace glared at Largo  Amber was ignoring her now. She was putting the dirty pants on again. Grace retreated out the front door to the rail. She crouched down and watched the cars flow by on Venice Boulevard. Before leaving for school she poked her head in the door. "Amber. Time for school."

Largo and Mom were on the couch together now. Mom looked worse off than usual, her hair a frightening tangle. Amber sat in front of them on the floor, staring at the TV. Largo lifted his beer, eyes locked on the screen. "I'll take her," he said.

That evening Grace went to Mom who was fixing a drink in the kitchen. "I think Largo did something to Amber."

Mom screwed up her face. She was already drunk. "Who the fuck are you to accuse anyone of anything? Amber is a tease," she slurred.

Grace's jaw dropped. "I think he's molesting her!"

Mom picked up a knife and took a step toward Grace. "You just want him for yourself, you little bitch!"

Grace backed out of the kitchen. Largo was still on the couch, watching *The Price is Right.* Amber was curled up on the other end of the couch. She was wearing the same dirty pants. She hadn't gone to school. She stared absently at the screen. Grace realized later that that was the day Amber surrendered. The spark of joy Grace envied in her would never return. It flowed down the drain with the bath water.

#####

Amber didn't know why *he* was taking her out for her birthday. She'd missed school two days in a row. *Is Grace mad at me?* Grace was at her friend Terri's. Grace never let her miss school, and she never missed her birthday. Amber balked at the crosswalk. *Who's going to sing Happy Birthday?* Amber's sandals were too tight, and Largo was walking too fast. *He was too much.*

He walked *too* fast, he held her hand *too* tight, he drank *too* much —like Mom—and he lied *too* much. He lied that he loved Mom, and he lied about what he did to her in the bathroom. And he'd made her lie too. And now they were going to get ice cream at Foster's Freeze because it was her birthday. Amber pressed the button for the crosswalk. Cars zipped by on Venice Boulevard Largo tried to go on red, but Amber held him back.

On green, Amber held Largo's hand across the street. As they reached the other side Largo looked down at her. She caught her reflection in his tinted lenses and made a face. "Too, too, too..." she said with each step.

"Stop that," he said, pulling her along. In front of Foster's Freeze, Largo faced her and talked in a hushed tone.

"What did I tell you to call me?" he said, dangerously.

Amber shrugged. "Daddy."

Largo let go of her hand and looked up at the menu board. "I'm getting chocolate. What are you getting?"

Amber thought of Grace. "I want an orange pushup," she said.

"Really? It's your birthday."

Amber looked down the street. "I'm not hungry."

Largo squinted at her, rubbing his chin. "You won't get anything later."

"I don't want any," she said, looking at his hands now.

Largo paid for his ice cream. They walked back to the apartment in silence.

Amber dragged her feet walking across the street. "Too, too, too..." Largo pulled her along like a doll. When they were on the other side, she wrapped her arm around a telephone pole. Grace wasn't going to be there.

"Stop playing around."

She tucked her chin into her chest, the thick smell of creosote choked her. The midday traffic made her dress flutter.

Largo licked his ice cream. "We'll see," he said.

When they got home Mom was sitting on the couch with a tumbler in her hand. "Where'd you two go?" she asked accusingly. Largo and Amber ignored her. She was drunk again. Amber went to the closet, grabbed her shorts and went to the bathroom to change. She wanted her own room. When she returned to the living room Mom watched her every step.

"Come here. Your hair is a mess."

Amber walked to Mom with her hands on her chest.

She faced the TV while Mom put her hair back in pigtails, fingers tumbling.

"That's better," Mom said, barely holding her head up.

Mom and Amber glanced up as Largo returned from the bedroom.

"Go put on your Brownie uniform," he said.

Amber recoiled. She shook her head. "When are you going to sign me up for Brownies?" she asked, pouting.

"You're not old enough. You need practice wearing the uniform." Mom smiled at Largo, crossing the living room to the couch. Amber caught something pass between them when he sat down. "Go get your uniform on," Mom said.

Amber went to the closet. Mom went to great lengths to keep the uniform in order. It was ironed and pristine in its original plastic. Amber especially liked the beret, which she thought made her look French, like Grandma D. It was an incomplete uniform. Mom took the brown shorts to fix them. Amber slid the short dress over her panties She pulled the shoe box with Buster Browns, sat on the floor and put them on with the little lacy socks. She stood up and clutched the hem and pulled the dress down as far as she could. She could still feel a draft from the front door as she walked back to the couch. They stared at her as she stood in front of the TV.

"What?"

Largo grinned behind sips of his beer. Mom watched him watch Amber. "Turn around," he said.

Amber shuffled in a circle. Her face burned.

"Now, don't you look cute!" Mom said. "Let's take a picture and send it to the boys and Grandma D."

Largo stood up suddenly. "I'll go get the camera."

It was overcast. The parking lot in front of the apartment was strangely void of shadows. Amber stood in the carport with her skinny knees banging together. The wind whipped at her dress and she was afraid everyone could see her panties. Mom and Largo stood a car length away trying to get her to pose. Amber held her arms tight to her sides, hands clenched at her belt line.

"Come on. Smile! Don't you want to send a picture to Paul?"

Amber nodded. Anything to make the moment pass. When the flash exploded she looked up to see Sally and her brother Chuck on the landing, leaning on the rail waiting for her. Largo and Mom were huddled together whispering now. They didn't notice her rush back up the steps.

Back in the house, Amber changed into her Toughskins jeans. When there was a knock on the front door, she guessed that it was Sally from next door. She threw the door open and stepped back. A skinny Jimi Hendrix look-alike grinned down at her. "Hey. What's your hurry," he said with a soulful voice—like a disc jockey. He walked in as if it were his home. Largo lumbered in behind him. A customer, Amber thought.

"Sit on the couch, Herbie. I'll get the scale."

Amber turned before closing the door. She was glad she'd changed. Herbie was staring at her now. She walked next door.

Sally was her best friend. She had an abnormally scratchy voice for a nine-year-old. She also dressed like a teenager, sporting halter tops and tight cut off jeans. Largo said she was sexy.

"Hi, Amber. What do you want to do?"

"Hi yourself. I got cigarettes! Let's go to the basement."

"Where did you get 'em?"

"My Mom's purse, where else?"

The basement was where all the kids in the complex hung out. It was a dank, private place, with puddles in spots on the concrete, and a cinderblock wall running the length of the building. A row of windows let in a dusky light.

The girls plopped down on an old abandoned couch along the wall. Discarded items, from an old washing machine to an entire kitchen cabinet, were strewn across the swath of concrete. Amber pulled a pack of Viceroys out of her jeans pocket. She tapped one out and handed it to Sally. Sally lit it, took a drag and handed it back. Sally exhaled, blowing the smoke low across the concrete floor. Amber took the cigarette between her thumb and forefinger the way Mom did it. She felt older when she did that and imagined she looked like Mom. She was mixed about that—looking like Mom.

After a few moments of silence, Amber spoke up.

"Grace hasn't been home in two days."

"Where is she?"

"She's at her friend Terri's." Amber sighed.

"Does she know it's your birthday?"

"She never forgot before."

They listened to the floor above, to the landing, and the concrete steps to the second story. With the cigarette close to the filter, Sally took the pack and lit another one.

"Do you miss your family?" she asked.

"Yeah...Paul," Amber replied, her hands tucked between her knees. "My Dad took him away. He didn't want me and Grace."

Sally exhaled loudly and passed the cigarette to Amber.

"That's fucked up. At least my Dad visits." She adjusted her halter top and threw her head back. "What's up with Largo? He's cute, right?"

Amber didn't answer. She got up and walked to the wall where she picked up a piece of chalk. She drew flowing lines across the wall, one after the other. Sally watched her for a while, lighting another cigarette.

"Largo's Largo," Amber said dryly, staring back at Sally.

"What are you drawing?" Sally asked.

"A tree. Grace says trees are the most loyal things in the world."

Amber began drawing flowers on the branches.

"What are those things at the top and the bottom?"

Amber stood back and looked at her drawing. "Seeds."

They both froze and looked toward the laundry room. "Do you hear that?" Sally whispered.

The girls ran behind a pillar on the other end of the basement.

They huddled in tight, hugging the cold concrete and each other. Amber smelled something awful. She looked down. It smelled sour and she wondered if she smelled like that too.

An eerie, whining noise came from the stairwell. The girls peeked around the pillar. Something was moving in the stairwell, an injured cat maybe, or a bird caught by a cat. The sound stopped. They ventured forward to the stairwell, eyes wide, connected at the shoulders. They reached the door and edged through it.

"*Gotcha!*"

The girls screamed, fleeing to the other end of the basement.

In the doorway, Sally's older brother Chuck was doubled over with laughter.

"Ha ha! Scared ya!" Chuck was thirteen, one of the big kids.

Sally rushed forward and slugged Chuck in the belly. "You dick! You scared the shit out of us!"

Amber smiled at Chuck.

"Hi, Amber," Chuck said. "How's it going?"

"Just messing around." Amber watched Chuck closely as he moved to the couch.

"Well, I'm gonna get high," Chuck said. He pulled a bag of weed from his waistband, loaded a pipe, lit it. He held it in, then blew it out slowly.

Amber and Sally joined him on the couch. He got up and dragged an orange crate over for a table. He took another hit and leaned back.

"Can we have some?" Sally asked.

Chuck loaded another bowl. "I don't know. You get stupid when you're stoned. And she's too young," he said, pointing the pipe at Amber. He took another drag. "Damn. That's some good shit. Alright...here."

Sally took the pipe. She inhaled slowly, holding it in. As she exhaled, she sank deeper into the couch, staring at the wall where Amber had drawn the tree.

Amber watched Sally. Sally extended the pipe toward her. Amber took it gingerly, copying what she saw Sally do. She took a shallow hit. She felt it immediately. Her vision narrowed, and she felt like she was under water. She looked up at the sunlight coming in through the row of small windows. The light captured tiny dust particles floating, adrift and unattached, but multitudinous. It reminded her of the day they moved from Magnolia, she and Paul playing with the dust in the sunlight, while Grace picked up their clothes. She sank into the couch, rubbing her cheek on the scratchy cushion.

"Are you feeling it?" Chuck asked no one and everyone.

"I can't feel my legs," Sally said.

"Wow," Amber said, staring at her feet. "I've got chubby toes."

That started a laughing fit that lasted until Sally wet herself. They drifted back upstairs where Amber waited on the landing between the two apartments while she changed. The stereo blared in her apartment. It was going to be a hot day at the beach. She peeked in the window to see if Grace came home yet. Herbie was gone and the bedroom door was closed. When Sally came out they set off to 7-Eleven for munchies.

# 3

Grace felt guilty for being at Terri's. It was after all Amber's birthday. Even though Terri's mother was a bit off—plastic flowers and empty wine bottles covered every sill in the house, even the bathroom—she felt loved there. Mrs. Sanders hugged her like a lost daughter every time she saw her. Grace adopted them as her *Family*.

When Grace finally returned to the apartment, dragging her feet across the landing, she knew Amber was the only one keeping her there.

They were in the bathroom again. Only, this time, when she knocked, she heard the shower and was surprised when Largo walked out with a towel around his waist, dripping from head to toe. "Where's Amber?" she asked him.

Largo jerked his thumb toward the shower.

Grace looked in, Amber's silhouette confirmed it. At that instant, Mom walked by Grace and yelled in, "Don't use up all the water!"

Grace closed the door behind her and peeked in the shower curtain. Amber was scrubbing herself red. "Are you okay?"

Amber started. "Oh. It's you. You missed my birthday."

"I know. I'm sorry."

Amber soaped up the washcloth and started over.

"Are you okay?" Grace asked again, wanting a different answer besides this cold reception.

"Stop asking me that, please." Amber closed her eyes and soaped up her face.

Grace went to the closet near the door and changed out her overnight bag. She put her dirty laundry in the plastic bag she kept on the floor for Amber and her. As she was placing her fatigues and underwear in the bag, she recoiled at the sight of a pair of underpants. There was a thick patch of blood in the crotch. She kneeled to inspect them. There was so much blood. She began to rise, and stopped up short. Her worst fear. A tornado whirled in her stomach, building. The shower was still running. Amber wouldn't say anything. Grace turned toward Mom in the kitchen. Mom, smoking and staring out the kitchen window, as Largo raped her daughter. Grace stood up. She was stuck between two places, leaving, or staying for Amber. Grace folded the soiled panties and hid them in a corner of the closet, resigned to ask Amber about it later. She found a pair of fresh underpants, t-shirt, and shorts and walked them to the shower. Amber was standing in the shower with the water off, shivering. "Nana. Can you get me a towel please?" Grace relaxed. Amber was sweet again. She placed the clothes on the back of the toilet and closed the door. It was too early yet to ask, she knew.

"Do you want to go to the beach?" she asked, presenting more enthusiasm than she felt. She handed Amber a towel. "For your birthday."

"Can we get snow cones?" Amber asked.

"Sure."

Grace stayed in the bathroom until Amber was dressed. As they walked out of the bathroom there was a knock on the front door. It was Herbie. Mom gave him a lusty hug, pulling him by the hand to the bedroom. On his way, he winked at Grace and kissed Amber on the top of the head. Amber cringed.

"Where do you think you're going?" Mom asked, turning back.

Grace turned to watch Herbie and Largo, realizing Mom was talking to Amber. She looked down at Amber, who shrugged and pulled Grace toward the door.

Mom blocked their path. Grace couldn't look Mom in the eye. It was too much to stare into those deranged portals. "We're going to the beach," she said.

"She's not going anywhere. We have a guest."

Amber's hands fell limp to her sides.

"I want to take her to the beach for her birthday."

"We had a cake for her yesterday!" Mom lied, her voice rising.

Grace took Amber's hand. She attempted to step around Mom. They were nearly the same height now, but Mom had her by ten pounds, with another hundred pounds of crazy.

Mom grabbed Amber's arm. Grace knew she couldn't fight her.

The door flew open suddenly. "Marie!" It was Sally's mother from next door. "I've got Vodka!" she sang, strutting past them. Sally's mother took Mom's hand and pulled her to the back bedroom. At the same time, Grace pulled Amber out onto the landing. They ran to the stairs and didn't look back. When they were at the bottom step they heard the door slam.

Out on Venice Boulevard Amber smiled up at her. "Nana, I'm glad you came back."

By the time they reached the boardwalk, they were both drenched in sweat. The boardwalk and beach were a cacophony of sounds, smells and sights. Two portable stereo systems competed for air time: "The Long and Winding Road" by the Beatles on one side and "Ball of Confusion" by the Temptations on the other. Intoxicating aromas of pot, petiole, Coppertone, sweat and salt air swirled about them, while flocks of balloons, banners, and gaggles of kids sprawled on the grass, along with skaters on the boardwalk jiving to the beats, dogs on and off leashes, a hurly burly of youthful prerogative.

Grace breathed in deeply, absorbing the sun and scene, while Amber was transfixed by a sand-moored iron skeleton playground. A pyre, the burned down pier, occupied the North side of the beach. A towering crane worked alone, sifting through the aftermath of blackened timber and bone-white concrete foundation.

"Can I go play?" Amber asked, suddenly her age again, and sprinting across the grass.

Grace nodded. The salty wind flowed through her long black hair. She scanned the groups of young people lounging on the grass, letting go, without any parents around. She saw Terri playing guitar, surrounded by ten or so kids from their school. Grace took off her shoes and headed across the grass. As she approached she recognized the lyrics from "You're So Vain". She began singing along as she sat in front of Terri. Terri lit up, rising to greet her.

"You made it! Was your mother mad?" Someone else picked up the guitar and started to pick.

"We got out of there just in time," Grace said.

Terri shook her head. "I've got a joint. Do you want to get high?"

Grace looked at the playground. Amber hung from a low bar staring at her.

"Just a few hits. It's Amber's birthday."

A group of men in speedos, bulging muscles and slicked back hair strutted by. Grace and Terri exchanged faces and broke out laughing. Terri lit the joint and they both took several hits, then passed it to the surrounding kids. Grace looked out to sea. A small sailboat floundered just offshore. The breeze flowed through her hair and she closed her eyes to absorb the warmth of young bodies huddled together. She was suddenly filled with waves of joy, surrounded by friends, digging the vibe. When she opened her eyes Terri was smiling at her. "I love getting high," she said. Grace glanced over Terri's shoulder.

She panicked, unable to see Amber, annoyed that she couldn't just let go. "I'll be right back," she said. Terri followed her progress across the grass to the play area. Grace ran the last few yards, stood on the lower rung of the monkey bars and scanned the beach. She gave Terri a thumbs up and headed for the shore.

Amber was several yards up from the shore break, pouring a pail of water over the castle of a stocky little boy in droopy shorts. He was catching the water in his open hands, laughing with glee at the cascade they were making together.

Grace felt their joy. She wished she was young again. The responsibility she felt for Amber tore her in two; she loved children, but she still wanted to be one.

Grace strode between sunbathers to join Amber and her new friend.

Amber looked up to see Grace smiling next to her. The boy in the droopy shorts tilted his head, shielding the sun with his sandy hand. "Hi," he said, "You're pretty. You look like Cher."

"This is Paul," Amber said.

"I'm not Paul. I told you, my name is Roger."

Amber looked at Grace and smiled, wider than she had all day. "Let's pretend...okay?" she said.

Roger pulled up his pants. "Yeah, let's pretend that you are Gumby," he squealed.

"Gumby! Gumby! Gumby!" they chanted.

Grace smiled. "Okay, Gumby and Paul, who wants a snow cone?"

#####

The apartment was dark as they stepped up the landing. Grace tried the front door, and it was open so she crept into the darkness, Amber trailing her. She wanted to time their return with Mom's nightly blackout, and the chances were good that Mom would be unconscious. Over the threshold, she drew back at a wave of fresh cigarette smoke reaching her in the darkness. She heard the blow before she felt it, but even then it was too late. The last thing she remembered was the shadow of the iron rising overhead for another blow—and the sound of Amber screaming.

The next day she awoke in the hospital, foggy and lost. She knew they made it home, but that was the last thing she remembered. Fragments of the day at the beach bobbed to the surface. Grace tried to lift her arms. She began to panic—where was Amber? Her head was pounding. She peered out of slits. The brightness hurt. Foggy still, she couldn't tell if she was alone. Her head would not stop pounding.

Grace tried to sit up, to shift her weight, but the casts on her arms and the straps supporting them would not yield.

"You're awake. Thank God. Can you hear me?" A nurse stood over her. She could see the lips move, but the voice didn't quite match up.

She felt a cool hand on her forehead.

"Here, let me loosen these for you." The nurse adjusted her arm straps and checked her bandages. "You've been out since last night. Do you know what happened to you?"

"No. How did I get here?"

"Your neighbor called the police when they heard your little sister screaming. That's what the officer said."

Grace swallowed and even that hurt. Yesterday. Amber's face rose in the mist, but that was when they'd left for the beach. That was when...

Grace began to sob. The panic rose from her stomach to her chest, and she suddenly had the uncontrollable urge to throw up. The nurse produced a tub from below her bed.

After throwing up, Grace lay back and closed her eyes. Too many images floating together, rising too fast. She could feel her pulse in her fingertips. "Can I have some aspirin. Please?"

"There's nothing we can do about that, sweetie. We gave you a sedative to calm you. An aspirin won't do any good at this point. You have a concussion."

The nurse placed her hand on Grace's forehead again. Grace sighed. *Mom. Largo. Amber.*

Her heart sank when she realized that yesterday's attack meant she could not stay at the apartment anymore. Amber was lost, for who knows how long, from her.

Grace followed a line from her chest to her toes. Her arms were both in casts and her right shoulder was wrapped. There was no damage from the waist down. She could barely open her mouth. A sudden flash of memory accompanied a wave of nausea. Mom. The iron. The attack happened so quickly, she'd had no chance to defend herself. Grace closed her eyes and dozed in a timeless malaise.

A male nurse arrived with a food tray. "Lunchtime," he sang.

"I can't eat."

"Young lady, you need energy to heal. No way this" (he swung his finger up and around her damaged limbs) "is going to heal on its own." He put the tray down and placed a straw between her lips. Grace grimaced at the chalky liquid. He smiled and skipped out of the room.

Grace smiled as best she could. It was the warmest interaction she'd had in a long time. She was immediately shaken back to reality with the thought of where she might stay when she left the hospital. Her few things were back at the apartment. She was beginning to well up when she noticed a flower arrangement by the window. The flowers were shockingly beautiful, the purples, yellows, and oranges so iridescent. She thought she was hallucinating. For the second time since she woke up, her heart was warmed by the kindness of strangers.

By the next day, Grace was stir crazy. It had been a brutal attack. Grace awoke in the middle of the night screaming and had to be sedated. She wet herself during these episodes and could sleep for only a few hours at a time. They'd given her every kind of test imaginable and found no permanent damage. She would have light scarring on her arms, but no visual marks on her face. They were talking about discharging her.

After lunch, two uniformed officers stood in the hallway
outside her door. They looked so serious she thought she might
have forgotten a joint in her pants pocket. She'd been napping and
their conversation with the nurse woke her. The nurse saw that she
was awake and ushered the officers to her bedside. She placed a
pillow behind Grace's head and stood by the window pretending to
admire the flower arrangement.

"Good afternoon, Ms. Rentano."

Grace nodded.

"We'd like to ask you a few questions if you feel up to it."

She nodded again. She was glad the nurse was there.

"Who did this to you?"

"My Mom."

"Would you like to press charges?"

Grace hadn't planned on this. She looked up at the nurse who
was now rearranging the flowers. The officer's gaze bore into her
as they waited for an answer. The younger officer stood still, pen
poised above a leather-bound notebook. The older officer smiled
down at her.

"What he means is, do you want to see your mother charged
with assault, which means she will be arrested and tried for a
felony, which could mean jail time."

Grace imagined Amber alone with Largo. "No. I can't press
charges. It was an accident." The nurse was staring at her now; she
stepped forward to offer Grace water. She lingered with the straw
on Grace's swollen lips.

After a moment the older officer nodded to the younger. The
younger closed the notebook. "If you change your mind, give us a
call." He left a card on the bedside table, as they were leaving.

Grace stared up at the flowers on the table by the window. So
many colors. The sweet musky scent lifted her spirits. Looking out
the window she wondered, *Where am I going to stay? I can't go
back. What am I going to do with Amber?*

She noticed the crucifix on the wall to the right of the TV.
She hadn't noticed it before, and now she felt a kinship with it,

both having been banished. Grandma D prayed in times of trouble. "Help me. I don't know what to do."

The room was quiet. The crucifix didn't move. In a few moments, the nurse came in with another bouquet of flowers.

# 4

"Amber Rentano!"

"Here!"

Mrs. Chapman's 3rd grade class, at Walgrove Avenue Elementary, boiled with laughter.

"Ms. Rentano. I already know you're here. Please focus on the lesson."

Amber stared around the class absently. Everyone was looking at her. She pushed her hair back over her ears and turned to Sally, her best friend. "What?"

"Amber, if you would please move your seat up front. There will be no talking during the lesson. Is that clear?"

Amber stood up, pulled her tan skirt down, squinted at Sally, grabbed her backpack, and headed up the aisle. Amber hated school. No one liked her except for Sally. She could barely see the board. This morning, she'd purposely spilled Pepsi on the front of her blouse, but Mom made her go to school anyway and she'd been walking around all morning with a big stain on her chest.

Mrs. Chapman cleared her throat, pointing to an empty chair in the front row, close to the door. Amber shuffled, keeping her eyes on the floor tiles, stepping in each next tile until she reached her new seat. She pulled her skirt down again, turned back to glare at a giggling Sally, and sat down. *Why are they looking at me?*

Mrs. Chapman shook her head and resumed the lesson. Amber stared up at the clock. *Mrs. Chapman hates me. She's always calling my name.*

Amber leaned down and pulled the zipper pocket of her backpack. She took out a pack of Wrigley's, unwrapped a stick and put it in her mouth. She dropped the wrapper under her seat and took out her notepad. The page she'd been working on was dog-eared. She took the pencil from the wire spirals and resumed her doodle, a series of circles surrounding her name, written at the top of the page. She continued writing circles until Mrs. Chapman told them to take out their reading books. Amber closed the notebook and flipped to the page number on the board. She liked how fast she could find the page.

Amber looked around the room, back toward Sally who was still looking for the page, as were a few other students. Amber smiled up at Mrs. Chapman, who was also waiting.

The page had a picture of a black horse with a white star on its nose. She recognized it from the TV show. She put her index finger on the title.

*b-l-a-k, Black! bee-you-tee. I got it!*

"Who would like to read the title?" Mrs. Chapman waved her finger over the class.

Amber raised her hand, waving it as high as she could. She tapped her patent leather shoes on the tile.

"Okay. Amber, go ahead, dear."

Amber giggled nervously. Those closest to her smiled, exchanged glances.

It was her first time reading aloud in class. All eyes were on her.

"Go ahead, Amber," Mrs. Chapman encouraged her.

Amber stared at the letters on the page. She put her index finger on the word and began, "Black!" She stopped and looked around. Next word. "Betty!"

The class erupted. Mrs. Chapman held her hands up to calm them, pursing her lips. Amber looked around, then smiled up at her. She was so proud of herself.

Mrs. Chapman glared at the class. It was all so confusing.

"Betty! Betty! Betty!" the class chanted.

Mrs. Chapman walked to the board and wrote Amber's name. The class fell silent.

Amber's mouth dropped open. She stared at her name on the board. She'd fallen into some trap she hadn't seen, and everyone had been waiting to see her fail. Even Mrs. Chapman was in on it. She knew the words, they just didn't come out right. Amber crossed her arms over her desk and buried her head. She stayed that way until the final bell.

Sally caught up with Amber on the sidewalk in front of the school. Amber was in no rush. She dragged her feet, wondering how she could have been so wrong. She hadn't meant to read the words wrong. It just happened.

"You worry too much," Sally said, linking her arm in Amber's. "Let's go to 7-Eleven. That'll cheer you up."

Amber and Sally skipped up the street. They both made a face at a boy they knew from recess. They slowed at the crosswalk. "I'm getting a Rainbow Pop," Amber said. "Why is everyone so mean?"

Sally pinched her. "Are you kidding? That was so cool. You busted everyone up."

Amber didn't feel cool. She pulled her arm away from Sally. "What's wrong?"

"I wasn't trying to be cool!"

Sally took her arm again. "You'll feel better when we get home. Chuck'll be there."

Amber smiled. Chuck was her next best friend. He was nice to her, and he always treated her like a princess. When she got home, she would tell Chuck. He would understand.

44

Inside 7-Eleven, Amber and Sally walked up and down the aisles. There was too much to choose from. When they got to the aisle farthest from the cash register Sally made a confession.

"I don't have any money."

"Me neither," Amber whispered.

Sally pulled a fistful of candy out of her jacket, with a smirk. "Five finger discount."

Amber shrugged and screwed up her mouth. She walked away from Sally, over to the magazine section, pretending to read a magazine with David Cassidy on the cover. The trill of the bell on the door made her jump. Sally joined her in pointing out cute shots of David at the beach, on a motorcycle, and eating ice cream. They eyed the man at the register, culling the nerve to bolt from the shop. When a group of loud teenagers came in they dashed out the door. Outside, Amber and Sally raced to the corner. They stuffed their mouths with candy, giggling all the way home.

They went straight to Sally's apartment to get Chuck. He was lounging on the couch talking with his mom. Amber wondered if Mom and Sally's mom did their hair together. She had a partially bleached mop of hair with black edges and roots. It reminded her of a skunk. She sprawled spread eagle in a bean bag chair smoking and drinking a can of Pabst. "Tell Marie I've got something for her," she bellowed.

Amber and Sally waved for Chuck to follow them. The three darted out the door, before Sally's mom could get up. Amber stuck close to Chuck, anxious to tell him about school.

In the basement, they walked to the wall facing the small windows. They'd added a coffee table to accompany the couch. Off to the right where the storage cabinets were was an old mattress with a few scratchy Red Cross blankets on it. Amber, Chuck, and Sally spilled onto the couch.

"Why are you two so jacked up?" he asked.

The girls started laughing. "Here." They emptied their booty onto the coffee table.

Amber handed a Sugar Daddy to Chuck. "Your favorite."

After they'd all eaten a few pieces, Chuck pulled out a joint. "Wanna toke?"

"Yeah!" Amber said, with a showy pout for Chuck.

Chuck lit the joint and passed it to Amber. He looked at his sister. "What happened to Amber?"

"Ms. Chapman got mad at her again. It was great! Everyone was laughing."

Amber glared at Sally. "It wasn't her fault," Sally added.

Amber took a hit and passed it to Sally. After a moment she exhaled. "It was my first time reading in Ms. Chapman's class." She looked at Sally. "It was my first time, right?"

Sally nodded, holding the smoke in. She passed the joint to Chuck.

Amber continued. "I've been practicing." She winced.

Chuck passed the joint back to Amber.

"All I read was black betty," she sighed, before taking another hit.

Sally exploded, sending smoke across the room. She laughed uncontrollably, losing her breath until the laughter turned to a hacking cough.

Chuck stared at Sally and Amber. "Black betty?"

Amber reached over Chuck and shoved Sally. She sat back down, taking the joint from Chuck.

"It was an accident," she groaned.

"She meant Black Beauty. We were reading the story. Amber thought it said black betty. The whole class lost it." Sally threw her head back, laughing in fits.

"I'll never read in class again. I hate school. They're so mean."

Chuck put his arm around Amber, drew her to him.

Amber leaned into his warm body. He'd never hurt her. In the three years, they'd known one another, he'd never said a mean word. "It was an accident."

Chuck hugged her. He took the joint from her and put it on a plate on the coffee table.

"Leave her alone, Sal. She's sensitive," he said, kissing the top of Amber's head.

Amber pushed her face into his chest. "Yeah. I'm sensitive."

Chuck shifted to roll another joint. Amber got up and went to the wall. Chuck and Sally followed her progress from the couch, exchanging a glance when she picked up a piece of chalk, in her own world again. She drew an oval under the tree, added another, adding a torso on both, arms, until two figures huddled under the lowest bough.

"What're you drawing?" Chuck asked.

Amber turned at the waist. "That's me and Grace," she said, pointing to the figures.

"There was a sister Grace...who had to go away. She got hurt and left her sister, she will come back some day."

"Hey, that rhymes," Sally exclaimed. "Is it a nursery rhyme?"

"No. Grace used to make up stories when we were little." Amber chuckled softly. "She always started, 'There was a sister Amber...'"

Amber drew birds in the trees, a sun, with clouds across the sky. When she looked back to the couch Chuck was dozing and Sally was fast asleep. She stared at them, wondering how they slept so easily.

#####

Later, after watching *The Mary Tyler Moore Show* with Largo on the couch, Amber decided to get more candy. She knocked on Sally's door, but no one answered. She walked to 7-Eleven alone.

At the counter, she smiled at Mr. Sambria's son, a teenager, whose name she forgot. He was cool because Chuck said he sold him cigarettes. Amber gave a short wave and headed for the snack section. She stopped at the magazine rack and pretended to thumb through a magazine with Leif Garrett on the cover. The jumble of words only reminded her of school; drawing confidence from her anger, she walked to the next aisle, grabbed a pack of Wrigley's and a Baby Ruth bar, stuffed them down her pants. The sharp edges of the candy bar wrapper scratched her belly as she strode toward the door. She peered over a box of Jiffy Pop, to see the owner's son preoccupied with a *Penthouse* magazine. Amber grabbed the Jiffy Pop, judged it was too large to fit down her pants, rushed down the aisle and shot out the front door.

Outside the traffic was light and there was a tickling breeze. Amber turned around the side of the building and leaned against the wall. She pulled the candy out of her pants, rubbing her pubis where the wrapper had scratched her. She tore the Baby Ruth bar open, looked up to take a bite when she noticed a squad car parked in front of the laundromat next door. The motor was running and the officer in the driver's seat was staring at her. She was about to run when the officer looked directly into her eyes and turned off the engine. Amber thought he was smiling at her; before she could react, the officer was out of his car and approached her.

"Hello, Missy," he said, cheerily.

Amber squinted at him, too frozen to stow the candy.

"Hello," she smiled, with a little too much teeth.

The police officer looked back into the 7-Eleven. "Where's your mom?"

Amber forced herself to take a bite of the Baby Ruth bar, to seem casual. "She's at home."

The officer laughed. He was young for a cop, Amber thought. His gun was so close she could touch it. The officer hooked his thumbs into his utility belt. "It's going to be dark soon. You shouldn't be out alone."

Amber took a healthy bite, too big for her mouth. She stared at the officer's badge, chewing loudly and feeling more confident as the moment stretched. *He has no idea.* She swallowed the mouthful too soon and coughed, choking a little. The officer stepped forward, with a hand reaching around to slap her on the back when at the last moment he thought better of it and straightened up. Amber looked up smiling through teary eyes She dropped the wrapper on the ground, then snatched it up. She walked to the trash can. The officer followed her to the front of the store. The radio in the squad car squawked, and a young couple walked past them. The officer returned to the squad car and responded. Amber watched him, while taking a stick of gum out of the pack. She shoved three pieces in her mouth, watching the officer closely. He looked troubled. Amber stuck out the pack and offered him a stick. The officer looked at her askance; it was obvious to him that this young girl was alone—her jeans were torn, her hair unkempt and streaks of dirt on her forearms, a sure sign of neglect. He took the gum and walked back to the cruiser. "Come on. Let's get you home."

Amber followed the officer. She'd never been in a squad car, although she had seen one of Largo's friends picked up at the apartment. Amber looked back at Mr. Sambria's son before getting into the passenger seat. His head was still immersed in the *Penthouse* magazine.

Inside the cruiser, Amber stared at the lights, the switches, the radio, the shotgun. She couldn't wait to see Chuck and Sally's faces when she pulled up in a police car. She took out another piece of gum and when the officer turned to back out, she spit her gum out the window. She smiled innocently when he turned back to her, which made him smile.

They drove down Venice Boulevard, past the old library, the Oak tree where she met Chuck after school sometimes, over the train tracks and past the stop sign they threw rocks at when they were bored. She guided the officer, pointing out the landmarks to her home. When the cruiser turned into the driveway, Amber felt the floor falling away like a carnival ride. She stared up at her apartment window. No Sally or Chuck.

The officer followed her gaze. "Is that where you live?" She stopped chewing and nodded. Amber imagined Largo and her mother lounging on the couch, or in bed. They were always home and hadn't worked in months. She expected to see one of the "visitors" lumbering up the stairs to the second-floor landing, "visiting" the apartment but only staying long enough to make a quick exchange before bolting down the steps. The officer observed her blank stare. "Are you alright?" he asked.

Amber looked back toward Venice Boulevard. She wished she'd asked him to drop her off at the beach. She didn't feel like smiling but she did anyway and nodded.

Grace was at the beach. She knew she'd gotten out of the hospital. Largo told her so. He'd been kind enough to tell her Grace was going to be okay. "Forget about her," he said. "We're your family."

It was her Mom she was worried about now. "You're my baby. I'll take care of you." She'd said it the morning after Grace went to the hospital, after the police came and asked Mom all those questions. It was all a bunch of words. All the words in the dictionary wouldn't bring Grace back now.

Amber wiped her hands on her jean shorts. "Thank you," she said, before pushing the heavy door open and skipping away.

The officer watched her closely as she ran up the concrete steps to the second-floor landing. A red flag went up when she stopped at an apartment door, hesitated, and knocked at the next door. A taller, older girl answered. Amber pointed back at the squad car, waved and smiled. The older girl, blonde and dressed well beyond her years, pulled her into the apartment. The officer made a mental note and sped away.

# 5

Grace was grateful for the drugs they gave her for the pain. The dull buzz buffered her fear, that Amber was alone with Largo now, not the least bit protected by Mom. Grace hadn't wanted to leave the hospital. She couldn't use her arms—they were thick with casts—and she had nowhere to go. She'd walked in a zombie daze out to the beach, mingling with the flow of kids moving West. A few asked about her casts, but most were runaways and refugees, preferring to accept without prying, in their leap from fire to fire.

The sky over the burnt out pier was a thick sienna. Grace stared at the grey glowing sun, wishing for it to come out. She settled on the street edge of the wall where all the kids gathered. Concerts and festivals were held there for its wind cover. Alone and hampered she hoped it might afford some shelter when nightfall arrived. Kids were lounging, smoking, playing music and getting high, on the beach, on the grass, and along the wall. Yet, she felt exposed. Her arms ached. Her spirits rose when the sun finally burst through the cloud bank, warming her face.

She glanced sideways, recognizing Herbie, sitting on an outcrop of concrete facing the Pacific. *He looks peaceful*, she thought. A sudden gust whipped up a wave of sand at her feet. She knew he would know where to get a blanket. He was the king of the beach. Grace crept along the wall until she was throwing distance from Herbie and the three teenagers he held in thrall. She leaned on her cast rising from the grass, and let out a yelp. Herbie looked up at her and smiled. *So peaceful*, she thought. Grace froze, staring at the girls around him. They all seemed her age, some worse for wear. "Come here," Herbie called out, curling his finger.

Grace hesitated. A few of the girls smiled warmly. Herbie stuck his chin out and waved her over.

Grace took stock of the scene. Herbie was in the center, with circles of kids surrounding the edges. He was a like the hub of a wheel. Several kids on the opposite wall were watching attentively. Back in Herbie's group one of the girls rose and came to her. "Herbie wants to talk with you," she smiled.

Grace allowed herself to be assisted to Herbie's side. She was lowered onto the grass by two of his girls. They put a blanket across her shoulders. It smelled of sweat and patchouli, *Pleasant*, Grace thought. Herbie faced her, cross-legged like a Yogi. He sat motionless with an avuncular grip on his groupies. The observers from the other side came over and joined them. "What happened?" Herbie asked. "Some cat beat you up?"

Grace rested her casts on her elbows, but there was no comfortable position, so she lay on her side. "No. My Mom."

Herbie motioned to one of the newcomers and they produced a joint. It was soon lit and passed to Grace. She took a hit and passed it to the girl who'd helped her sit. Grace could see Herbie from the corner of her eye, checking her out. She was suddenly sleepy, and it took all her will to keep her eyes open. Before she dozed a few of the girls lay down beside her.

When she awoke there was a fire next to the wall. It was a small, yet efficiently flickering pile of kindling. The kids were gone, and she and Herbie were left by themselves. The sun was below the horizon now and the orange-pink glow encouraged her. Herbie hadn't let on that he knew she was awake, so she shifted her legs around in an attempt to rise. "Let me help you, baby," he said, coming to her aid. He smelled like patchouli and coconut butter.

"Where is everyone?" Grace asked.

"On the beach. I didn't want to wake you."

Grace looked down the beach. Fires had sprung up, creating a fiery line along the shore. Specks of kids lounged and dawdled about the well-lit hubs.

"You can stay here tonight if you want. It's safe. We all sleep here." He stared intensely. Grace wouldn't look him in the eye. She didn't want him to see that she was scared, and didn't want to encourage him. "If you ain't got no pad to go to..." he added.

Grace shrugged. Herbie looked down the beach. Now Grace checked out his face. The lines were thick and his chin was sharp. He looked like a great chief in that moment, outlined by the azure sea, the pounding waves, and throngs of teenagers. He was older than the kids by a decade. He did resemble Jimi Hendrix. When he glanced back at her, Grace held his stare this time. A sudden gust whipped at the little fire, sending a handful of sparks along the base of the wall. Herbie got up and kicked sand into the fire. Grace let him lift her to her feet. He laid his arm across her shoulders and guided her to the nearest fire ring. She enjoyed his strength as they shuffled through the sand to his ring. There, he let go of her, letting her descend to the sand with the other kids, some abandoned, some runaways and some strung out. He laid a blanket over her and motioned for a few of the girls to snuggle with her. For the rest of the evening and until she fell into a sound and peaceful slumber, they smoked joints and told stories of their short lives. Grace watched Herbie, as the fire made dancing shadows on their faces. He was quieter than she'd imagined. She felt safe now, safer than she had ever felt before. She couldn't worry about tomorrow. It was so far away.

#####

The sun was high and the beach was a writhing mass of drug-fueled revelers. The boardwalk in front of Muscle Beach was packed. The muscle men held the crowd in awe, posing and strutting, oiled up and eating up the catcalls from men and women alike. A few beat cops moseyed up the way, greeting regulars, chatting up bikinis, dancing a few steps with the Hari Krishnas—being a presence. It was that timeless space between late afternoon and early evening. Grace and Terri made their way across the boardwalk to the grass in front of the sand dunes. The party was already underway.

Herbie held court, with a gaggle of mop-haired kids playing a guitar, drumming, and carousing. Several starry-eyed teenagers with a little too much makeup sat at his elbows. Terri and Grace sat down next to a few kids in a heated debate about who was better, Paul Simon or Bob Dylan. A joint was making its way around. One couple huddled near a park bench making out.

Grace felt at home, in spite of the sand fleas and cold nights. The joint came to Terri, she took a long drag, and passed it to Grace. Grace held on to the joint, watching the kids around her. There were the regulars —Herbie's disciples—a few new kids who, judging by their pasty skin, were new to the scene, and a few homeless kids, like herself. Herbie seemed drunker than usual. With his stylish hairdo and brass wit, he had more than a few of their schoolmates under his thumb. Today, however, he was in rare form. "Fuck Nixon! Fuck the Arabs!" he ranted. Watergate and the death of the Israeli hostages at the Olympics were in all the news.

Grace sighed. She took a long hit off the joint, held it, and exhaled. She closed her eyes, the grass soft and inviting, the world spiraling away.

Terri nudged her. "Send it around, stoner, stop bogarting the joint," she teased.

Grace passed the joint to the guitarist. He was a John Denver look-alike, but with a mustache. Grace and Terri started giggling at nothing at all. The two hugged and giggled, rolling in the sand. When they sat back up, the joint had made its way back to them.

They both took another hit. Herbie had peaked early. A group of girls guided him to his knees. He was quiet and sullen, badly in need of consoling.

Grace looked across the beach, out to sea. A small sailboat was flapping too close to the shore break. Out further, she could see the outlines of offshore oil rigs. Nearby, at the shoreline, a few toddlers were prancing in the white water. Their mothers sat on the edge of the waterline smoking and drinking from a thermos. The beach was packed with sunbathers supine, reclined and huddled.

Grace jumped up. She stepped over a dozing teen she'd never seen before and shook her hair out. She'd grown used to the ever-present sand, which she constantly dislodged throughout the day—one of the hazards of sleeping on the beach. Grace glanced at Herbie. He was fast asleep with his head in a lap. She felt warmth for him. He'd taken her in, fed her, kept her safe until her wounds healed. She scratched her arm where the cast had been.

"Let's go to Aunt Mary's house," Grace said to Terri. "I need to change." Aunt Mary was a friend of the kids on the beach. She lived in Venice near the Marina.

On the way up the beach, Grace and Terri caught wind of a Doors concert that evening near the wall. They grabbed a few Cokes, used the bathroom at the Oar House, and headed East.

After changing at Aunt Mary's, Grace decided to stop by Amber's school. She hadn't seen her since the beating. Terri helped write the note (from Marie Rentano) that would get Amber out of class. The Office Manager at Walgrove Avenue Elementary knew her—she'd seen Grace come for Amber. They waited in the office, with the giant clock staring down at them, with the mint green walls and slippery wooden chairs, glossed by the sweat and body oil of so many generations of kids. Grace felt like she was back in school, and in trouble. Her leg jiggled nervously, and Terri laughed because there were two circles of sand around her feet.

When Amber came up the hall she was dragging her backpack. Her face erupted when she saw Grace. "Hi, Amber. Happy Birthday!" Grace said, hugging her. Amber planted her head on Grace's chest. Terri gave her a hug. "Do you want to go hear some music?" Grace asked. Amber looked sideways at Grace, then Terri. A smile spread across her face. Grace herded them out the door.

On Rose Street, they began to run West, toward the beach. The sun was directly overhead as they reached the edge of the grass. They could already hear live music down the beach. They took their shoes off and walked along the grass until they approached the outer edge of the crowd. Grace held Amber's hand on one side and Terri held the other. They stared up at the warm-up band. Amber stared at the lead singer as if she were from another planet. "Are the Doors here yet?" Terri asked the nearest group of kids.

"Yeah. They're over there," a leather-clad teenager said, pointing to a van parked at the edge of the wall. The first band wound down after a long jam, and after a growing number of kids began to yell for the Doors. The band shuffled off the stage flipping the bird. Grace took Amber to the bathroom before the Doors came on. In the bathroom, Amber whined that she was hungry. Grace noticed how thin she was, and even at nine, she was already bleeding. Strange to be having her period so soon, Grace thought.

Grace and Amber reunited with Terri, who'd bought them chips. The Doors were already kicking into "Soul Kitchen" They decided to sit down by the wall to get out of the sun. Amber accidentally sat in a pee-damp patch of sand, so they moved down. Grace watched Jim Morrison sway languidly over the crowd, threatening to plummet on top of the kids at the edge of the wall. Terri danced in circles around them and Amber joined her, wet bottom and all. "He's really fucked up!" Grace yelled above the music, pointing at the lead singer.

It was such a perfect scene: a sea of kids swaying together, some with babies, stray dogs dodging amongst them, and everyone at least a little buzzed, but utterly awash in their place in time.

After the last chord of "The End" died out, Grace, Amber, and Terri trudged up the boardwalk toward Venice Boulevard. "Did you have a good time?" Grace asked Amber. Amber nodded. Her eyes were droopy as the sun loomed a few fists above the horizon. They took turns giving her a piggyback ride to save her swollen stump of a big toe.

At the top of the landing, Grace recognized her mother's drunken cackle. She broke into a sweat. The front door was open and the TV was blaring. Grace trod lightly, following Amber, with Terri behind her. Amber walked straight to the bathroom, leaving Grace exposed in the doorway. Terri waited outside. Largo and a red-headed teenager were on the couch. Grace had never seen him before but he looked an awful lot like Mom. He had a beer in his hand, and his eyelids were drooping as if he'd been up all night.

Mom acted as if nothing had happened. "Grace. This is your brother."

The redhead stared at her, suddenly awake and on the edge of the cushion. Mom watched them, smiling. She was really drunk and didn't grasp the weight of the reunion. "Go ahead. Give your brother a hug. He's come all the way from Texas."

Grace took one step into the room.

"I said...give your brother a hug. Stop being a bitch!" Her venom shrank the already tiny room. It was as if she and Mom occupied the same skin.

The blood rushed to Grace's face. She ran out the door, past Terri and down the stairwell. Terri ran after her, calling her name. Grace stopped at the corner. This was the last time, she promised herself. She hoped the best for Amber. She hoped she could see her again someday.

5

Grace received her diploma from Venice High in the mail. It arrived on a Saturday. There was no advancement, no parading across a well-lit stage, and certainly no parents to capture the Kodak moment. She'd never really been there. The leaving spread through her life like the fire at the Cheetah Bar. Not only did she leave school, she'd left the kids on the beach, just as she'd left Amber, and left her family. She'd moved in with Rex and his lover Kimo, after six months of living hand-to-mouth: a few nights at Aunt Mary's, a few at Terri's and as a last resort, on the sand next to the wall. The beach had changed. Heroin was everywhere. Herbie was dealing and the word was that he was pimping.

Now that Grace had bills to pay, she got a job at Der Wienerschnitzel. She got to take home day-old buns, wieners, and slaw. She made enough money to fund her new lifestyle and pay rent. It was after all the seventies. Sex, drugs and rock n' roll was the raison d'être for her generation. Living with Rex and Kimo was like having two older brothers who adored each other. They were inseparable and loved her unconditionally. They didn't judge her when she brought men home.

Grace found companionship and sex at the Oar House, her favorite bar in Santa Monica For the first time in her life, she felt she could be irresponsible—letting her desires guide her. Her favorite time of the day was when she got off work. Since she worked the noon to eight shift, she got home just as the night crowd began to stir. She took a shower, changed, and headed to the Oar House to meet up with Terri. Terri had changed little from the moment they met in the ninth grade at Venice High. She still wore her red hair long, with little bits of colorful thread and twigs braided in. She had shown Grace how to put on makeup. Grace had found out pretty quickly that men were drawn to her when she was made up.

One Friday night Grace and Terri walked to the Oar House after getting high on the grass on Muscle Beach. The sun was fading below a belt of maroon haze. Terri had a crush on the bartender, Andy, but Andy liked Grace, so he served them. They knew his schedule by heart. They arrived at nine, just as the bar was starting to fill up.

"What're you ladies having?" he asked, looking straight into Grace's dark eyes.

Terri put her purse on the bar with a thump. "'I'll have a gin and tonic, Andy."

Andy smiled at her and turned back to Grace. He picked up a bottle of Jack Daniels, his eyes glued to Grace's face. "What'll you have, beautiful?"

"The usual," she winked. She looked over her shoulder, surveying the bar. "Has Victor been in tonight?"

"Haven't seen the asshole," Andy said.

Terri smiled at Andy and flipped her hair back. "Andy, turn up the music. I like this song."

Andy motioned to a bouncer at the other end of the bar. The music cranked up. Terri swayed in her chair, staring at Andy. He looked back at Grace. "You were fucked up last night. Do you even remember who you went home with?"

Grace took a sip of Jack Daniels. She loved the way it burned going down. She leaned over the bar, knowing it squeezed her breasts together. "I so do remember. He was that surfer dude with the really fine butt."

Andy scoffed.

"No." Terri laughed. "That was Wednesday night."

Grace turned toward the door when a new group walked in. She turned back to Terri, took another sip, dipped her head and squinted. "Oh...right. It was that guy who used to date Tracy, the waitress."

"Scott," Andy said, shaking his head.

Grace glanced back to the exit. "Andy, what time does Victor usually get here?"

Andy looked up at the clock over the bar. "After ten."

Grace took another sip of her drink. From the corner of her eye she saw a familiar face stride into the bar. Images of last night started to surface: A smoky fire ring, the back seat of a VW bug, and Old Spice. Terri followed her gaze and turned to the exit. "Oh, there's Scott." She waved.

Grace turned to face the mirror behind the bar. She wrapped herself around her drink. Terri elbowed her as Scott made his way toward a group partying near the cigarette machine. One of the group pointed toward the bar. Grace did not like this part of her life. She wanted to have a good time, but the day after felt criminal. She hadn't mastered the art of the one night stand. Terri was no help.

"Hi, Scott. Did you have a good time last night?" Terri asked, as Scott stepped up to the bar. He whipped his long blonde mane out of his face.

"You tell me," he said, facing Grace.

Grace glanced over her shoulder. "Oh. Hi, Scott," she mumbled.

Terri nudged her.

"I had a good time last night," Scott said. He squeezed between Grace and Terri. She could smell his Old Spice. Andy smirked.

Grace had a rule. Never get with the same guy two nights in a row.

"What are you girls doing tonight?" Scott asked.

Andy moved down the bar. It was filling up, and the dance floor was starting to hop.

"Not much," Grace said, "We're trying to score some acid. Do you know anyone?"

"As a matter of fact, I do. Hold on, I'll be right back."

Grace and Terri watched Scott go to the pay phone by the cigarette machine. In five minutes he came back smiling.

"It's all set. We can pick it up now."

Grace hopped off her stool and downed her whiskey. "Let's go for it, dude," she said, mimicking him. *Scott was so proud of himself*, she thought. It might be the night to break rules.

Out at Scott's VW bug, Grace pulled down the passenger seat visor. She checked her hair, and makeup. She reapplied her lipstick, puckering close to the little mirror. Scott watched her for a while with his hands in his lap. After a moment she felt uncomfortable. "Well?" she said. "Let's get going."

Scott drove up Venice Boulevard, keeping an eye out for cops. At a red light, his eyes settled on Grace again. "You look hot, babe. Can you get me my poncho in the back seat?"

Grace put her lipstick away and stretched between the seats. Sand fell out of the poncho pockets. They both laughed—last night's hook up.

"Here, take the wheel." Grace held the wheel with both hands, keeping the car steady, as they flowed through traffic. Scott blindly pulled the poncho over his head. "Thanks," he said, resuming control. He took a joint from his pocket, lit it, took a drag. "Shotgun," he coughed. He placed his lips on hers, blowing the thick smoke into her mouth and down her throat as she inhaled. When they separated she giggled. He had lipstick covering his lips.

"What?"

Grace took her palm and wiped the lipstick from his lips. She rubbed her palms together. "There, all better." Fifteen minutes later they pulled into the motel parking lot. "Why are we going to a motel?"

"Randy got evicted from his apartment. He knows this guy at the front desk. Come on."

Scott bolted out of the car and was nearing the gate to the pool area when he looked back. "Come on, baby. It's cool. We'll only be a minute." He drummed his hand on the top of the gate. Grace got out of the car, looked at him askance.

Together they strode to a poolside unit. All the drapes were drawn in the lower units and the pool area was deserted. *Strange*, Grace thought, *on such a warm evening*. They stepped between a manicured hedge, onto a small patio with a sliding glass door. The curtains fluttered as Scott rapped on the sliding door.

Randy, a short, tanned Fonzie look-alike, pulled the curtain aside. He unlocked the door and ushered them in. "What's up?"

Inside, he locked the door, closed the curtain and waved them to a small floral patterned love-seat next to a mini fridge. The room smelled like stale beer and cigarettes. A sallow blonde in panties and a Snoopy t-shirt lolled on the king-sized bed. Randy pulled up a chair and opened a drawer in the bureau. He pulled out a Yellow Pages phone book. The book spilled open to a loose white page with row upon row of dancing bears. "Is this what you want?" he asked.

Scott's eyes lit up. He reached for the sheet. "Is it good shit?" he asked. "That last blotter you sold me was weak."

Grace let go of his sweaty hand. She'd never seen so much acid in her life.

"Yeah, man. This is the shit. Straight from Berkeley."

Randy pulled a vile and a mirror from the drawer. He tapped the vial on the mirror. Two clumps spilled out. "Want to party?"

Scott looked at Grace. She shrugged. Grace looked over at the girl on the couch. Her eyes fluttered. She was somewhere else.

"Cool," Scott said, rubbing his hands together.

Grace watched closely. She'd never seen anyone snort drugs. Randy chopped the stuff with a razor blade. He formed the powder into thick clumps half the width of a straw. Scott pulled out a dollar bill and rolled it into a tube with one hand.

Grace moved aside and let Scott lean in. The white clump disappeared up Scott's nose. He rubbed his nostrils between his thumb and index finger. He arched his back, sniffing and swallowing. Grace watched him curiously.

He leaned back into the love seat. "That shit burns. What'd you cut it with?"

"I didn't cut shit," Randy said, feigning outrage.

Scott leaned forward again. He held the rolled dollar out to Grace.

She stared at the powdery clump. All eyes were on her. Scott put the dollar in her hand. Grace put her purse down beside her. The girl on the bed opened her eyes a crack and smiled.

For some strange reason, her thoughts went to the last party they'd had at Highland Park. The face of her mother, still, in a frozen, lost, smile, faded as she leaned forward over the glass.

"How do I do it?" she asked.

"Hold the straw in your fingers, right up to the line, and snort it up your nose." Randy grabbed the dollar, snorted a clump and handed the dollar back to her.

Grace took the dollar. She looked up at Scott whose eyes were now glassy. He was smiling. Grace leaned forward and snorted the white clump into her nose. She'd never put anything up her nose. It burned.

"Go like this, and sniff in," Scott said, as he rubbed his nose and snorted.

Grace sniffed in with force. The white powder hit the back of her throat. She coughed and swallowed. The chemical taste nearly made her gag. In seconds, the top and back of her head tingled. Her body seemed to melt, the weight of every moment up until then went out the bottom of her feet, leaving her weightless, and blissful.

She looked up at Scott, who was watching her expectantly. "Mmmm. What was that?" she asked.

"You just snorted heroin, baby. You ain't no virgin no more."

Randy and Scott laughed. The woman on the bed sat up.

Grace leaned her head back against the wall. Everything she touched was pillowy. Even her vision seemed to be soft. "This feels wonderful," she murmured.

Grace peered at Randy and then at Scott. Scott was in a world of his own. "Can I have some water?" she asked.

Randy turned to the woman on the bed. He waved her toward the bathroom. She went into the bathroom and returned with a glass of water.

Grace measured her breath, in and out, to try to focus her eyes. Her head was numb and tingly, and she felt like she would float through the ceiling. She took the water glass and tasted it. She could barely feel her lips on the glass. The water flowed down her throat, a little out the side of her mouth onto her cotton blouse.

Grace giggled and wiped her mouth. A sudden thought entered her mind.

"What happens if you mix heroin and acid?"

A knock at the door froze the room. Randy put a finger to his lips. They all waited, wide-eyed. There were two short raps on the door. Randy relaxed and walked to the door. He gave two short knocks, and there was a knock in return. He opened the door a crack. Scott folded the sheet of acid, put it in his jacket and motioned Grace toward the sliding glass door.

At the door, Randy invited the visitor in. The girl on the bed relaxed. In walked a pimply teenager with oily hair and an oversized red vest.

"What are you tripping about?" Scott asked.

"I owe Victor money," Randy said, baring his teeth.

Scott nodded. "Victor."

Grace saw fear in their eyes. Victor was always sweet to her. What was their problem?

Randy moved on to the next customer. "I'll check you out later, Scott." He nodded at Grace.

Outside, Scott and Grace walked through the pool area. "Oh my God. That's so much acid. Are you going to do all that yourself?" she asked.

Scott seemed in a hurry to get out of there. Grace rushed to keep up.

"Of course not. It'll last a while." They took two hits each and drove back to the beach.

They parked on 18th Avenue a block from the boardwalk. Grace looked over at Scott. He stared at the beach with his mouth agape. Her head felt like it was glued to the head rest. She'd been watching the glow of the red traffic lights. "Are you okay?" she asked.

"Yeah. The acid is kicking in. How about you?"

"I'm just starting to feel it." She waved her hand in front of her face. Her hand trailed across her vision, surprisingly vivid. "It just kicked in," she said. Her voice echoed forever inside the little VW. She knew they were parked, but the car felt like it was skating along on a steel grey sheet of ice. "Yeah. It's hitting me. Let's go trip on the grass."

The boardwalk was crowded. Grace felt as if the crowd swelled every time she inhaled. The sun had already set. It took them what seemed like an hour to get from the car to a bench on the grass. Grace squinted toward Gold's Gym and marveled at the oversized men carousing in front of the sign. They seemed inflated, with steely muscles and constipated expressions. She had the strangest inkling that they were going to the gym to have sex with one another, and shook her head to dispel the notion. She moved closer to Scott, who gazed out at the beach.

"I'm tripping really hard," Scott whispered. His poncho hood covered his head. Grace thought he looked like a leathery frog.

"Me too," she said. She was in awe of the sensory overload: the colors flowing together, a babbling brook of voices, contorted faces riding a big moving caterpillar, the ocean a rippling two-dimensional sheet.

Scott got up and walked across the boardwalk to the sand. "I'm getting cold. Let's find a fire ring."

Grace flowed beside him onto the sand. As her feet hit the sand she felt like she was going to sink through the earth and fall out the bottom. "Scott. Help me," she said, grabbing his arm. Scott took her arm in his. They trudged to the nearest fire ring. A couple sat huddled close to the edge, their faces aglow and shadowy. Grace and Scott plopped down on the other side of the fire. Grace touched her face. She was smiling too much, she thought, as if her cheeks were touching her ears. She touched her ears to reassure herself that her face wasn't stretching too far. She leaned against Scott, who was staring into the fire, following the curling smoke rise into the night. "I have never tripped this hard," she whispered.

"Me too," he said.

Grace took a deep breath and closed her eyes. She saw sparks fly inside of her closed eyelids. She needed a break but knew from experience that one could not turn off an acid trip. One had to wait it out. The couple across the fire ring didn't seem to notice them. They were whispering and kissing under a hairy looking blanket.

Grace was grateful for the space between them, and that there was a sea of sand between them and the traffic on the boardwalk.

Grace stared up at the sky. It too seemed to be moving, but not in designs and shapes like the sand. The sky flowed in never ending striations of scarlet, periwinkle, and turquoise. There was a crescent moon, which appeared more like a smile than an orbiting body. Grace watched the moon, willing the smile to broaden. The couple lay down, covered now beneath the blanket. *It's getting cold*, she thought and inched closer to the fire. Scott stayed where he was, frozen, silent. Grace pushed her hands between her thighs for warmth. She stiffened at an alarming wetness between her legs She looked at her hands, bewildered. They were a thick red. She blinked to clear the vision, but her hands were still red. She felt her crotch, stretched out her legs, then stood up. Blood saturated her corduroy pants from her belly button to her thighs There was blood smeared on the instep of her Wallabee shoes. Scott stared up at her in horror. The couple stared at them.

"I'm bleeding!" Grace screamed. Her heart thumped out of her chest, and she struggled to control the rising terror. She felt no pain, rather a relief between her thighs.

Scott jumped to his feet. "What's going on, Grace?"

He too was trying to blink the disturbing image from his mind.

Grace hopped on her toes in the sand with her red covered hands in front of her face.

"Scott! I'm bleeding to death. I'm dying. Get help!"

Scott ran back to the boardwalk. Grace felt like she was sinking. The couple stared at her. "Help me!" she screamed at them.

The couple let the blanket fall away, the girl stood up, walked to Grace's side, and took her arm. She stared down at Grace's red crotch. "Does it hurt?" she asked.

"No."

The girl smirked. She whispered into Grace's ear. "You're having your period."

Scott dropped Grace off at midnight. Grace was still seeing colors. The red target on her crotch was a stiff plate. She wanted to talk, but Rex and Kimo were already in bed. Their door was closed and the stereo was cranked; that meant they were having sex, so Grace went to the bathroom and took a shower. She lay in the tub naked with her eyes closed until the hot water turned cold and she began to shiver. As she dried off she couldn't shake the adrenaline of nearly bleeding to death on the beach. She pulled back the shower curtain to find Rex urinating. She looked up at him and smiled. "I'm tripping," she said. Rex helped her to bed. Grace lay there listening to her heartbeat. Her bed was a big hug holding her tight. She didn't have to work the next day, Saturday. She could sleep for the whole day if she liked.

# 6

The second time Amber got caught shoplifting Mom let her stay in jail overnight. She was so young they put her in a cell by herself. The cell was a cinderblock room with metal benches lining the walls. She could hear snoring from the cell next to her, and low conversations: prostitutes talking about how to get an abortion and where to find the best drugs. She knew Mom would come for her. She knew she was the only reason Largo stuck around.

Amber was the only one to get caught. Sally and their friend Mindy shot down the alley when the squad car pulled up. Amber was the last one out the door. It was the same officer who'd given her a ride home. She'd seen him parked across the street from their apartment complex. Five days a week, he pulled up around noon, and then again at five, always with the motor running and his head bowed and eyes closed, appearing to doze. Amber overheard Largo say the "pigs" were on to him, and that they should do their business at the beach from now on. The house was quiet with Officer Bell out there.

Amber liked having Officer Bell so close. He smiled at her when she skated on the sidewalk. He was nice. She waved at him

68

when she stayed home from school, peering out the curtain minutes past noon, disappointed when he wasn't there. She drew chalk flowers on the sidewalk near his spot. He noticed, she figured, when one day she found a pack of gum in the eye of one of the flowers. It was unopened so she knew it was from him. When she came down the steps from the upper level she kept her eyes on the squad car, for the wave, and to see if he was too busy for a conversation. She could read his mood better than he could read hers, she thought, because if he could read hers he would take her away. When he looked up and smiled she went straight to his window. She trod softly across Sally and Chuck's doorway on such days. They called the police "pigs", but she saw this one as her knight in shining armor. She danced in front of the driver's side window, his undivided attention and smile driving the demons away. "Why aren't you at school today?" he always asked when she came down at noon. "I'm sick," she always said, and it was true because she'd started bleeding. "Can I sit in the car?" she asked one day. "Can't do it, Amber. Against regulations," he said, smiling sadly.

Mom didn't like Officer Bell parked in front of the apartment. "What does he say to you?" she asked, after seeing her with him. "He asks me about my day," she responded, feeling protective. It was *her* policeman. Mom gave her a look that day that froze her blood. She never mentioned Officer Bell again. The apartment was calm when he was there, that's all she knew.

After a few months, Amber began missing school regularly. She brought treats out to him at lunchtime: Butterfinger bars, popcorn she made by herself, a can of Orange Fanta, and a bouquet of dandelions. The truth was that when Officer Bell was there, Largo left her alone. This was a fact that spurred her vigilance. Even if it meant that Sally and Chuck came around less. "You can't keep missing school like this," Officer Bell said one day. He had a pained expression, and Amber was worried that he was mad at her. "It isn't right," he continued, looking back at the work on his lap.

"Don't you like me?"

Officer Bell gave her a look that spoke a thousand words. She'd noticed the shiny new ring on his finger, his hair was freshly cut and his mustache trimmed. He just shook his head. "I wish I could do more." He pulled away and didn't come back at five. He didn't come back Thursday or Friday. That weekend Largo was back to his usual self. Mom had a party and the police came. Officer Bell wasn't among them.

Amber listened closely to the prostitutes in the cell next door at the mention of *his* name.

"Largo gets the best shit on the beach."

"Girl...he gets it from Herbie."

"Herbie gets it from Victor, but don't show up at his pad. You too old."

Amber trembled on the steel bench. Everything about the cell was cold. The walls, the bench, the colors—grey and mint. The mention of Largo put a frost on things. *Mom should be here any minute,* she thought. She zipped up her jacket. The clasp fell off, tinkling on the tile floor. The women in the next cell stopped talking. In a moment they resumed. Amber picked up the clasp and began carving a heart in the bench. She began to form a story in her head. She knew the truth, but it would not fare well with Mom. She couldn't tell Mom the real reason she got caught shoplifting.

Her plan *was* simple. She would shoplift at 7-Eleven, Officer Bell would respond, and he would take her away. It was *that* simple. She would tell him everything: how her family abandoned her, how Mom was a drunk, and how Largo molested her. He would rescue her because, she knew, he loved her. Why else would he park in front of her house every day? She loved him too.

The plan failed from the start. Mr. Sambria wasn't even going to call the police. She had to talk him into it. "I've been stealing from you for years," she said, with a smile on her face. When he arrived, Officer Bell put her in the backseat of the squad car, where she'd never been. He didn't say a word as she told him her story. She added that Herbie abused her too. Amber stared at the back of his head the last few blocks. When he pulled into the station he got out of the car without looking in the rear-view mirror. She began to cry. The curtain was coming down, he was offstage now and the audience had left. Amber was alone more than ever, with this lost hope dangling around her neck. He wouldn't even touch her, calling out for a female officer to come get her. That was the last she saw of him. Officer Bell. *Her knight in shining armor.*

Amber etched lines off of the heart as if it were a sun that would warm the cell. The bench creaked as she dug in, making the rays deep. She looked up at the sound of the hallway door opening and closing. She heard footsteps, thick boots and the tap of heels. She hurriedly crossed out the heart, with all its thick rays. There was Mom, standing outside the cell looking old, with too much make-up. Her eyes were red and puffy. Amber stood at the bench, six feet between them. Mom didn't say a thing. Amber wanted her to scream, like she did at home. She wanted home Mom to meet public Mom right there in front of the police and the prostitutes. The officer opened the cell. Amber didn't budge. She and Mom stood there staring at one another. Amber shivered. The officer opened the cell door wide as if to free a wild bird. Finally, Mom turned and left. The officer stood there with his mouth open, looking between Amber and Mom. He cleared his throat when Mom opened the door at the end of the hall. The prostitutes were talking again. Amber rushed out of the cell, after her.

#####

A short time later they moved to Reseda. They left under the cover of darkness. Largo pulled his loaded Barracuda out of the moonlit driveway a few hours short of sunrise. The new address was a ramshackle bungalow behind a ramshackle house on a dusty dead-end street. A towering Eucalyptus guarded the driveway, the last surviving windbreak for fields that once grew the region's sweetest lettuce. Instead of rushing to unload, they slept in the car until the interior baked from the morning sun. Amber crept out from between two liquor boxes in the back seat, warped by ragged dreams and the strange new surroundings. The air was dry, inland air, so far from the beach.

Amber was the first to venture to the wood slat porch; she cupped her hands and peered in through the screen door. She could see through the living room, the kitchen to the right, and a windowless bedroom in the back. The stinging scent of cat pee and Pine-Sol stung her nostrils. *Where am I going to sleep?* Mom pushed by her with a grunt, headed for the kitchen sink to make herself a drink. An abrupt déjà vu transfixed Amber. It lasted seconds: Mom vomiting into the sink after her first shot of vodka, Largo on the couch with a Pabst, no space for her.

Amber slid down the door jamb and sat on the porch step. The sun baked her sandaled toes. Her stump ached. She hadn't even said goodbye to Sally and Chuck.

She wanted her new life to be different. Yet, on that first day, the moments mounted, confirming the same old story. Largo bulled toward her with two boxes from the car. She leaned back on her elbows and looked up into his bearded face. She was ten now and her body was changing. It had an effect on him, she noticed, but wasn't sure what the change would bring. Largo exhaled loudly and shifted the boxes to one arm. "Baby, move."

"Go get a box," Mom yelled from the kitchen.

Largo shrugged, then stepped over her. Amber kicked the gravel driveway on the way to the car. She sat in the back seat, waiting. Her sweaty thighs stuck to the vinyl seat. She thought it might be an okay place to sleep. The smell of diesel exhaust filled her nostrils. On the other side of the street was a busy truck yard. She watched a semi backing up to the fence. After the third attempt, the driver set the brake and got out of the cab. The driver had the same sideburns as her father. Some said he looked like the former president, Richard Nixon. Amber thought of him less and less, and it was moments like this that she wished she never did.

Amber got out and stared beyond the rows of trucks, and the mechanic's shop, toward a mountain range. She inhaled the dry valley air, longing for the fresh ocean breeze. The guttural hum of the nearby Ventura freeway did nothing to drown out the feeling that her life was hitting a downgrade. She sighed and turned to face the little bungalow nestled in bougainvillea at the end of the driveway. In that instant she noticed a sagging gardener's shack adjacent to the bungalow. It was just big enough to fit two queen-sized mattresses. It reminded her of the garage in Highland Park— a refuge that she and Grace shared.

Suddenly, a torrent of barking interrupted her daydream. A motley Terrier tore circles in the swath of grass in the middle of the yard. Amber smiled at the frenetic little mutt. She listened as she watched it make ever-widening circles, wondering who the owners were. She spied a hole in the picket fence next door. She followed the line of fence to a Raggedy Ann doll frozen in a briar hedge. Amber went to the doll but was a fraction too late. The terrier leaped and caught the doll's head in its tiny jaws. Amber grabbed futilely at the doll's legs. She was in no mood to be toyed with. Amber stood in the middle of the lawn as the dog made circles around her. It released the doll and dropped onto its belly, panting and wide-eyed. Amber looked up at the bungalow and back to the dog. She reached for the doll, but the dog growled. It wasn't worth the trouble, she thought. There were puncture marks over the entire doll's fabric skin and its signature apron was a tattered pale flag. She shrugged and headed back to the car. The doll was missing its eyes, and she wasn't going to sew on new ones. She was way past dolls anyway, she thought wistfully.

Amber peered into the car. Mom's purse was on the front seat. The zipper to the main compartment was open. The contents spilled onto the seat: a box of Tampax, a pack of cigarettes, lipstick and her mother's wallet. The wallet's brass clasp glinted. The terrier brushed her ankle on its way under the shaded underbelly of the Barracuda.

Without a second thought, she picked up her TWA bag from the back seat. Next, she grabbed her mother's wallet, opened it, took out the cash, some twenties and a few small bills, and placed them into her pants pocket. She stuffed the Tampax and cigarettes into her bag. She saw a lighter in the ashtray, so she took that too. Amber peered back at the bungalow. Mom was yelling at Largo.

It all happened so fast. Amber rushed up the dead-end street toward Reseda Boulevard At the intersection, she looked left, then decided to head back toward the sound of the freeway. She hurried along the chain link fence, relaxing with every step further from her new home.

Amber trudged along the sun-moored sidewalk as quickly as her little legs could take her. It was hotter than she'd ever remembered Venice being. After Grace left, she'd gotten used to walking the streets alone, and these vacant sidewalks lacked the waves of drifters and hippies that roamed Venice. A few cars passed by in either direction. Amber kept her head down. She stepped behind a telephone pole, the choking scent of creosote made her spit. With the coast clear, she lit a cigarette and resumed her journey toward the sound of the freeway. After another block and a little dizzy from the heat and the nicotine, she started to take note of her surroundings. It really was a small town, she thought. A field lined the sidewalk on her right while across the wide boulevard a 7-Eleven, a laundromat and a Chinese restaurant nestled at the foot of a small hill. Looking back toward her street, she saw the golden arches off in the distance. Up ahead she spied an overpass. *Where am I going?* she thought. A bus stop loomed at a stop on the overpass. *Maybe I can catch a bus back to Venice Beach!*

Amber kept a lookout for the Barracuda. *He*, not *She*, would look for her. *She'd* be half in the bag by now. Just as likely *She* would be pissed because she couldn't find her cigarettes and lighter. Amber decided to stop at 7-Eleven before she reached the bus stop.

She smiled at the crewcut man at the register. He wore an army fatigue shirt with DUNCAN stenciled above the pocket. She was thirsty and hungry so she bought a liter of Dr. Pepper, red licorice, and a pack of bubble gum. Duncan frowned at first when she produced the twenties, but softened when she thanked him for the change. Outside she noticed a few older cars in the parking lot. They looked abandoned except that one of them had new tires and a shiny bumper sticker—GET A HAIRCUT. The sun bore down as she continued up the boulevard.

At the empty bus stop, she looked over the embankment; a concrete wash flowed desolately below. Amber looked up and saw a bullet-ridden sign, LOS ANGELES RIVER. She stared at the chain-link fence guarding the gravel service road down to the river. Cars zipped by over the bridge. The cool shade of the underpass beckoned. Amber pulled on the gate until the chain slackened enough for her to squeeze through. A passing car honked as she yanked her bag through behind her. She headed down the concrete bank and ducked under the bridge. The cool of the shade caressed her face. It was like opening a refrigerator door. Amber sat down on the cold concrete bank, opened the liter of Dr. Pepper and took a long drink. She burped and laughed at the echo. She opened the licorice and stuffed a vine into her mouth. A flurry of wings overhead made her jump. On the underbelly of the bridge, Amber discovered a line of clay nests. She watched a small bird peek its head out, then dive out of the hole. A flock of birds followed, and together they swooped down to the surface of the water and arced back up to the sky. Amber relaxed onto her elbows, drank and ate and watched the flock dart en masse to the river below. Hunger abated, she lit a cigarette and watched the smoke roll toward the lazy river.

Amber was starting to doze off when she heard a shriek from downriver. She rose up on her elbows and craned her neck to see three older boys, all carrying skateboards, trailed by a girl a few years younger than herself. The girl had a tawny mop like one of the boys. The boy in the lead, who was just about to loft a 40-ounce bottle, spied Amber in the shadows. She sat up and slid her TWA bag to her side.

While Amber was deciding her next move, the little girl noticed her. She ran up the embankment and hailed Amber as if they'd been friends forever and shook her hand.

"Hi. My name is Julie. How are you today?" Her hand was sticky.

The three boys came up cautiously. The first one, with the bottle, stepped forward. "You got a smoke?" he asked.

He had longer hair than the other two and smudges on his upper lip and chin. The four of them waited for Amber to speak. She sat up and took out a cigarette. She handed it to the boy who turned out to be named Charlie. She looked at Julie and said, "My name is Amber."

Julie hugged Amber. "Can I have some?"

Amber pulled out another cigarette.

"She's too young to smoke and so are you," one of the boys, who was missing a front tooth, said. Julie introduced him as her brother, Frankie.

Amber pushed Julie off of her. "Mind your own business," she said to Frankie. She reached into her bag and pulled out a licorice and gave it to Julie. "Besides, he's not old enough to smoke either," she said, pointing to Charlie.

Charlie shrugged and threw the bottle down the concrete grade. They all watched the glass shards tinkle to the river's edge. "What are you doing here?" Charlie asked.

Amber took a long drag off her cigarette. "I'm waiting for the bus to Venice."

"There is no bus to Venice from here," he snickered.

The other two boys looked at each other. Julie's brother Frankie spoke up next. "Did you run away from home?"

The birds on the underbelly arced and swooped under the bridge.

Julie chewed on her licorice and watched them.

"I don't know."

"What do you mean you don't know? Did you leave home, or not?"

"I left, but I don't know where my home is. I'm going to find it," she said, feeling suddenly wise and independent.

Two or three cars passed over the bridge. Amber looked up. Charlie noticed. "You can hang out with us if you want."

"I'm going to Venice."

"What's in Venice?"

They all sat down now. Julie leaned into Amber. Amber liked it. She glanced down at the slow-moving river.

"My sister. We used to live together. She's older. She took care of me. She's beautiful, and she's really smart."

"Why don't you live with her now?"

Amber thought about it for a moment. "She can't. She doesn't have enough money. She lives with her friends and they won't let me live there."

Julie looked up at Frankie. "Maybe she can stay with us."

He ignored her. "Don't you like your mom?" he asked.

"I don't know."

Charlie reached into her backpack and took out a licorice vine. Amber looked the other way.

"What about your dad? Can you stay with him?"

Amber's head dropped. Julie put her arm around her. Amber rubbed her sleeve brusquely over her face. She didn't want her new friends to think she was a punk. She pulled her knees in and straightened up.

"My Dad doesn't want me."

Amber lit up another cigarette. She took a puff then passed it to Charlie. Charlie took a puff and passed it back.

"Well, that bus doesn't go to Venice."

Amber passed the cigarette back to Charlie. "I don't want to go back home."

"Why not?" Julie asked.

Amber thought of Largo, and the last time she tried to tell Mom what he was doing to her. Her heart clunked, remembering the beating. "Just can't." She pulled her bag onto her lap. "I've got money...wanna go to McDonald's?"

The kids nodded their heads and looked at Charlie. "Cool," he said.

Charlie got on his skateboard and headed down to the edge of the river, then swooped back up again. Frankie and the other boy joined him, staying a bit further from the edge. Amber and Julie followed them along the concrete river bank.

Back up on the sidewalk the children waited for the traffic to clear. They crossed, yelping encouragement to Julie. Amber felt like she was a part of something again. She grabbed Julie's hand as Charlie led them down the boulevard to the south end. The three boys rode their skateboards while Amber and Julie ambled together. Cars passed by and it must've been a curious sight, three boys flitting in and out of storefronts, jumping curbs, with two young girls chatting along in their wake. Amber was surprised at how empty the restaurant was. They settled into two booths with a view of the street. While they were waiting for their order to arrive, she took Julie to the bathroom. It was disturbing to find that Julie needed help and hadn't been shown how to wipe herself. She helped her wash herself and buckle up. Back in the booth, she continued her surrogate role. "Don't eat so fast," she said to Julie. "You'll get a stomach ache."

After they finished eating Charlie voiced the question that was on everyone's mind.

"Are you going to go back to your house?"

Amber was about to say that she was going to Venice but it seemed useless now.

"I guess I have to. I don't have anywhere else to go."

"Why don't we go to our house? We can have a sleepover," Julie asked.

Frankie frowned at her. He smiled at Amber. *He's cute*, Amber thought.

On the way to Julie's house, they smoked and finished off the rest of the licorice. Amber was happy to find out Julie and Frankie lived down the street from her. It would only take her a few minutes to walk home. They were on the South Side, near

McDonald's. As they approached the house Frankie stopped them. "My mom is a little crazy sometimes. Don't worry about it. She's really nice when she isn't drunk. But she drinks all the time...so be ready is all I'm saying." Julie fell quiet as they opened the front door.

Mrs. Turnbull was drunk. Amber thought there was something else wrong with her. She'd never witnessed anyone shift moods so rapidly. Even Mom seemed normal by comparison. One second she welcomed Amber like a prodigal daughter and the next she was threatening them with a bat. There was a case of Schlitz malt liquor next to her easy chair, and the discards were lying on the floor around her. The children crept out to the backyard. It was a lot like the one she had at her new place, only there was a large tree in the middle of the yard with a tire swing, and in place of the shed was a two car garage. The girls took to riding the tire, while the others smoked and drank a Schlitz they'd taken from Mrs. Turnbull. Amber loved how her new friends stuck together. It reminded her how things had been on Magnolia Street when she, Paul and Grace were inseparable. She felt safe for the first time in years. While Julie flowed joyously through the air, with Frankie standing on the tire behind her, Amber fiddled with a stick, jabbing it into the Bermuda grass between her legs. She dreaded the inevitable confrontation at home.

As the shadows grew long and cool and the sun sank low over the Topanga Mountains, Amber reviewed a plan she'd been working on since McDonald's. She would sneak into the house, crawl if she needed to, and lie down right inside the door. She counted on her mother to be too drunk to notice. Largo would be an entirely different challenge. When it was time to say goodbye Julie wrapped her arms around Amber's waist and wouldn't let go. She hung on to Amber, and let herself be dragged to the back porch. It only took five minutes to walk to her new house. She walked down the gravel driveway, past the shuttered front house, keeping her eyes on the darkened doorstep. She was thankful that the porch light was out. The tiny bungalow was still and silent.

On the porch, Amber peered in the window. Her hopes rose, as it appeared that no one was home. But then, she saw it—the glow of a cigarette, and as her eyes adjusted she made out a broad silhouette on the couch. Largo.

Amber buttoned up her blouse all the way to the top, and did the same with her jacket. She tightened her belt. She thrust the screen door open until it squeaked. Timidity had no place in their relationship. He'd never beaten her, but the threat was ever present. She opened the front door and entered as if coming home from a long day at work. She dropped her bag just inside the door and headed straight for the bathroom, with soft steps. It wouldn't help to wake Mom.  She paused at the bathroom door to listen. She jumped at the suddenness of his deep rumbling voice.

"Where have you been?" His buffalo head reeled. He patted the cushion next to him. "Come here."

Amber's heart leaped into her mouth. A pain shot through her abdomen.

Largo, a much worse scenario than any her mother could conjure. He didn't care where she'd been. He only cared where she wasn't when he wanted her.

Amber endured his need as he called *It*. She hoped it wasn't one of those nights. Amber walked over to the couch and sat at the far end. She immediately regretted wearing the shorts.

Largo took a drag. The glowing tip lit up the lower part of his face. He stamped it out on the table, not bothering to locate the ashtray. "Come on over here," he said. He grabbed her by the belt, effortlessly sliding her to him. It was going to be one of those nights. Amber went limp.

Afterward, she felt as dead and used as she always did. He tried to keep her close, his paternal touch with the heavy bicep around her neck—she was too afraid to move for fear that it would arouse him. She couldn't bear his touch, but it was in fact all she knew. He lit a cigarette with his free hand and passed it to her as if they'd just shared something.  Largo nodded off around midnight. Amber watched his head drift back, exposing his thick neck. She imagined going into the kitchen, getting her mother's one sharp knife, and slitting his throat. He snored so loudly Amber thought it would wake Mom who would in turn find her nearly on his lap. Amber slipped out from under Largo's arm. She dragged a blanket to a corner of the room and curled up. She imagined her day: the arrival, the new kids, the river, all so new. She tapped the images for hope, embellishing them as she fell into a fitful slumber.

#####

The next morning Amber awoke on the couch to the sound of screeching. She pulled the blanket over her head. Mom and Largo were having one of their hangover fights in the kitchen. She lay as still as possible, gathering the gist of the fight.

"I was asleep. How could you?"

"Your eyes were wide open. It's called a blackout, baby."

"You could've at least woke me up."

"You liked it and you know it," he leered.

The pit of Amber's stomach burned. She was fully awake now but she didn't want them to know it. She wondered if there was any licorice left. The leftover money was lying right there in her bag.

Mom took a Vodka bottle down from the middle shelf of the cabinet. "By the way, did you take money from my purse again?" she asked Largo.

Amber held her breath.

"You mean my money. Don't forget where you got it."

That was close. Amber exhaled. She peeked out toward the window. The morning sun forged shadows on the faded carpet. An acrid smell rose from under the blanket. It occurred to Amber that she was the source, not having bathed in a day or so. A cramp made her gasp. When Mom and Largo retreated to the bedroom, and she heard the bedsprings twang under their weight, she tiptoed into the bathroom. Amber stood under the shower, plugged the drain, lay down and felt every drop gently batter her. She lay there with her eyes closed until Mom banged on the wall. "Don't use up all the hot water, Amber!"

All fresh and ready for another day with her new friends, Amber ate Cap'n Crunch on the couch. Mom and Largo were talking and getting dressed. Amber went into the kitchen and grabbed a pack of matches from the counter. She accidentally knocked over a plastic tumbler and panicked when it clattered loudly on the linoleum floor.

"Amber, is that you?" her mother yelled from the bedroom.

"Yes, Mom."

"Where have you been?"

"I made some friends yesterday. They live down the street. That's where I was last night. Largo knows, ask him."

Mom murmured something to Largo. Amber knew he wouldn't say anything. Mom walked past her to the sink.

"Where are you going?" she asked over her shoulder.

"I'm going to my new friends' house." Amber opened the front door.

"Don't stay out too late. We need to get you some school clothes."

# 7

"That seems so long ago," Grace said to Terri who was sitting across from her at the Blue Parrot off Sunset Boulevard. The Polaroid photo she held was taken when they were fresh out of high school. "I was so thin. We were such babes." The best friends hadn't seen each other in months. Terri had been to Florida with her mother visiting family. Grace spent the time "finding herself" as she often told Kimo and Rex. It explained the late nights and anonymous sex. Many of her friends were married now. She was yet to have a steady boyfriend. At nineteen, she acted as if she were making up for lost time.

The bar was filling up quickly; it was Friday night, with lots of skin showing, typical Los Angeles summertime. A gaunt man, boyish, but well into his thirties, walked by wearing cut off jeans that showed his butt cheeks. Grace and Terri paused briefly to appreciate the sight.

Grace looked closely at Terri. "You got a perm."

"About time you noticed. Do you like it?"

"It's going to take some getting used to," Grace laughed. She stood up. "Look what my wonderful roommates Kimo and Rex got me for my birthday!" She posed, her hips a bit thicker, her breasts fuller than at any point after high school. The combat pants stretched over her butt nicely, she thought.

"They're coming tonight, right?" Terri asked.

"Why do you think we're meeting here?" Grace said.

The bartender placed two glasses of draft beer in front of Grace and Terri.

"There you are, ladies. Compliments of the hottie with the gorgeous arms," he said, nodding at a tall suave man near the stage.

Grace looked over her shoulder expecting Rex and Kimo but to her delight, it was Victor. She'd made out with him last night in front of Gold's Gym. She'd wanted to date Victor since the first time she'd met him at the Oar House. He was an aspiring actor who'd had a small role in a Sylvester Stallone movie. He also dealt most of the heroin on the beach. Grace jumped off her stool and ran to him. "You came," she said, wrapping her arms around his waist.

Grace dug her face into his hairy chest and breathed in his musk. She'd been following him around the Oar House for the last year waiting for him to ask her out. She'd gotten increasingly aggressive in the last few weeks. Victor held her at an arm's length.

"Lookin' fine, baby!" He twirled her. He let go and started for the bar.

Grace pulled his arm across her shoulders and around her neck. It'd taken this long to get him, and she wasn't about to let go. "Let's dance," she said, pulling him onto the dance floor.

The DJ turned up the volume and the dance floor was suddenly packed with writhing, pumping and jiving men, scantily dressed and glistening. Grace was the only girl on the dance floor. She danced in a circle around Victor. A tall thin boy with no shirt on and slicked back hair danced in close to whisper in her ear, "Lucky bitch."

Grace gave him a shove with her hip, threw her head back, strutting in front of Victor. He made a show of grabbing her breasts and gyrating into her. He undid a button on his shirt revealing a

gold necklace and chain. The song was winding down. Grace
pulled Victor by the hand to the bar where Terri, Rex, and Kimo sat
together. She hadn't noticed her roommates come in. She gave
them each a hug. Terri made space for Grace and Victor. Grace
waved at the bartender, ordered a round of shots, then put her arms
around Victor's neck. Victor winked at Terri. Terri held up her
engagement ring. Grace kissed Victor, tickling his lips with her
tongue. She pushed off when the shots came.

"Happy Birthday Grace," they toasted.

"And Terri's engagement!" Grace added.

A roar went up from the dance floor as the opening notes to
"Superstition" by Stevie Wonder kicked in. "Let's dance!" Grace
yelled.

Rex and Kimo were the first on the dance floor followed by
Grace, Terri, and Victor. The lights around the stage cast shadows
on their faces. The night was young, and Grace, young, full of life,
knew what she wanted for her birthday. She grabbed Victor's belt,
gyrated down to her knees and back up again. She kissed him fully
on the lips, throbbing. It'd been a week since she'd gotten any.
Grace pressed her breasts against his chest and corralled him with
her thighs. He was a foot taller but her fire consumed him. He
wrapped his arms around her as the song ended. Grace shivered
when his lips slid past her ear, down the nape of her neck.

Rex and Kimo kept close to Grace, aware of Victor's
reputation. Terri danced nearby, keeping an eye on her friend.

Grace licked Victor's ear. It felt right. She whispered, "Let's
go smoke a joint. Did you drive?" She knew he had a hot car.

Victor nodded.

Grace took his hand and guided him toward the rear exit. As
she sped off the dance floor, Rex and Kimo blocked her path.
"Grace. Can we speak to you for a second?" Rex said. They looked
worried.

Grace turned to Victor. "Dance with Terri. I'll be right back."

Back at the bar, Rex and Kimo cornered her.

Rex spoke first. "You know who you're dealing with, right?"

"He's no gentleman, honey," Kimo chimed in. "He sent Tracy to the hospital, remember?"

Grace looked from face to face. These were not only her close friends but her housemates. She knew they wanted the best for her, that they felt protective, but she also knew that Victor could be sweet, even generous. She'd never seen his "bad" side. She looked into Rex's, then Kimo's eyes.

"I know. But Tracy exaggerates everything. Look at him."

The three looked at the dance floor. Victor was dancing in step with Terri. He thrust toward her, pumping his hips. Terri kept her arms at stomach level and kept looking back at Grace and the boys.

"Look." She pointed at them. "He's a perfect gentleman."

Rex took her hands in his. "All we're saying is don't get too close.  He's a pimp and a drug dealer."

Grace hugged Rex and Kimo. "Thank you," she said, as she rushed to grab Victor off the dance floor.  Terri pulled her by the arm. "Be careful, Grace," she warned.

Grace grabbed Victor's hand and headed for the back exit. "I'll be back!" she yelled over her shoulder, tossing her hair.

Outside Grace lost no time in producing a joint from her blouse pocket. Victor led her to his cherry red Camaro, parked against the fence. He pressed her against the passenger door and kissed her deeply. She groaned and ground into him. He pulled away, opened the door, stepped around to the other side. Grace got in and lit the joint. She put one hand on the steering wheel, pressed her mouth against Victor's and gently blew the smoke into his waiting mouth. She played her tongue along his lips. Victor's hands slid around her body, first her waist, butt, and thighs. Grace straddled him. Victor pushed the bench seat back. Grace fit perfectly between Victor and the steering wheel. She began riding him with the joint in one hand, and the other behind his head. She nuzzled his neck, threw her hair back and offered her breasts to him. She took another drag on the joint. Victor bit her breasts as she rode him. He entwined her hair in his fingers and pulled. Grace was suddenly taken by his strength as her head snapped back. She bent to kiss him, but he held her head back, teeth bared His other hand crept up between her breasts, to clutch her neck. He began to tighten his grip, chuckling in a way that made her heart skip a beat. She was frozen above him, in his grasp, joint smoldering in her hand. She gripped his collar with her free hand.

A jolt of fear mixed with lust tore through her. She wanted him, but up to that moment, it was her hunt. Now, Victor held the initiative, and she was looking for a counter. As his grip tightened around her throat, Grace pressed her knee into his solar plexus. She meant to communicate, not to disable. As he released his grip, Grace lifted her knee. His surrender was gradual. When Victor finally let go he raised both hands above his head. "Damn, baby, I was just playing." He took a deep breath.

Grace slid her knee back to his side. She placed both hands on the back of the seat, suspended above him. She purred in his ear, "Gentle."

He pushed her off and moved the bench seat up.

"Wow," he said. "Who *are* you?" He took a drag from the joint.

Grace leaned over and kissed him on the cheek. He exhaled, shaking his head.

"Let's go back inside," he said.

Back in the nightclub Grace and Victor joined Terri, Rex, and Kimo at the bar.

Rex spotted them as they walked across the dance floor. He nudged Kimo, and soon all three friends turned to greet them.

Victor had lipstick smeared on his lips. Grace's hair was tousled, but she looked no worse for the wear. She sat down next to Terri. Victor tried to sit between them, but Rex slipped off his bench in front of him.

"Want to dance, big boy?" he asked.

Kimo slipped up next to Victor on the other side. They grabbed Victor's arms and guided him to the dance floor. "Come on, manly man, let's shake it."

It was already past ten o'clock, and dancers flowed en masse to the beat. Rex and Kimo guided Victor to the center of the floor. Victor took one uncertain glance back to Grace and Terri before surrendering to the surge.

Grace watched the boys jive and tussle a few yards away. She turned to Terri who was already half in the bag, with four shots and a beer. She tapped her engagement ring on the bar, watching Grace.

"How was it?" she asked.

Grace raised her chin, gazing up at the ceiling. She sighed. "Well, he's a good kisser."

Terri furrowed her brow. "What really happened? You can't hide anything from me."

"Well, we were in the car smoking a joint, we started making out and he got rough. It was sexy at first, but it didn't feel like he was playing." She paused, looking over at the dance floor. Terri shook her head.

"I don't think he was trying to hurt me. He's just so strong. I like that."

"What did you do?" Terri asked, placing her hand on Grace's arm.

"I overpowered him." Grace jumped off her stool and mimed a bodybuilder from Muscle Beach, arms flexed above her head.

"No really, stop playing. How did you stop him?" Terri pleaded.

"I put a knee in his solar plexus. He was a kitten after that."

"Do you still like him? He's a jerk."

Grace looked back at the dance floor. The song was nearing its end. Victor looked impatient. Rex and Kimo were jostling him and laughing.

"I've been waiting this long. Don't you think he's hot?" She squeezed Terri's arm. "Don't worry. I can handle myself. I just want to have a good time, that's all." Grace hugged Terri.

Kimo and Rex left around midnight. Terri's fiance came to get her shortly after. Grace gave her a long hug at the door. "We'll always be friends, no matter what," she told her.


######


Victor's house, the Victorian, had a reputation as a party house. In the fifties, a successful drug dealer owned it; he held lavish parties whose attendees included some of Hollywood's greatest B actors.

Now, the house was known for a different clientele and service. It was referred to as the "Bordello". Victor "rented" rooms to teenagers he'd taken in, accepting payment in a variety of ways. They found in him a firm paternal security. The home was also a source of heroin, for the kids on the beach. A steady ebb and flow took place at most hours, with a Victor-mandated break from four to nine in the morning. Business was good these days, but there was space for a new girl in the house.

Grace stared up at the lacy curtains in Victor's master bedroom, dreamily watching the sunlight fill the bay windows. Victor lay face down next to her, his arm draped across her breast. She sighed, in concert with his rising and falling back. She was suddenly very thirsty at the sound of running water, someone taking a shower somewhere in the house. She leaned toward the bedroom door and purred softly at the sight of her and Victor's rumpled clothes making a trail to the bed. She thought it strange— she hadn't noticed anyone when they arrived—drunken with lust, booze, and dope.

Her head jerked toward a voice on the stairs. She craned to listen and realized it was a conversation between several people. She was suddenly aware that the house was alive with people. From the front of the house, on their floor, she heard soft, bluesy music. From downstairs, toward the front of the house, she heard a blow dryer, and toward the back of the house, near what she imagined was the kitchen, she heard the soft lilt of a young woman. Below them, the noise was clearest. Someone was having sex. Whoever it was moaned in pain or delirium, maybe both.

Grace peered back at Victor. He gurgled softly, and she was grateful for the thought that she was among the very few to see him so vulnerable, so lovably peaceful. While the house erupted around them, Grace breathed in the solitude between them.

Heavy steps on the stairs broke her reverie. Victor lurched upright.

As the steps resounded down the hall, nearing, Victor reached into a bed stand to produce a pistol. He was on his knees, bouncing naked and still semi-hard when the intruder pounded on the door. Grace fell off the side of the bed in a heap.

"Victor! The cops are here. They want you now."

Victor grabbed a silk bathrobe from the bedpost and slung the door open.

"Shit!" Victor swore. "What the fuck do they want now?"

A short teenager with a scraggly beard cowered under his glare.

"They're at the door," he cringed.

Victor bounded past him.

Grace grabbed her new camouflage pants off the floor. She yanked them on and reached for her bra and blouse. She heard loud voices downstairs now. The skinny kid's gaze lingered on her breasts, then he turned and sped after Victor.

Grace listened in the open doorway. The hallway was vacant. The rest of the house was hushed; the blow dryer had stopped, the bed was no longer knocking below them, and not a peep from the kitchen.

Grace closed the door. She looked across the room for a possible exit. One of the bay windows was ajar. Other than that possible egress, the bedroom was a dead end. Then, she spied the closed bathroom door. It blended so well with the wall paper she'd missed it altogether.

Grace rushed into the bathroom and was immediately taken by its opulence. The tile on the bath was ornate and immaculate, and the sink hardware was finely polished brass. It was not what she expected from a struggling actor. Grace stared at the only window in the bathroom, over the toilet. The bottom of the screen was unlatched. She stopped to listen. Muffled voices emanated from the front of the house, footsteps on the stairs, in the hallway. Grace pushed the screen and was abruptly surprised that it did not spill onto the roof, until she saw the hinges, and realized she'd found Victor's escape hatch. Grace heard footsteps in the room now, stepped on the toilet seat, and put one foot on the sill. She was half out the window when a voice froze her in her tracks.

"Where are you going?"

Victor stood in the bathroom doorway smiling. "Was I that bad?"

He stood with the robe open, full frontal nudity.

Grace stepped off the toilet. She exhaled loudly. "I thought it was a raid. What happened?"

Victor returned to the bedroom. "It was nothing. Some dealer is missing. Do you want some breakfast? One of my girls is making pancakes. Come on." He waved her toward the door. He arched his brows. She smiled, stepping forward into his arms. She could feel him grow between them. "On second thought, pancakes can wait."


######

It was after the Joni Mitchell concert at the Corral Club in Topanga, and it was their two month anniversary. During the concert they sat entwined, close enough to hear Joni's intimate banter with her guitarist. Joni even winked at them as they made out between sets.

Afterward, they held hands all the way back to the house— pulling over once to make out under the sprawling boughs of a massive Jacaranda. The Victorian was alight when they pulled up. Music blared out the side of the house, with the living room windows wide open and voices careening out to the curb, where cars were double parked. Victor pulled onto the grass. Victor took her hand and led her up the steps into the foyer. She would have followed him anywhere at that point.

The living room was a high ceilinged lounge area that could hold twenty people comfortably. Victor had knocked down the wall separating the parlor and now the larger room was furnished to entertain multiple parties at once. Victor led Grace past the line of couches and glass top coffee tables toward the grand fireplace at the far end of the room. On a polished brick mantel were bare-breasted figurines in pantaloons, afros and large hoop earrings. A bearskin rug guarded the hearth. On the walls a collection of nineteenth-century portraits stared down on them, ridiculously formal and strident.

Victor sat down in a high-backed chair, next to a couch and coffee table, which made an intimate quadrant by the fireplace. When she sat on the couch, Grace noticed a few couples staring her way. She recognized only a few people, which made her wish she'd invited Terri. Victor reached into a cabinet, hidden behind the high-back chair. Grace observed the three or four separate parties occurring throughout the room. She recognized one of the women who'd made pancakes, Pam, and another who'd helped clean up the dishes, Vickie. They were dressed swankily and held their space like hostesses. Grace also observed that, while Victor was preoccupied, he continued to furtively measure his guests.

Grace moved closer to the edge of the couch toward Victor.

"Have you ever snorted smack?" he asked.

"A couple of times," she replied, rubbing her nose at the memory.

Victor poured out little piles of powder in rows onto the glass coffee table. He produced a straw from the cubby, inhaled two piles, and pinched his nose. His eyes teared up, as he relaxed into the chair-back. Grace watched him. She'd never seen anyone snort that much heroin at once. Victor handed the straw to Grace. Grace looked around the room and caught Pam's eye. Pam gave her a strange, indecipherable look. She watched Victor. He was in another world now and she wished they'd stayed under the Jacaranda tree. If he wasn't there, she knew she would have declined the heroin, but it was still early in their relationship and things had been going so well. She leaned over the coffee table and snorted the smallest pile. Tears streamed down her cheeks, such was the burn. Grace leaned back against the couch cushion. She closed her eyes for what she thought was a second when suddenly she felt a tap on her shoulder.

When she opened her eyes, there were only two parties in the room, the one under the bay windows, and Victor's. The room was quiet. Victor was on the couch next to her, nuzzling her breasts with his eyes closed. Pam hovered above them. Once again, she emitted a confusing aura: her sallow complexion (so strange in Venice Beach), her dead dark eyes, and a frozen sneer. Pam pointed at the remaining pile on the table.

"Are you going to do that?" she asked Grace, with a quick glance at Victor.

Now that she was close up, Grace could see the lines in her face. Her eyes were hollow, and she looked dangerously underweight.

"Hunh?" Grace responded.

Pam kneeled in close to the coffee table, the straw at the ready. The party under the bay windows was disbanding. Grace waved dutifully, as the girlfriend of Victor, then recoiled at the absurdity of it. She watched in a mix of horror and awe as Pam snorted the rest of the heroin. Grace watched Pam's head sway back, her eyes close, and in one swoop, she was out. The back of her head thudded against the thick red shag. Grace tried to catch her fall, but her system was addled by the powder. Now, she watched Pam lying there, curled up into a fetal position, devolving.

She looked around the room for help. The room was cleared, except for Victor, her and Pam. Even Vickie was off somewhere.

Grace shook Victor. He wasn't moving, and for a split second, she thought maybe he'd also succumbed. In a desperate flurry of energy, she pushed him off of her. Finally, he opened his sleepy eyes, taking a moment to recognize her. She held his face.

"Victor. Something is wrong with Pam."

Victor, perturbed, looked down at Pam. "Shit. She'll sleep it off," he mumbled, as his head descended to the armrest.

Grace knelt beside Pam. She bent next to her mouth and felt for breathing. There was a slight tickle of breath on her cheek. Grace looked up at Victor. His eyelids fluttered and a glitter of spittle was already forming in the corner of his mouth. She stood up, looked back down to Pam, and decided it was alright to leave her be for a moment. Grace walked out the double doors and down the hall.

In the kitchen, Vickie was entertaining two men at the kitchen table. One was kissing her breasts, while the other, wearing a calf skin jacket, had his face mashed into the dark fuzz between her legs.

Grace rushed in, still a little dizzy. "Pam is passed out. I think she's dead!"

"Her bedroom is the second on the right," Vickie murmured.

Grace threw up her hands. "Would someone fucking help me, please? She's dying!"

The man in the calf skin came up for air. "Put her to bed. She'll be alright." He bit Vickie's thigh. "Ain't no thang." He seemed to notice Grace's face for the first time. He gave her a wink and followed her back to the living room.

Pam was motionless. Victor was now stretched out on his back, snoring.

Grace stepped aside as the stranger lofted Pam over his shoulder in a fireman's lift. She followed him to Pam's room, where he plopped her on a bed strewn with dirty laundry. It smelled like vomit and sandalwood.

Grace stood in the doorway waiting. The stranger stared down at Pam. Grace waited for him to leave but he didn't budge. He looked up at Grace, smiling; he began to unbutton Pam's blouse. Pam rolled over against the wall. Grace wanted him to know there was nothing there for him. She was tired. More tired than she'd been in her short life. She wasn't going to leave Pam alone with this beast. The stranger reached for Pam. "Let's get a drink," Grace said. The stranger looked down at Pam, and back up at Grace. There was that wicked smile again. Grace waited for the stranger to abandon his post by Pam's bed. She pushed the button on the doorknob to lock the door prior to closing it. She'd done a good thing, she thought.

The next morning Grace woke up in Victor's bed. A harsh sunlight filled the bay windows. Victor snored softly next to her. She did not feel the elation of their first night. She had a splitting headache, and her stomach growled incessantly. Her body ached, but she couldn't recall having had sex. Then she remembered the drugs. Her next thought brought her off the bed. On her feet, she experienced a wave of dizziness that nearly dropped her back onto the mattress. She shook off the nausea, gathered her clothes and dressed in a hurry. The cotton dress she'd worn for the concert had a tear in the seam, and she couldn't find her panties. She tumbled downstairs to Pam's room. She frowned to find that the door was ajar. The sun cast a swath of light across Pam's body. Grace realized there were two people in the bed, and was horrified when she recognized the man, the stranger with the calf skin jacket. Pam was still facing the wall, but she was nude, as was he.

Grace walked down the hall to the kitchen. She tried to make sense of what she'd just seen, of what this place really was—the parties, the drugs, the sex, the hostesses, and on top of them all, was Victor, the king. She was safer on the beach with Herbie. She didn't want the truth to fully form in her mind, but the whisper of its meaning was undeniable. She sat heavily on a chair at the kitchen table. Half full and empty bottles formed a glass skyline, along with ash trays, and plastic keg cups. She determined to talk with Victor when he woke up. He couldn't condone rape, could he? She waded through the memory of the evening, looking for the precise moment that it had gone wrong—their dinner together, the concert, and back to the house. She rubbed her nose, recalling the heroin, Pam, and the strangers' faces around the room.

Grace took a plastic cup and went to the refrigerator. The house was still quiet. She found a bottle of orange juice and brought it back to the table. The sun spilled into the room, glinting off the bottles on the table, making colorful prisms on the floor. A horn blasted out on the street. Grace thought back to the concert while she poured a glass of orange juice. The colors were so pretty on the floor, Victor had been so loving during "Both Sides Now".

She brought the cup to her mouth, paused, and decided to add a little Jack. *To give me courage,* she thought. Grace sipped in silence. Halfway through her drink she began to cramp. She dumped the rest of the drink in the sink and let the tap run over her cheeks. The pressure from the counter felt good on her stomach. She walked past Pam's door again on her way back to bed, ignoring the evidence of an incident she'd tried to prevent.

# 8

They were all in the kitchen at Victor's Victorian. The windows were open, a fresh salty breeze and pancake smell swirled about the room. The table was replete with pancakes, orange juice, tall glasses of milk, and a wonderful bouquet centerpiece. Pam, Vickie, Grace, Victor and the scraggly teenager, Lance, sat at the table. Victor sat at the head of the table in his bathrobe, hair slicked back from a recent shower, while Grace flipped pancakes on a grill she'd picked up at Woolworth's.

At Victor's request, she'd called in sick to her job at Der Wienerschnitzel. Her boss let her have her old job back when he heard she was living with Victor. She felt if she had her own money Victor would respect her. Vickie took the message to come pick up her final check. She'd been fired.

"I can put you to work here," Victor reassured her. She didn't know what that meant, but she did know that the cramps that began at the party a week earlier had gotten worse. And now she'd contrived this "family breakfast" to distract her from what the pain meant.

"Pam, can you pour the orange juice, please," Grace asked.

Victor seemed to be enjoying the assembly of his intimates, as he called them. Grace smiled to see him glowing and in such a good mood.

Grace placed a large platter of pancakes in the center of the table. Lance and Victor dug in, while Vickie picked the smallest cake on the pile, slapped it on her plate, and lit a cigarette. She leaned back with a sour face, smoking and stabbing the same punctured pancake over and over.

Victor poured a pool of syrup onto his plate. Grace admired the spread, took her apron off and sat opposite Victor. In that moment, across from Victor, a full table, she wondered what it would be like to have her own family. Victor stared across the table chewing a mouthful of pancakes. Syrup ran down his chin before his tongue darted out to swipe the sticky drop. They'd made love in the middle of the night. It was painful this time. She'd initiated it because he was most vulnerable then, pliable and instinctual, unlike when he was awake—which was all about his power.

After six months together, she thought she knew him. There was the business-income from selling drugs and prostitution. She accepted this because she knew him above anyone else. He loved her, and his customers were all, for the most part, consenting adults. Now that she was nearly twenty, she wondered if he'd changed his mind about her, if he was ready to take the next step.

Grace watched him tenderly tuck a wayward strand of hair behind Pam's ear. He was kind, she thought, and even fatherly to Pam, and the other young ones, who came off the beach, into their home. Grace watched Vickie dissect her pancake, with a squinty eye on Victor and Pam. She'd occasionally glanced Grace's way, and they'd exchanged a practical mask of confederacy.

Lance ate quietly. He hardly ever spoke. He'd taken to Grace, like a wayward puppy, and she knew how to cheer him up when Victor was in a cruel mood.

Grace started clearing the breakfast dishes when Victor held his hand up for an announcement. "We've got some new stuff coming in tonight. Pam, Vickie, Lance, get the word out on the beach. Grace."

Grace leaned against the counter.

"We need your paycheck. Pick it up, and bring me cash."

Grace looked around the table. All eyes were on her. This was a first.

"I just called in sick. Can't I pick it up tomorrow?"

Victor slapped both hands on the tabletop. Everyone froze. "Do it," he said in a low voice. Grace stared around the table. No allies.

Victor arched his back with a toothy grin, rubbing his hands together. His voice softened, "Go after you clean up, okay, honey?"

Vickie snickered and stamped out her fifth cigarette. She stood up and tied her bathrobe.

Lance and Pam helped Grace clean up the kitchen. At the sink, she soaped the dishes, staring into the neighbor's backyard. The cramps were back. She took her mind off the pain by focusing on the little world next door. There was a jungle gym, a Tonka truck, and a small sandbox. They'd constructed a trellis, and the view was partially obscured by morning glory vines. But, she could still see the mini playground, and thought it peculiar, under the shadow of Victor's party house. She suddenly realized how sad she was. Not from the subterranean lovemaking, nor from the physical work she'd put into the house, rather, from the weight of the slow-forming truth. She'd been his girlfriend, but that was no longer the case. Pam was his project. "She's a money maker," he told her. She wondered if he'd soon say that about her.

Grace wiped down the counter. Out the window, two toddlers edged down the back steps of the house next door. She ducked out of sight and watched the mother at the top of the steps keeping guard over her pups. The toddlers stumbled toward the sandbox, and Grace was suddenly filled with an undeniable yearning to see Amber.

She turned away from the window and put the milk and orange juice back in the fridge.

She walked down the hall and paused at Pam's doorway. Victor was stretched out on her bed. Pam hunched over his naked thighs. Her hair cascaded over his open robe, as she bobbed mechanically. She gagged, and Victor stroked her hair, making cooing sounds. He jerked his head toward the door when he realized Grace was watching. He smiled and continued stroking Pam's hair. She resumed the piston-like rhythm.

Grace tore off her apron and threw it toward the front door as she ran upstairs. Grace went to the little room next to Victor's. The closet was filled with Victor's clothes, while a few of her outfits hung at the end of the bar. Grace pulled down a pair of khakis and a denim blouse. She turned toward the window and realized how small her life had become. A mattress lay below the window, a bloated laundry bag, a few art books, and her carryall. That summed up her material life to that point. She retrieved the brightly colored work uniform and stuffed it into her bag. She winced when she bent to put on her Wallabees. The pain was only getting worse. She could no longer discern between the pain of truth and the pain of her body.

A plan began to form, a possible remedy. She would go to the free clinic after she cashed her check. She would run and keep running. As she descended the stairs she looked back toward his bedroom. Through the bedroom and the bathroom beyond was the window—the escape hatch she'd used that first night. In hindsight, she wished she'd have taken it and kept going when she had the chance. She heaved down the steps already thinking what she would tell the doctor at the clinic.

Victor startled her at the bottom of the stairs. "Hey, baby. I'm going to need that money by one." He caressed the back of her neck, bent, and kissed Grace firmly on the lips. "That's my girl."

Grace met his kiss with stone lips. All she could think about was what she would do if she were carrying his baby.

Under a cloudless California blue sky, Grace walked up the sidewalk laden with the weight of uncertainty. She'd thought of having children, and until recently thought that might be possible with Victor. Her feet were sore already and she cursed her decision to wear her Wallabies on such a hot day. At Ocean Park Boulevard she adjusted her carryall. The cramps assaulted her midsection and the mid-day heat compounded her crankiness. She picked up her pace on the other side of the street with Der Wienerschnitzel a block ahead. She entered the front of the restaurant and was grateful no customers were at the counter. A new girl greeted her and she asked for her check. She looked around the restaurant. A few families were eating noisily at nearby booths, but most of the tables were empty. As she waited the cramps overtook her. She slumped dizzily. She had a blinding fever and the room was spinning. She placed both hands on the counter and dropped her carryall. She didn't want to throw up on the counter, but it seemed imminent. Grace leaned away from the counter, weaved, then fainted onto the tile. As she stared up at the ceiling, noticing the cobwebs, and the ketchup stains that had inexplicably reached the highest regions of the restaurant, she pondered her death at a fast food restaurant on Ocean Park Boulevard. The pain was so great she could not move, and it was clear to her that any way forward would require a Samaritan. Grace closed her eyes. The sound of rubber soles squealing on tile signaled her savior. When she opened her eyes her manager Billy stood over her. He and the new girl loaded Grace into his Mercury and in a blur, they were in the waiting room of the Venice Free Clinic.

Grace sat in the tiny room with a wastebasket in front of her. A nervous-looking teenager and a middle-aged man stared at her as if she were about to erupt. The intake nurse called her over and after fifteen minutes she led her into an examination room. A young doctor in scrubs and a sympathetic, yet condescending affect, checked her vitals. "What seems to be the problem?"

"I think I'm pregnant," she blurted between spasms.

"I don't do abortions," he said with a tight jaw. Grace opened her mouth to protest, but he launched into a series of routine questions, after which he asked her to change into a paper dress.

He did a swab, which she thought must be a new pregnancy test. Grace relaxed when he left the room. She felt the air conditioning kick on. It felt good on her face and she welcomed a sudden shiver. The young doctor returned with a Dixie cup of pills. He helped her sit up, dropped the pills in her hand and filled the cup. "Here. These are for your pain."

Grace smiled up at his sudden kindness. The mood had shifted and she soon found out why.

"I'm testing you for Gonorrhea. I need you to check back in with me in a couple days for the results." He handed her a pamphlet with a cartoon drawing of a confused amorphous blob with a question mark above its head. It was labeled Gonorrhea! Now what?

Grace stared at the word, Gonorrhea. She'd heard it once, in a sex education video in high school. Her symptoms suddenly made sense, the cramps, the fever, nausea. She'd assumed she was pregnant because on some level, she welcomed the change a baby would bring.

Back in the waiting room the nurse stared at her expectantly but kept her distance. Her weak smile revealed to Grace that the doctor had loose lips. She let Grace use the telephone. Grace dialed the number, but the line rang and rang. Terri wasn't home. She kept on the mute line, buying time until the nurse began to hover close by.

Laden once again on a bus bench in front of the clinic, Grace decided to go to Aunt Mary's by the beach. She'd always lent a hand to desperate kids. After an interminable trek, she arrived at Aunt Mary's, and she welcomed her without asking questions. Grace spent the next few days on Aunt Mary's couch waiting for the test results. They watched *Twilight Zone* reruns with the sound off, and Herb Alpert and the Tijuana Brass playing on the turntable. As the black and white characters strode across the screen, Grace mourned a *fait accompli* she couldn't quite accept as yet.

After the news, Grace went back to the clinic to get her shot. She bade goodbye to Aunt Mary, who gave her some pot brownies wrapped in wax paper for her pain.

Her carryall was all she had now. She'd gotten even lighter at Aunt Mary's, and the fresh start that began a week earlier with the last kiss was now in full motion. Her arm still burned from the shot as she stopped at a gas station on Ocean Park Boulevard. The attendant waved, an old friend from Venice High. She went to the phone booth on the side near the bathrooms. She couldn't call Rex and Kimo, or Terri, the thought of explaining what happened was too much to bear. They'd warned her. She felt like she'd abandoned them. Maybe someday, but not today.

Grace fished in her camouflage pants for a dime. There was only one person she could call, and she hadn't spoken with him since he returned from Vietnam. She called information first. The operator connected her without delay.

"Dad?"

"Grace, is that you? Where are you?"

"I'm in Venice." She began to well up. She squeezed her eyes shut, banishing her tears.

"What is it?"

"I need a place to stay," she stammered between breaths.

"Are you alright?"

Grace squeezed her eyes shut. She hit her fist against the side of the glass phone booth.

"I need a place to stay," she repeated.

There was a pause on the other end. A man in a business suit turned the corner on the way to the men's room. Grace turned her back to him and hunched over the receiver.

"Dad?"

"Grace."

"I hate to ask, but I don't have anywhere else to go."

"Can't you stay with your friends?" he asked, sounding apologetic.

Grace stared across Ocean Park Boulevard. A shiver of rage rose in her. She lifted the receiver, ready to strike it against the glass when the man in the suit came out of the bathroom. He rushed around the corner when their eyes met, the receiver frozen above her head. Her arm began to hurt where she'd gotten the shot. She placed the receiver against her ear as her father washed his hands of her.

"Why don't you call your mother? She needs help with Amber."

Grace absently rubbed her arm. She kicked the ground. Now she had to use the bathroom. She no longer felt like crying. She straightened up at the mention of Mom.

"Write this down," he said, a TV on in the background.

Grace pulled a pen from her carpet bag. She wrote the information on the inside of her arm.

"Grace. I'm sorry. You know I've got my hands full with the boys. You're an adult now. Go help your sister."

Grace thought of Amber, the blank stare the last time they'd seen each other. How would she be now, after all that time with Largo and Mom?

"Goodbye, Dad."

It was final. She'd never asked him for anything and he'd never offered. Grace leaned against the phone booth and closed her eyes. The fiberglass shield offered no relief from the afternoon sun; she jack-knifed to her knees, dizzy and drenched. She forced her limbs to comply, denying pain, she stormed into the bathroom.

A few minutes later, Grace came out of the bathroom with her hair tied back in a ponytail. Her makeup was freshened, and the fading glimpse of motherhood sloughed off with each step. A warm Santa Ana wind buffeted her face as she headed to the curb to thumb a ride. She stopped up short when she heard giggling from the gas pump. She readjusted her bag, turning to spot a microbus with smoked up windows. A shaggy character in tie-dye manned the gas pump, while a jovial commotion rocked the bus.

The tie-dye guy noticed her checking out the bus and smiled. He banged on the side of the bus. "Dude! Leave me some!"

Grace breathed a sigh of relief. She walked over to the pump as he put the nozzle back.

He looked at her bag. "Need a ride?"

"Yeah. I do."

"Where ya going, sister?"

"Reseda?"

"Your lucky day. We're going to San Francisco. I'm Tad."

"Grace. Thank you."

In five minutes Grace was sitting in the front seat of a VW microbus heading up the 405 freeway. In the back were two women and one man. Tad preferred the slow lane. Grace was relieved that they were mellow stoners. After a few hits of some really good pot, she zoned out on the road. A hazy recollection of her desperate moment on the floor at Der Wienerschnitzel rose in her mind. The cramps that occupied her every sense were now churned to a passable ache by the sputtering four-cylinder engine. A succession of Samaritans had risen to her aid. And now she was flowing toward a most unexpected reunion.

# 9

School started and Amber met with Julie every day at recess and lunch. She had one other friend, Kendra, whose mother walked her to school every day, but Julie was always there, and Amber liked playing the big sister. Frankie was a few years older. He mostly hung out with his boys, which of course included Charlie—who Amber hated, because he always walked away when she joined them.

Now, with Christmas break rapidly approaching, Amber waited for Frankie by the hibiscus bushes near the front gate. She tried to meet him every day but she had to stay after sometimes to do her homework. Amber fixed her new bra strap. Mom surprised her by throwing the bra on the back of the sofa while they watched Tom and Jerry Sunday morning. Now on Monday, she couldn't wait to see if Frankie noticed. She wore a dress that showed her legs, and even put on some of her mother's eyeliner. Amber waved at Kendra and her mother and remembered to check her backpack for her homework. She found the packet at the bottom of her backpack. She squinted at the jumble of words.

Mr. Henry. When class let out he'd called her up front. She was anxious to leave, and he seemed to be intentionally targeting her. Most of the teachers did target her, she thought. He informed her he was moving her seat again—away from Kendra. It wasn't her fault school was boring.

Finally, Frankie arrived. Amber's face changed when she saw him coming.

"What's wrong?" he asked. Amber always had something wrong.

"Mr. Henry is a dick," Amber pouted.

"Why? I had Henry. He was cool."

"He moved my seat again, away from Kendra. She's my best friend in class," she said, pushing her chest forward as she put on her backpack. Amber searched his face.

He stared back toward the hallway where a wave of students approached the exit. "Where's Julie?" he asked.

"I don't know," she said, shifting from foot to foot. "What are you doing after school?"

He looked back at her and shrugged.

She fixed his collar. He looked so handsome, she thought. "I saw you at recess," she said, winking. "What were you boys doing?"

Frankie stepped away from her. He adjusted his backpack and continued scanning the crowd for Julie.

She touched his backpack. "So, it's in there."

The nurse came out of the office and spied them. "Julie wet herself in class. We'll have her ready in a minute," she said.

Amber sat down on the edge of a planter. A pink hibiscus blossom tickled her neck.

Frankie dropped his backpack and sat next to her. Amber leaned in close. "Are you going to show me?"

Frankie smiled. Amber hugged his arm. "Show you what?" he laughed.

"Whatever you boys were looking at, at recess."

"You're too young to see that stuff. It's just for boys."

"I'll give you a hundred dollars."

Frankie nudged her with his knee. "Liar."

"Nah aw. My Dad sent me a check for my birthday. He signed it in cursive like you're supposed to."

Frankie shrugged.

"You don't believe me?" Amber asked, pouting. "You can ask my Mom."

"Maybe later."

Amber rose in front of him sticking her chest out. Julie would join them soon, and she wanted to give him another chance. Frankie picked up his backpack and poked her in the belly. "You look different. Did you get a haircut?"

Amber, Frankie, and Julie moved up the Boulevard, past McDonald's to the Turnbull family home. It was an unusual day for Southern California. The air was damp and the sun was an orange cotton ball. Amber and Frankie dropped Julie off and headed to the park. It was a two block rectangle of scattered trees of oak, pine, and eucalyptus, with swings and a merry-go-round in the middle. Frankie and Amber skirted the path, past a gaggle of kids, toward a small grove of oak trees, where they arrived at the gardener's shed. The gardener left the shed door open during weekdays, and after school Amber and Frankie went there to smoke and talk. They'd spent hours doing just that. It was Amber's favorite part of any day. Frankie hadn't kissed her yet, but she was hoping.

Frankie strained the rusty hinges until the door seized open. He stuck his head in while Amber waited in silence. The shed was empty, and they knew the gardener wouldn't return until dusk to lock up. Amber and Frankie sat down on a couple of empty metal cans. She took out a pack of cigarettes, lit one and handed it to Frankie. He took a drag and passed it back.

"A hundred dollars," she said, crossing her bare legs and holding the cigarette just right.

"Alright, but don't tell anybody."

Frankie pulled out a tattered magazine. He turned to a centerfold of a naked woman. Amber scooted her can closer to his. "That's no big deal."

Frankie flipped through the magazine, stopping to show her his favorite. "Why do you like that one?" she said, pointing. "She's so hairy."

"Everyone gets hairy when they get older. Haven't you ever seen your mom?"

Amber nodded. "I'm not hairy."

"That's because you're a girl. These are grown women."

Amber stood up and stretched her back. "Grown enough," she said.

Frankie watched her face.

Amber sat back down. "Where did you get it?"

Frankie shrugged. "Charlie gave it to me. He stole it from his dad." Frankie dropped the magazine on the floor. Amber handed the cigarette to Frankie. Her hand lingered on his while he puffed. He exhaled, and she noticed him look at her chest when he handed the cigarette back. Amber stood up and swiveled her hips from side to side. She liked the feel of her skirt swishing against her legs.

"You're weird," he said. Amber kicked the magazine away. She ruffled his hair.

Frankie slapped at her playfully; Amber danced out of reach, then back to him.

Amber stamped out the cigarette and sat on Frankie's lap. It took him by surprise; he fell sideways, righted himself, then put his arms around her waist. "What are you doing?"

"What does it look like?"

She craned to kiss him. He pecked her on the lips, then pulled away. "You're only twelve."

She closed her eyes and puckered. Frankie adjusted his legs.

Amber opened her eyes, exasperated. "Well?" She knew he wanted to.

"I..."

Amber smirked and slid off his lap onto her knees. She pushed between his legs, an inch from his face. She could smell him, fresh smoke and adolescent tang. She smiled, slid a hand to his crotch, staring into his eyes. He would have to like her now. She squeezed slightly, feeling the warmth, knowing from experience what effect it had on men. It was all wrong though. Frankie's eyes were wild pools, churning, unsure and unfocused. She pressed in to kiss him, but the motion upset his balance, and all at once they were tumbling. Amber ended up on top of him, giggling nervously, while he guffawed, with his hands under him.

They were so still now, the shed so quiet, the world ebbed in their first real moment. She laid her head on his chest as he wrapped his arms around her. *Finally*, she thought. When suddenly...

Bam!

Something or someone hit the shed. A series of raps on the shed door shot them to their feet. Silence. Then a familiar voice.

"Frankie! Are you in there?"

Frankie took a step back. "Charlie?" he whispered.

"Dude!"

"I'll be out in a minute...I'm busy."

Amber stared at Frankie. "Are you mad at me?" she asked.

"No, Amber. I'm not mad. I like you, but you're...young," he said, sounding contrite.

Amber leaned forward to kiss him again. Frankie pecked her on the lips and hugged her gently.

He pushed away, slipped out of the shed, leaving her with her arms wide and empty. The shed was suddenly very cold. She sat on a can hugging herself. She didn't want Charlie to see her; he would make fun of her and Frankie would never hear the end of it.

Amber walked home hollow and numb. He *was* angry. She could see it on his face. *He's using me* chimed in her head. The words circled like vultures, around and around, until she convinced herself it was true—the same old story. She trudged down the gravel driveway, spied Mom through the living room window, waving her hands over her head, a human tempest to be gauged and avoided. Amber skirted low along the side fence, out of view. When she reached the shed, she sat on the cinder blocks in front of the door.  She listened and watched two squirrels quarreling in the tree across the driveway. They reminded her of Sally and Chuck, the way they used to argue; she envied them and wondered if they thought about her. *They probably already forgot me. Nobody loves me. Grace hates me. Now Frankie too.*  Amber leaned forward and began to cry. Her shoulders shuddered as she rocked back and forth. She wanted to scream, to wail, to throw things, but she knew safety lay for her in the shadows, apart. *They'll be sorry one day,* she promised herself. *They'll all be sorry.*

#####

At twelve Amber hated her body. Where she had always been thin, she began to grow hips and breasts. The change frightened her. She blamed herself, seeking control over the uncontrollable. She rejected proffered meals, and when she did eat, it was from the collection of snacks she kept hidden in the shed. There were times when she couldn't stop eating, which led to the first time she made herself sick. She threw up in the trashcan outside the shed, and in that moment of lightness, she found a way to change how she felt. Soon, she purged daily like a sacrament. When she lost her baby fat Largo stopped using her. It solved a problem.

It was her little secret. Something she alone could do for herself. It was none of their business, she thought defiantly.  She spent hour after hour sequestered in the little shed, looking at magazines, smoking, bingeing and napping. That summer she moved all of her things into the shed and ran an extension cord for power. Frankie helped her set it up. She and Frankie were boyfriend and girlfriend. She snuck food back to her shed. Mom and Largo stopped paying attention. The following school year she was an infrequent student. Then, Paul came to visit.

The day of his visit Amber could barely contain herself. She binged the previous night and in the morning, lying with the evidence, two empty boxes of Cheese-its, she rushed past Mom and Largo and spent the next fifteen minutes in the bathroom throwing up as quietly as she could. Mom banged on the door at one point. "I don't know what you're doing in there, but you better knock it off," she warned.

Later, as she walked to 7-Eleven, on an errand for Largo, she thought of Paul, chubby little Paul, her older brother.

"He wants to see you. I told him yes," Mom had told her.

She observed herself in the windows of the cars she passed. She was satisfied with the outfit she'd picked out: a halter top, a pair of Osh Kosh shorts, and flip-flops. Her ribs showed, which delighted her. She didn't feel like a witless little girl anymore. She put on eyeliner, and her lips were moist with strawberry lip gloss. She hoped Paul would like the way she looked. *Seven years. He won't even recognize me.* She bent forward and flipped her hair back over her shoulders, the way Farrah Fawcett did in *Charlie's Angels.*

On the way back from 7-Eleven, she decided to drop by Frankie's. He would finally meet the brother she'd been talking about. Amber skipped up the driveway feeling light and expectant. She could hear the blaring TV as she strode along the walkway on the side of the house. Mrs. Turnbull was probably passed out, she thought. The birds in the yard seemed abnormally chatty. Amber pursed her lips, tasting the strawberry.

She sidestepped beer cartons, spilling trash bags and a collection of bike frames. She nearly tripped over a mini bike motor, near the side door of the garage.

She entered into a wave of static heat. It was a sweat lodge. The only ventilation, a broken window frame on the door. Amber waited by the door for her eyes to adjust. Boxes of old magazines, clothing, generations of Turnbull junk were stacked to create interior walls. No one looking into that broken window could have guessed that two kids lived there. Amber felt her way along the wall of boxes until they funneled into two separate chambers. She peeked over the boxes and saw Julie asleep on a mattress— partially covered by an old bedspread. She still sucked her thumb. Amber entered Frankie's side. He was sitting on his mattress, still unaware of her presence. Amber rushed into the room and tackled him, his cigarette falling onto the mattress. The move upended a small coffee table. An ashtray clattered on the floor, along with a forty ounce bottle and a Playboy magazine. Frankie threw her on her back.

He pinned Amber effortlessly. She loved how strong he'd become in the last year. He'd put on fifteen pounds and two inches. He was the biggest kid in eighth grade. "You little shit," Frankie whispered, as he retrieved his cigarette. Amber grabbed his crotch. Frankie winced. "Stop!" he yelled, then put a hand to his mouth.

"Shush!" Amber put her finger to her lips. "You'll wake Julie."

"It's about time she got up. She stayed up late so Mom wouldn't burn the house down."

Amber leaned back against the side of the garage. "I've got a surprise," she said, grabbing the cigarette from his mouth. She lit it and took a drag.

"What?"

"My brother is coming today. I haven't seen him since we were little." Amber bounced on the mattress. She handed the cigarette to Frankie. He held it between his teeth while he set the table back on its legs. Smoke filtered out his nose as he reset the bottle and the ashtray. He picked up the magazine and began thumbing through it, one eye on her.

"How old is he?" Frankie asked.

Amber slid next to him. "He's a year older then I am. He plays Pop Warner football. Why don't you play Pop Warner?" she asked.

Frankie tilted his head at Amber. "Why aren't you a cheerleader?" She thought about it.

"What time does he get here?" he asked.

"Mom says around one o'clock," she said standing up.

Julie appeared at the opening. She was as tall as Amber, but still had her little girl voice and cherubic face. She was in a onesie that was stretched to burst. The zipper on the front was broken and her belly protruded.

"Can I watch cartoons?" she asked, sleepily. She dropped in front of a small black and white set resting on a milk carton. She turned it on but the set remained blank. She twisted the extension cord, and the set blinked on. Bugs Bunny hopped across the screen, followed by Elmer Fudd. She giggled to herself, oblivious to Amber and Frankie.

Amber jumped off the mattress. "Well, I gotta get back." She leaned over and ruffled Frankie's hair. She hoped Frankie and Paul would get along. "I'll bring Paul by later."

Amber bent and hugged Julie. Julie slapped Amber's calf, eyes glued to the screen.

It wasn't noon yet, and Paul wouldn't arrive for another hour. As she shuffled up the gravel driveway she spied the Raggedy Ann doll near the hole in the fence. *Where has it been?* She scanned the yard for the little terrier that welcomed her the first day. It came around once in a while, and she'd gotten used to giving it scraps. Amber kept an eye on the hole as she walked across the grass. She felt a strange impulse to hold the doll. She retrieved it, held its waist in her palm and stroked the mop head with her fingertips. She picked burrs out of its hair, straightened the calico dress and white blouse. She noticed for the first time that someone had taken the time to repair a tear on her black boots. Amber's lips tightened at the realization that the doll had a prior life, that another girl must have cherished her. Still, it had no eyes. She took it to the shed, where she found an eyeliner pencil. She moistened the tip and drew on new eyes, taking extra care to make sure they matched.

"I'm going to call you Annie," she whispered. She went to a box marked "Amber's stuff." She pulled out her old Barbie dolls, the ones she and Paul used to play with. She lined them all up against her pillow, on the mattress on the floor.

An hour later Amber sat on the couch in the bungalow eating mouthfuls of dry cereal. She stared at the door, jiggling, unable to contain her excitement. Paul was late. Mom walked in from the bedroom, a tumbler in her hand. Largo was napping on the bed. "You're going to get fat eating all that." Mom buttoned her pants. "Just like your father...late."

Amber watched Mom in the kitchen. Mom was more agitated than usual, her complexion mottled and her eyebrows arched. She had an extra layer of pancake, Amber noticed, wondering what Mom was up to. She was gauging herself, holding back on her daily assault on her liver.

As Amber turned toward the door she heard a knock and jumped. The cereal bowl fell to the floor. She ran and flung the door open. She drooped at the sight of their neighbor, the one with the crazy eyes.

"Largo here?" he asked. Her shoulders sagged. She looked back at her mother in the kitchen.

Mom waved the neighbor off. "He went to the store. Come back in a couple hours."

Amber trailed the neighbor out on the porch following his progress up the driveway. The sun galvanized the abandoned house at the front of the driveway. Vapor waves rose from the roof. She looked beyond the truck yard, toward the freeway. *There's still time*, she thought. Amber went back to the shed and settled onto the mattress. *He'll like the Barbies.* She could see him laughing now. Amber fetched Annie. She traced her dark eyes with the tips of her fingers, admiring her handiwork. *They might not have time to visit Frankie.* She went outside and sat on the cinder block in front of the shed, Annie on her lap. She heard a car idling and looked up as her Dad pulled the station wagon up the driveway. She stood up abruptly, sending Annie to the gravel.

Paul looked so grown up and handsome in the passenger seat. He got out of the car and waited for her Dad to step forward. He walked beside his Dad until they were face to face. He was a head taller than her, his face a little thinner, but his distinct dark eyes and soft smile gave him away. "Hi, Amber," he said.

Amber beamed. *He remembered me.*

"Hi, Amber...do you remember your old man?" Dad stepped in front of Paul and embraced Amber. Amber kept her eyes on Paul and met his hug stiffly.

Mom came out on the porch. She'd brushed her hair; a new blouse and a fresh coat of lipstick presented an impression Amber hadn't seen in a while. "Hey, Joe. Come on in."

"Go play with your sister," Dad said to Paul. He patted Amber on the head. Amber led Paul to the shed. He walked a few steps behind her, tentative, taking in his surroundings. Inside, she placed Annie next to the Barbies, stood back, to see if he remembered.

Paul ran a hand through his wavy hair, just posing, it seemed, until his face lit up.

"We used to play with those, right?" he said, pointing at the pillow. He fell to his knees, suddenly six again. Amber noticed the crocheted vest he was wearing, *a gift from Grandma D*, she thought.

Amber knelt next to him. She couldn't believe he was here, in her room, Paul. It wasn't Magnolia, but they were still Amber and Paul. Something flickered inside of her. She didn't recognize it, but she knew it was hers. It hadn't been extinguished after all she'd been through. Paul pushed aside Annie and picked up one of the Barbies. His face went blank staring at it when suddenly he looked up. "Where's Grace?"

She lifted one of the dolls off the pillow, her favorite, the Barbie she'd given a haircut—the one with uneven bangs and a missing tooth she'd drawn in with a ballpoint pen. She hadn't played with it since he left.

"She doesn't live with me. She lives in Venice."

"Oh. Dad said you two lived together." Paul looked back toward the house, sullen.

Amber pranced her Barbie in front of his face. "I miss you," she made the Barbie say in a squeaky voice.

Paul smiled and put his Barbie back on the pillow. He adjusted the arms and legs in a comfortable posture. "Who's that?" he asked, pointing to Annie.

"She's my best friend, Annie. We play together. She likes you, see?" Amber squeezed Annie against his cheek.

Paul pushed her away. He was smiling now, with the flip of a switch they were attuned.

"Does she get along with the Barbies?"

"They fight sometimes, but they always make up," she replied giggling.

Amber fell onto her side, staring up at Paul wistfully as he glanced around her tiny shed. "I'm still decorating," she said, suddenly feeling bloated and fat. She wished she hadn't eaten all that cereal.

"You got your own place?"

Was he being sarcastic? She couldn't tell.

"I share a room with Bryan. He farts a lot," he said, making a face.

Amber sat up, pulled the hem of her shorts down. She wanted him to sit down so they could play dolls again. Paul just stood there looking around acting like her stuff was dirty or something.

A squirrel skittered across the roof. Paul looked up at the bare rafters and a light went on. "I can do twenty pull-ups. Do you want to see?"

Amber put the dolls back in the box. She kept Annie on her pillow. "Sure, I guess."

Paul leaped up and grabbed the rafter with both hands. He whipped off fifteen pull-ups, then huffed and puffed on the last five. He dropped to his feet and flexed. "See?"

Amber pulled out a pack of cigarettes. Paul's face changed. An awkward thickness enveloped them. "Mom lets you smoke?"

Amber smirked. "I do what I want. She doesn't care."

"Do you like living with her?" he asked, sitting down on a crate.

Amber fell silent as she took a drag. She exhaled toward the door, happy to have corralled his attention again. "It's alright. She buys me things, and I can go out whenever I want. I got this doll for my birthday." She put the cigarette between her teeth and grabbed Annie. She rested the doll on her lap; self-conscious now, she tossed it back on the pillow.

"Do you want to smoke?"

"Maybe later."

Amber mashed out her cigarette on the plank floor.

She rose quickly and grabbed Paul's arm when the blood rushed to her head. She pulled the hem of her shorts down. "Let's go see my friends," she said.

#####

Outside, the sun was at its peak. The truck terminal across the way was quiet. Amber glanced at Paul, and he back at her, as they moved toward the boulevard. It felt good to be moving, away, together, off on one of those days they used to share, with no clear end. Amber took his hand for a few steps, lighting up inside, until it felt like a three-legged race, out of step. She was glad when they arrived at Frankie's. They stood briefly at the side door of the garage; tightness in her chest, she looked into Paul's face, wondering what he was thinking. She could hear the little TV, inside, the bees on the bushes next to them. Amber hugged Paul quickly and led him into the stultifying darkness. Paul followed her back through the maze, his hand on her shoulder until they stepped into Frankie's room.

"What's up?" Frankie nodded over at Paul. He stood up, gave him a cool bro handshake. "Where you staying?"

"We're in Duarte," Paul replied.

Amber hugged Frankie and ruffled Julie's hair. She was coloring on the floor. "And this is Julie."

Julie looked up at Paul. "Who's that?" Julie asked.

Amber elbowed Paul in the stomach. "He's my brother."

"He's handsome," she blurted.

Frankie pulled out a bag of weed and loaded a bowl. "You smoke?" he asked, gesturing with the pipe.

Paul kneeled in front of the little coffee table, looking out of sorts. "Once," he said.

Amber looked at him sideways. Frankie took a hit off the pipe and passed it to Paul. Paul held it with his fingertips, inspecting it. Amber and Frankie exchanged glances, smiling. Frankie handed him the lighter. He made a face at Amber, who shrugged.

Paul wiped his mouth on the back of his hand, held the flame over the bowl and took a small puff. He coughed fitfully until Amber took the pipe from him and slapped him on the back. Frankie chuckled. "Good shit, huh?"

"Whoa. It's been a while," Paul croaked.

Frankie handed Paul a warm can of already opened Pepsi. Paul took a sip and abruptly sat on the floor across from Frankie. Amber walked around and sat on the mattress with Frankie. Frankie took another hit and handed it to Amber, who shook her head. Paul took another hit, smoother after his first. Amber couldn't believe her brother was getting high with her boyfriend. She watched him sag into himself, staring quietly at the coffee table. She'd never seen this Paul.

"So, you play football?" Frankie asked.

"Yeah. Pee Wee." Paul listed to the side, ready to lounge, but unsettled.

"I played football when I was little," Frankie said.

"That's cool," Paul said, leaning onto the coffee table. Amber thought he was going to sleep, his eyelids were so droopy. She got up and changed the channel on the little TV. Everyone stared at her as she returned to the mattress, smiling to herself.

Frankie shot her a quizzical look, then got to his feet. "Well, Nice meeting you, bro." He looked down at Amber. "I've got to meet Charlie." He loaded another bowl and left it on the table.

Amber protested. "We just got here."

"I'll be back later."

Paul sat up and extended his hand. Frankie gave him a high-five and headed out.

Amber and Paul watched Frankie leave. She smiled at Paul phlegmatically, lit a cigarette. There were no dolls to play with. He smiled back at her, leaning on his elbows. "Do you want to smoke another bowl?" she asked, pointing to the pipe.

"I'm good."

Julie turned up the TV and they both looked at her.

Amber blew cigarette smoke toward the garage door. Paul watched the smoke curl over the boxes and collect in the corner. "Do you want a smoke?" she asked, stretching the cigarette to him. Paul got up and sat on the edge of the mattress. He took a drag, a soft plume of smoke seeped out of his lips. Amber laughed. "You don't smoke, do you?"

"Not all the time."

"I've been smoking since I was seven," she said, matter-of-fact. She leaned back across the mattress, readjusted her shorts, then stretched her legs out.

Paul glanced at her, at Julie, then stared at the TV. Amber took another drag and laughed.

"Frankie has a dirty magazine collection. Do you want to see it?"

Paul looked over at Julie, then back to Amber. "Okay."

Amber offered the cigarette again. "No thanks," he said. "I find magazines all the time in the canyon behind our house," he added.

Amber reached under the mattress and grabbed a magazine. She sat cross-legged on the mattress. Paul slid up beside her.

"Here," Amber said, handing it to him.

It was a *Penthouse* magazine with a bare-chested woman with a top hat, bow tie, and cane. Paul thumbed through the first few pages, found the centerfold, and opened it, held it up. Julie glanced over. "Eeeew. That's nasty," she said, wrinkling her face.

Paul squirmed a little and put the magazine back on his lap. Amber threw a pillow at Julie. Julie stuck her tongue out. Paul hunched over the magazine, lingering on a cartoon. Amber took the magazine off Paul's lap to find Frankie's favorite model. Amber laughed. Paul lurched forward. He had a hard-on.

"No big deal. Frankie always gets hard when he looks at his magazines," she said, jerking the magazine away, falling on top of him.

Julie jumped up. "Can I see?" she asked, running to the mattress. Paul sat up quickly, a bewildered look on his face. He held the magazine over his head, while Amber kneeled over him, grabbing for it.

Julie dived across Amber and Paul. All at once, hands were everywhere, grabbing and tickling. Paul's mouth hung open, his eyes wide. Both girls were on top of him now, tickling him down there. Paul pushed Julie off first. He wasn't laughing anymore. He had a twisted look on his face, like he'd tasted something exotic and couldn't tell if he liked it or not. He was staring at Amber, staring at her legs. In an instant, she was on her feet lighting another cigarette. Julie went back to the TV. Paul leaned against the wall with his arms over his lap. The magazine lay open on the floor. Amber shoved it under the mattress. Amber put her hair in a pony tail while Paul fixed his pants. She paced, smoking, a frozen smile on her face.

Amber moved to the mattress next to Paul. He was still hunched, arms across his crotch. He wouldn't look her in the eye. Amber could see that he was trying to act casual, like everything was just fine.

"I've seen one," she said, thinking that it would ease him.

Paul leaned back, just a little. "Come on...really?"

"Sure. Largo...and Frankie. It's no big deal."

"That's weird."

Amber stared at him. "You're weird," she said, pulling away.

The room was a pall now. They both looked at Julie on the floor. Paul shifted next to her.  Amber's feet thrummed on the mattress. She sensed the loss before his feet hit the floor. "Sorry," she said, sarcastically, when he got up and pulled down his shirt. "Sorry," she cried, staring at him.

He wouldn't look at her. "We should go," he said.

Amber jumped off the mattress. She grabbed her cigarettes and stormed out the exit. Paul looked down at Julie, then followed.

They didn't talk the entire way home. Amber ran across the boulevard ahead of him, just to see if he would keep up. As they slowed on her driveway she turned to him. "Why are you acting so weird? I'm your sister. Don't you love me anymore?"

Paul froze. "I...you...of course I do." He looked up at the bungalow, and back at her. "Amber..."

"What?"

He just stood there shaking his head; his lips moved but no words came out. It was over, for now, she thought. Amber took his hand and led him as she'd always done. It was the way things worked with them. She knew it. He knew it.  She let go of his hand inside the bungalow. Largo was on the couch, while Mom and Dad stood by the sink talking. They all looked at Amber and Paul when they came in. Amber rushed to the bathroom. Dad stared at Paul. "Where have you two been?" Mom asked.

In the bathroom, Amber went to the toilet and threw up. She'd wanted to since he arrived. She sat back on the edge of the tub with her head in her hands. The feeling that she would never see him again settled on her shoulders. She rose to wash her mouth out, blew her nose and buried her face in a towel. A rap on the bathroom door made her jump. "Amber! Paul's leaving," Mom said.

The car was idling as she came out to say goodbye. Paul was in the front seat waiting. She lingered at the front bumper, feeling awkward and exposed, staring at him through the streaked glass.

Still no smile, as the car backed away. Amber waved, her elbows tight to her side. Her eyes welled up; she kept them locked on the windshield, where his face flickered in the reflection of the clouds overhead.

Amber took a step forward, grinning and waving. Paul raised his hand and wiggled his fingers. He was smiling now, not broadly —a fingernail smile—noncommittal. Amber took another step toward the street as the station wagon sped away. The chain-link fence across the street rattled.

Amber went into the shed, ignoring Mom's glaring presence in the window. Inertia from Paul's departure sucked the air out of her. Amber took a box of Cheez-Its from her TWA bag and began shoveling them in her mouth. The look on his face when they left Frankie's plagued her. *He hates you. He hates you.*

# 10

It happened abruptly with no announcement, fanfare or debutante ball. Amber just decided to be grown up. She started wearing dresses, carrying a purse and putting on makeup every morning. She tried sewing, dyed her hair, started a diary, smoked incessantly and lost a dangerous amount of weight. Her English teacher sent her to the nurse to get her eyes checked, and out of it, she was ordered glasses. They turned out to be owl-rimmed, which she thought made her look intelligent, even bookish. She cleaned up the shed to match her new appearance. Frankie helped her lay pallets on which she placed the old mattress. She took milk crates from school and built cubbies to house her clothes. The honeycomb of crates was a source of pride, a symbol of the next rung in the ladder out of her former self.  She completed the transformation of her space by hanging shipping blankets on the walls. It kept the wind out and blocked sound from the bungalow. Frankie said it was nicer than the rooms he'd made for him and Julie. Amber beamed when he said that. She couldn't change how she felt, but she could change what it looked like to feel it.

Her classmates didn't know what to think of the new Amber. They squinted at her the first day as if she'd been transported back in time, from the future. She wasn't the only girl in the seventh grade with a purse, but it was the kind of purse their mothers carried, a bulky vinyl bag with a belt strap. She and the bag were inseparable. After the first month of school, she realized the folly of carrying a half-empty suitcase around, because that was what it really was, a home away from home. There was no way she could fill such a cavity, so she downgraded to an oxblood shoulder bag she'd found behind the thrift store.

Amber thought less and less of Paul. She'd just moved on. The Barbie dolls were in a plastic bag somewhere in the honeycombs. He didn't call after the visit, and she assumed he wanted nothing to do with her. She didn't think much of Grace either. She stopped trying to call her. Hope was like a dying poinsettia. She had no clue how to revive it, so she stopped nurturing it.

Out of this distance, Grace showed up at the shed one sunny day when the Santa Ana winds blew dust over everything. She came unannounced and like déjà vu, they were sitting together on her mattress. Grace told her what happened. Amber nodded quietly while Grace held her hands and told her things that didn't sound like the big sister who'd bathed, soothed and protected her. This was a new Grace, broken, reticent, and diminished. Gone was the lion whose mane she'd clung to. She didn't think she'd ever stop talking. Amber wondered if Grace noticed how grown up she was now. When Grace stood to stretch, Amber did the same, reflexively.

They were a foot apart, nearly the same height now, although Grace had filled out and Amber swam in her dress. Grace held Amber's hands out to look at her.

"Amber! You look so grown up!"

Amber smiled, touching her glasses. "I have a boyfriend."

"What does Mom think?"

Amber sat on a milk carton and fished a cigarette and lighter out of her purse.

"You know Mom. She's in her own little world."

Grace watched Amber light the cigarette. She was shocked at how much she looked like Mom, although she'd never say that to Amber. They stared at Grace's carryall.

"Is that all your stuff?" Amber asked.

"Rex and Kimo have the rest of it," Grace replied, holding her stomach. She stood up suddenly, looking pale. "Where do you go to the bathroom?" Grace asked, looking around the shed.

"I use their bathroom," Amber said, gesturing with the cigarette. "I try to go when they aren't there."

They headed to the bungalow. Grace gave Amber a worried look as she opened the front door. She took a deep breath and stepped into the front room. Mom was in the kitchen waiting for her. She stared Grace down, years flowing between them like toxic fumes.

"You just keep out of my way, keep this one in line, and keep your hands off my man!"

The old familiar death stare punctuated the threat. Largo stood behind her with his wife beater t-shirt, eating her up with his eyes. Strands of grey flecked his hair now, and Grace hoped the years had been merciless. When Mom turned her back on them, Amber showed Grace the bathroom. Alone in the bathroom, Grace breathed a sigh of relief. The cramps were assaulting her less and less, and she was already thinking of ways to avoid the bungalow. She could hear Mom ranting in the kitchen. *How has Amber put up with this all these years?* she thought.

When she came out Amber was leaning against the door. She looked so thin and drawn. "Do you want to get something to eat?" she asked, remembering that she had two hundred dollars from her last paycheck.

Amber shrugged, her smile phlegmatic. This was the new Amber.

As they left Mom yelled, "You owe me fifty bucks for rent!"

Grace grimaced as they rushed out the front door.

Back in the little shed, early afternoon, they ate McDonald's
in silence. Streaks of sunlight striped the planked floor. The years
separating them had yet to catch up as they had so easily for
Amber and Paul. Amber had just asked Grace to help her get birth
control pills.

Grace tried not to look disappointed. Amber's scowl betrayed
a teenager on edge, and Grace had no idea what would happen if
she went over. "Are you sure?" she asked. Amber looked like she
was about to cry. If she did, Grace wanted them to cry together, to
release the vinegar of the last five years.

Amber searched Grace's face, her fingers entwined on her
lap. Grace shook her head. "Let's just eat for now, okay?" She was
miffed that they'd only been together for a few hours and Amber
already wanted something.

Amber adjusted her bra strap. It was going to be another hot
day in Reseda. She stood up and went to the door and peered out.
"Nana, can Frankie and Julie come too?" she asked, mouth open
wide.

"Don't make that face. People are going to think you're
retarded," Grace snapped. She covered her mouth. She sounded
just like Mom.

Amber slammed the door. Grace gave her a hug. "Oh, Amber.
I'm so glad to see you." The room was too small to be angry.
Amber stiffened, then put her head on Grace's shoulder. "Frankie's
your boyfriend...right? Sure he can come."

Outside Amber showed Grace the hole in the fence where the
terrier came in. The sisters paused at the sound of Largo's car
edging into the driveway. They looked past him to the truck yard,
walking along the grass near the shuttered front house. Amber and
Grace glanced back at the bungalow in unison, before rushing
down the sidewalk.

#####

Grace and Amber met up with Frankie on the way to the clinic. She was surprised at how big he was for a fourteen-year-old. She was surprised at how Amber and he hung on each other. She hadn't been that touchy with her boyfriends, and the sight of Amber leaping into adolescence made her skin crawl. She wondered painfully whether Largo's abuse propelled her along that path.

They passed over the Los Angeles River, where Amber showed Grace the spot she'd met Frankie on her first day in Reseda. Amber made a point to kiss Frankie in front of Grace to show how grown up she was.

The clinic was in a little mall with a Grants, a liquor store and a Buster Brown shoes outlet. A group of kids loitered in front of the liquor store; they greeted Frankie and asked Grace for a cigarette, ogling her breasts. Frankie waited with them while Grace and Amber continued on to the pharmacy.

The waiting room was dark, with the blinds shut and an oscillating fan set on high. It felt like a catwalk as they made a beeline to the counter. "How can I help you?" a woman in horn-rimmed glasses asked.

Amber rushed forward. "Can I get the pill?" she asked as if she were ordering fries.

Grace stepped in front of her, forcing a smile. "We need to talk with someone about birth control, please," she said.

"Here. Fill out these forms, and the doctor will be with you in a moment," the woman said with a pinched mouth, looking from Amber to Grace.

Grace and Amber settled into a pair of seats near the fan. Amber took out a pack of Dentyne, pulled two sticks and began to chew vigorously. Grace filled out the forms, looking up every so often, wanting to tell Amber to chew with her mouth closed, but not wanting to hurt her feelings again.

After filling out the forms Grace held Amber's hand. Amber stared straight ahead, chewing and tapping her feet. She pulled a cigarette out of her purse, put it in her mouth, but Grace shook her head, so Amber leaned back and crossed her legs, staring at an old man reading a *Field and Stream* magazine. Grace couldn't read her. Was she afraid, bored; the old Amber would have vaulted into a story about school, or what she wanted for her birthday. This Amber was a blank screen.

After the teenager next to the old man was called, Amber went outside for a smoke. Grace couldn't stop her. As soon as Amber lit up, Grace was called in, and fifteen minutes later they were on their way back to the shed.

"I'll show you how to take them. You still have to watch out that you don't get VD," Grace said. She watched Amber and Frankie as they walked ahead. They were so young. She was glad she had waited.

Back at the shed, Amber sat on the mattress staring at her toe and smoking. Frankie dozed next to her. "Do you know where we can get some pot?" she asked.

Grace shuffled through her carryall. "I've got a little, but you're too young."

"I've been smoking since I was seven." She took another drag and passed it to Frankie.

Frankie pulled a pocket knife out and started cutting a loose piece of his Converse tennis shoe.

"Can we get high now? Mom doesn't care. She gets high all the time."

Grace pulled out a baggie full of joints. Frankie and Amber looked at each other and smiled. "Told you she was cool," Amber said.

Grace lit a joint, took a long toke, held it and exhaled slowly. She closed her eyes for a moment. She handed the joint to Frankie. "Take it easy, that's really good weed."

Frankie took a drag and passed it to Amber. Grace watched Amber inhale, hold it, and exhale slowly.

So it was true. Not only did Amber smoke and have sex, she was also a stoner. Amber was a stranger, wise beyond her years, and getting wiser by the minute.

Grace looked at Frankie. "So why does Amber need the pill?" she asked point blank.

Frankie was already sagging into the mattress after only a few hits. "I don't know."

Grace looked at Amber. "I need them because I don't want to get pregnant," she said.

The little shed was hazy now, catching rays from the window over the mattress.

Frankie opened his eyes. "We haven't done it. She's too young for me," he said. A lecherous smile spread across his face. He stared at Grace's breasts. Grace parried with a glare.

Grace suddenly realized that the pill was insurance for Amber, but not to prevent her getting pregnant by Frankie. She'd completely misread the situation. It was Largo. Amber was worried about. After Victor and his *Gift* of Gonorrhea, she was in the same boat all over again. She stood up and opened the window over the mattress. The room gradually cleared. At least Amber wasn't sleeping around, she thought. She recalled Largo's baleful eyes in the rearview mirror as they left to get the pills. *When will it end?* she asked herself, standing up to stretch. Grace looked down at the mattress. Amber slept soundly, her hard edges softened by slumber. Grace saw a frail, dangerously thin version of Amber that made her want to cry.

After Frankie went home, Grace showed Amber how to take the pills. Amber seemed ambivalent, not like how Grace had been —liberated, empowered. Afterward, they cleaned the shed together. She missed the relative grandeur of Victor's Victorian, but the events of her final twelve hours there made the little shed a rustic sanctuary. If not for Mom and Largo it would be a welcome retreat.

Amber was in good spirits. She bounded around the little shack showing Grace where she kept things. With the door open, fresh air filled the little room, herding dust bunnies across the floorboards. Grace looked for a broom. "I don't have one," Amber said defensively.

"No big deal." Grace pulled her hair back into a ponytail, headed across the driveway to the porch. She knocked, softly at first, then with increasing force. Largo answered in his boxer shorts and a wife beater t-shirt. The stench of sweat and stale beer assaulted her through the screen door. He'd gained weight, and his hair was receding, but it was the same Largo.

"I need a broom," she said.

He held the door too long without saying anything, just staring into her eyes. Finally, he said, "Come on in. It's behind the kitchen door." He said it slowly, "beee-hiiind," stepped aside and gawked as she strode by.

Grace shot him a stony glance as she walked past him, her hands ready at her chest. She did not take her eyes off him for a moment. In the kitchen, she looked over the counter, taking stock of the living room: a sleeping bag was draped over the couch, a disheveled pair of overalls lay on the armrest, a coffee table with a row of beer cans, an overflowing ashtray. No sign of Mom.

"See anything you like?" he sneered, taking a long chug of his beer. He crushed it with one hand and grabbed another off the table.

Grace stood firm at the kitchen door, eyes scalding him, contempt feeding malice.

"Want a beer? Marie won't be back for another two hours."

Grace gripped the broom with both hands. The path to the door was clear. She also had the kitchen door behind her if she needed it. She marched through the living room, taking in the putrid air in short quick breaths.

Outside on the porch, she searched through the brief interaction for the precise moment she could have attacked him, at the very least confronted him, told him what a pervert and creep he was. The effect on Amber was glaring to her, but was it too late? Grace jumped off the porch. She'd gripped the broom so tightly, her fingers were numb. *What can I do?*

Inside the shed, Grace set the slide lock and crumbled onto the mattress. Amber rolled over to face the wall. Her good mood was gone. *At least Amber can sleep in peace,* Grace thought. Grace pulled a joint from her bag and lit it. She lay back admitting for the first time since her arrival that it was going to be a short visit. She needed to make other plans.

That night Grace lay alone on Amber's bed. Amber was spending the night at Frankie's. It was a full moon, light enough to make out the photos in the *People* magazine she'd taken from the clinic. The TV blared across the driveway from the bungalow. At midnight she could hear clattering pans in the kitchen and wondered who could be cooking at that hour. Largo's Barracuda roared to life, peeled out of the driveway, and then it was frightfully silent. She wondered how Amber managed to sleep all those years, with those two.

As she fell deeper and deeper into a nightmarish slumber she got a niggling feeling that she was being watched. The room was stuffy and close. She heard a crackling outside the window. Her eyes shot open and she saw Mom's dark outline in the window, with nothing but the flimsy screen between them.

"I am going to kill you!" Mom screamed with a large kitchen knife raised above her head. Grace rolled off the mattress onto the rough floor. The knife sliced through the screen and struck the sill. She scampered across the shed and cowered beside the honeycomb of crates.

Mom's face was a macabre mask lit up by the moon. She struggled to free the blade, in a blackout, spewing venom at her oldest daughter. "You think you're sooo pretty. Why couldn't I have tits like that! You lucky bitch!"

Grace flattened against the wall. A quilted fabric brushed her cheek. She recognized the touch of the shipping blanket Amber had hung. She ducked under and behind it. She knew she was trapped, but she also knew from experience that Mom's drunken rages were short-lived, that she would fade. In a moment Mom abandoned the blade and slumped against the outside wall of the shed. Grace listened to her ramble incoherently.

By twelve-thirty Mom stumbled back across the gravel driveway to the porch. Grace sagged with relief when she heard the screen door slam. She peered out from behind the thick blanket. The stark outline of the knife trembled as a breeze tickled the screen. Grace rushed across the shed to close and latch the window. A wave of anger took her. She twisted the butcher knife out of the sill, then dragged the mattress to the other side of the shed. Unable to stand being there another moment, she threw on her clothes, rushed across the yard, heading away from the house to the dead end. She stopped where the asphalt surrendered to wild grass. There were no streetlights. A sea of crickets dappled the night air. Somewhere out in the moonlit meadow, a doleful frog begged for a response. She lit a joint and paced along the edge of a wood barricade. She checked the impulse to sprint into the darkness, across the dew fresh field, flowing away into nothingness, becoming nothing that feels, but something that belongs. The moon overhead was high and bright. She looked up, blowing the fragrant smoke at the perfect round. She laughed at the idea of getting the moon high. Her laughter peeled across the meadow, melting into the void. She laughed again, for no other reason than to hear her laughter leave her. Grace leaned against the barricade, pulling herself together, out of hopelessness. She would have to leave, sooner than later. She regretted reaching for her family, instead of trusting her *Family*: Rex, Kimo, and Terri, trusting that they would forgive her for abandoning them in favor of an abusive asshole like Victor. It had been pride, she knew. Grace sighed, relieved that Amber hadn't been there. She wouldn't tell her. Amber had enough stories to fill a lifetime. It defined her.

Grace turned her back on the meadow, headed up the street, back to the shed. There was much to let go of. When she reached the edge of the driveway, she looked back down to the dead end.

She sensed something had just shifted within her, that it was a moment where everything in the universe was moving in the same direction.

For the next few days, she felt like an interloper. Amber sensed Grace pulling away, shadowing her about the shed—as she idled restlessly—until Grace embraced her to stop their nervous dance. She was heading back to Venice but hadn't been able to reach Rex to get her old room back. The shed was getting smaller by the minute. Grace took Amber to McDonald's. She told her she was leaving over a Happy Meal, thinking it might soften the blow. Amber ate the French fries, eyeing the bathroom door the entire time. On the way back Amber pointed to a Shell Station where kids hitched rides. Back inside the shed, they sat in silence, Grace on the floor with her carryall on her lap and Amber on the mattress chewing her fingernails. Grace rose suddenly realizing that there was no reason to wait any longer. "You don't *have* to leave," Amber said, standing with her hands in her dress pockets. "You get used to it." Grace gave her a quick hug, afraid she might change her mind. As she made her way up the street she had the strangest vision of Amber as an old woman, grey and lonely, still living in the little shed.

#####

The silvery old couple in the Nova dropped her off at the gas station on Ocean Park Boulevard. Her high school friend waved from the cash register as if she'd never left. She waved back, energized by the salty Pacific air filling her lungs. Grace couldn't wait to get to the Oar House to see all her old friends. The beach would be hopping; the weather was perfect, with clear skies and the sun yet to peak overhead. Grace followed her shadow to Main Street and veered left, parallel to the azure Pacific. She waved to some locals along the way, people she'd seen around over the years. It still amazed her at how friendly people were down at the beach. With the Oar House on the next corner up ahead, she caught sight of Pam going into a liquor store. She looked thinner and stooped. Grace rushed across the street, and just missed getting hit by a moped running a stop sign. When she reached the curb, she waited behind a mailbox. She couldn't risk being spotted by Victor. Pam came out with a bottle of wine. She headed up Main Street with her head down, the bottle clutched to her breast. Grace moved along opposite her. To her surprise, Pam turned up Marine Street away from the beach. Grace caught up with her on Marine, a block up from Main.

"Pam!" Pam whipped around and nearly dropped the wine bottle. She seemed relieved to see that it was Grace.

"Grace?" Pam stooped to give her a hug. "Where you been?"

Grace pulled Pam into a doorway. "I've been to see my family. Where's Victor?" she asked scanning the block.

"Don't worry about him. He's in jail. He finally got caught. The last shipment was a sting. He'll be in for a while."

Grace put her hand on Pam's arm. "Was he mad?"

"At first. They busted him after you left to get your check. He thought you were in on it until Vickie left. She was a Narc. Can you believe it?"

Grace couldn't believe her luck. "What are you doing now?"

"Uh...I've got a date..." Pam jerked her head toward Marine Street. She looked trapped. Her sleeve rose as she adjusted the bottle. Grace's heart fell when she saw the track marks on her arm.

"Well, it was really nice seeing you, Pam. Take care of yourself," Grace said, giving her a light hug.

Grace was disoriented after seeing Pam. The news of Victor was a godsend, but seeing her brought back unwelcome feelings from her time at the Victorian. She turned the corner and burst through the front doors of the Oar House expecting a warm welcome. The place was mostly empty. A new girl was behind the bar. She wore a bow tie and a black vest, her hair a deep purple, eyes deeply shadowed, right out of an Andy Warhol flick. Grace slid onto a stool. "Where is everyone?"

The new girl put a coaster down and stared at her. "Don't you know? Elvis died."

Grace stared back. Never much of a fan, she was about to say, when a group of five surf rats entered the bar with their hair dyed black and coiffed like The King. There wasn't a smile among them, and with their tank tops and shorts, the ridiculousness of the ensemble made her chuckle. They glared at her and settled at a table by the front window. They proceeded to order shot after shot of tequila.

Grace downed her whiskey, went to the pay phone to call Rex.

She walked up the boardwalk as the sun began to set over the Pacific. Rex wasn't home. The burnt out pilings of the old pier were gone. A shaved swath of freshly graded dirt, lined out with rebar and chord, prophesied the rise of a new era. The wall where Herbie held court was loaded into green construction dumpsters at the curb, deconstructed into head-sized chunks. Grace wondered where the party went. As she walked up the boardwalk toward the Santa Monica Pier a few skaters passed her. Continuing, she noticed a mile long string of vendors along Muscle Beach, hawking sunglasses, sunshades and skate rentals. She stopped to observe a mural when a gaggle of young skaters flowed by, laughing and performing twists and turns. She slumped down on a bench, suddenly feeling old and out of place. Now she was in limbo, a tourist, with no taste for the nectar of change.

Flagging from her journey and two shots of Jack Daniels, she fell asleep by a smoldering fire ring. She awoke in the dark to the sound of joyful screeches, wafting to her from a small crowd that lined the shore. She skipped into the surf to join them, as the water was exceptionally warm. The early moonlight glittered in the surf, as it slowly dawned on her that the moon had some help. "The grunion are running," someone yelled, and she could feel the tickle of a thousand silver brushes on her calves.

She befriended a group of greying hippies from San Francisco and slept beside them until dawn. In the soft early light Grace sat and watched the surfers with day jobs catch the early morning swells. She shared a joint with a grizzly old surfer with a ragged longboard. When they parted she promised to have a beer with him the next time they met.

Afterward, she walked up Ocean Park Boulevard to visit Aunt Mary. When she got there the house was boarded up and a "For Sale" sign stood erect in the front yard. She sat on the curb between a rusting Falcon and a spanking new Corvette and cried. She was jarred by a wet muzzle on the back of her neck and turned to find a large poodle giving her kisses. The lady behind the leash gave her a strange look, then asked if she needed anything. "I'm looking for an old friend that used to live here. Aunt Mary."

The lady commanded the dog to heel. It was nuzzling Grace's crotch. "She passed away last week. I'm sorry."

Grace returned to the gas station to call Terri. Terri's Mom answered. "She lives with her boyfriend over in Orange County. She never visits," she said, "but here's her number."

Grace squeezed the phone when Terri answered.

"Terri?"

"Grace?"

"Where are you? How have you been?"

"It's a long story. I'm sorry I haven't called."

"I'm living in Orange County with Tim, my fiance."

"Wow, that's really cool."

Grace started to tear up. Her decision to be with Victor had nearly cost her most precious friend.

"I'm in Venice. Do you want to get together?"

"Grace, I can't believe it. We're going to a party tonight near my mom's house. You remember Scott. It's at his house. Rex and Kimo are coming too."

Grace gripped the phone with both hands and jumped up and down.

"Terri, I really missed you. I've got so much to tell you. When are you coming up?"

"I'll be there around seven thirty. Why don't we meet at the Oar House?'

Grace hung up feeling better than she had in months.

#####

At the Oar House Bar Rex, Kimo and Grace hit the dance floor like old times. Disco was dead, so they danced to the Sex Pistols and Talking Heads. Where they'd been dervishes in the sixties, they hustled and popped in the seventies, and now with punk hitting overdrive, they sneered and jerked around the dance floor. When Terri got there they packed into Rex's florist van for the ride to Scott's. Tim, her fiancé, always had speed so he gave them cross tops to keep the party hopping. Grace had never been to Scott's house. It turned out to be a masquerade party, and there were costumes ranging from a bong to Cher, from Cheech and Chong to Richard Nixon. Scott was dressed as Frank Zappa. The house was on the other side of Highway 405, near Culver City. Scott's family had lived there for generations. There was a wonderful rose garden in the front yard, and trellises with morning glories and bougainvillea surrounded the backyard. A Cream cover band occupied the back corner of the yard, while Scott manned a keg on the deck. Grace headed for a small patch of grass in front of a stage of pallets and plywood. Terri joined her with a couple of beers. They stood in the back of a speaker, sipped beer and smoked a joint. Rex and Kimo arrived from the kitchen with a bottle of tequila and shot glasses.

"Where have you been, what happened to Victor?" Rex asked as he poured them shots.

Grace passed the joint to Kimo.

"Let's just say you were right about Victor. I survived!" she shouted and downed a shot.

"Love is blind," Rex said, as he kissed Kimo on the lips.

"Do you forgive me?" Grace asked with a pouty face.

"Enough drama, girlfriend. Let's party," Kimo said. He filled their shot glasses again.

"To the King!" he yelled above the band, holding his shot glass to the sky. "Elvis!" they screamed in unison, downing their shots.

The band kicked into "White Room". The backyard was packed now. Scott and a muscular Hawaiian looking guy came out from the kitchen with a new keg, pushing through the crowd. Grace couldn't take her eyes off of Scott's friend. There was something about him. She smiled at him as she and her friends moved to the side of the house to smoke a joint. Terri told them about Tim, how he was thinking of joining the Navy. Rex and Kimo told them about how they were trying to get married, to make it official. All the while Grace eyed Ron, Scott's Hawaiian friend. She was distracted as he talked with a group of women, gave a baggy to one of them, and then walked to another group. He was so powerful, yet gentle and charming. Finally, Grace turned to Kimo. "Who is that?" she asked.

"Who?"

"The gorgeous Hawaiian guy over there."

Kimo nudged her. "What do you think, I know every Hawaiian who's moved off the island?" he laughed.

"That's Ron," Rex interjected. "He's married, but I think they're separated."

Grace watched Ron move from group to group. She didn't date married men. She stared back at Terri who'd popped another one of Tim's pills in her mouth. She shook her head when Terri offered one.

"So, where are you staying?" Terri asked.

Grace sighed. "Nowhere. I need to find a place."

"Why don't you ask Kimo and Rex? They never rented your old room."

Grace laid her head on Terri's shoulder. Rex looked at Kimo. They started giggling.

"What's so funny?" Grace asked.

"We came to the party knowing you would ask. Your room is exactly as you left it."

As the party wound down, Scott started herding people out on the street. The band was packing up. Scott and Ron moved the keg into the kitchen. Grace made sure to follow them. Grace lingered near the door as guests filed out; she wanted to catch Ron before he left. At the door he smiled at her, too much of a gentleman, she thought, to ask her out with the divorce pending. Terri, Rex, Kimo, and Grace went to the Oar house for a nightcap. It was as if she'd never left. She finally went to bed at sunrise, back in her old room.

# 11

The bungalow was finally quiet. Mom and Largo had been fighting, a daily eruption that stretched the patience of their neighbors on either side. A police cruiser was parked at the dead end. Amber liked to think the battles didn't affect her; they'd been a part of her life stretching back to Magnolia where her Mom and Dad's eruptions crumbled the foundation. They were like a constant fever holding her in a balmy grip. It was the norm and she didn't know anything different. After midnight, she peered out the shed door. The driveway was a dull cascade in the moonlight. A single light glowed from the kitchen. She ducked back in when she saw a large shadow eclipse the front window.

The last ten months were especially stressful for Amber. It started when Grace left. She couldn't convince herself that she wasn't angry at Grace for leaving. Now she was angry at herself for being angry at Grace. She hated the hope she still clung to, that they would live together.

Largo had begun to deal speed. He used as much as he sold —a fact that shifted Amber's reality once again. It made him horny, and he wanted her frequently when he was high. She spent as little time in the bungalow as possible, and only when he wasn't there. At first, Mom liked the drug money. They went to parties again, which left the bungalow vacant for Amber. Along came the day when he badgered Mom to let Amber sleep with them which only made Mom drink more. Now, Mom blew up at Amber every time she saw her.

Amber stared at the front window. She couldn't shake the feeling that he was watching her. She could feel her heartbeat in her temples. She was using regularly now. The pills she took an hour ago worked overtime in her system. While it made Largo horny, it made her numb. It made her feel thin and took away the binges. She saw her mop handle thin wrist in the moonlight. She liked it.

Amber crept out into the driveway. She giggled weakly as she jumped at the sight of her own shadow, stepped deftly onto the planks of the porch, and listened once again. The neighbor's cat meowed. The fence near the truck terminal rattled. She opened the front door and slipped into the living room. She shot glances at the couch, the kitchen, and the blackened doorway to the back of the house. In the bathroom, Amber disrobed down to her underpants. She found a clean wash rag, gathered the soap from the dish, wiped her intimate parts, and rinsed them, all so practiced, and expedient. She dried herself with toilet paper and marveled at her thin silhouette in the mirror. She bent closer. Her eyes were black yokes in the dim moonlight. Her hair was long and stringy now. She put it back in a ponytail, running fingertips along the thinness of her neck. Thirsty, she gulped handfuls of water, until she heard a sound from the other side of the door. She knew the loose board under the hallway carpet, she knew the warning signals. Amber strained to hear over the pounding in her head. She put her ear to the door. The old house was settling. She winced and stared back into the mirror.

Frankie said he liked her face. She ran her fingers over her cheekbone, down her neck to her breasts. They'd grown in spite of her self-deprivation. Her hands rested on her belly. Amber pinched the small fat on both sides. She pouted at the mirror, suddenly angry at herself. She'd stopped getting her period. She no longer took the pill. Her stomach growled. Amber crouched by the toilet, thrust two fingers in her throat and vomited into the bowl. She flushed it quickly, threw on her shorts and shirt, and tiptoed into the living room.

Heading out the door, she noticed Largo's leather satchel on the side of the sofa. He must have left it there during the argument with Mom. Amber crept to the side of the couch listening all the while for that loose board.

She unzipped the main compartment, but couldn't see inside so she took out her Bic lighter, and held a flame over the satchel. She undid the clasp and looked inside. Small baggies in big baggies filled the main compartment. A stack of bills tied together with a rubber band was in the front pocket. Amber reached into a large baggie, took out two small baggies. She silhouetted them in the window and saw that they each held a palmful of pills. She stuffed them into her pocket, then froze. It was one thing to take pills, yet another, to take cash. The image of the sweaty Largo hovering over her filled her mind. Her jaw clenched as she slipped two twenties out of the stack. She did the clasp, returned the bag to its resting place, and crept out the door.

Outside the moonlight painted the yard and driveway a calming grey-blue. Amber returned to her little shed. She took one of the pills and lay on her back watching the rafters tremble. Tomorrow she would buy a new pair of shoes and pants at Mervyn's. Tonight, she wouldn't sleep, but it didn't seem to matter either way.

#####

School was just a nuisance now. She felt older than the other kids. All the adults called her Ms. Rentano, she thought, because she wore dresses and owl glasses, and carried a purse. It was her last year in Junior High. Frankie was in High School already, and Julie went to a special school. She felt like she was drifting on ice.

Amber peered up at the school nurse. She'd passed out during science class. Her third-period teacher, Mr. Gage, called the office, and the nurse arrived with a rickety wheelchair. He resumed the lesson on the reproductive cycle of snakes, while Amber was pushed out the door with her chin in her chest, pretending to be passed out, but hearing everything they said.  In the nurse's office for the second time in two days, she pretended to read a diagram of a human skeleton. It was a young girl, nothing but veins, arteries, and bones.

The nurse called Mom. "She passed out. Did she have any breakfast? She also has lice. She's going to need to stay home for a few days."

The nurse, a serious, dowdy woman with great jowls and kind eyes, glanced over at Amber. She'd seen the signs.

Amber smiled weakly up at her, and stared back at the diagram. She knew exactly how Mom would react. Anger was her default emotion. Amber crossed her arms, scrutinizing the skeleton girl. She smiled grimly at the pelvic bone, following the spine up to the neck, chin, and forehead.  She wondered if it was possible to be that thin, imagining skin over the sharp edges.

"Amber, did you have breakfast?" She went to a small refrigerator and pulled out a small container of cottage cheese.

"Yes," she lied. She stared at the food pyramid above the sink. "I had two bowls of Cheerios and a waffle. The waffle was so good, with butter and syrup. I have so much to eat at home, I don't know what to do with it all. Do you think I look fat?"

The nurse shook her head. "Amber, I want you to eat breakfast before you come to school. If you can't get any, come by and see me. I've always got something here."

Amber took a small spoonful of cottage cheese. She placed it on her tongue, and swallowed. "Can I have some water?" She gulped the water. The cool flow eased the burn in her throat. She lurched dramatically, holding her stomach. "What's wrong?" the nurse asked.

"I can't poop. Do you have you any Ex-lax?" she asked.

"We don't give laxative at school. Eat some fruit. The fiber will help." The nurse walked to the scale leaning against the wall.

"Amber, let's weigh you."

Amber rose from the chair and stepped on the scale. She stared at the red arm tapping ninety, then settling on eighty-five. She looked up at the nurse.

The nurse pursed her lips and jotted something on a clipboard.

Amber stepped off the scale. She wanted a cigarette in a bad way. It was after lunch, and Frankie was going to meet her by the benches. "Can I go now?"

"How do you feel?"

"Much better. Thank you."

The nurse signed the paper on the clipboard, pulled it loose, read it over a last time, and handed it to Amber.

"Give this to your mother. Make sure she signs it and returns it to me."

"What is it?"

"It's a lice protocol. It acknowledges that she knows you have lice. There are directions on the back how to get rid of them."

The nurse put a hand under Amber's chin. She brushed her thumb across her bangs.

"We're going to miss you, Amber."

Amber stared down at her shoes, her face apathetic, offering no decipherable emotion.

"And eat something, okay, Amber?"

Amber's lips tightened into a faint smile.

Down the hall, she decided to skip the rest of her classes. She walked out to the quad to meet Frankie. Students milled around open class doors waiting for the bell to ring. Frankie was waiting on their bench. She approached slowly, offering a wan expression

145

as she reached him. Her dark loose clothes whipped against her as she bent to kiss his cheek.

"Let's get out of here," she said. "I need a smoke."

Amber led Frankie to a spot in the back of the cafeteria where the dumpsters lined the back wall, with a small dock and an open drain where the unwanted milk was poured. It smelled like rancid cheese, which kept the area clear of loitering, except for underage smokers, and cafeteria staff.

They leaned against the wall and lit up. A silence grew while they passed the cigarette back and forth. A bell rang, which prompted no response from either of them.

Frankie spoke first.

"Have you heard from your sister?"

"No."

Frankie turned to face Amber. "Why are you so quiet?"

Amber shrugged.

Frankie scratched the back of his neck.

Amber erupted. "Do you like her? I can't believe you even talk to her! She's disgusting."

"Who?"

"Lisa!" Amber stamped out the cigarette. "Don't you like me?" she cried.

Frankie stepped back. "It's not about you."

"She's just using you to make me mad. She's with Charlie. He told me so when he came to get speed from Largo."

Frankie stepped closer. "What did he say?"

Amber adjusted her sweater. It hung loosely on her shoulders, and dangled like curtains over her bony knees. "He doesn't really like her but he thinks you do." There was a glint in her eye, and a smirk across her lips. "He wanted to spend the night," she added.

Frankie scrutinized Amber. He chuckled.

"Are you kidding me? Charlie's in high school." He looked out toward the manicured grass field adjoining the alley. A shadow crossed his face.

"You don't like him, do you?"

"He's cute."

"But he's almost sixteen." Frankie looked worried.

Amber liked that. He was easy, she thought. *My Frankie.*

She really smiled now, for the first time all day. "He likes me. By the way, look what I got."

Amber held up a bag of speed.

"Largo?"

"Yeah. I got it last night. Want some?"

Amber gave Frankie a bag. She knew what effect they would have on him. "Want to go down to the river?"

Frankie put the pills in his pocket. "Yeah, let's get out of here."

Amber and Frankie trudged up the busy boulevard, and stopped to buy Big Gulps at 7-Eleven. It was their after-school routine. They walked down Reseda Boulevard, crossed over the bridge, straddled the abutment, and slid into the shadows of the overpass. The river was especially grey, capturing the sagging clouds overhead.

They sat smoking in silence, watching the lazy current tickle bunches of reeds growing incredibly out of the concrete by the riverbank. The clay nests that lined the underbelly of the bridge looked exactly the same as she remembered them on her first day in Reseda. She knew the birds were in there, but couldn't see any as yet.

"Do you remember when we first met here?"

"You were so scrawny. You thought you were so tough," he chided.

"You were such a surfer dude." Amber stretched her legs out and smoothed her skirt.

"Have you ever been to the beach?" she asked.

"No."

They both laughed.

"It isn't very far. Grace and I used to go. There's a really cool beach in Venice. Everyone is so cool. There are these guys that lift weights. Everyone sits around on the beach partying and watching the weightlifters. Grace lives there now."

A dozen or so birds plummeted at once from their nests, formed into a flock, dipped to the river and up over the bridge.

"Where does the river go?" Amber asked.

"Out to sea."

"How do you know?"

"All water goes back to the sea." Frankie pulled out a joint and lit it, took a puff and passed it to Amber. She took a hit, held it and passed it back. She closed her eyes, imagining the river flowing through towns, and all the kids sitting on the banks watching the water, all at once.

"Rain goes to the gutter, the gutter goes to the river, the river takes it back to the sea where it evaporates into rain clouds. Didn't you learn that in school?"

Amber took another hit. "Everything goes back to the sea," she mused. "People too."

Amber wished she had something else to say. No words would come.

Frankie stared into space. A few cars thumped by over the bridge. A trio of wayward birds searched for the flock.

"My science teacher says that we evolved from the sea. But you're the only one I know who looks like a fish."

Amber punched him in the arm. She wrapped her arms around his neck. She kissed him on the cheek. "Sometimes you remind me of my brother Paul."

They peered up at the clouds, at the river again, at their feet swishing back and forth like windshield wipers.

Finally, Amber spoke up. "Do you like Lisa?"

"Do you like Steve?"

Amber took Frankie's hand. She leaned over and kissed him on the lips.

Frankie sat still. "Let's get out of here," he said. "I should check on Julie. She's been home sick from school."

Amber pouted. "What about me?"

"I'll come over later."

Amber held onto his arm. She hugged him. He smelled like bubble gum and sweat. She liked the smell. "See you later."

After he'd gone Amber watched the meandering river. She imagined it reaching the sea, where carefree kids played on the beach and waded into the warm shallows.

A horn from the bridge shook her back to the concrete embankment.

#####

"Where have you been?" Mom yelled from the couch.

Amber sighed. She'd snuck up the driveway, mostly on the grass, to avoid just this. "The nurse called me. She says you have lice. Get your ass in the car. We're going to get lice shampoo."

Amber started to get into the front seat.

"Get in the back. I don't want lice."

Amber wanted to run. She hesitated as she moved to the back seat.

"Hurry up!"

In a weighted silence they sped over the bridge and pulled into the Vons parking lot a half mile up Reseda Boulevard. "You stay here. I'll get it," Mom commanded.

Mom read Amber's mind. "Don't go anywhere!"

Amber fumed in the back seat. She scratched her scalp, imagining the little critters forming a colony near her crown. A mother with an infant and two tow-headed toddlers in a shopping cart stared at her as they trundled by. A cart boy pushed a row of carts dangerously close to the rear bumper. A van stopped briefly behind the car, then sped off.

When Mom returned her mood was even more sour. "I can't believe the trouble you put me through. When you get home, strip off those clothes. We'll take them to the laundromat." She threw the bag of supplies in the passenger seat. A gallon Vodka bottle burst out of the bag. "Shit!" She rammed the car into reverse and barely missed a silvery couple walking to their car. She glared at them and peeled out of the parking lot.

"That nurse is a bitch. Acting like she knows what it's like to raise a kid. Who does she think she is? Kids get lice all the time. She acted like I was abusing you. You think I abuse you?"

Amber stared out the side window. She knew better than to throw gas on that fire.

Mom turned around at the next red light. "Better not. I didn't have to take you. Nobody else would. I'm the only one!" she screamed, pointing at her chest. "Not your whore sister, or your war hero father."

Amber bowed her head. She closed her eyes so tightly she heard the sound of waves. "Are you listening to me?"

Amber could smell the alcohol on her breath. She opened her eyes to slits. She knew better than to answer.

"That's right. You better keep your mouth shut if you know what's good for you."

When she felt the crunch of the driveway under the tires Amber's heart started to pound. The thought of stripping down in broad daylight made her shiver. She got out of the car and stood in the shadow of the shed. At least the sun was out now. Mom stared at her, a jiggling stack of rage. She threw the shampoo on the ground next to Amber. Next, she went to the side of the house, and returned with the garden hose. By now, Largo was on the porch in his t-shirt and boxer shorts, enjoying the show. "Go ahead," her mother said. "Get your clothes off."

Amber looked up the driveway out to the truck terminal. No one could see her from there; she wished there was at least a single driver, a stranger, yes, but someone who might witness what was happening and put an end to it. "Can't I at least go in the house?"

"Yeah! Like last time?"

Amber stripped down to her underwear. Mom went to the side of the house and turned on the hose. Amber took one look at Largo whose head was nodding, ever so slowly. She stared at the terminal fence across the street, her hands covering her pubis. She leaped in shock when the cold stream struck her belly.

"Here!" Mom said, extending the hose. "Wet your hair."

Amber held the hose over her head, shivering in the late afternoon sunlight. Shadows were making their way across the driveway from the truck yard. Mom poured the shampoo into Amber's hair. Largo belched and leaped off the porch. He walked across the yard, a cigarette dangling from his raw lips.

"You need some help, missy?" Mom gave him a dark glare, which only seemed to encourage him. Amber retreated as he stepped toward her. Up close, she noticed the grey in his beard now. A vein pulsed in his neck.

He grabbed the shampoo from Mom. He made a show of massaging Amber's head with shampoo, and held the hose to the side, forming a foamy puddle at her feet. When it was time, he rinsed her off, gently directing the spray away from her eyes.

Mom scowled, lit a cigarette and stood back and watched. She seemed somewhere else now. She looked over at the Vodka bottle on the porch and rushed into the house. In a moment she stood inside the house, behind the screen watching them. She had a drink in her hand, blowing smoke out the screen into the driveway. Her stare bore into Amber.

Largo ran his hand down Amber's back, cupping suds off of her. Amber was frozen and shivering. She looked up at Mom in the doorway. Amber knew it would be all over soon. She was actually glad Largo was there. She stood still while Largo ran his hands down her legs and back up to her shoulders. "Do the hair again," he said. He kissed her shoulder as Amber reapplied shampoo.

They repeated the process, under Mom's death stare. When Largo started smoothing the suds on Amber's belly she'd had enough. She slammed the screen door open and leaped off the porch, eyes afire.

"That's enough, Largo...she's done." She threw a towel at Amber. Largo snatched the towel out of the air.

Amber looked up at Mom, then Largo. She smiled innocently and walked toward the shed. She was still nude, but she'd stopped shivering. At the shed door she gathered her hair and looked back at Mom. She knew what she was about to do would change things forever between them.

Mom trailed Largo, as he followed Amber. They stopped at the door to the shed.

Mom looked down at Largo's crotch. She slapped him.

Largo turned his head slowly and bellowed, "Fuck off, Marie!"

Mom jumped back, holding her hands up to her face. She leaped toward Amber. It was too late. Amber slammed the shed door.

Largo stared Mom down. Defeated, Mom stormed back into the house.

Amber knew the end was near. Soon, she would be free of the whole scene. Largo ducked into the shed. Amber knew the drill. It was time to perform. She'd performed for seven years, half her life. The curtain would fall for the last time.

# 12

Grace had turned a corner, and a whole new path lay at her feet. She was rid of her family, rid of Victor, and she felt like a new person. She got a job at Century City Mall at Ma's Cookies next to The Broadway. She was able to save some money and open a bank account. She bought a red convertible Karmann Ghia. On her days off she visited Kimo and Rex at the florist shop where Rex was the manager. She would sit at the broad linoleum tables, and learn how to create arrangements from the different varieties of flowers. She made her own arrangements with the discards.

There was another reason for going to the mall on her days off. Ron, the Hawaiian guy she'd met at Scott's party, worked at Swiss Colony. She knew when he got to work, his lunch break, and when he got off.

The florist shop was slow for a Thursday. Rex, Kimo, and Grace huddled together in the tiny workroom.

"That is gorgeous." Rex walked around the work table, eyeing Grace's masterpiece. He reversed direction and headed counter-clockwise, his eye leveled on the center of the piece.

Grace beamed under the bright fluorescent lighting. She'd worked on it for two days straight. It was her wedding gift to Terri and Tim. She held her hands together in a prayer posture, too excited to move until Rex had done his final inspection.

"You've come a long way, baby," he said, wiping a fake tear from his eye. "Lose those lilies though. That won't do for a wedding," he said.

"Can you believe Terri's getting married?" she asked.

"And to such a doll," Kimo said, walking in from the office. "How long have they been together?"

Grace got off the stool and walked around to the back of her creation. She started extracting the lilies from the piece. "Over a year now. They met on the beach. He was a lifeguard. Now he works at some factory in Pasadena."

"And how is your Hawaiian?" Rex asked, winking at Kimo.

Grace blushed. "He hasn't asked me out yet."

Kimo moved a sunflower to the back of her arrangement. "Why do you have to wait for *him* to ask you out?"

"I know...right? I'm sick of eating at the Swiss Colony." She looked up at the clock on the wall. "It's almost his lunch break. Kimo, can you put this in the cooler for me?"

Kimo came around the table to face Grace's creation. "You really are getting better, honey."

Grace hung her apron next to the phone on the wall. She undid her hair, shook it out, and flipped it behind her back. She put on fresh lipstick and rushed out the door.

"Ask him out!" Rex yelled.

Grace arrived at the door of the Swiss Colony a little short of breath. Her heart pinged in anticipation. She peeked in the window. *Good*, she thought, *he's working the counter.* She watched him help a customer choose a gift basket of assorted cheeses. He had his shirt sleeves rolled up, revealing his bulging biceps. She squeezed her purse. She watched him smile at the customer, a woman in her forties; judging by the way she touched his arm, she loved his biceps too. Grace loved how attentive he was, gentle, but strong.

Grace entered the restaurant and stood at the sign-up podium. Ron waved and she felt that reliable pang. She looked at her reflection in the window, correcting a few loose strands, took out a tissue, and dabbed a fleck of lipstick from her tooth. In the reflection, she saw a new girl approach the register from the back of the shop. She came up behind Ron, placed her hand on his shoulder, and whispered something in his ear. Ron rang his customer up, turned and walked to the back.

Grace whipped around. She and the new girl were the only ones at the front. Waitresses came and went, ringing up their customers. Grace didn't notice them. *Where did he go?* She went to the counter, feigning interest in the glass display under the register. The new girl just smiled and waited with her hands in her apron pockets.

*He's too helpful sometimes. Is he cheating on me?*

The new girl grabbed a menu and held it to her chest. "Seat for one?" she asked.

Grace felt a draft coming from the behind the register. *Where could he be?* Grace turned back to the plaza. A family and a few seniors meandered outside near the water fountain. *The back door!* she thought. On impulse, she bolted out the front door.

Outside, Grace turned down the side of the restaurant. It was a narrow walkway between the Swiss Colony and a See's Candy shop next door. She hurried along the path, stepping lightly, as the sprinklers had slicked the path that morning. At the edge of the building, she heard hushed but clear voices.

"Dude. That's some stinky shit. Acapulco Red?"

"No, bro...pure Hawaiian. I gotta go now."

Grace turned the corner expecting to see a couple of hippies. What she saw stunned her. Ron was standing by the back door taking money from a square looking guy with long sideburns and a corduroy jacket. The guy saw her, slapped some bills in Ron's outstretched hand, and shot down the alley in the other direction. Grace met Ron's gaze. He smiled, then folded the money, stuck it in his wallet, and closed the back door.

Grace leaned against the side of the building. Not again. She had no problem with Ron selling pot. She was more upset at herself for not figuring it out sooner. *No wonder he's always got plenty of cash.* Her immediate disappointment was quickly replaced by a greater sense of connection with Ron. She knew his secret.

Grace turned back down the walkway. As she turned toward the front of the restaurant Ron appeared with a broad smile on his face. Rather than being nervous and apologetic as she might have expected, Ron kissed her on the cheek. Grace wagged her finger at him. "You naughty boy," she said, smiling.

"You caught me. Can I bribe you to keep quiet?"

"With what?"

"Dinner."

"Is that all?"

Ron blushed. It was obvious to her now that while he was a flirt, he was actually shy when it came to making a move. "I...we..."

Grace took him by the hand. They walked together back to the restaurant. "I get off at five," he said. "Why don't we meet here?"

Grace could hardly contain herself. She returned to the florist to finish Terri's wedding present. Rex and Kimo teased her about dating a dealer when she told him about the transaction. "He's nothing like Victor though," Kimo said.

Later, in front of the fountain she counted down the minutes. *Will he kiss me again?* she wondered. When he came out the front door she noticed that he'd changed into a new pair of pants and shirt. His hair was freshly combed. She gave him a peck on the cheek, not waiting for him to make a move. They walked closely back to the florist, bumping together like two tethered ships.

At the florist shop, Grace led him to the work table. Kimo was in the office, but Rex was reading a catalog on a stool by the phone.

"Hi, Ron," Rex said, got up and hugged him. "It's so good to see you."

Grace walked to the cooler and took out her masterpiece. She looked it over, delighted that Kimo made a few adjustments. She gently placed it on the worktable, then took a few steps back. "It's my first big project. What do you think?"

Ron stood on the other side of the table with his hands in his pockets. "It's beautiful."

Grace turned it around so he could see the back side. "It's for Terri, my best friend's wedding."

"Terri and Tim?" he asked.

"Yeah. Do you know them?"

"My band is playing at their wedding."

Rex's jaw dropped.

Grace giggled at Rex, bouncing on her toes. Kimo walked in from the office. "Hi, Ron," he said, giving him a hug.

"Ron is playing at the wedding," Grace said, walking around the table.

"Don't forget to bring the Maui Wowie," he laughed, slapping Ron on the back.

That night after dinner they walked between Venice and the Santa Monica Pier. The tide was high and sandpipers were out in force, patrolling the surf like possessive mothers. Ron and Grace talked as if they'd known one another from another life and time. The conversation flowed, as they walked up and back until they settled on a bench in Venice. They watched the fire rings light up the beach, and the homeless stake their claims for the night. She would never forget their first kiss, with the Pacific shimmering, and the sandpipers scolding the tide. They kissed again at her door, pressing together, not wanting the night to drift into memory. She watched him drive off, and couldn't stop smiling on her way to bed.

#####

The wedding arch was erected in wet sand near the shoreline on Venice Beach. Grace and Ron stood in the front row of guests facing the Pacific Ocean. The tide came in abruptly after a great set of waves; Rex and Kimo pulled up the arch and the entire wedding party skittered up the beach to finish the vows. Grace held Ron's hand as they walked to his car on the way to the reception. The wedding was their third date. Grace was so charged up after the wedding she asked Ron if they could smoke a joint in his car. He obliged and when they arrived at Terri and Tim's house in Orange they were comfortably numb. Grace felt at home at Terri's, having spent many a night there. Ron went to the backyard to set up the band while she worked in the kitchen preparing aluminum sheets of lasagna, garlic bread, and salad. Terri's mother sat in a corner of the kitchen with a bottle of wine and a bucket of Colonel Sanders Kentucky Fried Chicken. The kitchen was so steamy Grace opened all the windows to let in the late afternoon breeze. Strands of hair fell down across her face and she was rosy from head to toe. Terri greeted guests in the backyard at a table set for the newlyweds.

Ron came in with an empty tray, that only moments ago held mini quiches. "If we ever do this, we're going to get a caterer," Grace said, pulling another tray of quiche out of the oven. She looked up at Ron to see his reaction, but he was somewhere else. The singer in his band was a flake and hadn't shown up yet. "The lasagna is taking longer than I thought. Lucky everyone is so fucked up."

Ron stopped and stared at her. He came around the butcher block in the middle of the room and wrapped his arms around her waist. "You are so beautiful," he said, nuzzling her neck.

Grace looked over at the pantry. "Let's have a quickie in the pantry," she said suddenly.

Grace led Ron by the hand into the small room. Terri's mother prattled on, but her eyes followed them. She stopped chewing and a smile stretched across her face. Grace turned to close the pantry door, catching Terri's mother's ebullient gaze. She smiled, closed the door, and unzipped Ron's pants. She massaged him, as he gasped, mouth wide open. She turned her back to him and raised her skirt. She gripped the shelf loaded with bags of flour and sugar and received him firmly.

Afterward, they parted with a smothering kiss. "The quiche is getting cold," she said. "Bring me back a joint when you get a chance."

Within an hour, the first three trays of lasagna were browned on top, with five additional trays on the way. While only fifty guests had RSVP'd, another fifty had drifted South from Venice. They were a motley group of stoners, veterans, and islanders. After dinner, Ron grabbed his guitar and got on stage for a solo. He'd written a song for Terri and Tim. Grace sat down next to Terri. It was such a beautiful evening. A mauve and orange sky glowed to the West. To the East, the hills were a long tract of grey-brown, speckled with early street lights. Terri had a green thumb, as did Tim. Rows of daffodils were rimmed by hydrangeas, with bougainvillea trellises along the fences. It was all so intimate and fragrant. Grace could smell jasmine and searched the yard for a slight whiff of fennel.

Ron finished his song with a passionate flourish. As the applause scattered the rest of the band joined him on stage. Ron's cousin Michael was the bass player. He'd arrived from Hawaii and was an instant favorite, with a voice that could charm a snake. He'd also brought some party gifts with him. As Grace scanned the backyard, she noticed thin Macadamia and chocolate boxes lying open on each table. She smiled to herself. They were a gift to Terri and Tim. Michael had shown Grace and Ron his method of packing Hawaiian bud under a row of chocolates and shrink-wrapping them. They looked like the duty-free souvenirs any tourist would bring home from the islands. The ubiquitous green sticky buds filled pipe bowls and joints on nearly every table, and certainly every table in the house. As the shadows grew in the backyard, and the sun took its rest, the party thinned out to intimate family and close friends, migrating into the kitchen and large paneled living room.

Terri and Tim passed out on a love seat by the coat rack. Grace, Ron, Kimo, Rex, and Michael lounged in old red velvet chairs and a plush couch, surrounding a glass top coffee table. A decimated box of the special Hawaiian chocolates, with smelly green buds, lay open. Michael strummed a ukulele, while Ron hummed a tune they'd been working on. A bottle each of red and white wine was half empty, with wine glasses scattered precariously across the glass top.

"So, when are you two getting hitched?" Kimo asked.

Grace lifted her head off of Ron's shoulder. He stopped humming. Michael kept playing, smiling at Ron. Ron shrugged. Grace looked around the room. Her head was spinning from the wine, an altogether pleasant sensation. All her closest friends were there. It was the best day of her life, she reckoned. The lasagna was a great hit, and Terri looked so happy slumbering, her face soft and blissful. Tim was a good guy, she thought. Terri was taken care of.

"We haven't set a date yet," she murmured into Ron's chest. She watched Rex pass the joint to Michael, who shook his head. "Don't you smoke, Michael?" she asked.

Michael smiled, running his fingers over the strings. "It's against my religion," he said.

Ron whispered in Grace's ear, "He's a born again."

Grace stared at Michael. She turned back to Ron. "But he still deals?"

Ron kissed her forehead. "He gave me his contact when he took the plunge."

Ron pulled his arm from around Grace. He stood suddenly and took Grace by the hand, helping her to her feet. "Let's go out on the patio. I want to ask you something."

Grace teetered for a moment, then followed him toward the kitchen door. Slipping into the kitchen, she raised her eyebrows at Rex.

Out on the patio, Ron pulled her to him. She melted into his arms and began to sway with the silent music of the stars and moonlight overhead. She could smell his Hai Karate aftershave, mingled with the lavender that grew wild around the patio.

"Did it bother you when Kimo asked you about us?" she asked.

Ron dipped his head and kissed her full on the mouth. She loved the taste of Hawaiian bud and red wine on his breath. They stayed chest to chest, feeling their heartbeats and nuzzling. Finally, Ron pulled away to face her. Grace's upturned face was clear and pale in the moonlight.

"Will you move in with me, Grace?"

Grace put her arms around his waist. "Of course," she said. It had been right from the start. It was as if they'd arrived at the same location at the same moment, from opposite directions, travelers from across the globe drawn together magnetically. She was going to ask *him* tonight. It felt right that he asked first. "What about..."

"Let's talk about that later," he said, chuckling. "We're in no hurry, are we?"

"No hurry," she smiled. Grace imagined waking up with Ron, his strong body next to hers, his loyalty and sense of purpose. Under the glittering stars, she imagined a child or two, maybe a dog, a garden, and a place for her to paint. Grace and Ron stared out at the bobbing blossoms in the moonlit garden. A slight ocean breeze teased the foliage to dance. When Grace heard someone cleaning up in the kitchen she kissed Ron and went inside to help. It was after all a perfect day.

#####

Early morning Saturday Grace opened her eyes to the sound of birds singing and an arm across her chest. Out of a dream about a trip on a ship, a dream she couldn't decide was good or bad. She was getting used to sleeping with him. She couldn't imagine sleeping alone again, and there was nothing in their love that said she would have to. They fit so well together. They lived in Venice Beach, paid bills with the shipments from Hawaii and her part-time job at Ma's Cookies. After Victor, it seemed like a dream. She couldn't have picked a better partner. Ron was going to a technical school, building a career that could support them for years to come. They'd planned it in bed, in the early mornings upon waking, days filled with promise. Grace was surprised at this new part of herself. She had not been one to make plans, living in the moment was her style. But Ron was a stabilizing force. He liked the structure, and she felt the effects of his influence in little surges of joy throughout each day. A joy she realized was the result of having a direction, and a shared life purpose.

Grace made it clear that she did not want to go back to school. Her experience at Venice High confirmed to her that she did not thrive in institutionalized education. Life experience was all she needed to know. She kept the home tidy and handled their finances. She visited Terri in Orange, and Kimo and Rex at the florist.

They'd been together six months when one morning she found herself trembling, on her knees on the tile floor of the bathroom. She was in a cold sweat, a vertigo she'd never felt. She remembered waking to the sound of the garbage truck out on the street. Ron was already out the door. Her head spun as she threw up, unable to reason what could have caused the sudden illness. She'd felt fine when they'd gone to bed. Grace splashed cold water on her face, then went to the medicine cabinet. She'd stopped having her period; she knew because she hadn't had one since she was fourteen when she started taking the pill. Her old pills stared down at her from the bottom shelf. Her legs were weak now, as she remembered she'd missed a week of pills when they took a trip to Vegas to see Ron's brother.

Grace went to the kitchen, made herself some toast and tea, thoughts jetting through her mind. The sudden horror that she might be having a gonorrhea flare up, and that she might have given it to Ron lifted her out of the chair. She went to the phone and called Terri.

"Terri. I think I have the clap."

"What are you talking about? You've been with Ron all this time."

"I've got the same symptoms. I've been throwing up all morning."

"Have you stopped to think that maybe you're pregnant?"

Grace rested her head against the wall. The receiver weighed a thousand pounds.

"I hadn't thought of that."

"You better get a pregnancy test." There was silence on the other line. "Tim and I have been trying."

"Well..."

"Are you going to keep it?" Terri asked.

There was something in Terri's voice that made her feel suddenly guilty. "I'll get the test," she replied, saying a rapid goodbye.

She was waiting on the couch when Ron came home that evening. The clinic had rushed her test. She had news but was unsure how he would take it. Her Karmann Ghia sat out front on the curb. She would need to get a station wagon. She demurred at the thought of losing her first car and promised herself she wouldn't be one of those mothers. What kind of mother *would* she be?

Ron threw his bag on the stuffed chair by the door. Always so connected, he came to her. She smiled up at him weakly, feeling suddenly small and frail in his arms. She didn't have to say a word. After a moment he stood up. No secret could linger between them, especially one of this sort. "Are you sure?" he asked, hands on his head. He giggled, and couldn't stop smiling. She had her answer. They went to the kitchen. She put hot water on as he paced in front of the refrigerator. Finally, she took his hand and led him to a chair. They stared at one another in silence as they sipped spearmint tea. The world outside beckoned: birds tapping at the window, the sun barreling in, the branches in the trees slinging autumn leaves about the yard. She felt the little life growing inside of her, even then.

#####

Ron proposed on the beach a stone's throw from the Oar House. It was a blustery day, and voracious seagulls zeroed in on stranded crustaceans skittering along the shore. Her hair whipped his face, and she was wondering why he'd brought her down to the beach on such an atypical Southern California day. He fell to his knees, *so gallant*, she thought, except that he knelt in a glistening pile of seaweed. When they stopped laughing he proposed, his expression etched in her mind. She laughed nervously at his seriousness, fell to her knees to join him, not wanting to be on a pedestal, wanting to be with him in every way at once.

That night in bed, the day's end whirring near, they made love with resolve, matching expressions and pace; they fell into a deep slumber in one another's arms.

The next day they went to St. Mark's to see a Catholic priest to begin the process. Grace was just starting to show. She wore the muumuu Ron's mother had sent from Hawaii. She explained to Ron that both her parents were Roman Catholic. Ron had an aversion to organized religion but respected that it was her first wedding and wanted it to be right for her.

A sallow-faced nun with a black habit led them along the outdoor path to the parish offices in the back. The grounds were meticulously kept: a pristine lawn, blooming pink camellias, and planters bursting with well-clipped rose bushes. They followed her to a quiet, mission style building at the rear of the church grounds. They exchanged glances as she led them through a shadowed door, down a long hall with portraits of dour men in crude wood frames, and wrought iron chandeliers lighting their way. It felt to Grace like they were invading an inner sanctum, off limits to parishioners. She held a child's myth of religion, a contradiction to the administrative cabal surrounding them. Grace and Ron trod softly through the dark hallway, eyes bright to the quiet nuns in tiny office rooms, and junior priests typing, washed in the patina of stained glass windows; past an austere break room with rows of plastic beige coffee cups, and a percolator bubbling lazily. The nun guided them further still, down a final darkened hall to a dead end and a large, impenetrable door. At the door, she turned and faced them, seemingly to take one final judgment, allowing them into the holy father's inner sanctum after a curt nod.

Grace quickly put her hair back in a bun. Ron forced a smile and shoved his hands into his pockets. They were herded into what turned out to be an unusually tiny room—a large closet. It was sparse, even by the ascetic standards of the priesthood. A short man with tightly cropped white hair and pink puffy skin sat behind a bare oak desk. His stiff white collar seemed dangerously tight, his face a deep red bursting out of the collar. The desk took up the entire back wall, with just enough room on either side to slip by. A large faded portrait of St. Mark, with lustrous black hair and beard, held the back wall, smiling warmly over the stern priest's spiked crop of hair. The dark eyes seemed to follow their every move as they lowered into two folding chairs. A slim inset window looked out on a hidden garden with a statue of the Virgin Mary suspended above a fountain. Father Mahoney looked up from a pile of papers. He shuffled them ministerially and motioned for them to sit down.

Grace continued to hold Ron's hand as they avoided looking at St. Mark. Father Mahoney looked like every priest she'd ever met. Imperious, endowed with an authority borrowed from righteousness. Mom and her Dad only took them to Christmas mass, and the task of getting their large family presentable was prohibitive in their eyes. She went to communion without actually having had her first communion, although she certainly wouldn't admit that today. Now they sat in front of Father Mahoney hoping for a sanctioned marriage, increasingly doubtful by the minute, not of their marriage, but of the need for sanction.

"Good Afternoon. My name is Father Mahoney," he smiled. "Have we met?" he asked, reaching into a file drawer. He produced a single piece of paper and placed it on top of the pile.

"No, Father. We've been to the church a few times. We're new to the area," Grace lied. "We'd like to join the parish...we're engaged to be married."

"Congratulations." Father Mahoney looked up from the paper. It was the questionnaire they'd been asked to fill out, the first step in the holy marriage process. "Mr. Marcos and Ms. Rentano. I see that only one of you is Catholic."

Grace looked at Ron and back to the priest. "I'm not, but I'd like to give it a try," Ron said, smiling, but completely serious.

"I am," Grace replied.

"Well, you both must be Catholic to be married in this church." Father Mahoney looked directly at Ron.

"Are you a Christian?" he asked.

Ron looked at Grace, then back to Father Mahoney. "No. I'm Presbyterian. I mean, my mother was."

Grace squeezed Ron's hand. He'd wanted to skip the church. He wanted to have a justice of the peace do their wedding on Venice Beach. She looked up at his earnest face, responding to Father Mahoney's inquiries with such honesty. She loved him for it.

"My parents were married in the church and I'd like to as well," Ron said.

Father Mahoney took his glasses off and placed them on the questionnaire. He leaned back in his captain's chair.

"Mr. Marcos will need to convert to Catholicism. That is the only way you will be able to get married at St. Mark's. We have a strict policy."

"How long will it take?"

"That depends on your sincere desire to become part of the faith. The inquiry stage could be brief, but then there is the rite of reception, the catechumen, the rite of election, then the initiation. One could complete the process by the end of April next year."

Ron freed his hand from Grace's grasp. Grace looked sideways at him. He ran his hand through his hair and exhaled loudly.

"St. John's is right down the street. You might try them," Father Mahoney said, leaning back in his chair.

Grace stood first. "Thank you for your time, Father." She reached out to shake his hand, but his reluctance was palpable. He drummed his fingers on the desk and stood up, waving them to the door with a plastered smile.

Ron cleaved to Grace, smiling uncomfortably. The priest opened the door for them. The nun was waiting on the other side. She straightened her habit, turning to lead them away in one motion. She led them back through the sanctified burrow, to the side door leading to the pristine church grounds, and to the street beyond. When they stepped across the threshold into the bright afternoon light, squinting out of the cool darkness within, the nun thanked them and locked the door behind them.

Out on the street, Grace and Ron walked home in silence. They passed lawns with busy robins and loud mockingbirds, unafraid of their slow-moving presence. A block from their street Ron spoke first. "He had liquor on his breath."

Grace missed a step and laughed. "Father Mahoney or the nun?"

"The priest. He smelled like altar wine. I could have sworn he had a bottle on his desk."

Grace poked Ron in the arm. "You're lying... he did not," she laughed.

Ron took a joint out of his shirt pocket and placed it between his lips. She took his hand again as they turned up their street. A car passed, then another. They were a block away now, safe from the eyes of the church.

On the porch, she put her arms around him. "Isn't Michael part of a church?" she said, looking up at his strong jaw and long shiny black hair.

Ron lit the joint. Orange and brown striped skippers skirted along the surface of the grass, dipping and rising in the waning afternoon sun. "Yeah!" he said, his face brightening. "I'll ask him."

After dinner, Ron called Michael while Grace cleaned up. Grace listened. It was a short conversation. After hanging up Ron sat at the kitchen table with his head in his hands and a strange look on his face.

"What did he say?" she asked, wringing the dish towel.

"It wasn't what he said, it was how he said it."

Grace sat across from him. "How's that?"

"He said he knew we were going to call. I don't know. He invited us to come to a service at the church."

"Did he say we have to convert?" she asked.

Ron got up to get his guitar in the front room. "He didn't say."

#####

Their first visit to the New Christian Apostles Church was memorable, in that it was the exact opposite of what they'd experienced at St. Mark's. Grace thought the reverend was nice. He didn't wear a collar, like the Catholic priests, and the only discernable fashion accessory was a thick wooden cross that hung from his neck. His light beard and effervescent smile set her at ease. Ron was skeptical, even though Reverend Duane played the guitar. He sang songs he'd written about Jesus and the joy of being saved. It surprised Grace that Ron grew sullen toward the end of their visit.

Ron brooded all the way home. In the door, he stormed into the bedroom.

Grace was shocked. She thought Reverend Duane was a perfect antidote to Father Mahoney. They were invited to a concert the following Saturday. She couldn't understand Ron's reaction.

Grace stepped lightly outside the bedroom door. She knocked but heard nothing. She went into the kitchen and poured herself a glass of wine. Reverend Duane said everyone received Jesus in their own time and way, that life was a journey whose destination was a mystery, and that mystery was the seed of all joy in the world. "It is better to wander in search of than to accept blindly without question," he'd preached.

She put a pot of water on the stove for pasta. When she heard the bedroom door slam, Grace went to the living room. It was so unlike him to show anger.

Ron was sitting on an ottoman roughly plucking his guitar. He had a pensive, confused expression. He seemed to be struggling with some invisible force that she could not relate to. Grace walked behind him. He stared in silence as he fumbled a melody he'd mastered long ago.

"Can I get you anything?" she asked.

"Do we have to go back there? Do you believe all that Jesus crap?"

Grace sat on the armrest. She put a hand on his knee. "I just think he's nice," she said plainly. "I think he'll marry us."

The sun shone in through the curtained front window. A shard of white light split the curtains and sliced across Ron's face. Squinting, he rose abruptly and put the guitar back on its stand. He shook his head and returned to the bedroom, closing the door behind him, softly this time. Grace returned to the kitchen to check the water. The phone rang as she pulled a package of pasta from the cupboard. When she picked up the receiver, Ron was already talking on the phone in the bedroom. It was Michael.

Grace hung up the phone, relieved. Michael wasn't only Ron's cousin, he was his best friend.

Grace forgot about Reverend Duane and the morning worship. She set the table and started a batch of oatmeal cookies, Ron's favorite. Tomorrow, on Monday, she was going to fill in a shift at the florist. Kimo and Rex were handling the flowers for a wedding, and she was going to put together the chapel decorations. She planned the tiny bouquets in her mind, recalling which flowers would be in season, and locally obtainable.

After an hour pondering and sketching notes and lists, Grace wondered how Ron was getting along. She listened for his voice in the bedroom. She was tempted to pick up the receiver but thought better of it. She got up, walked across the living room, was about to knock when the bedroom door flung open. Ron stood there with tears flowing down his cheeks. He had the most serene expression she'd ever seen, and his eyes shone clear and bright. He took her in his arms and held her. Gone was the dark and confused stare, he'd brought home from the morning service. Whatever Michael had said, it did the trick, she thought.

They stood together in silence for what felt like hours. His chest heaved against her breast. When she pulled away, she saw in his face a lightness of being.

"What happened? What did Michael say?" she asked.

Ron guided Grace into the living room, to sit on the couch. He was unusually gentle. He was always gentle, but his touch reflected an inner calm she'd never felt from him.

"I want to join the church," Ron said, without prompt. "I want us to join the New Christian Apostles Church."

He smiled at her, in a way that made her a little self-conscious. His eyes were so clear, she wondered if he'd been drinking in the bedroom. "Are you sure?" she asked skeptically. "I mean, you just spent all morning talking about how fake it was."

"Grace. Something happened. I can't explain it. I just feel it. I was sitting on the bed after Michael hung up. The light was coming through the window. I felt so alone, and suddenly, I don't know how, but I felt like there was something, someone else in the room. Whatever it was, I could feel it in my soul. I have never felt anything like it."

Grace leaned away from Ron and studied his face. It scared her how sincere he was. A sudden, unexpected change had come over him. Grace placed her hand on his cheek. His eyes welled up and his smile broadened. He'd always been pleasant, if a little cynical. But he'd always been kind and helpful to others. His joy brought tears to her eyes.

"Do you still want to marry me?" she asked softly.

"Reverend Duane will marry us. Michael already talked to him about it."

Ron hugged Grace tightly. She stroked his neck and arms.

When they separated, he took a shower, and she finished preparing dinner. As she grated cheese she wondered if it would happen to her, this sudden awakening. She only wanted to get married. She was happy as things were. She wasn't looking to be saved, she'd already been saved. It was settled. They were getting married, and now she entertained images of the ceremony. All their friends would be there.

After dinner, they sat on the couch and talked about baby names.

#####

Grace noticed an instant change in Ron. While unexpected, she welcomed it, and all the force it had on their relationship. The ferocity of his belief only seemed to draw them closer. While his change was a baptism of fire, she was slipping open-armed into the tepid shallows. Every Thursday Grace and Ron went to the little church house, where congregants of the New Apostles assembled for Bible study. On Saturday night they met for a meditation circle, and every Sunday they went to day-long services where congregants brought food, prayed, sang and worshipped. They all agreed that Reverend Duane was a guiding light. Children were everywhere. They were not only welcome, congregants were encouraged to bring their young to every event, even the meditation. A few followers provided child care, and Grace quickly found her niche playing games with the toddlers, and teaching them art during Bible study and the Sunday service. They were making new friends and realized how many were old acquaintances from the boardwalk and the beach.

When they returned home from the little church they'd sit on the couch and talk about their new friends. The church was the center of their lives and Grace hadn't seen Kimo and Rex in a month. "Why don't you invite them to our next service?" Ron asked.

Grace took out a joint and lit it. She liked the way it eased her after a day of being on. Ron picked his guitar. "Reverend Duane invited me to be the music director. He gave me a list of songs he'd like us to play. With Michael on bass, we only need a drummer to round out the band."

Grace sank into the couch and exhaled. She handed the joint to Ron, but he shook his head politely. He'd been foregoing their evening ritual for the last week and she was beginning to think that he'd quit.

"You don't smoke anymore?" she asked.

"I just don't need it," he smiled, matter of factly.

"Well, you don't mind if I do, do you?"

"I guess not." His smile was weaker this time.

Grace sighed. She took a hit and looked out the front window. Ron picked out a tune she'd heard Reverend Duane play during a service. She smiled. Ron was a quick study, and she could imagine him on stage, playing alongside Reverend Duane. She was so proud of him. Yet, there was a nagging feeling that her old life was no longer welcome on this new path. Ron was changing faster than she was. He constantly quoted the Bible and was resolute about saying grace throughout the day before every meal. He even insisted they pray in public when eating out. She felt she was gaining traction, but at a much slower rate. She was resigned to accompany him until they walked together. Grace took another hit and extinguished the joint.

She took out a journal she'd started after joining the church. She thumbed through the pages, appreciating her sketches, while listening to Ron perfect one of Duane's songs. After a while, she looked up.

"Are your Mom and Dad coming to the wedding?" she asked.

"I invited them. They haven't committed yet."

"I know they don't like me."

"It's not you, honey. You arc *haole*. Once they get to know you they'll love you like I do," he smiled.

"Are any of your brothers coming?"

"Michael's coming. How about your family. Who have you invited?" he asked.

Grace stopped at a blank page in her journal.

"No one yet. The only ones that'll come are my Dad, Paul, and Amber. I'll invite the boys, but they're all off doing their own thing. I don't think they'll come. We'll see," she said, starting to trace a rose she'd sketched the previous day.

Grace put the joint away. She took the bag and rolling papers, stood up and went into the kitchen. She found an old coffee can she'd been saving to keep spices, and stowed the pot and papers in the cupboard behind an old box of pancake mix. She would miss their evening ritual, smoking and talking, but the promise of a life together made it an easy decision. Besides, she was starting her second trimester and she didn't want a stoned baby. That night, Grace collected all the paraphernalia she'd hidden around the house. She was surprised at the sheer physical mass of their "pot lifestyle". She filled a small trash bag with bongs, pipes, screens, pipe cleaners, chocolate boxes, and all the seeds she'd been saving for a dream she'd had of growing her own strain of fine cannabis. It was trash day. The street was lined with trash cans. Grace pulled a bag out and covered the bag containing the evidence of her former life.

In a cleaning mood, she went into the bedroom closet intent on making space. In the only box she kept for family things, Grace found a picture of her and Amber at Venice Beach the day they'd seen the Doors. When she bent to pick up the box she felt a sharp pain in her abdomen. She stood, took a deep breath and lifted the box as if nothing happened. Grace took the photo and walked into the living room.

Ron looked up and stopped his picking. "Are you okay? You look like you just saw a ghost," he asked.

Grace forced a smile. She tucked the photo between pages in her journal. "Can you remind me to call Amber? I want to make sure she gets to the wedding."

It happened two days later. After a sleepless night, she promised Ron she would go to the clinic. The blood began to flow in the shower as she sponged her legs. Ron was in the kitchen when she called out to him. He rushed to her side. Grace was standing in the tub with the water off.  He blanched at the sight of a steady flow of clotted blood pooling at her feet. Grace reached for a towel and doubled over. He gave it to her and helped wipe her down. Grace shivered uncontrollably, although she was burning up.

Later, as she lay in bed on two layers of towels, staring up at the ceiling, counting the flycatchers in the corners of their bedroom, she accepted the dreaded possibility.  She kept falling back on her bout of gonorrhea, that it was punishment for her former lifestyle.

They prayed in the front seat of his old Pinto as it warmed up. Grace closed her eyes, listening to her body scream its protest in waves. Whatever God Ron believed in was her God too, and no God would let a child die to parents who wanted it so badly. At each stop light she stared at the red circle willing it to yield to something greener, something that grows and flourishes and brings forth life. She was drenched when they pulled into the parking lot. The waiting room was busy but she couldn't recall waiting, only that the nurse held her hand, and Ron helped her onto a table with rough sheets that smelled like bleach.

Afterward, she awoke in a corner of the tiniest room she'd ever been in that didn't have hangers. She was alone, but the door was ajar and she could hear voices. When Ron came in he was followed by the nurse and the doctor, who looked like they'd been scolded by some larger than life force. Ron lifted her into a wheel chair. Grace was still too groggy to guide her legs. The trip home was nothing like the trip there. She stared out the passenger window strangely comforted by the passing telephone poles. Ron didn't say a word. There were none that could survive the journey between them.

That Sunday Reverend Duane held a wake for the lost baby. The entire congregation was there. Their new family brought tidbits and meals for the entire week. They had so much food they bought a freezer and kept it in the corner near the back door, the one new thing in the house. In the evenings Ron joined her on the couch. They talked about how lucky they were to have found God. They agreed that when he wanted them to have children, they would be ready.

# 13

On her fourteenth birthday, Amber sat at a pale Formica table that smelled like Pine-Sol. Fluorescent lights buzzed overhead, and five strange, exiled girls ranging from thirteen to seventeen sang happy birthday over a flaming blue sheet cake. She was too weak to blow them out, so Freda, her girlfriend, blew them out for her. The meds made her listless, but she liked the calm, underwater feeling, like a mermaid in an aquarium.

Burbank was twenty miles from Reseda, but it might as well have been the moon. She hadn't seen or heard from Mom since she was taken out on a stretcher in the middle of the night, arms strapped to her sides. When she opened her eyes, alive and free, surrounded by strangers, she thought her former life *was* the dream, that her first thought would set in motion a new life, the real life she was meant to live. She thought of daisies, not real ones in a field, bobbing with stingless bees collecting bland nectar, but daisy prints. When her eyes adjusted she realized she was staring at wallpaper, and the turmoil in her stomach brought back the anger, the pain, and the memory of swallowing pill after pill in a fit of rage. It was her final exit strategy.

All the residents at the Mother Earth Teen Recovery Home called her Squeaky—because when she talked, her voice came out as if from a tightly held balloon. They'd scratched her throat when they pumped her stomach. Amber looked from face to face. She smiled at Mrs. Winters who tried to be a Mom, but it was like playing with a doll stuck in its store box, a TV Mom who couldn't come through the screen to change things. Amber loved her smile and how she smelled like the hippies in Venice.

Candle smoke drifted up to the ceiling. Amber liked the smell of the burnt wax. The moment dragged on too long, so she began to stand to go back to her room. "Sit down, dear, we haven't had cake," Mrs. Winters said.

Freda reached over Amber's shoulder to grab the knife, to cut the cake. Her face jolted upward, eyeing the attendant standing by the kitchen door. The handle-bar mustached attendant nodded.

"Birthday girl gets the first piece," she said.

Amber licked her lips. She had cotton mouth and her tongue was thick. She reached for the cherry Kool-Aid in front of her, but her arms were so weak, she couldn't quite grasp the plastic cup. The cup toppled over and a red sea flowed toward the crack down the middle of the table. A few of the girls laughed, prompting Freda to slam the knife handle down hard. The attendant rushed over and took the knife.

"Sorry," Freda said, then kissed Amber on top of the head.

Amber smiled but her lips were so chapped it hurt. She took two bites. "Come on, you've got to eat. You're getting too skinny. I like my girls plump," Freda said, smiling luridly around the table. Amber accepted the last bite from Freda, then asked if she could be excused.

Freda helped her to her bed. There were two beds in every room. Her roommate was a girl from Simi Valley who'd slit her wrists. She was home on leave. Freda put a pillow under her head. At the door she flashed Amber a pixie smile, "I'll be back in a jiffy." Amber stared at the bathroom door. Someone had scratched an X across it. The new paint didn't cover the mark, only authorized it with a latex coat. Amber pulled the covers over her and turned on her side. So many thoughts, bobbing and weaving in her mind. She could hear the girls laughing in the kitchen and wondered if they were talking about her.

Amber looked at the card on her bed stand. Frankie. The card was so sweet. Freda wanted to tear it up. Amber rested it on the mattress, inches from her face. It had a photo of a puppy that looked so adorably sad. She mimed the sad face, smiled when she imagined Frankie doing the same when he bought it.

Things had not turned out like she'd planned. Grace was supposed to come get her. She promised. Amber couldn't let it go. It started with the lice. No. It started with Largo. No. It started...but even if she'd been a perfect girl, and done everything Mom said, and everything Largo wanted, dressed like all the other girls at school, did her homework... Grace was not coming.

Amber held a final image of Mom as the ambulance backed out of the driveway. It was the first time she could remember her looking like a mother: worried, wringing her hands, distraught, as if every blackout she'd ever had, and all the pain she'd administered arrived en masse, in one redeeming expression. In that moment Amber felt a tinge of pity but wasn't sure if it was for herself or Mom.

Amber opened the card again. She could still smell the pot Frankie had stashed in the envelope. They'd confiscated it before it reached her, and a long conversation with Mrs. Winters followed. Her case manager was informed and her smoking privileges were suspended. Oh, she still smoked, but it was Freda who kept her supplied.

On cue, Freda filled the doorway, with that winning smile that got her out of so many scrapes at the house. Amber knew what loomed behind the smile. She remembered her first week there. Freda was a seasoned veteran, girlfriend of a butch lesbian, Benny. Amber glanced at the closet door. It had been too thin to muffle the girls' passion. She'd caught Benny going down on Freda in the closet, right there. Amber had slammed the door and rushed out of

the room. But later, Benny cornered her in the bathroom and
warned her to keep quiet. As tough as Benny was, there came a day
when Freda beat her down. Benny had her eye on one of the
younger girls, and Freda wasn't having it. If anything, Freda was
loyal. Brutal but loyal. Benny was found unconscious in the
shower one evening after dinner. She never returned to Mother
Earth after a trip to the emergency room. Now Amber was Freda's.

"Want to smoke?"

Amber turned toward the wall. Freda lumbered across the
room, squeezed her hand under the mattress and pulled out a pack
of cigarettes. She opened the window, lit a cigarette, inhaled, and
leaned in, lip to lip with Amber. Amber opened her mouth slightly
pursing her lips like Freda had shown her. Their lips sealed
together, the smoke flowed from Freda's lungs to her mouth, into
Amber's mouth, and into her lungs. Amber exhaled back into
Freda, and in turn, Freda blew the spent smoke out the window.
Freda held the smoldering cigarette out the window the entire time.
In five minutes they'd shared a cigarette that way. Amber felt right
when they smoked together—adjusted, connected. Freda called it
"kissmoking".

"What's wrong?" Freda asked. "It's your birthday."

"I'm alone," Amber said after a swig of Listerine. Freda kept
a small bottle on her at all times.

"No you're not. I'm here." Freda got up and closed the door.
She returned to the bed and wrapped herself around Amber.

"My family."

"Fuck them."

"You know what I mean."

Freda offered the Listerine bottle again. Amber declined.
Freda finished off the bottle. Soon she snored into Amber's neck.
The attendant with the handle-bar mustache awoke them for
dinner. It was against house rules to fraternize, but he let it slide
because it was Amber's birthday.

#####

Amber sat at the kitchen table with Freda, crocheting caps for the senior home down the street. Freda didn't care for it, too domestic, she said. But Amber found it remarkably relaxing, an activity her therapist recommended. There was something Amber wanted to tell Freda. She couldn't muster the courage to tell her that she wasn't a lesbian. She could only think of Frankie and the birthday card still sitting on her bed stand weeks after her birthday. Freda cursed and started tearing her stitches out, for the third time. Amber wished the rest of the girls would finish their counseling session in the living room, and join them. She would break up with Freda with the others present, to buffer the charge.

The phone rang and Freda jumped up to answer it. Amber watched her face change.

"I'll get her." Freda glared at her, extending the receiver.

"Yes?"

"Amber...it's Grace."

"Grace. Where are you? Are you coming to get me?"

Grace sidestepped the question. Amber sounded like she was in a box.

"Amber...how are you? Mom told me where you are."

"I'm alright. I'm bored. When are you coming?"

There was a pause that neither knew how to fill.

"Amber. I'm getting married." The words seemed so distant and apologetic. There was another pause, as Amber sighed into the phone, twice to make sure Grace heard. Grace waited, unsure whether Amber had hung up or fainted. "Do you want to come to the wedding?"

"I don't know if they'll let me. Can you come get me...please?"

Amber glanced at Freda, with the receiver in the crook between her ear and neck. Freda glared at her. "It's my sister," she whispered. She held the receiver again with both hands.

Grace was still talking when she put the phone back to her ear. "Let me talk to the house manager. We'll see if you can spend the night."

"You promised you would come get me," Amber pouted.

"I know, Amber. Let's just get you here and see what happens. Okay?"

Amber held the receiver to her chest. She looked up as Mrs. Winters entered the kitchen. She'd been monitoring the call. Mrs. Winters, a woman in her early forties, in blonde dreadlocks, a uniform of floral patterned skirts and loose cotton tops, adorned in beads, with yellowed false teeth, spent most of her day in the makeshift office off the laundry room.

"I'll take it in my office," Mrs. Winters said, padding back to her little room.

Amber smiled and stitched in silence. When she was done she chewed her fingernails and stared at Freda's work. Freda looked worried, vulnerable somehow. A goodbye hung in the air between them. Amber was relieved that she wouldn't have to break up with Freda. She would leave without a fight. For now, she helped Freda finish the cap she was making, showing her for the hundredth time how to create tight stitches, how to get into a rhythm.

Grace and Mrs. Winters spent nearly an hour on the phone discussing Amber's condition, house rules, her status at the home, the program she was working with to address her anorexia and bulimia, and how she related with the other residents. She described the medications prescribed by the doctor, which helped with Amber's agitation.

Grace listened patiently to ask the only question she needed an answer for.

"Can I take Amber for a few days? I'm getting married. Her family will be there. It would do her a lot of good to see them."

There was a pause on the other end. Grace could hear muted voices, the other residents, she imagined. Just outside the office door Amber sat on the washer straining to hear what Mrs. Winters was saying. The counseling meeting just adjourned and the other girls shuffled by, a cloud of banter, on the way to the kitchen for snacks.

Finally, Mrs. Winters responded. "Well, we do have leave procedures. I'll be honest with you, Ms. Rentano...Amber is in a fragile state. We know about the Bulimia and the drug use, but I sense that she's experienced a great deal of trauma. She hasn't told us anything, so we haven't been able to help her through it. She's very stubborn." After a brief pause, she continued, "Will there be drugs present in the home or at the event?"

"No. Of course not. I am a Christian." Grace immediately regretted using that tack, knowing that Ron would not approve. He wasn't there though, and she had no such compunction. "There will be moderate drinking. It is a wedding, after all."

"How long would she be away?"

"The wedding is in two weeks. Can I pick her up Friday afternoon, and bring her back Sunday afternoon? I assure you she will be in good hands. I took care of her myself until my Mom took her when she was six."

Mrs. Winters explained the rules for residents on leave. Grace would have to sign forms, she said, releasing the Mother Earth Home from any liability, should Amber be hospitalized outside of the facility's jurisdiction.

When Grace hung up she walked back into the living room. Amber would be her responsibility once again. Only this time, she was a medicated teen with a troubled past. Grace didn't know if she was up for taking care of her little sister and planning her wedding. She wanted it to be a quiet affair, but she knew Amber would never forgive her if she missed her wedding.

#####

The Friday before the wedding Grace and Ron drove up Highway 5 toward Burbank. The facility was a short distance from the airport, so when they reached the exit, jets were overhead, ascending and descending.

"Should we hide the snacks?" Ron asked, innocently.

Grace turned to face him at a stop light. His soft, innocent expression. "I love you," she said. "We'll see. I don't want to treat her like a patient. For all we know she was just acting up to get away from Mom and Largo."

"Should we at least get her cigarettes?"

Grace thought about her stash. It had remained untouched for weeks in the Folger's can behind the pancake mix. Ron would never find it because he never cooked, but Amber could be quite nosey; she remembered one incident long ago, and it made her laugh. Then it occurred to her how much Amber *had* changed, and not for the better. *You were pretty messed up too.* Grace constantly wondered if she could have made different choices...to protect Amber. She knew it was a conversation she and Amber would have.

"We'll see," she said, staring up at a rapturous couple on a billboard advertising "Kool" cigarettes.

They got lost just after the offramp. Ron stayed calm, eventually guiding them to the house, which stood out in a middle-class subdivision, with its front yard garden of sunflowers, tomato vines, and squash. The front door was bright yellow and the lavender trim gave the house a frivolous Disneyland aura.

Grace lurched out of the car, relieved to escape the confines of the Pinto. She'd gained ten pounds since the miscarriage and knew Amber would say something. She slammed the door a little too forcefully and clutched her leather tote bag. Her chest tightened as she walked across the sidewalk and up the driveway. Ron caught up with her at the yellow door.

Staring at the peace sign door knocker, she resolved that she was as much a mother as a sister, always had been, and those roles were about to play out once again. Ron knocked. A voice inside announced them. "They're here!"

Grace straightened the brush welcome mat with her toe, then hugged Ron. *I wanted a baby,* she thought.

The door flew open and there she was, Amber, a skeleton with owlish glasses, but with the same cherubic face and absent smile. She leaped into Grace's arms, pushing Ron aside. Grace ached for her. When Amber let go, she stepped toward Ron, turned her head sideways, and then hugged him. As she turned to lead them into the house, Grace and Ron's eyes met. Grace shook her head at the sight of Amber's clothes hanging off of her. She was nearly as tall as Grace but half her width. They followed her down the long hallway past the kitchen to a little office beyond a laundry room. An adolescent with a tight crewcut sat on the dryer with her arms crossed, swinging her feet, kicking the dryer. She scowled, mugging at Amber, Grace, Ron, and Amber again. She seemed to be waiting: for an audience, permission, or a blessing.

A woman with false teeth and dreadlocks came out of the back office. She side-stepped the swinging feet and stretched out her hand to Grace.

"Hi...I'm Mrs. Winters, you must be Grace."

Mrs. Winters looked at the young woman on the dryer sternly, her jaw clenched. "Freda...go to your room," she commanded. Freda sloughed off of the dryer, mugging at Amber all the way to the kitchen. Amber smiled at Ron. They followed Mrs. Winters back to her office. The room was so small that Ron had to stand behind Grace who sat in one of the two fold-up chairs in front of Mrs. Winters' desk. There was a large gold Buddha on the corner of her desk. Amber sat in the other chair, her knees pulled up to her chest. Mrs. Winters repeated the house rules for overnight leave and showed Grace where to sign on each form. Amber sat patiently holding Grace's free hand. She was silent until they went to her bedroom to gather her overnight belongings. She showed them her bed, her side of the closet, her side of the bureau, and then took a red TWA tote bag from the shelf in the closet. She filled it with a handful of garments from the bureau, then took a pair of pants and a blouse from the closet.

"Do you have a dress?" Grace asked.

Amber's eyes welled up. "I left most of my clothes at Mom's," she said defensively. "I'm sorry." She looked up at Ron, suddenly a wrinkled toddler. "Maybe I shouldn't go." She pushed her hands into her dress pockets, staring toward the door.

"Amber...stop it! Of course, you're coming. I have a dress you can wear. Let's get out of here."

Amber's face shifted like a traffic light. She stepped closer to Grace.

"Do you have a cigarette?"

"Yes, but let's get going."

Ron stood by the door with his hands stuffed in his front pockets. He turned to look at the scowling girl with the crewcut in the doorway. When she cleared her throat Amber introduced them.

"Freda, this is my sister Grace and her fiancé Ron."

Freda nodded at Grace and Ron. "How long are you going to be gone?" she asked. Ron raised his eyebrows at Grace.

Amber lied. "I don't know, a week or so. I might never come back."

Freda stiffened, but her face remained a cold mask. "Call me," she commanded.

Amber turned and picked up her tote bag. She slung it over her shoulder and led them past Freda, down the hallway. She stopped at the opening to the kitchen, turned to her right and yelled goodbye to Mrs. Winters, whose muffled response was unintelligible behind the office door.

Later in the car, Grace asked Amber, "What was that all about?"

"That's Freda. She's a lesbian. That place is full of lesbians. Can I have my cigarette now?"

Amber sat behind Ron, who was driving. She stared out the window as the cars whizzed by on Highway 5. Grace took out a pack of cigarettes that someone had left at their house after a party. She passed one back to Amber along with a lighter.

"Where do you want me to blow the smoke?"

Grace looked over at Ron. He shrugged.

The car was a Pinto coupe, so the backseat windows did not roll down.

"Blow it out my window," Grace said.

Amber watched Ron in the rearview mirror. She caught his eye as he gauged the traffic behind them, and switched lanes. Soon, the old Pinto filled up with smoke. Ron rolled down his window. Grace wished she had a joint. By the time they reached Ron and Grace's house in Venice, Amber had listed every grievance she held for the Mother Earth Home: "They don't let us eat when we want to, Mrs. Winters smells like boiled eggs, Freda treats me like a pet. I'm not a lesbian...I'm just doing it because she makes me." Her pace slowed as they turned up their street. "I'm hungry. Do you think I look fat?"

By the time they pulled into the driveway she was asleep, spread across the back seat. Grace looked over the seat. The car was church quiet now. Ron gripped the steering wheel, waiting for Grace to make the first move. It was a shame to wake her. There was a slight flutter of her eyelids, and Grace wondered what wild world she was living in her dreams.

Ron got out of the car and pushed the driver's seat forward. He stretched into the back seat, eyes on Grace, who nodded. He slid his arms under Amber's thin, yet sturdy frame, and lifted her effortlessly out of the vehicle. Ron followed Grace into the house and laid Amber on the sofa. Amber opened her eyes to slits in Ron's arms. She pushed her cheek against his chest. As soon as she made contact with the checkered fabric sofa, she sprang to her feet and flowed to the kitchen. Grace followed her.

"I'm hungry," she declared again.

"Sit down, I'll make you something," Grace said.

Grace circled around the kitchen table and opened the refrigerator. She pulled out a carton of eggs. Amber sat at the kitchen table following Grace with sleepy eyes. Her stomach growled. They both heard it. "Do you want some eggs?" Grace asked.

Amber stared at the refrigerator. "What else do you have? We eat eggs every day at the home. Do you have any Captain Crunch?"

"No. How about some Cheerios? You used to like them."

Amber shrugged. Her owl glasses made her eyes look too big for her face.

There was a Venice Beach magnet on the refrigerator door. Grace noticed her looking at it and smiled. "Do you remember when we went to Venice Beach?" she asked.

Amber shrugged. "Yeah. We saw the Doors," she said, her mouth a thin line. "Do you have any cookies or Cheese-its?" she asked, as her stomach rumbled again.

"Did you have breakfast?" Grace asked.

"I told you we have eggs every morning." Amber punctuated her words with a fake smile.

Grace knew she was trying. *Who knows what goes on in that little head? She can't help it,* she told herself. But *she* couldn't help it either. It was nearly impossible not to react to Amber's sourness.

Amber looked toward the kitchen door. "Where's your bathroom? I have to use it."

Grace could hear Ron playing his guitar in the living room. Both she and Amber paused for a moment to listen.

"It's past the living room down the hall on the right."

Amber slowed as she passed Ron in the living room. "Wow, you're really good." She smiled. She held her hands together at her belly. She fixed her bra strap. Her dress was so loose. Her knees were so knobby they jutted from the hem of her dress.

Down the hall, she entered the bathroom, closed the door, and locked it. She knelt by the toilet, inserted her index finger down her throat and expelled the paltry breakfast into the bowl. Her throat burned so she took a handful of water from the bathroom faucet and gargled. She stared at her reflection in the medicine cabinet mirror. She smirked and quietly opened the cabinet door. After rummaging, she found a box of chocolate Ex-Lax. She chewed two pieces and washed them down with a handful of water. She found Grace's brush in a basket on the toilet. She feathered her hair. It was down to her shoulders now, and she thought the length made her face seem thinner. She tucked it behind her ears and checked her teeth. She hated her teeth, so infantile, and stained.

On the way past the living room, she smiled again at Ron. Back in the kitchen, the smell of fried eggs and bacon turned her stomach as she sat at the kitchen table. She grimaced and squirmed, the wooden seat made her rump sore. She sat on her hands and watched Grace work the frying pan, the same way she used to.

"When's the last time you saw Paul?" she asked

Grace paused and turned to face Amber. She hadn't heard from Paul in ages.

At that moment Ron came in from the living room. He sat down across from Amber. He smiled politely then watched Grace preparing lunch.

"I haven't seen Paul since we lived at the Magnolia House," Grace said. "How about you?"

"Didn't I tell you? He and Dad came to Mom's house before you came to live with us. Same old Paul. He didn't say much. He acted like all boys do. I think he wanted to have sex with me." Amber looked at Ron and then at Grace waiting for a response.

Grace dropped the spatula. "I doubt if he wanted to have sex with you. He's your brother."

Amber smiled at Ron. She jerked her head toward Grace. "How do you know? You weren't there."

Grace moved toward the table with the frying pan. "That just doesn't sound like Paul."

The air in the room was thick, equal parts frying oil and tension.

"He's changed." Amber screwed up her face when Grace slid two eggs onto her plate. "Dad hates me...he wouldn't even look at me."

Grace sighed. Ron patted her back as she divvied up the remaining eggs on their plates.

"Can I have another cigarette?" Amber asked. She looked nervously at Ron and fixed her bra strap again.

"Why don't you finish your eggs first," Grace said, returning the pan to the stove and sitting down next to Amber. She watched Amber pout and push the eggs around on her plate.

"We'll smoke a joint after we do the dishes," she offered. Ron looked up with a mouthful of eggs and frowned. Grace was surprised she'd said it. She shrugged, thinking, *What else could I do?*

After lunch, Grace washed and Amber dried the dishes. It was the first activity they'd done together in a long time. It felt like they were pretending, Grace thought. It wasn't just that Amber was older, she seemed preoccupied. She'd been easy to distract when she was little. But now Amber appeared at odds with herself. Grace wondered if it was the medication. It was impossible to connect. She couldn't find the right words to pull Amber out of her shell. When the dishes were put away, Grace pulled a pack of cigarettes from a kitchen drawer. She was glad she kept the cigarettes and made a mental note to buy another couple of packs.

Outside, they sat on the porch step. Grace was proud of their yard. It was her sanctuary, and a warm feeling spread through her to share it with Amber. The Wisteria wedding arch was in full bloom, her Bird of Paradise swayed in a light breeze in the side planter where a pea vine was bearing purple blossoms. Amber watched her closely. "I like your backyard," Amber said.

Grace handed her a cigarette and the lighter. Next, she took out a joint from her blouse pocket. She waited for Amber to light her cigarette, holding out her hand for the lighter. She lit the joint and blew the smoke toward the back fence, toward a clothesline that held a pair of her panties, Ron's old t-shirts and a few pairs of ankle socks. She exhaled the next lungful toward the next door neighbor's yard, not wanting the pot smell to absorb into Ron's t-shirt.

Amber inhaled the cigarette and shivered. The front of her dress was damp from drying dishes. She squinted at her outstretched legs, the knobby knees and shoestring calves. She smirked at the stub of her amputated big toe, the one that'd been cut off by Steve's bike chain.

Grace nudged Amber and handed her the joint. She followed her gaze to the stump.

"Do you remember when you lost your toe?" she asked.

They laughed when the neighbor's screen door slammed. Amber switched her cigarette to her other hand and took the joint. She took a hit and wiggled her stump.

The girls laughed together. The sun was high and bright now. They leaned back on their elbows. "I remember the hospital. That doctor was a pervert. Do you remember that?" She took another hit off the joint and handed it back to Grace.

Grace shook her head and put her arm around Amber. "You've been through a lot, haven't you?"

Amber turned to face Grace.

Grace held the joint in her other hand, away from Amber. She suddenly felt cornered.

Amber stared at her, looking tired and twice her age. "Do you believe me now?" she asked.

"Of course I do." She looked away, ostensibly at the neighbor, but in her head, she looked far beyond the little backyard, and the porch in the afternoon sun.

Images of Amber through the years skated by. "Of course," she said. Then she remembered Victor, her momentary captivity, the murky faces, and a dull pain rose in her.

Amber took another drag off her cigarette. She stared at Grace. "Dad has no clue, does he?" she said, her chin jutting.

"No...he doesn't." Her own voice had gone so low, rising from a hardened place in her chest. It was a voice she only used with Amber. "I don't think he wants to."

There was nothing left to say, Grace thought. Yet she searched for words, scanning the opaque shadows and empty spaces in the yard, the pot drawing her deeper and deeper into herself. She could find nothing within her grasp to bring back what they'd lost over the last nine years. She focused on the Bird of Paradise again. How could something be so prehistoric and so inspiring at the same time?

Amber stamped the cigarette out, grinding the butt out with the pad of her foot. She kicked the ember onto the grass. "It was fun in Magnolia though. Do you remember when Paul started that fire?" A light shone in her eyes for the first time since they'd picked her up.

Grace stood up. She slapped the back of her legs and butt. "And that was a 'happy' moment, right?"

Inside, they washed their hands in the kitchen sink with Ivory Liquid. Grace walked Amber to her room across from the bathroom, strangely warped by thoughts of their Dad going off to Vietnam. She hadn't had such thoughts in years and chalked it up to Amber in the house, and too much pot after a long layoff. In Amber's room a futon lay on the floor, a bouquet of sunflowers stood out in a blue vase on a battered dresser. She showed Amber where she kept the linen and helped her make up the futon. Afterward, they stood together in the middle of the room, staring out the window at the neighbors' hedge lawn—as if nature could heal their wounds. Grace dared to hug Amber, a wringing attempt to reset; Amber began to twitch and Grace offered to braid her hair. All these were met with a thin smile and a shrug. It was impossible to read Amber behind those owl glasses and the past.

#####

She hadn't been alone in a room since she'd decided to die alone in the shed. It wasn't a strange feeling, just annoying that they'd decided to care—strangers really— enough to save her from the brink, only when the brink was sucking on her toes. Amber stared at the door. She thought Grace would never leave. She listened to her slippers shuffle back to the living room. She knew it wouldn't be long, until the whispers started. She looked around the room. The closet door was broken, secured to the back of the empty closet. *I should be grateful.*

She went to the window, opening it as quietly as she could. The ground outside was dry dirt and leaves. *That's good,* she thought. Amber lit a cigarette and leaned her elbows on the sill. She listened. She hated surprises. The conversation started in the living room. She craned to hear what they were talking about. She didn't believe for a minute that this was her new home.

Amber blew smoke toward the chimney of the house next door. Down the street, a bunch of kids played touch football. On impulse, she started to put her foot on the sill, then thought better of it. She changed into a loose pair of Dittoes and some Mervyn's knock-off sneakers. The kids outside were getting louder and she hoped they were moving closer. She paused to listen to the conversation she knew was taking place in the living room. Hushed voices always meant trouble. Yelling and screaming, you could trust. She pressed her cheek to the back of the closet to hear better. The broken closet door shifted and she just caught herself from spilling headlong into the scuffed wall. Amber stepped out of the closet and stretched. She'd wrenched something in her back. She went to the bedroom door, cracked it and waited. Their voices were louder than she expected.

"I don't have custody. What are we supposed to do?"

"He is her father."

The door creaked as Amber shifted her weight. She snuck into the bathroom, catching a glimpse of their upturned faces as she closed the door. *I knew it,* she thought. Amber found eyeliner and lipstick in a basket on the back of the toilet. She preferred lip gloss, but she wanted something to brighten her lips. She grabbed the toothpaste from the medicine cabinet and squeezed a dab onto her tongue. She'd never gotten used to the taste of bile, but it was worth it, shedding weight at will. Amber feathered her hair again and stomped into the living room.

Grace was amazed at how big Amber could sound for such a waif. "Where are you going?" she asked.

"Oh...outside." Amber gave them a deadpan smile and slammed the door behind her. *Now they have something to talk about*, she thought, heading across the lawn.

#####

Grace had to change the date for the wedding. Reverend Duane had a death in the family back East, and he needed to go home to tie up loose ends. Mrs. Winters was kind enough to extend Amber's stay. At Grace's request, Dad made a call to release Amber into Grace's custody. She could stay with Grace but had to meet weekly with her case manager.

Grace was overwhelmed with wedding plans and realized one day while shopping with Amber, how much she still depended on her old friends. Rex, Kimo, and Terri came over to the little house on Woodlawn Court to help out—even though their "spiritual family" at New Apostles was willing to be there twenty-four-seven. Grace wasn't ready to introduce Amber to her church community yet. She had a plan to bring Amber into the fold slowly, with a vision of Amber choosing to accept Jesus. What she'd been forced to be in her young life was enough to warp any young mind. Grace wanted to offer a new life when the time was right.

Amber had a mixed reaction to all the adults running in and out of the house. She loved the extra attention but acted as if they were intruders, taking Grace away from her. She spent hours at a time on the back porch smoking. They'd all be in the living room talking and she'd storm out of the house, slamming the door behind her. Grace just didn't have enough time for her. No one ever seemed to have enough time for Amber. Rex and Kimo lavished her with attention, and Terri helped her learn how to bake cookies. It was never enough.

Now, walking up and down the aisles at Vons, Grace wished one of them had tagged along. Amber's diet was abominable. Her staples were Cheese-it snacks, chewing gum and diet Pepsi. She smoked constantly and Grace's attempts to put weight on her bones went right down the toilet. Unlike the carefree toddler she'd cared for at Magnolia, this warped version was an entirely different species.

Grace wheeled the shopping cart down the snack aisle. She peered sideways at Amber—who'd insisted on carrying her own basket. Grace watched her—five solemn steps ahead of the cart—filling her basket with items Grace had no intention of paying for. The explosion was imminent. Amber lurched forward, her ponytail swishing from side to side as she struggled with the spilling hand basket. At each aisle, she changed her mind, leaving in her wake the detritus of indecision. At aisle 5 a stocker joined them. He waited at the end of the aisle for them to move on, and when they did, he gathered up Amber's discards and restocked them. Down the hygiene aisle, she made a point of announcing her brand of tampon and took that exact moment to beg Grace to get her contraceptives. "You don't want me to get pregnant, do you?"

Grace stopped the cart at the hardware aisle for a breather. The polished tile floor was newly waxed, smooth enough to skate on. The fluorescent lights reflected brightly on the shiny floor. Strangely, Amber lingered by the paint thinner with her mouth wide open, suddenly able to read the labels with microscopic lettering. Grace flowed by catching a whiff of Amber's acrid breath.

Amber hunkered down in the magazine section, resting on her haunches, thumbing through magazines with underage boys and girls whose parents made money off their royalties. Her over-filled basket sat next to her. She opened one of the diet Pepsis and slurped loudly.

"Amber. Put that away. We've got to get back and start dinner. Rex, Kimo, and Terri will be there. Let's get going."

"What about my cigarettes?"

"I can only afford one carton. You'll have to make it last."

Amber stuffed the last magazine in the bottom row. She lurched to her feet, groaning audibly.

Up too fast, Amber swooned with nothing but Dentyne and a diet Pepsi in her system. Grace leaped forward to catch her arm. Grace was shocked at how her hand circled Amber's arm. She held it for a moment, hoping Amber noticed her shock but released it when Amber started to pull away.

Amber gulped her soda and left it on the floor next to the magazine rack. Suddenly in a hurry, she stomped after Grace, brushing her hair behind her ears and clearing her throat loudly. At the end of the aisle she remembered her basket, turned and glared at it, willing it to come, the basket a stubborn toddler. She pulled her shoulders back and retrieved it. She marched toward the check out line to join Grace. Grace smiled weakly. "Are you feeling better?" she asked.

"What do you mean?"

"You nearly passed out."

"I'm fine. You're the one getting married," Amber slurred.

Grace turned her back to Amber and winced. She asked a bag boy to get them a carton of cigarettes. She and Amber stood in silence, watching a lady with boisterous kids dangling from her cart pay and trundle out the automatic sliding doors.

The mood continued all the way home with nary a word between them. Amber jumped out of the car when Grace turned off the engine. "What about your stuff?" she asked as Amber reached the front door. Grace opened her mouth to yell, but Amber was already inside. Standing at the front of her Karmann Ghia, she waved at her elderly neighbor across the street, a silvery dame, who'd lost her husband but still managed to have her large family over every year for Christmas. As she pulled bags of groceries from the trunk, Grace wondered if she'd ever get there.

#####

Grace stood in front of the full-length mirror in the bedroom. A bleached rectangle cast a wedding train on the carpet behind her. The sun filled every window. The house was strangely quiet. The calm before the storm. There was never an exact number of how many people would show. Everyone was welcome—she and Ron agreed—and always would be. But she hadn't seen her blood family in nearly a decade. They might show, or not. Grace felt obliged to invite them, wanting to share her community, but not wanting to play big sister or hippie daughter on her wedding day. Rex, Kimo, Terri had come early to set up. At least she wouldn't be alone.

Grace leaned into the mirror. Her image: a slightly pudgy, raven woman, with kind eyes and rosy cheeks; a woman she'd become by luck and strength of will. She looked maternal, she thought, in the lacy white dress. The floor creaked in the hall, and Terri burst into the room with tears in her eyes. "You are soooo beautiful," she exclaimed, spreading her arms wide to embrace her. When they pulled apart, they sat on the bed and talked. "Do you remember when we first met? It was your first day at Venice High. You looked like a Chola."

Grace dabbed her eyes. "What about you? Janice Joplin."

Terri tucked a fallen lock of hair behind Grace's ear. She jumped off the bed, pulling Grace to the mirror. "Let's fix that..."

A knock on the door startled them. "Come in," Grace said.

Kimo rushed in, beaming. "Sweetie, you are gorgeous!" he said, his fingers touching his lips. "The spaghetti sauce is on the stove, and the pasta is covered and ready to warm in the oven."

Terri let Grace's hair down and began braiding it. "Do you think that'll be enough food?" Grace asked nervously.

"Don't worry. We got it covered," Kimo said.

Grace smoothed her dress, while Terri finished her hair. She marveled at the embroidery on her sleeves. "You really outdid yourself, Terri. I love this dress."

"Can you believe I found it at a vintage thrift shop?"

"No. It's totally gorgeous!"

Grace hugged Terri tightly. She jumped off the bed and threw her hands into the air. "You know what I want right now though?"

Terri touched her arm. "What? I'll get it for you."

"A glass of wine and a joint. It's going to be a long night. I haven't seen my family in years."

"Tim brought his stash. I'll be right back," she said, rushing out the door.

Grace went to the bathroom to put on her makeup. In a few moments, Terri returned with two joints and a glass of Rose. Grace downed the wine and led Terri to the kitchen. She did a double take as she entered the kitchen. "Oh my God, look at all this!" she said, lighting the joint. She blew the smoke toward the open window over the sink. The kitchen table was full of chips, salsa and guacamole. Six large bags of salad cooled in the refrigerator and trays of garlic bread were covered and stacked in the pantry. Satisfied with the dinner preparations Grace went into the backyard to inspect the wedding decorations. Ron, Tim, Kimo, and Rex were working like bees. A plank stage on cinderblocks was already loaded with speakers and instruments. The rest of the yard was in varying degrees of set-up: folding chairs and tables strewn about the lawn, lavender streamers sagging languidly in the afternoon breeze. Tim, Terri's husband, had brought over two kegs in the back of his old Datsun pickup and was hooking them up. Rex and Kimo were decorating the wedding arch with flowers they'd gleaned from the florist shop.

Amber sat in the back corner by the fence, chain-smoking and staring off into the distance. "She's been sitting there all morning, hasn't said or eaten a thing. Is she alright?" Kimo asked.

Grace squeezed his arm. "You wouldn't know it, but I think she's as nervous as I am about seeing our family."

Grace looked away from Amber, at the decorations around the patio and yard: a canopy of white and blue Hydrangeas covered the patio, a fresh gravel path led to a wedding arch constructed of driftwood and adorned with blue and purple Wisteria garlands.

Grace followed the path to the arch. She put her hands to her mouth, speechless. Tears trickled down her cheeks. She put her arms around Kimo. Rex approached them holding a pair of clippers and a fern sprig. She hugged him too. They stood together admiring the loaded arch. Ron, who was onstage working on the sound system, joined them. He put his arm around Grace and hugged her close.

Kimo and Rex ushered him away. "You're not supposed to see the bride until the wedding," Rex said.

Ron kissed Grace and returned to his work on the sound system. Tim and Terri stepped out onto the patio. Tim brought trashcans and placed them around the yard. He and Terri set up a beverage table and began loading wine and glassware onto it. Tim went to the stage to help Ron. Terri went back into the house to use the bathroom, and in a few minutes rushed back out onto the patio looking for Grace. Grace and Terri helped set up tables until the guests began to show.

Reverend Duane arrived with his new girlfriend. He sported a hemp shirt and his trademark wood crucifix dangled on a bed of chest hair. He seemed even lighter than usual. His arrival began a steady stream of church friends and hippies from the beach.

Reverend Duane held the microphone at arm's length. Ear-piercing feedback hushed the wedding guests. Grace and Ron stood under the wedding arch. Tendrils from the Wisteria and Morning Glory shielded the late afternoon sun. Slightly tipsy, Grace squeezed Ron's hand and when she looked up at him there were tears in his eyes. She took a deep breath and leaned against his shoulder. There were no words to describe the love she felt, flowing through her, enough to stem the tide of sorrow she'd carried for so long. Ron kissed the top of her head. Reverend Duane was beaming before them. His mouth moved but she didn't hear a word, responding giddily on cue. When she finally said "I do" it seemed after-the-fact, incidental to what they felt. They'd kissed too many times to count, but when Reverend Duane announced them man and wife, they kissed as if they were alone on top of Mt. Mauna Kea. The night was young. They kissed once again, kicking off their first party as Mr. and Mrs. Ron Marcos.

# 14

Paul had yet to arrive, and everyone was rushing around. Everyone except Amber. It was the worst morning of her life. Grace was ignoring her. She knew for certain Ron was avoiding her, and Terri's husband Tim kept giving her funny looks. She didn't know if he was hitting on her or just hated her being there. Amber kept asking herself why she was there. She wanted to leave but didn't have anywhere to go. At that moment, she could honestly say she would welcome the mattress on the floor in the shed in Reseda. At least Frankie would be there.

She watched Terri rush across the yard to Grace, glared at Grace and Terri whispering under the wedding arch. There was no getting between those two. She eyed the wine that Tim just put on the table. Amber stamped out her cigarette, and strode across the yard, stepping on blossoms where they lay, chin to her chest, jaw twitching. The kitchen was empty for the moment. A cacophony of voices at the front door set her on edge. She spied Tim's stash on the counter and helped herself to several joints. She really wanted some speed but hadn't found a connection. None of the kids on the street knew where to get it. Amber sat at the kitchen table and helped herself to a large bag of Doritos. The salt felt good on the back of her throat. Voices from the backyard and living room threatened to converge in the little kitchen. She stood, and was heading to her room when Grace and Terri entered the kitchen from the hallway.

"Amber. Did you make that mess in the bathroom?" Grace asked.

"I don't know. Why are you asking me?"

"There's food and shit all over the bathroom." Grace took a deep breath. "Are you all right?" she asked.

Amber stood wide-eyed with her mouth open. She was a little light-headed, and her stomach boiled. "I got sick. Okay?"

Grace and Terri stared at her. Pity, anger and dismay swirled between them.

Amber hated how they were looking at her like she was crazy or something. "Stop it!" she yelled.

"Well?" Grace said.

Amber tucked her hair behind her ears and fished for another cigarette. Her hands shook as she put it between her lips.

"Aren't you going to clean it up?" Grace asked, her voice rising.

Amber shrugged. She started to light the cigarette, but Grace snatched it from her.

Ron came in as she was about to throw it out the door. He looked between Grace and Amber. "Amber...you can smoke later. Please clean up the bathroom," he said.

Amber shrugged. She put her lighter in her dress pocket and stomped toward the back of the house.

"I'm not crazy," Amber muttered, eyeing the crowd at the front door. She walked into the bathroom and stood frozen by what she saw. She quickly closed the door behind her. The epicenter of the disaster was the toilet. It was plastered in feces and vomit. An explosion of matter spanned across the shower curtain, the wall, the tub and over the tile floor. An empty carton of chocolate laxative was in the trash, empty Lay's chip bags and Oreo cartons were scattered in every direction. Amber felt sick all over again.

The scene was abjectly primal and pathological. She tried to relate to it, but the connection was no longer there.

That morning, she remembered waking up and drinking two diet Pepsis. She remembered eating the Oreos in her room while smoking out the window. She remembered finding a potato chip bag in the kitchen, eating some, putting on her dress, hating how she looked, eating laxative in the bathroom, then staring down at the toilet bowl. *Why is everyone making such a big deal?*

Amber found Comet under the sink. She slammed the cabinet door, hoping Grace heard it, knowing she was in there, taking care of things. After toweling up the mess, she stepped into the shower. She sat on the edge of the tub and soaped her feet. She stared at her stubby toe and froze. Her hands clenched the washcloth, as tepid water dripped down the front of her one good dress. She felt the soggy joints in her pocket. In a sudden fit, Amber threw the washcloth against the closed bathroom door. "I hate you!" she screamed. She listened, for a response, but heard only the thrum of her heartbeat. She stowed the cleaning supplies and stormed across the hall.

Back in her room she put her hair in a ponytail, and slipped into a pair of sandals. She felt weak at the thought of going back out there into the crowd of Grace's friends. *When is Paul getting here?* She knew he was coming. She overheard Grace say so in the backyard, when everyone was working to make her day special. Framed by the wedding arch, Grace didn't know she was listening.

Amber gazed out the window to the street. A car passed by, and she thought she saw a familiar boy in the back seat. He had dark hair, but Paul would be much older now. She was suddenly very tired. She had begun to doze when the doorbell rang.

A familiar voice resounded in the hallway. She couldn't summon a face, but remembered hearing the voice in the last few weeks. He spoke again and she recalled Michael, Ron's cousin. Amber straightened her dress and readjusted her bra straps. Grace was at the front door now, she could hear her slippers shuffle on the hardwood floor. The bustle of another group crossing the threshold drew Amber upright. She poked her head out of her doorway and listened. "Dad, Paul, thanks for coming!" she heard Grace say. Amber rushed out of her bedroom door, glancing at the bathroom. At the end of the hallway, Amber gazed at a handsome teenager with the shadow of a mustache and long black hair. He wore blue suede shoes and corduroy pants. She hardly recognized him, until he stepped tentatively into the room behind Dad.

Grace gave Dad a shallow hug. "There's my oldest," he proclaimed. Amber shuffled toward them, not wanting to interrupt the reunion. She waited until Paul hugged Grace and stepped aside. That was when he noticed her. Paul stared at Amber, but Grace still held his hands.

"Paul, you're so grown up," Grace said, as she held him at arm's-length.

"Yeah," he stammered, glancing at Amber.

Amber marched to Paul's side. She scowled at Grace, then took Paul's hand. She pulled him to the couch in the living room. They watched Grace guide Dad to the backyard.

Amber folded her feet under her and faced him. Paul fidgeted with his shoelaces, legs crossed on the cushion between them.

"Hi, Amber. How's it going?"

She smiled widely, wanting him to feel glad to see her. "Fine."

"So Grace's getting married," he said, running a hand through his long hair.

"Yeah. Ron."

"Do you live here?"

"Yeah. Let's go see my room."

She led him to her room. They sat on her bed with the window open, the curtain fluttering.

"Grace's getting married, huh?" he said again.

"Yeah. I like your shirt," she said.

"I got it at Mervyn's. Five bucks. I got a job."

"I don't have a job yet."

Amber gazed at Paul's face. He'd lost his chipmunk cheeks. His neck was muscular now, and his eyes were even darker than she remembered. They both looked around the room, unnerved by the sudden closeness. She felt like she was seeing it for the first time, through his eyes: the tiny, empty closet, two drawer bureau, bare walls, and yellowed lace curtains.

"How's Frankie?"

Amber smirked. She was a little embarrassed about the last time they'd been at Frankie's when she and Julie had teased him. "I don't know. He never calls me."

Amber bounced nervously. It was something they used to do at the Magnolia house, bouncing on the bed, but now she was buzzing inside, and no longer knew how to be his sister. Finally, she leaped off the bed. "This is boring. Let's go get something to drink," she said.

Paul followed Amber, as he'd always done—surrendering to her whims.  She had the ability to make the most boring occasion fun, even exciting. Amber led him into the kitchen. She stopped and spied the garlic bread, covered with tin foil, in the pantry. She could hear Dad chatting with Kimo on the patio. She winked at Paul, and took a piece of garlic bread out of the pan and gave it to him. She raised her hand to lick the butter off but, instead, wiped it on a towel. He scarfed down the bread noisily.

"You're a pig," Amber laughed. He went to wipe his hands on her dress, but she slapped them away. "Brat!" she teased.

Amber rushed out to the back door with Paul on her heels. She spied Grace with a wine glass in her hand, looking happy and beautiful. She was standing next to Ron, talking with Tim and Terri. The yard was elbow to elbow now, an eclectic collection of guests mingling, and admiring the decorations. Amber stared at Dad. Paul looked just like him. She still couldn't believe he was her father. She looked nothing like him.

Paul followed her gaze. "Wait until he's had a couple," he said, nudging her arm.

Amber scrutinized his face. She couldn't tell whether he was warning her, or joking.

"He's going to get fucked up," he whispered, leaning in close.

"Mom and Largo are drunk all the time." Amber shuddered involuntarily. She really wanted a smoke. She didn't think her Dad would approve, so she pulled on Paul's arm. Paul stared at the wine bottles on the beverage table. No one paid much attention. He met Amber's gaze. They giggled. Amber stayed on the porch. Paul walked over to the beverage table, took a wine bottle by the neck, held it tight to his thigh, and edged his way to Amber. They rushed through the house to her room.

Amber took out a cigarette and lit it. She opened the window and exhaled. She offered it to Paul while he undid the foil around the wine cap. He shook his head. "Makes me sick." He twisted the flimsy lid off and dropped it on the floor dramatically. Amber laughed. He was trying so hard. She wondered if it was his first time getting drunk. She wasn't much of a drinker. She preferred pills. She played along. Paul took a long swig from the bottle. He swallowed hard and coughed. He held the bottle at arm's length and appraised the level of his first gulp. "Let's get fucked up," he said. He handed the bottle to Amber, kneeling in front of her.

She put the bottle to her lips. She tilted it slightly, just enough to taste the sour liquid. She swallowed, suppressed a slight cough, and passed it back. She felt bloated immediately.

"Cool," he said, with teenage pride. He took another chug, spilling a purple streak down his chest. Their attention was suddenly drawn to voices near the side of the house. Amber closed the window. She pulled the curtains tight, hunching down on her futon, with a pixie smile. When their eyes met they both giggled. Voices also rang down the hall, from the front door. The house was bursting with well-wishers. The wedding would start at any moment.

Amber took another drag off her cigarette, held it, head lolling, for a place to exhale. She sought a plastic bag in the closet, blew the smoke into it and tied it up.

"That's fucked up," Paul laughed. He stood up and took a swig. He arched his back, ran his hand through his hair.

Amber thought he looked like a model. *He must spend a lot of time in the bathroom,* she thought.

"You have such beautiful hair," Amber said. She knew it would make him happy to hear her say so. Paul pushed his chest out and took another swig. He handed it back to Amber. She took a sip, screwing up her face. It made her stomach burn.

"Do you want to smoke a joint?" she asked. The room was starting to spin so she sat on the bed.

"Yeah." he rubbed his hands together. "Steve sells it. Do you have any?"

"Sure." Amber took the joint she'd stolen from Tim's stash. She straightened it with her thumb and index finger and handed it to Paul. It was always good to have some pot around. "Here...you light it."

Paul took the joint, gleefully. He took a deep drag, expertly now, not like the last time when everyone laughed when he coughed. He closed his eyes and exhaled into the ceiling, then put his hand on the bed to steady himself. "Whoa...what a head rush. That's some good shit."

Paul sat down next to Amber. He was suddenly quiet, with his hands between his thighs and his eyes glazed over. The quiet felt like remorse to Amber. Their time was always brief. They could party, sure, but that changed nothing, and he would go back to his middle-class life, his Catholic School, and his swimming pool. He would leave her. Amber and Paul stared at the door. Live music blaring from the backyard broke the haze. "I like this song," Amber said. They stood up at the same time. Paul took another swig and handed it to Amber. She took a sip and stamped out her cigarette. Paul took one last hit off the joint, spit on his fingers, pinched the roach to smother the tip. They waved pillows and magazines around the room to clear the air. At the door, she gave him a quick hug, a weak Heimlich maneuver. They crept down the hall, aware of their buzz and slaked with the moment they'd just shared.

The house was a blur of happy faces. A melange of laughter, smoke, food, and infused conversation met them in the hallway. They headed for the backyard, overwhelmed by the congestion: people arriving, jostling—a steady flow of traffic, mostly gregarious, mostly inebriated.

Out the kitchen door, Amber spied her older brothers, Steve and Bryan, mulling by the keg. They were young adults now. Amber saw them as far-off planets she'd visited once, unsure if she wanted to go there again.

Grace joined them on the porch. She yelled to someone on her flank, "Let's get dinner out on the table. People can start helping themselves."

Amber and Paul stepped aside to let her and Terri pass. Grace smiled at them, the wrinkles around her eyes thick with stress. "Let's go see Steve and Bryan," Amber said.

Steve came forward as they approached. He and Bryan each took turns hugging Amber. Neither was ever as close as Paul and her, but it warmed her to be among them. Steve teased her about her glasses. "You look like a librarian," he said. Amber stood among them soaking up the attention as if she'd just stumbled out of the Sahara. Bryan had just finished telling the story of how she'd lost her big toe when Grace announced dinner. It wouldn't last and within an hour they'd all be back in their little worlds; she, going nowhere, with no one and nothing to live for. When they left she would no longer exist.

Suddenly aware of bitterness rising in her, Amber broke from her brothers, edging her way through the crowd. Her face was a hardened mask, but her eyes were ablaze. She went straight to the kitchen where Grace and Terri were laying out trays of garlic bread, pasta, and sauce. When Grace saw Amber approaching she cringed. After a quick glance at the yellow chicken clock above the refrigerator, she winced. It was Amber time. Terri stared at the tray she'd just set down. She knew better than to look Amber in the eye when she was set to blow.

"Nana. The boys are so mean. They don't treat me like a sister!"

Grace was cornered. "Amber. It's my wedding...please," she whispered.

Amber picked up a wine glass and threw it on the floor. "Why doesn't anybody listen to me!" She stared at Terri. Terri rushed out the door, shaking her head at Grace.

Grace bore into Amber. "So help me, Amber, if you ruin this for me it's over!"

Amber stormed back out onto the patio. Grace stood still in the kitchen, her chest heaving in her wedding gown. She picked up a tray of spaghetti, took a deep breath, and headed to the tables. As she stood in the middle of the yard, she saw Paul chugging a beer near the keg. She waved him over.

"Can you watch Amber? She's acting crazy."

"What do you want me to do?" he asked, burping into his fist.

"Just stay close to her. I don't know what she's going to do...please? She adores you."

Paul smiled and patted her shoulder. "Sure thing, Nana."

Grace watched her little brother push through the crowd. Amber was pacing around her folded chair in the corner of the yard. She sat down when she saw Paul approaching. He said something to her; she glared up at him. He sagged noticeably.

The backyard was in full party mode and near its capacity: guests lined the fences on both sides, guests filled the round tables, a wending dinner line formed in front of the patio, bending back toward the stage. Ron was on stage, joined by Michael, and a few friends from church. Conversations tailed off as they led grace on a squelching microphone.

Exhausted, Grace slumped into a seat at the marital table on the patio. She gazed around the yard at the round tables they'd rented. Most of the guests had passed through the dinner line, and the tables were full. Conversations were terse amid the clicking of plastic ware and satisfied grunts. She glimpsed Amber and Paul by the keg.

Amber's shoulders slumped forward, and she was chain smoking, her foot tapping. Grace was close enough to hear her blather. "I didn't ask to be here...I'm not even in the wedding...I can not believe I'm even a part of this family...you all act as if I was Mom...I wish I had some speed...I wish I was at the group home...at least they gave me meds...why won't Grace talk to me?"

*Poor Paul*, Grace thought. *He's never seen her like this.*

Ron nudged Grace. He stood up to make a toast. He smiled broadly, tapping his glass with a plastic fork. Paul caught Grace's eye and came forward, kneeling next to her.

"She wants speed," he said, conspiratorially.

Grace stared into his face. "I...thank you."

She looked at Terri's table. She waved her over. "Does Tim have any ludes?" Tim carried Quaaludes for Terri's mother. He always had a supply on hand, for emergencies.

"Give some to Paul. Amber wants speed, but that's all we have." Grace watched Terri push back to her table. A tall woman with a pitch black bouffant pointed toward the house.

Terri signaled for Paul to follow her. They rushed to the living room and found Terri's husband Tim lounging, beer in hand, with two guys and a girl. Tim stowed a mirror under the table as they approached.

"Grace needs you to give Paul some ludes for Amber. She's freaking out."

Paul stood behind her with his hands in his pockets. Tim looked up at him, and they nodded.

"Sure. No problem. Anything for Grace." Tim reached under the couch and produced a tan satchel. He unzipped it and pulled out a baggy with a dozen or so pills. He dropped two pills into Paul's palm. "If I know Amber, she's not going to take these if she thinks they're downers. She likes to tweak."

Terri kissed Tim on the forehead and rushed back to the yard. Paul clutched the pills, following close behind her. He found Amber ranting at a couple who'd ventured too close. Paul positioned himself between them.

"I've got something for you," he whispered, inches from her hot face.

Amber's mouth stopped moving.

"Let's go to your room," he said, jerking his head toward the house.

Amber stormed past Grace and Ron, glaring as if they'd just slapped her.

Back in her room she closed the door and tugged Paul's hand to follow her to the futon. She pulled him down next to her, abruptly calm in anticipation. Paul held out the pills. Amber took a deep breath. She winced and rubbed her temples. She felt out of control. There were so many people there, so many people she knew, but didn't know her. Unwelcome thoughts exploded in her head like fireworks. There was nothing to hold onto. She felt so alone and unhinged. She tried to make her voice sound calm. "What-have-you-got?" she asked.

"You wanted speed, right?"

Amber held a pill close to her lenses. "What are they?"

"Robin eggs. That's what they called them."

Amber popped the pills into her mouth. She took a swig from the wine bottle on the floor and threw her head back. She stared impassively into Paul's face.

"Paul."

"What?" He asked, as he took a swallow of wine.

"I can't help acting crazy sometimes. Do you think Grace will let me keep living here now that she's married?"

He picked up the crooked joint off the window sill. He paused before lighting it. "I don't see why not." Amber laid her head on the pillow and stretched her legs out. She welcomed the clouds moving across the ceiling. The pillow seemed to wrap itself around her head now. Paul was still there, which was a good sign.

Outside, and all around them, the party seemed to be an echo traveling away. The heavy snore of the crowd turned to muffled whispers. The room darkened a shade as a cloud crossed the sun. She felt heavy. It took an effort to bring a cigarette to her mouth. She realized that the pills were not speed, but something Grace gave her when she couldn't sleep. She looked up at Paul who was taking a hit off the joint. "I'm going to take a nap," she said, eyelids fluttering.

Paul took the unlit cigarette out of her mouth. As he did so, her head listed harshly. Paul watched Amber, motionless on the futon. He sat gently on the edge of the bed, taking hits off the joint, not ready as yet to leave her. When he finished the joint and the bottle of wine, he spread a blanket over her and rejoined the party.

# 15

"It snowed in the Sahara this morning!" Ron yelled from the kitchen between spoonfuls of steamed rice. The *Los Angeles Times* was spread across the table.

Grace rushed in, late again for her volunteer art class at the New Christian Apostles Day Care. "Has she come out of her room yet?" she asked. Ron shook his head without looking up.

Grace finished putting on her earrings at the sink, staring out the window across the yard. *I can't believe it has been a year*, she thought, feeling every bit the young wife.

Ron came over from the table and kissed her on the cheek. He smelled fresh from his morning shower and dashes of the Old Spice she got him for Christmas. Grace squeezed his butt when he turned to go. "Later," he said coyly, over his shoulder. Grace heard the front door slam as Ron left for his job at Kodak in the valley. She went to the cupboard and pulled out Cheerios and Sugar Frosted Flakes, and set them on the kitchen table with a bowl and spoon. It was *her* morning routine for Amber—she wasn't giving up just yet. She didn't know where Amber was getting the speed, or if it was just her anorexia and bulimia that kept her from eating regular meals. They'd agreed that if Grace put it out, Amber would try to eat something. She never ate when Grace was there.

Grace opened the kitchen door and listened. The morning air flowed in, cool and fresh on her cheeks. It was going to be a beautiful day. Only a smattering of stubborn clouds lingered near the mountains. She thought she heard Amber stir from the hallway. She resisted the impulse to wake her. She'd tried for a year to wake her from a seemingly incurable state of hopelessness, a condition that set in right after the wedding. Amber resisted any type of professional help. Ron was the patient one, she thought. Grace closed the door and locked it. Amber had to wake up sometime. She was fifteen— a little girl trapped in a woman's body.

That afternoon Grace stood in the dark by her bed folding laundry. Sunlight encroached across the bedspread like a rising tide. She'd been home for an hour, and tip-toed around the house not wanting to upset the peace. As she returned the hamper to its spot in the closet, she heard Amber's door slam, followed by the swish of Amber's slippers in the hallway, tamping the same triangle between the bathroom, the kitchen, and her bedroom. There were days when no words passed between them.

The volume on the black and white TV in Amber's room doubled. *Family Feud*, Amber's favorite. Grace sighed. Ron was a hero. He cleaned up Amber's messes without complaint. Grace threw up at the sight of vomit. This time she looked into the bathroom, relieved that it was still pristine, then listened at Amber's door.

Amber spent hour upon hour in her room with the TV the only sign of life. They'd gotten her medication from the clinic, but she refused to take it. "You're the problem...I'm not the problem!" she'd screamed.

They encouraged Amber to attend services at the New Christian Apostles Church. Reverend Duane started a teen discussion group, and he invited Amber to join them on Wednesday nights. Amber went once, but ended up storming out.

"They just don't know," she'd said. It was a misunderstanding, but misunderstandings seemed to follow her like gnats. Grace secretly considered an exorcism.

Grace finished the first basket of clothes, walked down the hall to put the next batch into the dryer. Amber's door was ajar. She paused, avoiding the squeaky board, yet Amber looked up anyway.

"You all right in there?" Grace asked.

"Yeah."

"Did you go to school today?"

"No. I'm sick." Amber sniffed. She turned back to her magazine.

Grace edged to the threshold, leaning casually against the jamb. She knew if she pried Amber would go off the handle.

"Are you going to group tomorrow?"

"Naw. Reverend Duane creeps me out. The other kids won't talk to me. It's too churchy."

Grace ventured a step into the room. "I was that way too at first," she said, and then cringed. She'd already said too much. "I mean...it takes getting used to."

Amber frowned. "What are you trying to do? There is nothing wrong with me! Why does everyone act like I'm sick or something?"

Amber swung her legs off the futon. She pushed something under her covers, crossed her legs and stared at Grace.

Grace resisted the impulse to go to her. Reverend Duane said that love was the only answer, but she knew Amber could turn love into something unrecognizable and offensive. *She can't help it*, she told herself.

"I got a new *People* magazine from Rex's shop. Do you want to see it?" They both liked *People*.

Amber rose and swayed, steadying herself on the futon frame. She followed Grace into the living room. The *People* magazine was on the table. Amber stared at the cover for an interminable moment, took the magazine back to her room and shut the door.

Grace listened at her door, waiting for an explosion. Embracing the momentary peace, she put the wet clothes in the dryer. It was the most they'd talked in days. She went into the kitchen to start dinner, Ron would be home any minute. When she opened the refrigerator she was shocked at what she saw. There had been a block of cheddar cheese. It was gone. There had been a dozen tortillas. They were gone. A Tupperware of chili she'd taken out of the freezer was also gone. She closed the refrigerator. She leaned against the refrigerator door trying to collect herself. If it were anyone but Amber she'd have blown her top. Grace flattened her palms against the chilly refrigerator door, shackled for the moment by an intense desire to keep her cool. To react was to set forward a chain of events that would only make matters worse. She finally exhaled and went to the cabinet. She'd hid a bag of tortilla chips. They were gone.

Grace stared out the kitchen window. This was no mystery to solve. The wisteria bloomed on the wedding arch, framed by ringlets of sky blue. She opened the window. The salty sea breeze cooled her cheeks. She gripped the edge of the tile counter, resisting the impulse to rush into Amber's room. She sighed. *How can I bring a baby into this house with Amber here?* The house, their lives were hostages. The baby was on hold. Grace thought of calling Amber's case manager, or Mrs. Winters...

It seemed so natural to talk of having children with Ron. They both came from large families. She figured he would make a great Dad. Grace wondered what it would be like to have a child like Amber. Ron didn't seem to think about such things. He went with the flow.

The volume was up again in Amber's room, not a good sign. Amber was in the bathroom again.

*What would a mother do? I'm not her mother.*

Grace went to the trash can but found no evidence of Amber's latest binge. She knew what awaited her in the bathroom.

She swallowed the bile rising in her throat. They couldn't keep spending their hard earned money on groceries only to have them regurgitated into the toilet. The bathroom door slammed.

Amber's TV went silent as Grace crossed the living room into the hall. She knocked.

No answer. She knocked again with greater force. Then, Amber flung the door open. She had bags under her eyes. Her skin was ashen, her expression a thousand volts of crazy. Grace was transfixed. All Amber's drawers were dumped out on the floor, the curtains lay in a heap, the contents of the closet were piled in one corner while her bed was completely stripped—the mattress turned on its side. A red sore in the corner of Amber's mouth caught Grace's attention. She hadn't noticed it before. Her hand went to her lips.

"Amber. What's going on? What happened?"

Amber swiveled quickly into the room and back again to Grace.

"What do you mean?" she stammered. Her eyes revolved in their sockets.

"Everything is torn apart," Grace said.

"I lost something," she said, nonplussed. "Did you take my Raggedy Ann doll?" Amber lurched forward. Grace recoiled, not recognizing her little sister in this feral being.

"No. Of course not."

"Well, someone took it. I need it."

Amber stared up at Grace's frozen face. Their eyes converged on the trash can she kept by her bed. A plastic tortilla chip bag peeked up out of the trash can.

Amber's eyes bugged out and her jaw tensed.

Grace raised her hands to her chest.

Amber's expression shifted yet again. "Did you take my doll?"

"Amber...calm down."

Amber gripped the door, glaring at Grace. Grace had just enough time to pull her foot away as the door slammed.

"I don't believe you!" Amber screamed through the closed door.

Grace heard a crash like thunder. She knew it had to be the dresser drawers. She imagined Amber pinned under them, heard no cry, so she stormed down the hall to the kitchen. On the way, she paused at the bathroom door. She placed her hand on the door, took a deep breath and pushed. The door swung open to a Jackson Pollock dietary explosion. Grace's hand rushed to her mouth involuntarily. She stepped back out of the bathroom as a wave of nausea and horror gripped her. There was something terribly wrong. The irreducible truth was expressed so clearly on the walls and tile. Amber was killing herself. It was the first time Grace felt not an inkling of compassion for Amber. She felt only anger.

Grace fled to the kitchen. She grabbed a bottle of wine from the fridge. She poured a glass and downed it. She raised her face to the ceiling and closed her eyes. An ersatz calm flowed through her, sadly ephemeral. It couldn't compete with the adrenaline pumping through her veins. She took a deep breath, poured another glass and flung the back door open. A row of stricken pigeons scattered from the telephone line along the back fence. Angry tears flowed down her cheeks. All she could think was that Ron would be home any minute and it was only a matter of time until he had enough, and no amount of love could keep him from fleeing.

This time, Grace did not knock. She slammed Amber's door open. Amber was kneeling on the floor facing the television, clutching a pillow and rocking.

She turned and stared mutely at Grace. Grace heard a low whining sound from somewhere in the room. She paused when she realized that it came from Amber. Strangely, it hardened her resolve.

"Amber. Clean up the mess you made in the bathroom," she spat.

Amber turned back to the TV without a word. Her foot began to twitch.

"Did you hear me? Clean it up before Ron gets home!"

Amber began rocking faster. She whined loudly now—a trapped animal.

Grace lunged forward and knocked the TV over. She took a step back when suddenly Amber rose to her haunches. The whining stopped, replaced by childish humming. It was a child's nursery rhyme she hadn't heard in years, the eerie juxtaposition of which stroked a cold chill up Grace's spine. "What are you on?" Grace demanded.

Without warning, Amber grabbed the TV and thrust it out the window. The trailing cord smacked the pane, causing a slight crack near the latch. Amber began beating her head against the wall. The air in the room shifted like a passing cloud over the sun. In that instant, Grace lost a sister and gained a patient. She was compelled to rush forward, to aid Amber, but her feet were cemented to the floor. Breaking the spell she lurched forward, taking Amber into her arms. "Amber, stop!" Grace screamed. A splotch of blood appeared on the wall. Amber was bent on flattening that invisible nail. Just as quickly as it began, Amber stopped and turned on Grace.

"You never loved me! I should never have been born. Whey did you leave me! I am nothing like her. She's crazy! I'm not crazy!"

Grace stumbled sideways. Amber sprinted out of the room. Ron would be home any minute. Grace ran after her.

At the front door, Amber hunched over the doorknob, working it like a fire-starter. The mechanism was lost on her in her feral state. Grace approached her, postured as she might catching butterflies. She seized up when Amber pierced her with eyes so wild, she was compelled to run in the other direction. Amber's nightgown stuck to her sweat drenched body. The rage, her physical state, her past, the drugs, all converged. She pulled the doorknob but it wouldn't budge. In her last moment of clarity, she undid the deadbolt. She flung the door open—blinded in her tracks, blinking desperately—then threw herself off the porch, down the walkway, head whipping side to side. The neighbor's dog barked madly.

Grace stopped on the porch to gather her bearings. That's when she saw Ron frozen in the driveway, holding the door of his Pinto, his face transfixed as Amber scampered down the street. At the end of the block, Amber threw herself on the neighbor's lawn, flailing and stripping her nightgown off, revealing a pale skeletal frame, translucent and veiny.

Ron shot down the driveway. The image of Ron's face in that moment would never leave her.

Grace ran back inside the house, to call the police. She picked up the receiver but couldn't think of a number to call. She pulled out the Yellow Pages and found the fire department number. She called and after three rings a dispatcher responded.

"My sister has gone crazy. She's running down the street naked."

"Is she hurt, Ma'am?"

"Not physically. She's...sick." Grace couldn't believe she'd finally said it out loud. "Hurry! Can you send an ambulance?"

"Keep an eye on her and a unit will be there shortly. Don't let her out of your sight."

Grace hung up the phone and ran outside. *What have I done?* she thought.

She heard the sirens and in seconds the ambulance and police cars converged in front of the house on the corner. Grace ran toward them. She'd never called the police in her life. In fact, she'd avoided the police for most of her adult life. Now, as she approached the scene, she watched an officer escort Ron to a squad car. Two officers were holding Amber on the ground. She continued to struggle. Two male ambulance attendants approached with a stretcher and lifted Amber like a dry leaf. Seconds later, they loaded her into the ambulance. She was strapped down, losing the will to battle, drained and docile.

Grace went first to Ron. "He's my husband. That's my sister. He was helping," she pleaded. The patrol officer relaxed. He turned his back on them and walked over to the group of officers discussing how to write up the scene. One of the officers broke from the uniformed scrum and approached them. He held a clipboard.

"Good afternoon, Ma'am," he said to Grace. He nodded at Ron.

Grace bounced on the balls of her feet, adrenaline charging through her. "Where are they taking her?"

The policeman looked back at his fellow officers. They were already heading toward their squad cars. "She'll go to the psych unit at Mercy. She'll be held there overnight for observation. Here's the number for the hospital." He handed her a card without looking up. "They'll inform you of her rights, and tell you everything you need to know." He smiled weakly and began filling out a form. He jotted impassively, occasionally plying Grace for information.

Grace paced. They were alone now, her, Ron and the police officer. The neighbor from across the street appeared to water his lawn. She felt the day slipping away; a fresh salty breeze brought distant giddy voices from the nearby boardwalk. Ron put his arm around her. She had no energy now and if it weren't for Ron there next to her, she might have just lain down on the grass and slept. He guided her into the house and onto the couch. He brought her a glass of wine. She lay there sipping and staring at the curtains. She held up the card for Marina Mercy Hospital. The officer recommended they call later in the evening when Amber would be medicated.

Ron took out his Bible and read aloud. She suddenly remembered the bathroom. She took a long drink of wine, pulled herself to her feet, and lurched down the hall.

Ron looked up from the Bible. He watched her, lines etched around his eyes.

Grace did an about-face when she reached the doorway of the bathroom. She passed Ron on the way to the kitchen, went under the sink, grabbed a roll of paper towels and returned to the bathroom. Ron replaced the bookmark in his Bible. He calmly strode to the bathroom. At the door, he found Grace on her knees, with one hand over her mouth, dabbing the floor with the other. She was bone white. Ron knelt by her. "I'll do it, babe. Go lie down." She stopped dabbing and looked into his face. Her eyes filled. She realized she'd just lost something to save something. Ron helped her to her feet. They embraced. They were alone and poised.

# 16

She'd gained twenty pounds since moving in. Still, Dad piled Amber's plate with chocolate cake and vanilla ice cream. Amber gaped at the mountain of calories. Paul stared at her from the setting to the right of Dad. He never gained a pound, and flaunted it by emptying his plate and stretching his biceps, waiting to be excused.

Dad didn't believe in "Bull-Limb-ia". Amber looked around the table. It was a large family style table, passed down from Dad's grandfather. Steve was in his separate world, oblivious and ravenous, shoveling food into his mouth as Amber pondered the pounds floating from the plate onto her hips. She'd been at the house on Mt. Edison for over a year. It wasn't her home. Amber looked away from Paul intentionally. He was no longer an ally, especially with Dad around. She began the process of emptying her plate, afraid of offending Dad. She offended Dad easily, she knew, possessing the inescapable curse of being Marie's daughter. Paul leaned back in his chair. He'd changed, she thought, stuck up. Beyond him was the swimming pool, and beyond that the canyon, with its tumbleweeds, creeks and rolling sage hills.

The first month there she tried to assert her old command over him. It used to be, "Let's build a fort." He'd tag along, pulled by the gravity of her personality. But now he had only two things on his mind, getting laid, and getting fucked up. She realized she was an outsider, a rescue kitten in a house of toms. There was no changing the air in the house.

"Paul. Go get me paper towels."

Paul made a face at Amber from the kitchen. She flipped him off.

"Ladies don't do that," Dad said.

"Amber. Did you finish sewing my pants?" Steve asked from the end of the table.

Amber avoided Dad's gaze. He was suddenly very interested. Grandma D was teaching her to sew. "It's a valuable skill," Dad said.

"I'll do it tonight," she replied. She stared at the melting mess in front of her.

Paul stared at her plate as if it had legs. He spent most of the day on the couch smoking pot with his school friends.

*Stoner*, Amber thought.

"May I be excused?" Amber asked.

"Yes. Go finish Steve's pants, would ya?" Dad said.

Amber took her plate and emptied it into the kitchen trash. Dad watched her the whole way. "How are your grades?" he asked.

"Fine!" she yelled, already up to the landing. "What a dick," she said, as she closed her bedroom door.

Paul. They'd never be best friends again. She recalled her first days at the house on Mt. Everest Street, when she was still hopeful. She pranced out of the bathroom wrapped in a towel; he'd been waiting in the hallway, acting like he had to use the bathroom. She smiled because he was in his tightie-whities and had a semi. He covered it up with a casual, dangling hand, so obvious, she thought. She'd walk by his room in the evening and he'd be lounging on his bed staring up at the popcorn ceiling.

One evening she peeked her head in, and he awoke from his reverie with a lurid grin. At sixteen Amber knew she'd turned a corner. She was a woman. Gone were the days of hiding behind a pout and watery eyes. She preferred the reaction of men, the instinctual warp of recognition when she entered a room. The effect was no less febrile on her brothers, as she pranced around upstairs in her cotton shorts, an outfit she'd never wear downstairs. She plopped on his bed, wondering who her brother had become.

Her answer came a short time later. The air in his room became thick, as they talked about boys at her school, and Darryl, the boy next door, and why Darryl wouldn't have sex with her. "He's probably gay. You're cute. I'd do you," he said, grinning.

Amber shrugged, bouncing slightly on the ancient hand-me-down box spring. She took her owl glasses off. "You think I'm pretty?"

"Pretty enough."

"Pretty enough for what?"

Paul lay on his side. Her knee nudged his thigh. They were two hands apart. He adjusted his pants. Amber shook his arm. "You know what I mean."

"What are you...horny or something?"

"What if I was?"

"Girls don't get horny, only whores do."

Amber frowned. "Just because I'm horny doesn't mean I'm a whore."

All of a sudden she felt too close to him. Someone in the kitchen was banging pots in the sink. Amber jumped off the bed and punched Paul's chest. He rolled on his back. He was hard.

"Does it turn you on talking with your sister about sex?"

"No duh."

Amber jumped back on the mattress, bouncing on her knees like they used to do. She wanted him back. She'd lost Grace and Darryl—her only friend—was acting weird. She wanted Paul back. "Show me it," she demanded.

Paul's mouth fell open. "What? You're kidding."

"It's no big deal. I've seen plenty."

To her surprise, he pulled it out. She grasped it like a chicken neck. He lay there, frozen, mouth still open, short breaths. As she looked down at him, his head pushed against the headboard. *He likes me now.* She was about to do something for him, something to make him hers again...something. The landing creaked. Steve passed Paul's door. Amber jumped off the bed and Paul lurched to his side, frantically zipping up. They both stared at Steve's back, as he closed his bedroom door. When she faced Paul, he had a pained expression, like Frankie, the first time she touched him in the gardener's shed. Although brief, it was a defining moment. Amber rushed out of his room and closed her bedroom door, banished for her efforts.

After that, and for years to come, a barrier stood between them. Months passed without a moment of kindness between them. All the while, Amber knew her life there was tenuous. The slightest tremor could unroot her again.

#####

"Dad's going to be pissed if he smells that," Paul sneered, sticking his head in her bedroom door on the way to the bathroom.

Amber shrugged. The smoke hung about her. "Dad's at work." She knew he was trying to rile her. "Fine," she said, when he wouldn't leave, stamping the cigarette out on a wet square of toilet paper. She waited until he was in the bathroom, hungover, grumpy and preoccupied with his hair. A shard of rage cut through her chest. She swallowed, lit the cigarette again, rolled up a towel and crammed it tightly under the door. The smoke billowed out her window, over the pool and through the chain-link fence.

She watched the canyon beyond the patio. It was so peaceful. The peace called to her, but she had homework to do. Darryl was still at school, tutoring. Amber lay back on her bed. She'd brought a box of Vanilla wafers home. She finished the cigarette, exhaling

225

the last drag toward the open window and rolled the cigarette butt
into the wet tissue. She put it in a sandwich bag then placed the
bag in the top drawer of her dresser. She opened the bag of Vanilla
wafers and began eating them in handfuls. As she settled on
finishing the bag Paul burst in.

"I told you Dad is going to be home soon. He's going to have
a shit fit if he smells smoke!"

*Enough!* "Get out of my room!" she screamed.

"It's not *your* room. It's Dad's house!" he yelled.

"I don't care! Get out!"

"Make me," he challenged, his feet firmly apart, his chest
puffed out.

Amber reached under her bed. Paul's nunchucks. He'd made
them out of a broom handle and a short chain. Kung Fu was a
popular TV show at the time. The rage spread into every cell of
her body. She leaped off the bed, cutting the air with circles of
eight. The chucks flew in an arc, and as he raised a forearm to
block the strike, she deftly flipped the chuck into his rib cage. To
her surprise, he didn't flinch. As he reached for her shoulders, she
pummeled his ribs with three rapid blows.

They both stood there for a moment, staring into one
another's eyes. The house was silent except for their breathing, a
foot apart. Feelings, too heavy to bear alone, flowed between them.
Then, Paul slapped her. It was a blow that lacked commitment.
She laughed.

Paul shook with anger. He wrestled the chucks out of her
hands. Amber bolted out the door, over the landing, missing steps
down the stairs, bounded across the living room and leaped out the
sliding door. She started around the pool, eyeing the back gate as a
possible egress.

Paul was no longer on her tail; he stood now, inside of the
sliding glass door, calm and collected, his hand on the handle.
Paul, in the safety of his glass castle, mutely watched her. In that
moment Amber never felt as alone. Amber flew to the window,

beating it desperately with her fists. He stared at her with a piercing smile. Her chest heaved and tears ran down her cheeks.

"Let me in! Let me in! Paul...please let me in!" she screamed. She felt like everything was lost in that moment, although there was no accounting for what she had, or was, in the world.

Paul's lips began to move but she couldn't understand what he was saying. She pulled on the handle. She could see Steve now, rushing up behind Paul. Amber let out a gasp, something old and cold that she'd been holding.

"*What are you doing?*" Steve yelled at Paul. Paul stepped aside as Amber pressed against the glass.

Steve slid back the door.

Amber stomped through the living room with her head down. She avoided their gaze. She said nothing to Paul for the rest of the week. It wasn't until the Santa Ana winds arrived that they could look one another in the eye.

#####

Amber wore Paul's old Pop Warner windbreaker on her last day of school prior to the Winter break. The old team name was faded, but she liked how the loose nylon and polyester covered her curves. It was a gift, a peace offering. On that last Friday, everyone seemed to move slowly, her excitement building an attractive aura around her, suggesting that dropping out might be a mistake after all.

"You look nice today," Coach Billows, her P.E. teacher, said as they did jumping jacks. She'd found a temporal peace in her decision. It was concluded that she wouldn't graduate from high school, at least not in the near future. "I just can't do it," she told Dad after the beginning of the new school year when students are supposed to be rested and bright. She felt only defeated. The result was that Dad stopped forcing her into a posture she could never hold.

From September to December Amber and Dad crossed paths once a day, and like the boys, who were out doing their own thing, Amber stopped eating dinner with him. She paused at times at the bottom step, on the way up to her room, keenly aware of his abject solitude, as he ate alone in front of the TV. In those brief moments, she felt sorry for him, and herself, at the common thread they shared. Solitude. She knew he'd rather not have had children. Back in her room, she reveled in the embrace of no expectations. For a brief moment, she experienced what it might be like to actually like being alive, to feel joy. It was a short-lived reprieve.

Amber spent her days with Darryl, who'd graduated early, with Grandma Dupree sewing, or getting high with Steve in his room. She enjoyed her time with Grandma D. The gentle old lady from Canada was a blood connection she could never have predicted. She was Mom's mother, and when they sat on the couch in the living room, with her sewing kit laid out on the coffee table, she'd tell Amber stories about Mom. "She was the smartest girl in her class every year. She was the prettiest too. She had a voice like a songbird. She did like the boys..." she'd say, adjusting her glasses, as her head dipped. Amber saw the loss in Grandma D's eyes and wondered if it was hereditary. Grandma D, with her wig and false teeth, and her daughter who'd born her grandchildren and abandoned them. She carried the weight of a lost child with a stalwart smile.

Amber helped Grandma D darn Dad's socks, sew on loose buttons and patches for his work clothes. She almost felt guilty for being stoned when they were together. It was a trip, she thought, watching her grandmother's sparring fingers bring button, cloth, and thread together.

"How is school going, dear?" Grandma D asked, her penciled eyebrows raised.

Amber paused, the stitch a sudden challenge. "Okay," she lied.

228

"Oh."

"I'd rather not talk about it."

Grandma D picked up her retractable scissors, snipped a loose thread, and knotted the ends. "Have you talked to Grace?"

Amber looked up at her grandmother. *She really has no idea,* she thought.

"No. She hates me." Amber looked out at the shimmering pool. "She's married now. She doesn't have time for me."

"Oh?"

"Yeah." Amber looked up at the clock in the kitchen. Steve would be home in half an hour. She felt a slight buzz in her belly. It was Friday. Dad was going to his girlfriend's house, and Paul would go out with his friends, leaving Steve and her alone. Steve had mushrooms. They were going to trip tonight. Amber finished a sock, coupled it with its pair, and smiled at Grandma D. Now she had finished work to show Dad when he got home.

"Well, your father will be home soon. Your brother is going to give me a ride home. I better get my things together," she said with a smile. Grandma D hugged Amber. "I am so glad you're with us, my poor dear. It's been hard for you, hasn't it?"

Amber made a puppy dog face. It was an anachronistic impulse. Embarrassed, she turned sideways, peeled the scrunchy off her wrist and put her hair back.

"May I be excused?" she asked. Amber kissed Grandma D on the cheek. She fled to the upstairs bathroom. Her stomach growled. Framed by the wall-length bathroom mirror, she took off her owl glasses and frowned at the bags under her eyes. She pinched her cheeks to make the blood flow. She patted her pointy chin, her round cheek bones, slapped her jowls, and clenched her jaw in an exercise she was convinced would remedy the effects of gravity. She stood sideways to the mirror and took off her t-shirt. *I am fat.* She turned around to look at her butt in her jeans. "Shit!" she cried.

Amber locked the bathroom door. No one knew except Steve. He put two and two together: the mess, the gagging, and gargling. Bulimia. It was in the news now, a social phenomenon. Parents were confronting their teenage girls all over America. She begged him not to tell.

Amber knelt by the bowl, stuck a finger down her throat and purged the contents of her stomach. She experienced the same rushing euphoria she had the first time when she was twelve. It was a possessive feeling, one of ownership, a reclaiming of sorts. Amber stood up, scrutinizing the toilet bowl for evidence. She spun layers of toilet paper around her fingers and dusted the rim. Back at the mirror, a slight drizzle glittered on her chin. She washed her hands and face, feeling at once light headed and lighter. She stared at her face once again, swallowing cups of water to soothe her throat. To complete the process, she squeezed a dab of toothpaste on her tongue, gargling the bile away.

In her room, Amber put on a pair of loose jeans. Next, she slipped on a button-down checkered blouse that she wore to show cleavage. She heard the kitchen door slam, coming from the garage. She went to her cloth purse. She didn't carry it much but found it safe from wandering fingers. She took out two tabs of Dexatrim and swallowed them dry. She went into the bathroom. She wondered what it would be like to have a normal mirror again, one that didn't take up a wall, forcing her to confront herself every time she entered. She checked her hair once again—decided to put it back in a ponytail. She found herself dressing and acting as a boy since moving into the house of men.

Downstairs Dad was in the kitchen rattling pans. He still made way too much food, with the freezer full of leftovers. A thawing Tupperware of stew sat on the chopping block. Grandma D was on the couch talking with Steve. Steve slouched, with his work boots up on the coffee table. Grandma D kept glancing at his boots between sentences.

"Amber. Did you dust today?" Dad asked her.

Amber walked over to Steve and punched his arm. Steve swung for her. Dad stopped what he was doing. "Amber! Did you dust today?" Dad glared at Steve. Steve stopped smiling and swung his feet off the coffee table. Grandma D pressed her veiny hands tighter on her lap.

Amber froze at the end of the counter. *His tone.* "A little," she lied.

"If you want your allowance, get it done. And don't forget the bathrooms." Dad turned his back on her, dumping the stew into a pot, at the kitchen sink.

Amber made a face at Steve and shrugged.

"Steve...take your grandma home. Hurry up if you want dinner," Dad said.

Steve got up. "C'mon, Grandma. Let's get you home."

"Amber, get me my jug," Dad said as Steve and Grandma D shuffled out the kitchen door.

They were alone now. Amber kept her distance. It always felt like she owed him something, for being her father, for having provided the sperm. Amber went to the faux fireplace near the dining table, the heater with an electric brush cylinder that tickled plastic to produce the effect of crackling flames. She lugged the gallon jug of Burgundy back to the counter. Dad watched her every step, sizing her up. As she handed him the green tinted jug, he looked her in the eye.

"Go change your shirt," he commanded.

Amber's jaw dropped. The double standard. It wasn't the first time he'd objected to her clothing, her weight, her hair—or any reason, it seemed, to put her in her place. He never did it with the boys.

"What's wrong with it?" she objected.

"You look like a whore."

Amber bristled. His mood determined what she was at any given moment: whore, virgin, little girl, dutiful daughter, pound cat. "Whore" was a word he used most often to describe Mom.

Upstairs Amber put on a down vest. She lingered by her door —pent up, wanting to be out or high, considered another tab of Dexatrim or a cigarette. He would be gone in a few hours. She got a cigarette from her purse and got the trash bag from under the bed.

It was a system she'd devised after the fight with Paul. She lit the cigarette, took a drag and blew the smoke into the trash bag, tightly sealing it. She did this three times in succession. She put the bloated bag on the floor of her closet. She went into the bathroom and brushed her teeth.

Later, downstairs, she watched TV with Dad. He'd settled in with his second tumbler of wine, which always made him rambunctious for a good half hour; followed by an hour or so of vicious teasing, bordering on sadism.

Paul came through the kitchen door. Amber rose and settled back into her seat when she saw that it wasn't Steve.

"Are you going out again tonight, boy?"

"Yes, sir. We're all getting together at the beach."

"Well...be careful." Dad looked at Amber for a moment, his mind somewhere else. "And wear a condom for Christ's sake."

Paul rushed upstairs as Steve came in the kitchen door.

Steve and Amber exchanged looks.

"I'm serious," Dad continued, unaware that Paul had already retreated. "The last thing you need is to get a girl pregnant."

Steve struck a pose in the kitchen behind Dad's back. He pointed to the ceiling. The upstairs was the outback of the house. While Dad ruled the downstairs, he never went beyond the bottom step. He conceded the top floor, an armistice for a war he couldn't win.

Amber met Steve in his room. As she closed the door, she glimpsed Paul coming out of his room. Their eyes met for a fraction. He looked sideways at her and scrunched up his nose. She stuck her tongue out and slammed the door.

Inside, Steve lounged in an overstuffed chair—an heirloom from their great-grandparents. His room always smelled like smoke and butt. He was disgusting, she knew, always scratching and digging, but he was her only ally in the house. As she sat on his bed, she looked around. Not much changed, week by week, another layer of his silt: dirty work clothes lay in a pile by the closet, dead beer cans behind his chair, a boom box and a teetering stack of cassettes—late 70's Neil Diamond, Don McLean and American top forty. The lone window overlooked Mt. Edison, a view skewed by a ratty curtain that served as a hand towel and a screen for their clandestine activities. A germinating pot plant lay on the sill. A small cooler sat next to his chair.

Steve scratched his crotch. It repulsed her to be in the cramped room. He partied with her, even loaned her money, but he was a pig. It was better than being alone.

"Want a beer?" Steve asked, pulling a sweaty can from the cooler.

"No. Do you have a wine cooler?"

Steve flipped open the beer and took a long drink. He inhaled loudly and burped.

He reached into the cooler again and brought out a wine cooler.

"You remembered!" Amber smiled.

He opened it for her. Amber took a sip. "Did you get the mushrooms?"

Steve reached under his seat cushion. He pulled out a baggie full of gnarly mushrooms. They were grey, blue, purple. He abruptly opened the baggy, took out two pinches of mushrooms, stuffed them in his mouth and began to chew them. His face contorted as the taste infiltrated his buds. He held his nose and chugged his beer. "Nasty," he said. He handed the bag to Amber.

Amber examined the contents. She pulled out a long stringy mushroom with its tiny cap intact and slipped it into her mouth. She chewed it slowly, making a face. Steve laughed, chugging his beer.

"Take another one. You won't even feel that."

Amber squinted at him. "Are you sure?"

Steve waved his hand. "Go on. Don't be a pussy."

Amber reached into the bag and pulled out another cap and stem. She chewed the mushroom into a muddy pulp. She swallowed the wretched mass and chased it with a long sip of cooler. Steve eased back into his easy chair. He got another beer. A smile spread across his face as his glassy eyes leveled on her. Amber sipped her cooler, swinging her feet. "I'm bored," she whined.

Steve chuckled. "You won't be." He lit a joint and opened the window. He blew the smoke out. He offered it to Amber. Amber took a small hit and froze. Steve jerked his head toward the door. The stairs creaked. It was impossible to tell which step Dad had ascended. His voice boomed up the stairwell.

"You kids be good. I'll be back tomorrow." He was going to his girlfriend Renee's place for the weekend.

"Okay, Dad!" Steve and Amber yelled back in unison. They both settled in, waving their hands in the air.

"Now we can really get fucked up," Steve said. The garage door banged shut, foretelling an evening of delicious abandonment.

As Amber handed the joint back to Steve a rainbow trailed her hand. Like the suddenness of a closing shade, the air in the room and all its surfaces began to glow in Technicolor. Everything seemed so fat and polished. Steve's face was super round, and his eyes blazed. His hair appeared to be growing out of his head and getting longer.

"I'm rushing," she said, sitting as still as she could. Every cell in her body was a new being, seeing the world separately in its own distinct way. She shared every individual perspective with her cells. She could feel each breath enter her body, and each exhale filled the room with her. She was no longer Amber, not the static being she'd hardened into, but an aqueous child of possibility.

Steve giggled, hands massaging the armrests. He set his beer next to the chair and began waving his hands in front of his face.

"Do you see trails?" he asked. His glowing face appeared to dawn out of his neck. "I'm hot," he announced, rising to his haunches. He took off his pants and opened the window.

At first, Amber thought she was hallucinating. When Steve slumped back into the chair there was a bulge in the crotch of his tightie-whities. He was oblivious. Amber watched Steve cross himself with his Budweiser can over and over, eyes popping.

Amber felt like she was looking down a tunnel. Leaning back on the bed she peered down her torso and thighs to her feet, so distant and falling away. The distortion didn't bother her though. What bothered her was nausea. Her stomach gurgled in protest. "I feel funny," she giggled nervously.

Steve jerked his head at the sound of her voice. "Don't throw up. It'll ruin your buzz."

Steve held the beer in his lap with both hands. He stared at Amber's chest.

He was trying to cover up his bulge, she thought.

"Why are you doing that?" she asked, pointing at his crotch.

"What?"

"Why are you covering up your boner?"

Steve put his hands on the armrests. He stared at her. "You're my little sister."

"So. Do you think I've never seen one? I don't care."

Steve squinted at her. "Where did you ever see one?"

Amber sighed. Now she regretted bringing it up. The topic was a familiar slope that always ended in the same gulch. "I saw my first one when I was seven," she said, swooning from another wave of intoxication. Her voice sounded distant and canned now. Memories of the little girl in the brownie outfit, rough hands and the smell of Ivory soap flashed through her.

Steve crossed his legs. He recrossed them twice before giving up. He placed his beer can between his legs. "Who would show a seven-year-old their unit?"

"Largo, Mom's boyfriend. It's no big deal," she said, placidly.

Steve put his hands behind his head and lifted a leg over the armrest. Her next move was mechanical. The slope had taken her to this point, not yet at the gulch but descending rapidly. Amber eased to the floor. Her face was a dull mask. She slithered to him. The grain wood floor had a current of its own. A feeling took her over. Impossible to articulate, it was familiar, a part of her that rose like steam from her soul. It was neither comfort, nor power, rather, a pure impulse that she never balked at, or questioned.

"See," she said, placing her hand on his bulge, "no big deal."

Steve's jaw dropped, as Amber slipped her hand inside his underpants. She gripped him, her knees already whining. Steve's face twitched, eyelids fluttering. He recoiled slightly, as she started jerking it. He relaxed as she slowed to a steady rhythm. He exhaled loudly.

Amber watched Steve's face boil like a cloud. She was glad his eyes were closed. It would be easier that way. She knew what guys wanted. They didn't care who did it, as long as it was done. Amber rose up on her haunches for leverage. She worked between his legs like a boy scout making a fire, chuckling at the faces Steve made. She wasn't sure, at times if her strokes hurt or pleasured. She clenched her teeth as he spilled over her fists. And suddenly, her arms were weighty, and she just wanted to lie on the bed. The act banished her buzz and she wanted it back.

Steve handed his work shirt to her. His face was rubber, lips like raw slugs ready to burst. He put on Chapstick, circling his mouth over and over, dumbstruck, staring at the ceiling.

"Are you mad?" she asked.

He looked at her eyebrows. "Nah."

That was it. Amber lay back on the bed searching for whatever he saw in the popcorn ceiling. It was always the same, afterward. As the air began to crackle between them, she drifted into the ravenous maw of her thoughts, consumed by the gnawing truth that with one little act, her days were numbered on Mt. Edison.

##### #####

Within a month Amber was delivered to Venice Beach. Dad instructed them to drop her off at Grace's. Steve drove, Paul sat in the front, she in the back. They smoked a joint after getting on to

I-5 North, passing it in a rudimentary triangle. Amber held the joint, inhaling heavily. Steve cranked "Psycho Killer" as they cruised in the fast lane through San Clemente Canyon.

They stopped in Oceanside for a burger and a smoke. Amber paid at the register with the money Dad gave her, an exorbitant amount. A payoff, they both knew. She didn't thank him. Stared into his eyes for the first time in her life. He didn't expect thanks.

In the parking lot, Steve and Paul stood by the car. Steve pulled two beers from his ubiquitous cooler; they both downed a beer, while Amber had a smoke. It might have been the neutral turf or the fact that she might never see them again, maybe the jutting tip of something even greater, but that's when it started. Amber glared at them over the roof of the car. They turned their back on her and continued to talk.

She threw the butt near the drive-in window and slammed her fists on the roof.

"You never wanted me there, did you?"

Steve and Paul stared mutely at the scenery.

"Admit it. I've never been a part of this family."

Steve reached in the driver's side window and turned up the stereo. Paul shook his head. "Be cool, Amber."

"I don't care what you all think of me. Dad treats me like a slave. He let you boys do whatever you want, but when I got home even a minute late he'd give me shit. Does that sound fair to you?"

Steve chugged his beer. Paul hummed along with the song. They both jumped in the car at the same time drawing from the same impulse.

Amber stared at the passing landscape, seeing only reds and greys. The words spilled out of her. "Why didn't you stick up for me and say something to Dad? Do you know why I didn't go to school? Because they made fun of me. I had no friends because Dad wouldn't buy me clothes. I had to wear Grandma's homemade clothes! *Home-Made-Clothes!*"

Amber lit a cigarette. She blew the smoke toward the front seats. Paul opened his window. Steve stared slantwise in the rearview mirror.

She smoked feverishly. Her head swiveled from side to side.

As she recognized landmarks, Amber began to cool. She hardened as the salty breeze coming from the Pacific tousled her hair. After exiting at Highway 90, they flowed down Lincoln Boulevard. "Stop at that Der Wienerschnitzel," she said, pointing over Paul's shoulder. "I've got to pee."

Amber sat up in the back seat, spinning her head around, eyes wide, bouncing.

"That looks familiar," she said, pointing at a seedy motel.

They pulled into the parking lot of the Der Wienerschnitzel. The lot was packed, so Steve stopped in the red zone on the side of the restaurant. Paul stepped out and pushed the seat back so Amber could squeeze out. Steve and Paul watched Amber run into the restaurant with her TWA bag.

In the bathroom, Amber put on makeup. She changed into a halter top, shorts, and a pair of jelly sandals. She put her hair in pigtails. *They won't see me if I sneak out the back,* she thought. It had been years since she'd been to the boardwalk. She was almost free. The fry cook didn't take a second look, and the manager in his office got up and locked the door behind her. She bolted out the back of the Der Wienerschnitzel toward the dumpster on the far side.

Amber walked down a side street and headed west through a residential tract parallel to Venice Boulevard. She smiled, squinting at the midday sun, pulled out a pair of sunglasses and stowed her owl glasses. *A new life,* she thought, smiling broadly, slapping her jellies up the sidewalk on an adventure. The houses with their perfect lawns and picket fences, were not, and would never be, hers. She was done trying to be a part of that world. She was on her own, independent for the first time. *I don't need anyone!*

#####

Amber got her wish, to live in Venice Beach like Grace. The unrelenting sun beat down from a cloudless sky. The boardwalk. The back streets and alleyways. The constant motion. Herbie watched her from his lawn chair, next to the little surf shop, a block from Gold's Gym. Amber didn't like the costume, the makeup, the entire getup he insisted upon. "It attracts Johns, baby. You can wear anything you want when you're off the clock."

She always seemed to be working. Amber admired herself in the storefront window. Meth made it easy to stay thin. She felt her ribs through the red striped tube top. She spun around to look at her butt cheeks in the tight white vinyl skirt. She really liked the way she looked. A stream of tourists flowed behind her. She smiled at a gawking husband.

A whistle from Herbie's perch spurred her down the sidewalk. She could hear him in her head, *Get to work!* He was kind at times. *He loves me*, she thought.

At eighteen, Amber couldn't care less about the work. Herbie took care of her. She didn't see the faces of the men who hired her. She did her job, on her back mostly, and at the end of the day, Herbie gave her spending money.

Amber walked up the boardwalk stepping with a purpose in her cork wedge platforms. An infected sore on the inside of her thigh mocked her progress. A metallic blue 64 Chevy Impala lowered and popped on performance shocks, bobbed up beside her as she reached the corner. She gazed warily at the driver, a Cholo with ray bans and a wife beater t-shirt. Three teenagers in blue plaid and khakis were all teeth in the back seat. A hard-faced woman with dark, thin painted eyebrows leaned forward from the passenger seat. "Wanta party, baby girl?" asked the woman. Her breasts heaved in her t-shirt. Amber looked across the street at Herbie. He gave a thumbs up, but Amber's stomach turned at the sight of the boys in the back seat, younger than her, with daggers for eyes. She took a step backward, adjusting her tube top.

"What's a matter, baby, aren't you working?" asked the driver.

Amber heard a loud whistle. She knew what it meant.

She smiled at the driver. The boys in the back seat ribbed one another. She caught a glimpse of something grey in the middle boy's hands. The boys leaned forward in their seats as she huddled into the window. "What are you looking for?" she asked, flashing the smile she'd perfected over the last six months.

"What you think, bitch? Get in the fucking car!" the driver demanded. The woman with the penciled eyebrows punched his arm.

"I mean, we just want to party with you, baby," he sneered with slits for eyes.

The teenager in the middle of the back seat held up a roll of duck tape. "Yeah. We just want to take you for a ride, baby girl," he snickered.

The woman slapped the duck tape out of his hand. "*Callate puta!*" He slumped back into his seat. The teenagers on either side of him erupted in laughter.

Amber unconsciously scratched the sore between her thighs. Her stomach growled. She hadn't eaten all day. She'd done two lines before hitting the street. She stood and turned toward Herbie, who was making his way toward them. Amber swooned. It had been happening for the last week, nausea, tender breasts. When she threw up back at the apartment, Herbie bought her a pregnancy test. It had to be his, she thought, and almost welcomed a baby with him. *Am I fucking crazy?*

Herbie stopped at the corner, pulled a *Penny Saver* from a stand twenty feet away. His body language was clear. She'd rejected one John earlier—a drifter with crazy eyes. "You don't get to choose who you fuck!" Herbie had yelled, the implicit threat of violence all too clear. *You don't get to choose* resounded through her, at the sight of Herbie looming across the street.

"Come on, baby, get in." the woman said, her voice all at once saccharine and menacing.

Amber smiled weakly. "I..."

The woman with the spilling breasts leaped out of the passenger seat, strode around the front of the Impala, and grabbed Amber by the wrist. Amber's legs turned to stone. The woman dragged her back to the passenger side. Amber dug her heels in, losing one of her platforms along the way. It happened so fast. Amber had no intention of getting in the car with this group. She heard a shout from the opposite corner. One of the teenagers from the back kicked the front seat forward, his outstretched hands clutched at her. She splayed her limbs wide like a fawn rising for the first time. She felt a blow on the back of her head and the street tilted. She searched the sidewalk for a friendly face. A group of elderly tourists on the opposite corner pointed in her direction. *Don't let them get you into the car!*

The Chola kicked her in the side. She fell to her knees, head pounding. The heat from the asphalt seared her knees. Forced upright, she was thrust toward the back seat.

"It's okay, baby. We just want to party," the driver charmed her through clenched teeth.

Her skin prickled. The look on the faces of the teenagers in the back seat, the Chola pushing from behind, the blood trickling down from her scraped knees, the driver pulling her arm; she imagined herself bound in some seedy motel room, blinds blocking out light and safety. *I am going to die.*

Amber grasped the roof of the Impala and kicked out with all her might. The one remaining platform caught the Chola soundly in the stomach. Amber spat in the driver's face—he loosened his grip on her arm, just long enough for Amber to break free. Amber leaped out of her platform shoe and fled to the other corner in her bare stocking feet. She heard the Chola curse, and the Impala peel out.

Barefoot, bruised and bleeding, she leaned against the stop sign watching the Impala turn right on the next block. She looked across at Herbie, jaw clenched, steaming toward her in long ominous strides. She searched the street for her shoes. Herbie would charge her for them. She wiped back tears streaming down her face. She cursed herself for being weak, just then, when she needed to pull it together. Amber found one shoe at the corner, and the other on the sidewalk. She buckled the straps when a blow to the side of her head felled her.

"Bitch. I told you to do your job." Herbie pulled her to her feet and hustled her down the sidewalk. Amber slid along on her toes, resisting but too afraid to battle Herbie. He'd taken her in. He'd given her a place to stay. Now, they were going to have a baby together.

When they got home Herbie locked himself in the bathroom. That meant he didn't want to share. When he came out he held the pregnancy test in his hand. "You little bitch! Why didn't you tell me?"

Amber cursed herself. She'd wrapped it in toilet paper, was afraid that she'd used too much, and that he would bitch at her for that. Amber put on her owl glasses. She'd changed into sweats and was waiting for him to finish so she could take a shower. Now, she went to the kitchenette and got him a beer. "I don't know. I, I wanted it to be a surprise," she murmured, shuffling to him, extending the beer.

He took it absentmindedly. "Yeah, it's a fucking surprise. I got no use for a pregnant ho."

Amber slumped. "Do you want me to make hot pockets for dinner?" She went to the tiny fridge and waited.

Herbie just shook his head. "Baby, you don't get it. You're not my bitch, *you are my ho*. That means, no baby." He paced by the bathroom.

*He's afraid to even get near me*, she thought. Amber opened and closed the door on the mini-fridge. The frosty air kissed her raw knees. The traffic outside seemed to get louder as the air in the apartment grew thick.

"I want to keep it," she finally said. She took out the frozen hot pockets and ran them under the tap to defrost. Herbie shook his head, three steps to the couch, and the TV volume went up, which meant the conversation was over. Amber rubbed her belly. *I better eat something,* she thought. *I wonder if it's a boy or a girl.* Amber smiled at the paper towel roll as her fingers got pruney and the hot pockets turned soft. *He'll change his mind.*

#####

"Grace?"

"Amber? Where are you? We've been worried."

"I'm in Venice. I'm living in Venice."

"What? It's been three months since Steve lost you at Der Wienerschnitzel. Where have you been?"

Amber drew strength from the growing silence between them. There was no good answer. No clear way forward. She hadn't planned the call. When Herbie *commanded* her to abort the baby, she reacted.

"I'm pregnant. Do you want it?"

She listened to Grace's halting breath on the other end. She was in a phone booth, and it seemed suddenly otherworldly to be in a glass box on a busy corner trying to give her baby away. The baby wasn't real yet, just symptoms competing with her anger, sadness, and longing. She took Grace's silence as reluctance.

"You always wanted a baby...didn't you?" she pleaded. She could stay with Herbie with the baby out of the picture.

"This is such a surprise. Who is the father?"

"You don't know him...does it matter?"

"Amber?"

"What?"

"Is this what you want?"

Amber picked at the clumps of chewing gum stuck to the underside of the pay phone.

"I don't know. Can't you just take it?" she implored.

Silence again. Amber sensed someone else on the line now. It must be Ron.

It was a mistake to call. Amber slammed the phone down and instantly regretted it. She could taste the meth drip in her throat from the lines she'd snorted to brace herself for the phone call. Herbie was trying to appease her with drugs and she hated herself for letting him. He'd won again. Amber shuffled toward the clinic blinking wildly at the harsh sunlight and her even harsher resolve.

# 17

Grace had always been a mother. She mothered dolls as an only child, and when the parade of babies came home, each with less and less fanfare, she descended into the shadows, materializing gradually to care for her siblings. Now, at thirty she was ready to have her own.

At their first visit the fertility doctor commented on her maternal stature. "You certainly have the hips for it," he said, glancing at her waist. He was the first doctor, in a revolving door of bleached smocks and framed credentials. They changed doctors, tried the positions, in vitro, test after test until a nurse at Mercy asked her if she'd ever had an STD.

"You know certain types of STDs can prevent you from being able to conceive." It was a flippant comment but it changed Grace's life. It was like a shifting gale, sending her in the opposite direction. Grace went home that night and sat on the back porch. She'd thrown away all of her pot, had quit drinking, cut out red meats, drank water religiously, lost five pounds and was walking every day, to the beach and back. She'd never felt so healthy.

As she sipped from a glass of Chardonnay, the first in months, Grace started to cry. Mom could have babies effortlessly, while she was denied the one thing she felt she was meant to do. When Ron came home she was stretched on the couch hugging a pillow, staring up at the ceiling. When she turned over her eyes were puffy and red. He stroked her hair, but she was irritable; still, she let him do it because he had to be given something to do. When his touch got to be too much she went into the kitchen to start dinner. The sight of pork chops pink and limp in the sink made her nauseous, so she started boiling water, without any plan, no particular intention. She had just sat down when Ron came in with his Bible. "Sara couldn't get pregnant either. Remember? I don't think we should give up. If God wants it, it will happen."

"I don't want to talk about it. I'm done." Grace started looking through the cupboard for something to put in the boiling water.

Ron went to the sink. "I thought we were having pork chops."

Grace leaned her head against the cabinet.

"Honey? Are you okay?" he asked.

Grace could feel the steam wafting across her breasts. "No," she said calmly, resigned. "I am not okay. We've been trying to have a baby for a year now. We've done everything right. My mother could have a million babies and throw away every single one. What the hell is wrong with me?"

Ron turned the burner down. Always the practical one. "Maybe it's me?"

Grace lifted her head. She turned to him. "That's sweet, but you heard the nurse. I think she's right. It's the gonorrhea."

That night they lay in bed, a cold valley between them. There was something caustic in their touch. They'd eaten in silence and gone straight to bed. He refused to leave her alone, shepherding her to the couch, to the bathroom and then finally, to bed. "You need a good night's sleep," he said with stitched brows, looking as if the world were ending and a good night's sleep could cure the plague. "It'll be alright in the morning."

Grace slept raggedly. In the middle of the night, she crept out to the couch and stared at the ashen world outside. A family of raccoons drifted across the lawn, their white parts glowing like foam on the beach. The largest black ghost looked after her kits disappearing en masse into the hedge, a departure Grace felt in her chest. She went back to bed. In the morning she fried Spam and white rice for Ron, his favorite. *No use both of us being sad,* she thought.

##### 

A few days later, Reverend Duane came to the Sunday School room. Grace was doing an art project with ten or so children ranging from four to twelve years of age. Bottles of paste and multicolored scrap paper filled a low table by the door. The older children helped the younger ones paste outlines of their hands, pointing to a spot on the page, a depiction of "The Creation" by Michelangelo. Reverend Duane pulled her aside. "Is everything alright? Ron tells me things aren't going so well."

Grace looked deeply into his eyes. He believed so completely in the God that moved in strange ways. For a brief moment, she felt an alloy of love and sadness for him. "I want to meet with you and Ron after today's service," he said, gently touching her arm. His kindness flowed through her. Throughout the lesson, she strove to pass it on to the children in spite of the thickness in her chest.

After the service Grace and Ron sat at a folding table in the kitchen area of the hall. Ron took his time offering them cookies and coffee, and to Grace, it felt like he was priming them for something. Ron kept his Bible on his lap, as they both watched Reverend Duane wipe down the counter, finally settling across from them, unaware of a piece of paper towel stuck to his shoe. Now, he offered his hands to them, and in a tight triangle, they prayed. Afterward, they separated and Grace felt no better.

"How long have you two been trying to conceive?" he asked.

They looked at each other. "Over a year now," they chorused.

"Grace. You are a mother. You are motherly. You don't have to conceive to be a mother, do you?"

Grace wanted to strangle him. *Don't you think we've thought of that?*

She sighed. "We want our own."

"There are so many children out there that need good parents."

"I know." Grace thought of Amber.

Reverend Duane reached into his vest pocket. He pulled out a pamphlet with a paper clip and a card attached. He detached the card and placed the pamphlet on the table.

The pamphlet's headline was "Are You A Foster Parent?"

It had a beaming couple on the cover holding a baby, ecstatic and complete. He pushed the card across the table.

"This is a friend of mine. She has foster children. She can help you." Neither of them rushed to pick up the card. Finally, Ron picked it up and held it close so they could read it. It was a business card for a government agency. Grace stared at it. Numb. After a moment, they prayed again. Only, this time, Reverend Duane said a prayer for them, and when they separated Ron drove them home in Grace's Karmann Ghia.

Out of the blue, Amber called to tell Grace she was pregnant. She asked if Grace wanted the baby. Grace barely recognized her voice. It was such a surprise. When Amber hung up, Grace and Ron celebrated this unlikely providence. She secretly regretted her lack of faith. A day went by, and another, and another, and the memory of the desperate, murky phone conversation with Amber faded until it seemed unlikely to have happened at all.

They were both in their thirties now. They weren't getting any younger. Ron was doing well in his job. The New Apostles Church was the center of their existence. The past was tucked neatly away in the little cardboard box she kept in the hall closet. Amber was an adult, ostensibly, on her own. Grace had heard Mom hooked up with a long-haul trucker and was zig-zagging across the country. Dad and the boys were a dot on the map, down South in San Diego. All that was missing for Grace was the warm weight of a child on her hip.

The state of willingness and surrender came to her one day as she arrived home from teaching an art class at Sunday School. She rushed in the door, ebullient from the morning's lesson. The art her "babies" had made, inspired by her passion and a touch of the divine, made her vibrate. She knew *He* worked in her life. She placed her keys on the old console table near the door. The mirror reflected the living room. She kept old receipts, loose change and collected mail there. The table was an object of permanence that she rarely noticed, but in that convergence of light and her reflection, a seam of possibility opened in her. She could be a mother and she was the only thing preventing it. Grace rustled through the drawer and held up the pamphlet. She called the number, and just like that, hope began to grow again.

They went to Foster Services to see about adopting a child. They wanted a baby. They would go to any lengths. They waited in lines. They heard of babies available for adoption from China. At first, they wanted a mixed race child, Asian and White, so it would look like them. They submitted and resubmitted all the right paperwork to a growing album of familiar faces. Grace knew all the receptionists, counselors and nurses by their first name. They called her the immaculate mother. After a year of meetings, their name rose nearer the top of the list. Time stood still, week after week passed, phone call after phone call until they told her that they would call her, and to just be patient.

For the first time since that moment in the hallway, when receiving another woman's child became her only hope, she broke down and admitted to Ron that she was being punished. That her life to that point, the countless one-night-stands, and abuse at the hands of her family could not be forgiven so easily. It was in the backyard and Ron held her as he always did. She couldn't see the beauty of their yard: the bird of paradise, the wisteria, nasturtium, the morning glory and the sunflowers Ron planted for her birthday, all vying for her attention. Grace was blind to them, her face burrowed into his chest. The colors seemed to have drained out of the world, colors that saw her through years of pain, colors from paints, flowers, yarn, children. She saw the world in that moment through a sepia screen, dull and unforgiving. Ron guided her to the kitchen and sat with her, offering doses of encouragement; then to the couch and finally, he laid her in bed, where she slept for two days, subsisting on broth and saltines. On the morning of the third day, they received the call.

Mimi was a blonde-haired, blue-eyed one-year-old who stole Grace's heart the moment she laid eyes on her. That day, Grace held her in her arms, Mimi clung to her— nuzzling her chin with her hot little head. Grace had goosebumps as Mimi clutched her with her inconceivably tiny fingers. Her life began to fill and gain momentum, the act of giving oneself completely.

It was early Thursday afternoon, after a long morning remaking the crib, checking and rechecking the pantry, the refrigerator and the cupboards. The weight of raising a child rested firmly on her shoulders now, and it felt like she was preparing for a lifetime. Grace sat knitting a cap for Mimi as the neighborhood kids came trickling home from school. Ron sat across from her, playing a soft melody, humming to himself. She opened the curtains affording a view of the street and entryway. Earlier in the day, Grace went shopping for food she thought would be appropriate for a one-year-old. Mimi's record showed she had no allergies, and she was partial to Cheerios and cottage cheese.

Grace went to the door, opened it, adjusted the welcome mat, and stepped back in. She walked back down the hall and gazed left into Mimi's room. *Amber.* There would be no space for her now. It took Grace days to get the smoky smell out of the closet and walls. The new pink walls with grass and flowers she'd painted herself made her smile. She walked to the center of the room; a ponderous melancholy began to rise as she wiped dusted the baseboard for the third time, decided to open the window, noticed a nest in the tree across the fence, and closed it again. Amber was her first child. She would do better.

Grace stood at the window feeling the warmth of the sun on the pane.

At the sound of a car on the street she bolted to the front door. She fought the impulse to fling the door open, to run out onto the street and take her baby into her arms. But things were not final—the process, their life sifted through cheesecloth, follow up visits, so much still up in the air. The doorbell rang. Grace jumped. "Ron! she's here!"

Ron came to her side. She smoothed her skirt. For once, she didn't feel fat. She felt like a mother. Ron stepped back as she opened the door.

The case manager, a middle-aged woman who smelled of Jean Nate and menthols, held little Mimi in her arms. Mimi shifted, eyes wide as she soaked up the interior of the house. Grace took Mimi in her arms. They went to the living room, where the case manager smiled as they signed the papers. Mimi stayed in Grace's arms the entire evening until Grace laid her in a crib in their bedroom. Mimi didn't eat much that first night: a little milk from a bottle, a spoonful of cottage cheese and a few Cheerios. Grace didn't want to push food on her, but she was worried that Mimi was already too thin, and small for her age.

Mimi slept the entire night. She awoke at sunrise, standing in her crib calling out, not Grace's name, rather, a plaintive cry that drew Grace to her like a shot. After breakfast Grace ran a bath and dressed Mimi in clothes donated from the families of the New Christian Apostles Church. Mimi watched her make lunch from her high chair. Grace followed Mimi around the house, as she explored each room. She didn't call her Mommy until Sunday. It was at church and during the sermon, Mimi surprised her by whispering, "Mommy,potty" in a plaintive voice.

After a week the house typically went silent at eight o'clock. Ron watched from the doorway as Grace read to Mimi in bed. Mimi lay with her eyes open and closed, dozing, being a good girl, all tucked in. When Mimi settled into a deep slumber, her face so still and her tiny hands balled at her chin, Grace pulled herself away and crept to the couch. Ron joined her. They snuggled, listening to the house creak, wrapped in the quilt Grandma D had made as a wedding gift.

With the lights out, they could see the mauve eastern sky through their front window.

Grace sighed, Ron's warm sturdy frame still and comforting next to her. Grace felt as if a new world had descended around her. A world of promise and hope. She hadn't been able to sleep last night, and probably wouldn't tonight. Ron began to snore softly. In the other room, Mimi worked a small saw of her own. Soon, Mimi and Ron contrived a syncopated slumber—the snoring a sweet melding of the two loves of her life, the new and the old worlds coming together. She woke Ron and led him to their bed. She crept into Mimi's room and went to the crib, her first night sleeping alone.

Mimi was on her side, so still. She shifted slightly, pawing at her pillow, settling. Grace wondered what she'd been through, and what mother wouldn't want her. She resisted the impulse to kiss Mimi. Ron began to snore and Mimi joined him.

Grace went to the kitchen. Too excited to sleep, she opened the cupboard with the pancake mix. She grabbed the canister with her stash. There was only a baggy full of shake. She began rolling a joint when she heard Mimi yelp. Grace rushed to the crib to find Mimi shifting once again. She waited at the rail for her to settle. Ron was on his side now. Outside the yard was all shade and silhouettes. The sky held the sun's last breath over the horizon.

When Mimi settled, Grace crept back to the kitchen. She finished rolling the joint, put it to her mouth, and froze. She hadn't smoked since the wedding. *What am I doing?* she asked herself. She put the joint back in the canister, put the lid on, and dropped the whole thing in the trash can. It wasn't just a new person in the house, it was a new life. Grace stared at her reflection in the kitchen window. Her hair was longer than it had ever been. Her face had filled out, her breasts heavy, and her hips wide. She was still pretty, she thought, but she was no longer a young lady. Her eyes were as dark as ever; she looked deeply into them as if she could see the future. It felt as if she was just beginning to be who she was intended to be.

The next day Grace packed Mimi up to go to daycare at the church. She had trouble putting the baby chair in the back seat of the Karmann Ghia, so she called Ron at work. After getting talked through it, she strapped Mimi in and set off to church. The New Christian Apostles Church had expanded in the last few years, a benefit of the growing trend of young people seeking alternative worship outside of the mainstream religions.

Grace carried Mimi in through the main hall, through the kitchen, into the Sunday School classroom. Children ranging from ages two to fifteen ran amuck: playing tag, finger painting on the floor, reading and praying. At first sight, the chaos was unsettling, but Grace could see through the overlapping activities and was accustomed to the underlying order they'd worked so hard to develop. "Let them find order within choice," Reverend Duane said.

The tempo of the room slowed as Grace walked through. She was soon surrounded on all sides, the center of curious eyes. "Who is that, Grace?" one of the children asked.

"It's my daughter, Mimi."

"She doesn't look like you," a freckled face said.

Mimi hid her face in Grace's neck.

"Aw, she's so cute."

"I didn't know you had a daughter. Praise Jesus."

"Yes," Grace said as she started toward the back wall, "Mimi is a gift from God."

Most of the students went back to their activities. A few followed. Mia, a teenager Grace had taken under her wing, walked with her to the sink. "Can I hold her?" she asked.

"Let's see," Grace said. She transferred Mimi to Mia. Mimi whimpered, her eyes riveted on Grace. Mia shifted her to face

Grace. Mimi touched Mia's nose. Mia laughed. Mimi smiled back at Grace. Grace kissed her on the cheek. She walked to the sink and began preparing paints and brushes for the mural she'd started on the back wall. Mia held Mimi close by, so she could watch Grace work. Every so often a couple of students approached to visit Mimi. Throughout the day Mimi became increasingly comfortable with her new surroundings. At one point she wanted to be set down so she could join a small group of toddlers. Grace stopped painting to watch Mimi interact with the other children. She was a gentle, a shy girl, but held her own.

"I think you got lucky with that one," Mia said.

"Don't I know it," Grace said, blowing a wisp of hair out of her face. "We are blessed."

#####

Easter morning, the main hall bustled. Throngs of brightly dressed congregants, wanderers and searchers, outcasts and fresh converts, women with flowers in their hair, men with rope belts hugging leather-clad bikers, denim-vested women with beads in their hair, all packed into the hall. Ron and Grace arrived early with Mimi, now three and fully immersed in their Christian community. Ron carried Mimi, while Grace carried an assortment of sweet treats she'd baked specially for the occasion.

The large hall was filling up quickly. Ron motioned to a young man with a ponytail and a wooden crucifix around his neck. They walked toward the stage to check the sound system. He paused at the fire exit to assign duties to a small group of teenagers. Grace beckoned Mimi to follow her to the kitchen. Grace loved the kitchen in their little church. It was fully equipped for commercial use with two Hobart mixers, a Waring food processor and blender. She would equip her kitchen in just the same way if she ever had the money. She went to the wall of refrigerators and stored the pies she'd made. Margaret Lum, an old

classmate at Venice High, and Vincent Mallory, a friend of Rex and
Kimo's, waved from the doorway. The room was abuzz; small
cliques performed necessary tasks to make Easter Sunday festive
and bountiful.

Vincent and Margaret approached her. "My, how big you
are," Vincent declared, bending down and pinching Mimi's cheek.
Grace hugged Margaret.

"She's my big girl," Grace said, hugging Mimi to her.
"Margie, can you take Mimi in the back room to play with the
other kids, please? I've got to get the buffet going."

Grace and Vincent set about organizing the trays of food,
taken from the row of wall refrigerators. They'd joined the church
around the same time, both survivors of the Venice Beach scene. "I
got my two-year chip last night," Vincent said.

Grace's mouth dropped open. "Vincent! That's wonderful.
Praise the lord."

Vincent beamed. "Don't *you* have some good news? I heard
it through the grapevine that you've got another baby on the way."

Grace pulled a stack of trays from a shelf overhanging a long
row of stainless steel work tables. "His name is Ben. They're
bringing him on Wednesday."

Vincent gave Grace a hug. He took a tray from the stack and
starting arranging fruit on it. He meticulously laid out rows of
strawberries, banana circles, orange slices and apple wedges in
quadrants.  Grace deftly arranged a row of centerpieces for the
tables to be set up after the service. Vincent lingered next to Grace
waiting for her approval. She glanced at his work, nodded, as she
deftly clipped the stem of a long stem rose.

Congregants came and went, some stopping to congratulate
her, others to offer to baby sit.  She set them to work on trays at the
other stainless steel table.

Grace began to clip the stems of sunflowers, placing each in
the row of glass vases. One stem was especially stubborn. She
swore under her breath. "Here, let me do that," Vincent said. Grace
wiped her hands on her apron. She sighed.

"What's wrong, honey. Something bothering you?" Vincent asked.

"Ron lost his job." She set the vase aside and mechanically started on another. "We're going to have two babies and no money coming in." She started placing fern sprigs into the vases. "That's terrible news," Vincent said, touching her arm. He went to the refrigerator and brought back two containers of vegetables in cool water. An older woman with flowing white hair approached them from the nearby work table. "Grace, where do you want these cold cuts?"

Grace pointed toward the row of refrigerators. "Put them in the second fridge, over there."

She began trimming lavender stems. "I don't know what we're going to do."

Vincent smiled, knowingly. He put an arm around Grace's shoulder. "I have a feeling everything is going to work out. You are in God's hands."

Grace hugged him. "You're right. I should have faith. Ron sure does."

Grace found herself distracted during the service. Mimi mirrored her agitation, twitching and running to the bathroom. Reverend Duane droned on about compassion and renewal. She had hoped for an inspiring message, and was relieved when Ron led the worship band in a jazzy version of "Amazing Grace". After the service Grace guided a crew of congregants in filling tables along the walls with trays of food. Throughout the transition, Ron played his guitar on stage, blending worship songs with top forty hits. Grace paused when the tables were set, every table adorned with her centerpieces, a loving touch, her creativity a gift and a blessing. She watched Ron from the back of the hall. The joy of playing flowed from him. The sight of her man, the joy he brought with his music, the embrace of the community, united in spirit, brought tears to her eyes. A slight touch at her skirt wrested her attention downward.

"Mommy...why are you crying?" Mimi asked.

"Mommy's not crying, sweetie. Mommy's happy," she said, taking Mimi into her arms.

She carried Mimi to a table near the stage where she could watch her Daddy. Grace went to fill up three plates of food. When she returned, Ron and Mimi were playing Patty-cake.

After the meal, the room began to quiet in anticipation of closing words from Reverend Duane. He and his wife sat at an adjoining table and he appeared to be reading from a journal. A few volunteers began to quietly clear the trays.

Reverend Duane rose to his feet. "I'd like to thank our volunteers for their gracious service in creating this holy feast." The congregation bubbled with raised glasses. Reverend Duane faced Grace's table. "I would like to give special thanks to the Marcos family, Grace, Ron, and Mimi."

Applause filled the hall. Reverend Duane waved his hands, smiling ear to ear.

"I also have an announcement. Grace and Ron are expecting a new arrival on Wednesday."

Reverend Duane pulled an envelope from under the folds of his frock. "Today, we welcome our new member with open arms, hearts and..." he held up the envelope, "...our wallets." He handed the envelope to Grace. "Grace and Ron, your hard work and faith have meant so much to The New Christian Apostles Church. Please accept this gift for your growing family."

Grace took the envelope, with one hand over her mouth, tears rushing to her eyes. Ron stood up, Mimi in his arms. Grace looked from face to face. The kindness was overwhelming. Reverend Duane hugged her. She made the sign of thank you, turning to the congregation, not seeing anyone clearly but feeling every one of them. She heard the applause and felt utterly embraced.

Later, Grace led Ron and Mimi through a gauntlet of well-wishers out of the hall to the car. Grace was as light as a feather, coasting toward a life she could only have imagined. Ben was a very lucky boy, she thought on the drive back to the house.

#####

Grace had never heard of Rochester, New York. She was a West Coast gal, born and raised in the California sun, Beach Boys, the Doors, and Sunset Strip. In Rochester, Eastman Kodak was *the* employer. After three years at the West coast office, Ron took a position in operations near the Kodak Tower. It was a chance of a lifetime at a *Fortune* 500 company. There was a glitch in their ascendancy, a lack of steady income, and Ron was excited to remedy that. Grace was proud of Ron, his ability to master complex technical machinery. The ever-present manuals he kept near his guitar case, the nightly ritual of studying was beginning to pay off. Over the last five years he'd built a solid resume, and their future was bright.

Like a pioneer wife, Grace shouldered the family, which now included Ben, her newly adopted son, and her first, Mimi. The move was scheduled for Saturday, the only day her friends could help. A biblical journey across the heartland lay ahead. They were leaving their church, their community, their family, their friends, their entire existence up to that point.

It was a classic Venice weekend. The sun rode the rooftop baking the driveway where the U-haul sank lower and lower onto its axle. Rex, Kimo, and Terri came over to help them. They would party when the truck was loaded. Grace was grateful for the fact that Reverend Duane allowed alcohol in moderation. Ron still enjoyed an occasional beer, and she planned to open a bottle of wine she'd been saving.

The kitchen was the last room in the house to pack. Ron, Kimo, and Rex had gone to Vons to pick up steaks and beer. Terri was off getting her a going away present. Ben rocked in his highchair gurgling, and Mimi, four now, did her best to carry items back and forth: a bag of flour, a coffee can, bags of noodles and pancake mix from the counter to the kitchen table. "Thank you, Mimi," Grace said, planting a kiss on her forehead. Her heart swelled at how Mimi embraced the move without a single grumble or tantrum.

Grace went to the sink to wash her hands. Out in the yard, the Wisteria never seemed to stop blooming, covering their crumbling wedding arch. They talked about disassembling it, putting it up in the backyard of the new home in Rochester. They were leaving so much behind. Tonight, for a ritual offering, they would burn the arch. Reverend Duane would offer a blessing. Their entire community would be there.

Ben started to squirm in his highchair, his chubby toes curling with excitement at the busy house. Grace deftly placed a handful of Cheerios on his tray as she heard the dryer buzz and then the phone ring.

She picked up the wall receiver. "Hello?"

"Hi, Grace...it's me, Amber."

Her heart began to pound. Grace twisted the telephone cord around her wrist and twisted it back again watching Ben drop Cheerios on the floor while Mimi patiently picked them up. "Hi, Amber. How are you?"

"I'm living in San Diego, at Grandma D's. Dad needed me to take care of her. Her brain is starting to slip."

Grace rolled her fingers on the wall, waiting for it to come: the drama, a problem that needed solving, or worst of all, a place to stay.

"Oh, that's great, Amber. Do you like it?"

There was a pause on the other end. Grace could hear muffled, hurried voices. Amber returned in a flurry, her voice a gear higher.

"It's okay...she keeps trying to dress me up like a little girl. She calls me Marie all the time. I can't stand it."

Grace listened, trying to withhold judgment. Amber was talking at a breakneck clip now and she was starting to get a headache.

Amber continued, "I get out of the apartment as much as possible. She tries to make me go to church. Dad won't let me stay at the house, he says Grandma needs me but I know it's because he hates me. I love Grandma but she's a little crazy. I am not Marie. I'm nothing like Mom." Silence again. Grace could hear angry, muffled voices and imagined Amber's hand over the receiver.

"Amber...I'm moving to New York. I've got to hang up..." She said it into the space, hoping Amber would at least downshift. Amber could go on for hours.

When the silence stretched and she heard Amber's muffled voice responding to some peripheral cohort, Grace hung up. The receiver was nearly back in its cradle when she jerked it back. "Goodbye," she whispered, but at that point, it seemed like she was smoothing something over. She stared at the phone, so alive seconds ago. While she was happy to hear that Amber was being taken care of, she knew that Amber was holding back, that she'd called for a reason. *Whatever it was*, Grace thought with relief, *it mustn't have been that serious.*

Ron, Kimo, and Rex laughed in the hallway, laden with plastic grocery bags and three pizzas. She helped Mimi pick up the remaining Cheerios. She took Ben out of his high chair and went into the living room. "Let's go read a book, Mimi. You've been such a big help. You can choose one of your books."

She sidestepped Ron on her way to the living room. "I'll join you after I put the kids to bed," she said over her shoulder.

They milled about in the backyard debating the best way to burn the arch. The kitchen table and chairs were out on the patio and Ron was playing his guitar. The air smelled thick and loamy from the mound of fresh dirt; the open hole near their wedding arch was waiting to be filled with its charred remains. Grace opened the bottle of wine, and sat on Ron's lap, grateful that they weren't taking this final step alone. She watched as a sudden salty warm breeze tickled the overgrowth; the sun warmed her skin and she closed her eyes, savoring her last hours in California. The winters in Rochester were harsh, she'd heard from the realtor, but Spring and Fall were beautiful.

When the guests arrived, they helped load the final set of boxes stacked in the living room. Kimo, Rex, and Terri helped dismantle the arch, and each guest threw a slab of wood onto the fire. Reverend Duane said his prayer—she was somewhere else, staring at the fire as it rose. And for a moment she regretted it all, the rapidly approaching departure and responsibility—the brief hesitation flowed up with the embers to oblivion, as she watched Ron nodding and smiling at Reverend Duane's words.

They'd decided not to have a last supper together; the finality and symbolism of such an event was too much for them. Kim, Rex, and Terri helped shovel dirt back onto the smoldering embers. She watered the new soil, tamped it with her bare feet as Terri joined her. They marched in the mud like pagans in an Autumn ritual, finding themselves alone and hugging. By then the moon was high and the wine was gone. "I'm really going to miss you, Gracie," Terri said, face-to-face. Emotionally and physically exhausted, they passed out on the carpet in the living room wrapped in movers' blankets.

The next morning Grace woke the children up to bathe them in preparation for the long journey. They had five hundred miles to cover in the first leg.

Once again, Amber came to mind, as did Paul. She shunned the memories as she lathered Mimi and Ben's hair. Amber was Dad's problem, for now, she reminded herself. Paul was finding himself.

When the kids were tucked into the backseat she did a final walk through. The house was as vacant as the day they arrived five years ago. She'd been so frightened and uncertain after Victor. Grace stood gazing out the kitchen window watching their garden shimmer in the early morning breeze. Ron came up behind her and put his arms around her waist. He kissed her neck. "It's getting late," he whispered. She wanted to remember his hot breath. She pivoted, held him and closed her eyes. She wanted to remember the color of the walls, the hum of the refrigerator, the longing that brought them to this point of departure. She wanted to remember what made them a family.

# 18

As Grace fell asleep in the passenger seat, heading up Highway 5, Amber was one hundred and thirty miles South, in Old Town, San Diego. She was living with Grandma D in a senior apartment complex across from Immaculate Conception Catholic Church.

The bathroom was her ad hoc office. Grandma D left her alone when she closed and locked the door. *What happened?* she thought, plucking her eyebrows down to a thin line. She hated that Steve and Paul picked her up again, hated that she needed them to. Herbie crossed the line when he made her work the day after the abortion. Paul's face, when he saw her, teetered between disgust and pity. She hated that she needed her family, but told herself they owed her.

She'd changed. The glaring 100-watt bulbs Grandma D kept in the bathroom showed the slightest detail of her face. Marie wouldn't recognize her, which delighted her, and under the interrogative light, she barely recognized herself. Her naked thighs were thin and grey, blue veins streaked her translucent skin. No trace of the baby fat that once made her seem childish and cute. She had a stud in her nose, her hair was cut short and mod. She wore thick eye shadow, and her nails were done up the color of peas. She kept a bag of her clothes in a corner of the hall closet.

Grandma D was sharper than she looked. With her crooked wig and false teeth, she played the part of the tottering senior to the tee. But Grandma D had taken her in, taken her to church—introduced her with pride. "You didn't have a chance living with Marie," she often told her. Grandma D and Mom were not on speaking terms. It was beyond animosity. They hadn't spoken since the divorce over fifteen years ago. Grandma D compensated by sewing Amber outfits from the J.C. Penney catalog. The preteen style, with its puffy short sleeves and buttons all the way to the neck. Grandma saw what she wanted to see. Amber could see why Marie ran away.

Amber sat on the toilet and picked a scab on her chin. Her stub of a big toe ached from her shift the previous night. She needed to get a move on if she was going to make her first set. Ramon, her handler, would have something to say if her manager complained. Grandma D thought she worked at Taco Bell down on Taylor Street. The transition between the two disparate worlds was exhausting. Amber kept a trash bag with her work clothes in the bushes near the church. The parking lot was quiet between services, only tourists streaming between Juan and Calhoun Streets could see her ducking behind the hedge.

Amber snickered as she dabbed the open sore. Marisol, her new best friend, was the quintessential Catholic virgin. Grandma D encouraged their friendship. Marisol, a raven beauty, who looked like a J.C. Penney junior model, the daughter of respected parishioners... moonlighted as a stripper. Amber put on a trainer bra and a g string. She leaned in close to the mirror to apply eyeliner. They'd met in the rectory after the noon mass. While Grandma D chatted up her parents under the soft glow of the rectory chandeliers, Marisol invited her to a party at a nearby motel. A dark secret bonded them like no previous friendship. Dabbing her chin with a square of toilet paper, Amber wondered what attracted Marisol to her. She was just as fooled as anyone;

264

Marisol, with her pixie smile and Buster Brown shoes, brought in sixty bucks a night at Les Girls.

At the party that night, Amber met Ramon. It was the most meth she'd ever seen. It was a seedy crowd, but strangely, she felt like she belonged. Amber stayed long after Marisol left for her shift at the club.

Amber was hooked. Ramon got her a job dancing at Les Girls. She performed at private parties set up by Ramon. Mostly, she had sex and did drugs. She bragged that she was a "working girl", that she made money, and supported herself.

She was Ramon's little "Chiquitita". She'd found a home in San Diego's underbelly. She had as many friends among the prostitutes, strippers, and junkies on Sports Arena Boulevard as she'd ever had in Venice or Clairemont combined. Ramon was generous as long as she put out.

Amber walked into the tiny living room sporting Grandma's newest creation, pink polyester bellbottoms and vest with matching bow tie and pink sandals. Grandma looked up from her sewing. Lawrence Welk filled the room with his baritone.

"I'm going to Marisol's, Grandma," Amber announced as she bent and kissed Grandma D. She wiped a smudge of lipstick off Grandma D's forehead.

"That's nice, dear," Grandma D said, smiling at the screen.

Down the steps, crossing the street, Amber nearly got hit by a sight-seeing bus. Asian tourists stared at her through the tinted glass as she knelt and fished through the hedge. Barely concealed in broad daylight, she changed into a leather skirt, tube top, and platforms before stowing her Grandma D clothes in the garbage bag. She stepped back onto the sidewalk and headed down Juan Street. Past Bazaar Del Mundo, the sounds of a Mariachi Band and the hoots and howls of Tequila-pickled tourists sparked her steps. Amber turned onto Taylor Street, off to the first real job she'd ever worked.

Amber enjoyed being a stripper. The attention was intoxicating. She'd lost weight and at five feet tall she looked underage, a quality that made her an instant draw on stage. All the other strippers treated her like a little sister. Dancing kept her toned, something she'd never been. Ramon worked for the club, providing a steady stream of girls and meth for management and patrons. She knew she wasn't his only girlfriend, but she loved him.

As Amber crossed the parking lot she saw Ramon in his car, behind the wheel, with a cute new girl in the passenger seat. They were talking in low tones. The girl was crying softly, Amber noticed, as she walked closer. "You're too young, baby," Ramon said. His tone was gentle, apologetic. "This ID is crap." He waved the ID in her face. "Get a better one and we'll see."

Amber cleared her throat and they both turned. Ramon had a murderous expression. She'd caught him off guard. His face flipped when he saw it was Amber. "Hey, baby! Crystal's a no-show. Go get dressed. I'll be right in."

Amber waved to the girl in the passenger seat, but she was inconsolable. Inside the club, her eyes strained to adjust to the nocturnal world. The bar held a few patrons, and the twenty round tables scattered across the main floor were sparsely occupied. Ten or so regulars lined the stages, the same evenly spaced retirees, who never tired of the smell of sweat, cheap perfume and meted flesh.  Amber walked past the bar to the lockers. Cody her favorite bouncer was working, she saw from the schedule on the wall. It took minutes to strip and slip into a bikini. She took a few steps in front of the full-length mirror next to the time clock. She punched in and headed for the stage.

The three stages were flat cylinders, four and a half feet off the ground with bar stools surrounding all sides. Amber strutted to the middle stage as Ray, the bartender and part-time MC, announced her. "Straight from Hollywood, California, barely legal, Amber..."

Like flipping a switch all eyes were on her and Amber became a different person. No drugs or human touch gave her the sensation she felt dancing above men who wanted her more than their own families. The look in their bloated faces, the bulges, the lust they sprayed on her as she taunted and teased from one edge to the next, always moving, eye contact for the hand that held the largest sum. She liked that Cody was there, standing by the door. Amber squatted in front of a crusty surfer with a silver mop of hair and gyrated her crotch in his face. Just as his free hand slid up her ankle she launched to the next patron, snatching the fluttering green bills as she went. After working the rim of the stage, she danced to the pole in the center to start her show. She'd learned it from Crystal: treat the pole like the biggest cock you've ever seen, want it like a million dollars, and whatever you do, don't forget to get the money before you leave the stage. She taught Amber the struts, the kicks, the stretches, the twists, but Amber knew it was her dancing that made them pay. Ray played her favorites, the Scorpions, AC/DC, Def Leppard, and White Snake. Halfway through her set, she'd already collected fifty dollars, mostly from a group of businessmen, who were drunk when they came in. One of them resembled Marisol's father, a local accountant. Amber was relieved when her first shift ended. The club heated up for her last two sets. Ray left a few lines on a mirror for her behind the bar.

It was a typical night. She was excited to have enough cash for the shopping spree she and Marisol planned in Fashion Valley the following day. Ramon was waiting for her by the time clock when her set ended. It was as steamy as an armpit in the back room. They closed the windows after the sun went down, rendering it stale and humid. Amber's limbs ached but the promise of a party quickened her steps.

Ramon led her to a windowless room backstage, topless and with nothing on but a g-string. He laid out lines of meth and she was so high on adrenaline and speed, that she blew him without being asked, such was their routine. He asked her to spend the night with him at the motel. In the two months she'd known him, it was a first. She was honored that he chose her. Yet, she declined.

Amber felt loyal to Grandma D. She promised herself that she wouldn't sleep away from the apartment, as a sign of respect.

But the stress of maintaining two lifestyles was too much. With her job and Ramon, she didn't need Grandma D. She had a locker at the club. The groundskeeper at Immaculate Conception threw away her stash of clothes. The topography of her life was sliding toward Sports Arena Boulevard and Les Girls.

Within a few days, Ramon's invitation morphed into a demand. The first night she spent at the motel, she didn't leave the room for three days and nights. It was the most meth she'd ever done. At one point she lay in the tub with the shower flowing over her, her brittle hair in her hands and her heart thrumming. It was an attempt to come out of the downward spiral; what got into her she couldn't say, except that they'd done so much meth, she couldn't imagine going out in the light of day. Toward the end she saw spiders on the wall and stopped trying to remember the names of the men Ramon tramped in and out, to be with her. Ramon dropped her off in front of the apartment on Juan Street, disoriented, willing tears to cleanse her crusty red eyes. She crept in the door, greeting Grandma D with a contrite smile. She collapsed on the couch and watched Lawrence Welk do a soft shoe with a milky blonde girl. Sleep deprived, yet unable to slumber, she stared at the lilting German with the conductor's stick, drained by the juxtaposition with lurid visions cycling through her mind. "You're getting too skinny," Grandma said, with her inflected Canadian accent. "Let me make you something to eat...maybe some toast."

"No thank you," Amber croaked, staring absently at the TV.

A night's sleep and a few meals later the full weight of her lifestyle sank in. "She's the only one in my family who really cares about me," she'd told Marisol. "I can't abandon her."

Grandma D never raised her voice. To her, Amber was a victim of Marie. She was her "precious" granddaughter. "Amber will find her way," Grandma D always said.

Early one Summer evening Amber set off on foot toward Taylor Street. Grandma D had just brought in the waistline on her favorite skirt for the fourth time and she liked the way it flowed about her knees. It was warm enough that she'd left her sweater on the back of one of Grandma's dinette chairs. Bare shouldered and feeling better than she had in weeks, she made her way up Taylor Street toward Rosecrans. It was her first shift after a few days off. She'd gone to the movies with Marisol, shopped in Fashion Valley, all sober, at Marisol's insistence. As she passed a shop window she smiled at herself, appreciating how young and thin she looked. Something in the image made her pause and take notice. Her teeth. Amber ambled to the wide window display as the wind of passing cars on Taylor Street made her skirt swirl. She bared her teeth at her reflection, instantly taken aback by how yellow and stained they'd become. She rubbed them with her index finger but couldn't produce enough saliva to spit. She ran her fingertips over her jaw and cheekbones, acutely aware of the angles they made. *I look like a movie star*, she thought. She jumped back when the reflection faded, and beyond the glass a woman in sweats and a Padres t-shirt vacuumed. The old woman looked up and smiled at her. Amber pretended not to see her. She stooped to adjust the sandal on her missing big toe. It hurt most of the time now, being a dancer. Amber continued on to Les Girls looking forward to seeing Ramon. As she walked across the parking lot, she noticed Ramon's car by the front door. He preferred to park in the back, so Amber thought that was strange. She hoped Cody was working tonight as she walked in the front door. She smiled at Pete the bouncer and strutted backstage looking for Ramon. She wanted to get high before her set. The dancer on stage, Candy, gave her a cute wave, putting her foot behind her ear. The crowd was small for a Thursday night—she recognized a few regulars at the bar.

Backstage, the locker area was vacant, and the office door was closed. Amber was immediately on guard. She recognized Ramon's voice, its high pitch signaled danger. The manager's tone was equally charged.

"You've been fucking cheating me for the last year, you fucking punk!"

"I bring you girls and dope. That's the arrangement!"

"Your girls are all dope heads. They're ragged. You need to cut back on the shit!"

"Don't tell me how to run my business! I knew your father. His father knew mine. We built this fucking business!"

Amber stepped behind a stack of kegs. The hallway reeked of stale beer and Ben Gay. She wasn't going to get her lines. She pulled her hair back into a ponytail, the way Ramon liked it. She tiptoed to the bathroom across the narrow hallway. She was closing the door when the office door flew open.

"Get the fuck out of here and don't come back!" the manager yelled at Ramon, who stomped toward the stage.

Ramon didn't even notice her standing there. She was going to call his name when the manager spotted her.

"And take that bag of bones with you," he yelled. Amber cowered into the bathroom as the manager rushed forward. He grabbed Amber by the shoulder and pushed her after Ramon. Amber could feel her heartbeat throb in her collarbones. Her jaw twitched uncontrollably as she tore from the manager's grasp, speeding after Ramon as fast as her sandaled feet could carry her.

Outside in the greying twilight Amber caught up with Ramon at his car. "Get in!" he commanded.

Amber got in the passenger seat shaking. Ramon peeled out in reverse, nearly hitting a man in a cowboy hat and a lime green leisure suit. As they left the parking lot he reached under the seat, produced a pistol and put five shots into the Les Girls marquee. They peeled down Hancock toward Sports Arena Boulevard. "Slow down," she begged. Ramon gave her a menacing stare. Amber tightened her lips. She knew where they were going. She gripped the door handle. Her legs tensed as they screamed down Pacific Coast Highway. Ramon ran a stop light and in a fit of paranoia whipped the car over the curb, onto the dirt and shadows of the I-8 underpass. The engine ticked away the silence. Amber held her breath, hoping her stillness would calm him. Ramon stared out the windshield with his fingertips dug into the steering wheel. The settling dust revealed the tagged concrete underbelly—

an ersatz sunset for angry youth. Amber searched her periphery for an out, unable to turn her head for fear of becoming a target of his rage. She raised her hand to open the door, her eyes on the embankment. She jerked her hand back when Ramon threw his pistol out her window, and peeled back onto Pacific Coast Highway.

# 19

They rented a house near the University of Rochester. It was an American Foursquare built in 1923, but what attracted them the most were the sunflowers growing in the front yard garden, in contrast to their neighbors who had plush lawns and meticulously kept hedges. With a three-year-old and a four-year-old, and plenty of foot traffic surrounding the University, Ron put in an extra deadbolt on the front door. They were happy for the garage in back, where most of their unpacked boxes were temporarily stored. They spent the first weekend driving around Rochester, Mimi and Ben pointing at all the sights—colorful trees, pampered Victorians, and large brick monuments—while Ron and Grace were locating grocery and hardware stores, the library and the post office. They also explored churches in the area, but saw only historic and conservative edifices. They missed the little community that Reverend Duane had created. He had recommended they contact a former member of the New Christian Apostles Church, who'd moved to Rochester a few years ago.

The Monday after they arrived Grace called Jeff, the former member. They'd missed church five Sundays in a row, and there was an empty feeling as they ate breakfast. She called him after

Ron had gone to work, and she had set the kids down on the rug in the front room for *Sesame Street*.

"Yes, I remember Duane. He was different in those days. Does he still have his ponytail?"

Grace laughed at the image of Reverend Duane with a ponytail.

"We don't have a New Christian Apostles here. Most of the churches are well established, but I am a member of a community that embraced me when I arrived from California. We have Wednesday Bible Study and the band practices on Fridays. Duane tells me your husband is a musician."

"He is. I also taught Sunday school."

From there, it was a simple, fluid transition into their new spiritual community. They became fast friends with Jeff, his wife Carol and their two teenage children, Simon and Megan. Their daughter babysat for them, and the kids loved the Johnsons.

The Marcoses fell into a steady routine of service at church, Ron's work, home schooling and setting up their little home. Rochester was the opposite of Venice: all four seasons, family and academia. Grace thought of getting her teaching credential. She strolled through town, thrift store shopping, pushing along Ben, and answering Mimi's myriad questions. Mimi was ready for school. Grace went to the public school down the street to register her for kindergarten. When she contacted the local school district for ideas on how to prepare Mimi for kindergarten, she found them rude and dismissive. She decided to homeschool Mimi, and then Ben, rather than placing them in a system she didn't trust. Each night when Ron came home from work he'd tell her of all the new skills he was learning.

#####

Within the next few years, as the kids became increasingly independent, Grace dreamed of her own career. She felt confident that she could walk into any classroom and teach. Yet, she wasn't quite ready to go back to school. The kids still needed her. Mimi was a confidant overachiever. Ben, extremely precocious for his age, was already reading. Mimi was in ballet, and Ben had begun piano lessons. When Ron came home from work, they'd sit in the front room, with the kids snoring softly in the other room. It was Grace's favorite time of the day—the quiet wordless stretches, her creating lessons, he practicing guitar for Sunday service. She felt like they'd hit their stride as a family and could go years doing exactly what they were doing; if only Mimi and Ben could stay as they were, impressionable and innocent, and Ron continued to thrive at work, as she rose victoriously out of her former self.

Thursday evening, the kids were in bed and she'd just opened *A Road Less Traveled*, an inspiring book recommended to her by a visiting pastor. Ron was at band practice, and the purring refrigerator lulled her. The phone rang. It was Carol. She'd just seen her the previous night at Bible study, and it was disturbing because Grace knew her to be an early sleeper.

"Carol. Is everything okay?"

Carol was distraught and barely intelligible.

"What do you mean he's dead? What happened? Do you want me to come over?"

Grace slid her feet off the couch, clutching the phone.

"Okay. I'll come by with the kids in the morning. If you need anything, anything at all, call me."

Off the phone, Grace stood up, her hands covering her mouth. She wanted to do something, but Carol refused her offer to come over.

When Ron came home he found her on the couch clutching the book, staring at the ceiling.

"What's wrong?" he asked.

"Simon is dead. He borrowed Carol's car this afternoon and she hadn't heard from him all day. He ran a red light and the car was totaled."

Grace went into the kitchen not wanting to wake Mimi and Ben. Ron followed her. Grace stood with her back to the sink staring at Ron. "What should we do? Do you think Reverend Pam knows?"

Ron sat at the table. He put his hands together. "Let's pray for them."

Grace came to the table and took Ron's hand. She moved her chair closer. His hand was warm and calloused from the work he'd done in the yard. She closed her eyes but all she could think about was Carol, Jeff and their only remaining child, Megan. "Heavenly father..."

After praying Grace got up and put a kettle on for tea. Ron watched her. It was time to come together as a community. They called Reverend Pam, and a service was laid out for the following day, including a list of duties and assignments to support Carol, Jeff and Megan. Grace set about making lasagna to bring in the morning.

Grace got up early, fixed breakfast for Ron, and got the kids ready for a long day away from the house. She packed a daypack with snacks, a change of clothes for both kids, homework and coloring pages. As she drove down past the University of Rochester Nursing building, Ben pointed out buildings he knew by name, and Mimi wrote in her journal. The drive across town took longer than usual; there was a short detour for construction, and by the time they arrived there were already cars parked in front of Carol's house. Grace unbuckled the kids, set them on the curb and grabbed the lasagna off the seat. The front door was ajar. Through the foyer, the house was quiet, except for a low murmur from the living room. The detached banter of young children in the backyard wafted in from the open kitchen. Grace went into the kitchen and put the lasagna on the table with all the meals from other members of their community. She was pleased to see the trays of cookies, pans of brownies and casserole dishes, with enough food to cover meals for the family for at least a week.

Ben tried to get on a chair to see the table's contents—the smell of which filled the room, a mixture of baked pasta, tomato, sweet chocolate and buttery lemon. Mimi looked up at her mother, imploring, so Grace took two oatmeal cookies, gave one each to Ben and Mimi and sent them to the backyard to play. She was pleased to see Megan watching the young children outside. Her face seemed drawn and her eyes were ringed from lack of sleep. She waved weakly at Grace, avoiding eye contact as she turned her attention to Mimi and Ben.

Grace went to the living room to find Carol. She was anchored on the couch, distraught and absent. Grace went straight to her side. The other women in the room were a collection of the old church ilk, mostly in their forties, perfectly coiffed. Grace always felt isolated from this older type, which made her connection with Carol—who was also young and from California —that much stronger. Grace hugged Carol, holding her head on her shoulder until Carol began to sob softly into her neck. There was a teapot on the coffee table with a plate of lemon bars, and five envelopes—sympathy cards—and a box of tissues.

"I didn't get to say goodbye. What am I going to do?" Carol looked from face to face. The ladies shifted and nodded, and touched her arm with their fingertips as if they could draw the pain out of her by the slight contact. Grace took her hand. The mother of the other children playing in the backyard sat on the other side of Carol. Together, she and Grace took turns holding Carol. After a moment one of the elderly, kind women suggested they eat something. Grace thought it was a good idea. She'd only been there a short time, but she'd forgotten to eat, in their rush out the door.

After lunch Grace stayed behind when all the other ladies left. Carol and she sat on the back patio in wicker chairs while a robin mined for worms on the small patch of grass next to the swing set. An old Cottonwood tree dominated the far half of the yard. A tire swing hung from its lowest bough, vacant and wistful. Megan excused herself and went to her room. They watched Ben and Mimi take turns swinging and pushing one another. "Megan and Simon used to play like that," Carol offered. Grace was relieved that she was starting to open up. It was one of the few things she'd said all day, and Grace had begun to worry. "Grace, what am I going to do? It's always been about the kids. Simon was going to go to college next year. Megan is all I have now."

Grace turned her chair to face Carol. How would she feel if she lost Mimi or Ben?

"You're a good mother, Carol. You have Megan, and Jeff needs you. You're not alone. You've got a whole community to help you through this." Grace patted her knee. Carol leaned forward and buried her face in Grace's heavy breasts. Grace relaxed into the creaky wicker. Carol wept until Mimi and Ben came to them, hungry again. After feeding the kids, Grace did the dishes while Carol sat at the kitchen table baring her soul. They'd never talked this way, Grace thought, and felt profoundly at ease.

Carol broke the connection, going to the bathroom. When she returned she sat pensively at the table. Grace could see she had something to say. The kids at the table grew quiet as well. Carol broke the silence with words that would change Grace's life forever.

"I wish I'd had another child," she said in a calm, emotionless voice.

Grace paused, hands clutching a dish and dripping. "Why?"

"When you have three, if you lose one, at least you still have two. Now we only have Megan and she's going to be all alone."

Grace nodded. The words stuck. She proceeded to sweep the floor in silence, guiding the broom around Mimi and Ben's swinging feet. On the way home, passing the detour once again, and later as she put Mimi and Ben down for a nap, Carol's words kept circulating through her head. *I wish I'd had another child.*

That night, she and Ron lay together in bed. Ben and Mimi snored softly in the other room, and the house ticked and popped as old houses do when the temperature drops. Grace imagined what it would be like to bring another child into their family. How would Mimi and Ben react? Ron worked so hard. Would he welcome another child? Ron lay on his side. He was already fast asleep. She spooned him, thinking of how she would tell him that she wanted another child.

#####

Their friends said she was crazy. Not to her face, but casual conversations often trailed into an unremitting silence as she offered unsolicited updates on the new adoption. She was in her mid-thirties and her family was humming along on a smooth track. Ron didn't exactly say no. It wasn't a fight, they didn't fight, but it was the first time Ron did not exactly say yes. He withdrew, perplexed, working an incalculable equation it seemed as he took on additional hours at work. *She* wanted another child. He only wanted her. Another child meant less for Ron. She understood. It came to her in the Pediatrist office, in a room filled with nervous mothers and fortunate children. She had to take care of Ron too. She would be the complete wife: caring for the children, doting on her husband, a traditional arrangement—one that she'd balked at with respect to her sixties sensibilities. It was *her* tribe. She devised a plan by the time she reached home.

Grace began to approach each new day with intention. She'd wait by the stove when he walked in with his work uniform neatly ironed, and she'd set his coffee down, a spoon, cream, and sugar in a neat line. She'd kiss his freshly shaven cheek. Not to entice, but to engage: brief massages, a pat, a compliment. When he returned home, she gave him jobs to do around the house. He liked to be busy, to know that he was appreciated. Who didn't?

After a week of this, him coming in with paint speckled hair, or rust dust on his cheeks from the plumbing, dirt caked nails from building flower beds, she bathed him in love and attention. In bed, when Mimi and Ben were tucked in, they talked about the plan they'd made in Venice. He declared that it was not up to him, but

"God's will" for them to bring another child into their home. "It'll be easier this time," he said.

The next day she went to the Rochester Office of Child and Family Services. Grace hoped it was just a matter of sending their paperwork from California to New York, but her hope was dashed after a long wait in a cramped, overused room. A kindly woman with a retro-bouffant handed her a stack of forms and a battered clipboard. She went back to the waiting room fooling herself that she had the stamina to complete the task in one sitting. Three pages in, she packed up and swung by Carol's to pick up Mimi and Ben. It would take her three days to turn in the paperwork. It would have taken her a month, she thought, if it had been her first time.

The second time the agency lost their paperwork she demanded a meeting with a Case Manager, paperwork or not. Chelsea was young and spry, with a freshly minted MFS framed over her desk. She explained that she already had a full caseload, but would submit Grace's paperwork personally, seeing that they'd already been through the process, and cleared in another state. Grace resisted the impulse to fix Chelsea's collar the entire meeting. She went home encouraged now that she had an ally in the system.

It took two months to meet the first child. A long line of children, whose files and faces were much too full, too many horror stories, damage that could never be resolved by anything other than a constant infusion of love. She realized how lucky she'd been with Mimi and Ben. A kernel of doubt appeared, whether she had the requisite love to raise a child with so many challenges. She returned home and hugged Mimi and Ben, so grateful.

#####

The trial was on every local news network, a constant barrage of horrific details. The three boys, ages eight months to three years, had been beaten, raped, tortured and abandoned in a motel room. It was the case of the century in Rochester, Grace was enthralled by it. She kept up with the trial after she put Mimi and Ben down for the night. Ron sat quietly in his chair, with his manuals, shaking his head. When the sentence was read on the last day, she watched their father erupt in court and declare that he would kill anyone who took his boys.

The introductory meeting in their front room seemed truly ordained. The boys were so sedate she thought they must be drugged. Later, she realized they were still in shock. Grace started calling them "my boys" after they left. When they rose to leave the youngest reached for her, not yet able to walk, and the other two clung to her skirt. She had no doubt and neither did Ron. The case manager wanted her to know every detail of the boys' past prior to signing the papers. There was near certainty that the youngest had a cognitive disability as a result of the abuse.

Within a month of that first meeting, the boys were dropped off and from that moment forward, they were a family: mother, father, four brothers and a sister. John, Thomas, and Michael all wore cloth diapers. The church donated a dryer, because it was the dead of winter and the boys were going through diapers so fast, the clothesline in the basement couldn't dry them quickly enough. Mimi had the hardest time of it, being the only girl. "You will always be my special girl," Grace soothed her, as she tucked her in that first night.

The house was instantly transformed. While Ben and Mimi were active children, the boys had been pent up. Where Mimi and Ben had seethed, the boys exploded. They escaped to their rooms initially, surrendering the rest of the house to the boys. Grace watched her first two avoid the living room when the boys were present. They were polite, she saw, and at night Ron assured her that they'd come together at some point. "It is, after all, God's will."

Within a few weeks Mimi started to carry Michael when they went out, and in those moments Grace saw reflections of herself as a girl again, in Magnolia. Ben didn't play the way the boys did. He was measured and introspective.

One day, the distance between Ben and the boys closed. Ben sat at the piano going through his daily routine. He was preparing for an upcoming recital. While he played Bach's Well-Tempered Clavier #2, the boys rushed in at the opening bars. Grace watched from the doorway as they began to dance around the room. Ben's tight jaw began to soften as he sensed the joy behind him. He finished with a florid adaptation, something he'd never do alone. He spilled from the piano bench and they all tumbled in a pile on the floor. Ben piled on top, the big brother at last. Grace lingered on the piano bench resisting the impulse to pull them apart. That night in bed, she cried when she told Ron what she'd witnessed.

The trial was still in the sentencing phase. Grace kept the boys inside the first week. The surrounding neighborhood was in transition. The homicide rate in Rochester was in the top three in the nation. Gunshots were a common backdrop. Grace heard a siren after breakfast. She looked out the living room window and was shocked to see a gathering of police cruisers in front of their house. She thought it was the neighbor across the street again. She was surprised when Chelsea, the case manager called. "Are the boys okay? I saw your house on Channel 8!" Grace took frantic stock of the boys. John and Thomas wrestled on the couch. Michael was in his baby carrier on the table. Grace peeked through the curtain. There were flashing lights up and down the block now, and a small phalanx of uniforms gathered by the stoop. "They're all fine."

"Well...there's been a shooting. The whole block is taped off," Chelsea said.

Grace looked up the street. Several squad cars pulled away, while a news cameraman trailed a reporter on the way back to an emblazoned van. A yellow police tape fluttered on their mailbox. She glanced back at the boys on the floor now, stacking blocks and knocking them down. Their home was so peaceful compared to the activity on the street.

Chelsea groaned. "I thought it was their father who'd come for you."

"Isn't he in prison?" Grace asked.

"He's down at County waiting to be transferred. I'm calling Channel 8. They risked your lives...putting your house on the news. Stupid!"

Grace hung up and stared at the lingering assembly outside. The trial had come to them. Her heart beat loudly in her chest. She took a deep breath, took Michael out of his baby carrier and sat on the couch. He gurgled, blowing bubbles out of his mouth, his broad smile lighting up her face. She let him play with the ends of her hair, as it dawned on her that their life in Rochester was lost. They'd done everything right. The boys hadn't been outside once since they'd arrived. She couldn't keep them locked in indefinitely. *They* weren't homicidal.

Grace instructed the boys to play in the pantry. She put Michael's baby carrier on the kitchen table. Mimi and Ben came in from their rooms. They stood in the doorway, scared, shoulder-to-shoulder. It was clear to Grace that they had to flee. When Ron came home that night they agreed to get a realtor and start looking for a new home.

# 20

The Best Rest Motel was walking distance to Grandma D's apartment in Old Town. It overlooked I-5, just off Pacific Coast Highway. At first Amber liked to sit in the window behind the stale stiff curtain watching the cars whizz by, breathing the exhaust, and watching the meandering clouds over the Pacific. About noon, she'd walk to Grandma D's, share a snack and TV, and return to the motel for the sunset. There wasn't much else to do. She'd smoke by the ice machine when housekeeping came to clean the room, hoping for a chance encounter. A little after rush hour Ramon picked her up for work. She'd be ready, dressed to kill. He brought her to "private parties" to entertain. After their infamous exit from Les Girls, that was the only work she could get.

Ramon started rationing her drugs after that night. "You too skinny. You a skinny old woman," he'd say, although she was barely twenty-one. He showed up with cheese pizza, always cheese pizza, and she began to wonder if he had a girl friend at Pizza Hut down the street.

He had other girls, she knew. "You don't love me, do you?" she asked when he'd bring a new girl around to the room to party.

He just shook his head and smiled, which made her want to slit her wrists.

One day, on one of her visits, Grandma D didn't answer the door. Her hearing had never been good. Amber leaned against the wall in the hallway, dozing over a *People* magazine she'd found in the lobby. When Grandma D finally opened the door, she barely recognized her. Amber no longer resembled the little girl she loved. Grandma D was on her way out, didn't offer Amber anything to eat, closed the door behind her, and shuffled off to her friend Agnes's on the first floor. Amber shrugged it off, but she ached inside for Grandma's reassuring smile.

Back at the motel room, Amber thumbed through the Yellow Pages phone book. She wanted to call Pizza Hut to see who worked there. Instead, her eye fell on an ad for a Chat Line. She'd seen infomercials on late-night TV. She sat in her chair by the window and called the number.

That first call was an unexpected pleasure. She was desperate for a connection. Any connection. To her delight, she connected with a friendly stranger named Max. They spent the afternoon chatting as if they'd known each other for years. He warned her of the crazies she would meet. She felt like she was cheating, but she was also liberated by this new line of human contact. How empowering to be sought, to have an admirer at your fingertips, day or night. She was so engrossed in the interminable banter that she didn't notice Ramon enter the apartment. Max said he wanted to talk again and they made a phone date. Ramon could see the change, and when she turned down her nightly lines, he squinted at her, sensing a fissure starting to form. The next day Amber went to the thrift boutique in Old Town and bought herself a "new" old dress.

From that point forward, when Ramon left in the morning or didn't come home at all, she began a new morning routine. She got up early, got dressed, cleaned the apartment, and walked to 7-Eleven for snacks and a liter of Pepsi. The rest of the day she napped, and talked with complete strangers, telling her life story, embellishing as she pleased. Amber enjoyed flirting with the men, most of whom were married and interested in younger women. It was the highlight of her day. Ramon became suspicious and surly at her newfound confidence.

Her addiction to meth was a separate issue. After the sun went down, her body craved it. She couldn't turn it off. Ramon had plenty of work for her. He put an advertisement in the back of *The Reader* under the heading PRIVATE PARTY. It drew a broad clientele of lonely businessmen, cheating husbands and sexual deviants. She made as much as she did at Les Girls, but spent it all on meth, which he supplied. It was impossible to deny the toll it took on her body and soul. Meth invaded her new routine. She snorted a few lines within minutes of waking, stumbled outside for a quick smoke, cleaned up, and got on the chat line. The routine lasted for a month.

Amber knew she had a drug problem, and that it was affecting her health. It showed most in her face. She was a floating skull with lips. She spent less time in the bathroom, to avoid seeing herself. Then one night Ramon made her sit in the back on the way to a party at the Holiday Inn. It was a first. That evening she stood on a balcony overlooking the twinkling San Diego skyline, Mission Bay, and the Sea World tower, lit up and jutting into the sky. The party took its usual course, on its way to the bedroom. Ramon had left with a new girl, and the clients huddled on the couch with a teenager named Tina. All she could think about was Ted, one of her callers, and an offer he'd made. "Why don't you move up here and let me take care of you?" She wasn't sure if he was playing her. He was a regular, and the connection seemed strong. He had a steady job at Boeing, and spent most of his time with his large family. Amber knew he was desperately lonely, but didn't trust him just yet. He lived near Seattle.

"It's too cold up there," she said, not sure how to respond. Now she wished she'd taken him seriously—encouraged him. Up to that point, she'd told him a sad tale of how she'd been abandoned by her family, and how she'd survived by cleaning houses and caring for her sick grandmother. It was all true to some extent, she thought, but when he repeated the offer she felt a need to come clean. The need pulled at her like a tide going out, she felt she owed him for the kindness he'd shown her.

The next morning, Ramon returned to the hotel room to find her finishing up the drugs he'd left on the table. She was alone while the clients and the teenager were snoring in the bedroom. He just shook his head, a look of disgust on his face.

In the following week she tried to cut back on the meth but found it nearly impossible when she started putting on weight. Ted did call her back. She resigned herself to set things right this time. She tested him to see how far he would go. "I really like you but you might not like me so much when I tell you what happened to me when I was little."

"I would like you no matter what happened. You know that."

Amber paused until the phone was hot against her cheek. "Are you still there?" he asked.

"Yeah. I just don't know if you're ready to hear this."

She sensed his impatience. His offer was still fresh in her mind. She had nothing to lose. "I was molested. My Mom's boyfriend started molesting me when I was seven."

"My God, what did your mother do?"

"She said I was lying. Largo and I had sex until I was thirteen."

Amber paused. She could hear Ted on the other end. He was huffing into the phone now, and she could imagine his chest puffing out.

"That's rape, Amber. Not sex. He raped you. Asshole."

Amber heard a series of thuds, like a sack of dirt being beaten with a bat. Amber imagined him punching his couch cushion, in a nice apartment, with a nice colored TV and a dining set. It delighted her that he cared so much.

"I guess so," she whispered.

They finished the conversation that night promising to be there for one another. He was her "knight in shining armor".

The next time they spoke she told him about Ramon. She was afraid to tell him that she was a meth addict. When he told her he smoked the occasional joint, she saw an opening. "I have something else to tell you. I'm trying to quit crystal meth." She waited for Ted to respond but the line seemed to have gone dead.

When he finally came back his voice had changed. It was lower and serious, and he sounded like he was about to cry. "Amber. Nobody's perfect. I'm sure not. I think you are an amazing person."

Another pause, only this time she sensed that they were flowing together. Amber twisted the cord around her finger waiting for it to come.

"I love you."

Amber jumped to her feet, swooning from lack of sleep or food. "I love you too," she yelled. She'd never heard the words, not from Charlie or Frankie, and certainly not from her family. "I love you," she said again, just to see how it played on her lips. To make sure he heard it. The words would never sound the same.

Then it happened. Her knight in shining armor leaped into her arms. He chose *her,* Amber Rentano.

Amber pressed the phone to her cheek. It hurt her cheekbone, but she didn't want to miss his very next words. "I'm going to come down there and get you. We should be together. There is nothing that can keep us apart. I can help you kick meth. I won't accept no. I have a truck. I'll take the week off. I'll be there tomorrow evening," he said.

Amber held her breath until he finished talking. She was dying, she knew now. She'd hid behind her pain, her anger, and her rejection her entire life. It had taken her to this bottom. When she heard her words "I will be here waiting" in the receiver she hardly recognized her own voice. It sounded at once foreign and familiar like a relative who'd called the wrong number.

When they hung up Amber went into the bathroom. San Diego was already falling away, taking her old life with it. She peeled off her clothes and ran a bath. She closed her eyes and fell asleep. She awoke underwater, sputtering and cursing herself for nearly ending the new life before it began. She toweled off and lay in the pajamas Grandma D had bought her for Christmas. If Ramon came by, she would lie and say she was sick. As she lay dozing on the bed, she thought of how Grandma D might miss her. The truth was, there was absolutely nothing keeping her in San Diego.

#####

Ted was exactly as she imagined him. He reminded her of a young John Goodman, strong, with a big heart. Her belongings fit in two boxes, which he strapped down with bungee cord in the bed of his Ford Ranger. They held hands as he sped up Highway 5 North, destination: Tacoma, Washington.

After La Jolla he settled in for the long haul, with both hands on the wheel and eyes on the white line. He wasn't in a hurry, but he was resigned to their new life together. He fancied himself courageous and chivalrous now; he'd taken the leap of commitment, and in Amber, sound asleep in the passenger seat, he'd found his broken angel. At San Clemente, he pulled into a Vista Point to check on her—she hadn't stirred in over an hour. He leaned in close, marveling at her frailty. Her chest rose and fell; satisfied, he set off again.

The trip was a jostling dream for Amber. She awoke at the motel in Corning, ate two French fries, otherwise slept the full length of California, the breadth of Oregon, and the base of Washington. In withdrawal, she was incapable of processing the immensity of the sudden change.

Amber slept the entire first week in Tacoma. Ted insisted she use his bed, although the couch was more comfortable. He brought her broth until her body craved solid food. When he went to work, the house—a three-bedroom shack on the main drag—she felt like an interloper. She called Ramon, as if hearing his familiar voice could ease the hunger of withdrawals. She hung up when he answered, went into the kitchen and ate three pudding cups.

Their first meal in Tacoma together was at a Denny's off Highway 5. She ordered white toast and he had the Chicken Fried Steak. She wore the old dress and sweater his mother and his sister donated. When she went to the ladies room halfway through the meal, she heard someone throwing up in the stall. She checked her makeup, and hitched up her skirt, wanting to show her thighs. She put a hand on the stall door but thought better than to interrupt someone else's misery with hers so close behind.

Over Sunday dinner at his parent's house, he met Ted's family. The ten brothers, sisters, cousins, and his parents all talked at once, with never a harsh word between them. The living room was a shrine: trophies, banners, photo albums, and portraits, dating back three generations. There was even a coat of arms over the fireplace.

"Are they always like this?" she asked in the backyard where they'd gone to smoke. The pines towered above them, dancing in a line as the wind promised a storm.

"We're very tight," he said, not sounding proud, just matter of fact.

All the women were in the kitchen when they returned. Amber dried the dishes while Ted's sister pressed her for her history. "My family has been in California for a hundred years," she said. "I have a big family." When they settled in the front room she felt like one of the family.

"She's nothing like your last girlfriend," his mother said.

The following week she cooked for Ted for the first time. It was her first roast. It was a dry and wrinkled wedge by the time she laid it in the center of the table. Ted just smiled. He'd cooked for himself since leaving home to work at Boeing. After doing the dishes they went out on the rickety porch as traffic streamed by on the busy street just beyond their lawn. Street lights glowed on the porch, green, red, yellow and back again. They smoked, inches apart as if they'd been together, an old couple waiting out their years. In the morning she made him bacon and eggs, and from that day forward he never cooked a single meal. They both gained considerable girth leading up to their special day.

#####

It was meant to be a humble affair. Ted's family, the Molesons, set up the entire wedding—from the arch to the ring girl. They had it covered. Amber was slowly getting used to her new skin. She muddled her way as a wife by watching her adopted family. The Grange Hall was Mr. Moleson's idea. It was a Moleson family tradition dating back to pioneer days. The decorations were a gift from Mrs. Moleson's sewing group. Flowers were handpicked or donated. Ted's niece was the flower girl, and his sister Melba was Amber's maid of honor. Mrs. Moleson let Amber wear her wedding dress. They were nearly the same size. The Moleson family grew in scope the week leading up to the wedding, relatives arriving from as far away as Boise, Idaho. The Marysville Molesons provided the catering.

On the day of the wedding, Amber got up early and made Ted pancakes. It was raining again and she wanted to spend the day in her robe and slippers. The coffee pot overflowed onto the floor. She beat the mix so briskly, it splattered everywhere. She needed a task to occupy her. The entire wedding was out of her hands. Ted walked in fresh from a shower and grabbed a beer. He never drank in the morning. It was a first. "We're getting married today!" he stammered as if the magnitude of it required an early start.

After cleaning up the breakfast dishes Amber sat on the toilet and smoked. Ted was in front of the closet mirror trimming his beard. The hum of rain muffled her senses like a hood. She could stay in the bathroom all day, a familiar cocoon. She could call the whole thing off. She felt like she'd bought tickets on a merry-go-round and picked the wrong horse, bouncing along on some beast of burden, the brass ring a taunting star in the sky. *You should be grateful*, she told herself. *He saved your life.*

Amber could hear Ted singing now. He never sang love songs, but today he tortured "Open Arms" by Journey. He stalled on a high note as Amber came out of the bathroom in a cold sweat. "What's wrong?" he asked.

"I think I just got my period," she said, rummaging through the bureau for a pair of panties.

Ted went into the kitchen for another beer. "At least you're not pregnant," he yelled.

Amber went to the wedding dress hanging by the window. It was beautiful enough, she thought, but she would have liked something less traditional, less white. No one was that clean.

Ted bellowed from the front room, "We better get going. My brother wants us in the hall early for photos."

Amber wanted to call Grace. Did she feel the same when she got married? She went to the bathroom and put on her makeup. *Grace doesn't want to talk to me*, she thought. *If she did, she'd be here.* Amber had invited her entire family to her wedding. Mom and Dad were the only ones to RSVP. Paul hadn't RSVP'd—she had a few choice words for him. Grace said they couldn't afford to fly out.

When she finished putting on her wedding dress she walked into the kitchen, all white and innocent, her owl glasses magnifying her hazel eyes. Ted was on his fourth beer. He froze by the refrigerator and cried tears of joy, a meaty paw over his mouth. She wrapped her arms around him. "Mr. and Mrs. Theodore Moleson," he whispered. Amber put his beer back in the refrigerator and helped him put on his coat.

"We have plenty of time," she said as they pulled out of the driveway.

The interior of the Grange Hall was like the bowels of a great ship, cavernous and sectioned with massive beams angling overhead. Voices of the early arrivers mingled, echoing off the whitewashed walls. Amber and Ted were greeted at the great doors and escorted to an anteroom next to the kitchen. "Don't you look beautiful," Mrs. Moleson exclaimed, holding Amber's face in her hands. Melba gave her a weak smile and slid behind Amber to fix her hair.

Ted had found a beer and was joking in the corner with the pastor. As he approached Melba dashed forward, escorting him back to the main room. "It's bad luck to see the bride," she said, squeezing his arm.

The noise in the hall filled the anteroom now. Someone was doing a sound check. Amber peeked through the doorway, wondering if Mom and Dad had arrived. She only recognized a few people from Ted's extended family. The ring bearer was playing tag near the wedding arch, a pink polyester canopy hung from the rafters.

Amber went to a window and lit a cigarette. She was surprisingly sedate. Mrs. Moleson stood nearby chatting with the pastor. The day was picking up steam. It didn't feel like her event. She was there to complete her commitment to Ted, for saving her, for offering her a new life. It completed her transformation. She loved him for what he'd done. The least she could do was to declare it to the world. The rain outside was letting up. From the open window, she heard a cackle from the back row of cars, near the boggy pasture bordering the Grange. A couple emerged from a row of cars, and suddenly she was reduced to a three-year-old in the midst of a whirlwind. Her wedding pumps were suddenly wheeling her across the hall to the entrance. In seconds, she was on the steps, face-to-face with her parents.

Mom and Dad Rentano took a step back as she rushed forward. Amber's mouth dropped open, searching their faces for recognition, shocked at finding raw fear. Finally, Mom broke the ice. "Amber?" Dad stepped forward and gave her a peck on the cheek. Mom squeezed her hand, holding her at a distance. Amber could smell liquor on her breath. She was leathery and must have put her lipstick on in the dark—she'd missed her mouth. Dad stepped away from Mom, a chagrined look on his face. "I'm proud of you, Amber. Where's the lucky guy?"

Amber led them into the hall, disoriented by their proximity. She'd held that they were mortal enemies, and now they arrived like an old married couple. If they got along so well, why the hell did they get a divorce? The table she reserved for them was near the bar. She wanted Mom's steps to be few, especially as the night stretched on. She watched Dad free Mom of her sweater. Amber was invisible again as he went to the bar for a beer and a glass of wine. Ted was mixing it up with his father and cousins near the back door; Amber waved him over and introduced him to Mom and Dad. Mom was so different, she thought. She actually looked happy. Dad was nearing sixty, all silver on top. Oregon and retirement had been good to him. Dad abruptly stood and shook Ted's hand, nearly upending his beer. Mom sat with her legs squeezed together, her nails looking fresh enough to smear.

"Pleased to meet you, Mr. and Mrs. Rentano," Ted said.

Mom and Dad exchanged faux scowls and laughed. "Divorced," they chorused.

Mrs. Moleson appeared next to Ted. "You must be Mr. and Mrs. Rentano," she said, casting an expectant glance at Ted. Mom had a dangling cigarette in her mouth, but stood up and hugged Mrs. Moleson. The cigarette poked Mrs. Moleson in the ear. Dad kissed Mrs. Moleson on the cheek, sending her off toward the front of the room with a head of steam. Ted followed her.

"They seem nice," Mom said, rolling her eyes. Dad had his arm across the back of her chair. There was a definite connection. The "what if" of them kept bouncing around in Amber's head. They chatted like old flames at a high school reunion. She stormed outside for another cigarette.

Mrs. Moleson found her in the parking lot sitting on the rear bumper of a Mercury station wagon. All of the light had gone out of Amber. She wanted the day to be done with so she could return to her safe little house, away from drama and her insidious past.

"Come on, dear," Mrs. Moleson said, guiding her to her feet, "It's time."

Years later, whenever anyone asked her about her wedding, Amber blanked on the vows. She could recall the parking lot, the motherly hand of Mrs. Moleson, the ruddy faces of Mom and Dad, the fleshy Nordic faces of the Molesons, that everyone had danced, and that they'd eaten leftovers for weeks. She remembered cutting the cake and stuffing a wedge in Ted's face, gaping mouth stretched to receive a Buick. She remembered when it turned from a Disney romp to a Grimm fairy tale.

After the vows, Amber blew up at the photographer for asking where the rest of her family was, and wouldn't let it rest until Ted promised to take her to Disneyland in Anaheim. Later, Ted came to her. "You better cut your Mom off...she just called my Mom an uptight bitch," he whispered. Amber went to them, pleading: there was no way she could predict the reaction these two volatile solids would create. The ozone around them had thickened impermeably. Dad got in an argument with one of Ted's Idaho uncles. Ted's family stopped going to the bar because Mom assailed anyone who passed by her. A few had already left, and the remaining fifty made a show of scooting their tables further and further toward the kitchen. She remembered escorting Mom and Dad to their car, a mixed bag of embarrassment and gratitude hanging from her neck.

On the way home, she stared out the windshield, exhausted. She hadn't drunk at the wedding but she wanted one now. She smoked in the car at 7-Eleven, while Ted got her a six-pack of Budweiser. The windshield wipers stuttered across the dry glass. She nearly put the car in gear as she reached over to silence them. When Ted got in, she snapped at him for keeping the car running. Her wedding day was the happiest day of her life, and she was pissed off. There had been no Paul. And worst of all, no Grace.

# 21

Amber settled into a plodding domesticity that would last until the final days of their marriage. After the wedding she kept in touch with Mom, by way of Mom's intermittent calls for cash. Mom was homeless now and Largo was long gone. The years went by in a miasma of accumulation and routine. They made large purchases: washer, dryer, TV, matching Harleys, a boat, and a growing collection of accessories, filling the garage. The stress of terminal debt was the theme of their union. They joined a motorcycle club and stopped attending the gather-ups when Amber had a fall out with a few lady bikers. Amber found herself alone most of the time, and at first welcomed the solitude as a way to reduce stress. Hours went by where the only voices she heard were her own, and the TV.

She'd always had an unrelenting inner voice. Back when Largo abused her, the voice was a current running through her. When she lived in the shed in Reseda, it eased her fears: *Grace will come back soon.* In the group home, it was a murmur, mollified by a steady stream of medication. In Venice and in San Diego it was appeased with doses of meth. But now, it *was* her. The absence of drugs or medication allowed Amber's taunting inner voice to go unchecked. The solitude became untenable, although she could never admit it. *You are broken...everyone hates you...*

On the outside, Amber floated through her day with curt responses and an ever-ready smile. But on the inside, the voice kept up a steady grating banter, an insatiable confidante that warped her sense of reality and self. A seemingly simple life was a constant battle between good and evil. Evil could flip good, and back again in the course of a conversation. Dear friends were banished for a few unconscious words. An unintentional snub was a capital offense.

The voice thrived in darkness and solitude and drove her to isolate. She blamed all of her erratic behavior—hypersensitivity, over-reaction, seeing threat where there was none—on her past. "You need therapy," her mother-in-law said, "I had therapy after my sixth child. I swear I would have killed one if I hadn't." She refused to speak to her mother-in-law for months after that.

Days glided into years. Ted came home from work and she made meals and kept the house clean. They both fell asleep in their recliners. Their banter flowed from a shallow bank. A standing dinner engagement with his parents every Sunday was the highlight of their week. Life was exactly as it should be, she thought: husband, home, family (his). But there was always that illusive, indefinable missing piece.

One day on her weekly shopping trip, Amber came across a battered calico in front of Ralph's grocery store. The local SPCA stacked cages with weepy eyed felines, heavy headed expressions that pricked her heart every shopping day. She'd passed the line of cages for the last few years, and on a whim, squatted to peer in at a mottled kitten. It was love at first sight. He rubbed his warm rough nose across her finger tips and purred so loudly she thought he must be sick. When she brought Reggie into the kitchen that first time Ted snubbed his nose at it. "I'm not cleaning the litter box," he said. *As if he would.* Reggie became the target of her affection, tapping within her a flow of love she never knew existed. It was the first being who accepted her unconditionally. Ted was jealous from day one, resenting that the master of the house had a tail.


On a typical weekday morning Amber settled into her recliner as she did every morning for the last thirteen years. Their wedding photo stared back at her from the end table. Ted had just left for work. The house smelled like bacon and fried eggs. The state of Ted's empty recliner was how she felt, used, sagging, replaceable. Her body could not bear children. "It was the abuse," she said, when people asked. It took her six years to realize the only thing she loved about him was that he was still there. She squinted at the photo of them, so young, her so thin, he, broad-shouldered, with a slight paunch. Amber listened for the roast she'd put in the oven that morning. The fat was just starting to pop. She lay back in the recliner and took her morning nap. Sally Jesse Raphael blared from their 28" TV. Sally's voice, commanding the room, made her feel safe.

Amber woke up to the sound of applause. The show was over, time to check on the roast. She peeled the tin foil back and spooned the liquid fat over the top to keep it moist. She'd learned the trick from her mother in law. *They're your real family.* Amber started to drop back into the recliner when she got the sudden urge to get online. She'd convinced Ted that she needed a computer to do their finances. The internet was rapidly becoming a safe escape. She went to the office and sat down. Her feet hit against one of the multitudes of boxes stuffed in every crevice, lining the walls and rendering the room useless, except for a claustrophobic square in front of the desk.

She glanced at the telephone message machine. Nothing. She picked up the mouse and clicked the America online icon. She waited...as the computer jingled—establishing a connection. She jiggled the mouse impatiently...*I hate this room, there's no light...*

looked back at the answering machine and grimaced. It was her birthday in two months. *Why doesn't she call me?*

Amber thought to call Grace, but instead, typed in Largo's name in large caps. There were too many Largos. She decided to do an image search. The image at the bottom of the page was a mugshot. She slammed the phone down. It felt like she'd been punched in the stomach. Her hand covered her mouth reflexively. "Shit, shit, shit..." Amber lurched to her feet and paced the tiny dark room. *What am I going to do...?*

She went to the kitchen and got herself a Diet Pepsi. The office pulled at her. Back at the computer, his face seemed to have grown.

"You Shithead! I can't believe no one has killed you yet." She took a long drink. "Do you have any idea what you did to me?"

Amber looked back toward the front door. The mailman would be there any moment. He liked to talk and would miss their daily conversation. *He* was a good listener. But on the screen was the man who changed her. *Now what?* Amber chugged the rest of her Pepsi and got the hiccups. Her stomach burned. Largo's shaded eyes stared back at her. She was certain he was able to see her, knew how he warped her. Amber's reflection hung over his, on the screen. She burned with the dark whim of her image devouring his. She scrolled in search of more. It was the only image of Largo. She printed it and put it in a manila folder in the desk drawer. She exhaled for what seemed the first time all day. It occurred to her to call Mom. She balked at the idea; Mom hated Largo now, and her number was always changing.

Amber played *Mario Brothers* until Ted got home. When she heard the key in the lock she shut the TV off and got him a cold beer from the refrigerator. Back in the living room she handed him the beer.

"Melba called. She wants to know if you want to meet them at Jake's to watch the Seahawks game."

"What did you tell her?" Ted asked, taking a long chug. He turned on the TV, and all that came on was the blank game screen. "Can you switch the TV so I can watch it, *please*."

Amber came in with oven mittens held to her chest. She turned off the Xbox and switched the TV over to cable. "I told her we were going shopping for a new microwave."

Ted chugged his beer and channel surfed. "We have too many channels," he yelled. Amber joined him in the living room.

"Turn on *The Simpsons*." She lingered over his shoulder. "I saw him today."

"Who?"

"Largo. The guy who molested me."

Ted stared at her when a commercial came on. "What'd he say?"

"He didn't say anything." Amber chewed on a string dangling from the oven mitten. "It was a picture I found on the internet." She watched the back of Ted's head.

"Why are you looking for him?" he asked.

Amber stepped around the chair. "I'm not sure. Maybe to tell what an asshole he is for molesting me."

She wanted something from Ted, wanted something from Largo, wanted something.

*He doesn't care or* he *would do something.*

"What do you want me to do?" he asked.

"You said you would kill him if you ever met him."

"That was such a long time ago. We've got too much to lose now," he said, looking around.

Amber returned to the kitchen. She manhandled the roast into the sink. Grease splattered her dress. She didn't know if she wanted him dead. She wanted to hurt him, but she also wanted him to see how well she was doing.

*Ted doesn't love you or he would offer to do something.*

After dinner in front of the TV, and after the entire FOX weekday lineup, Ted turned off the TV.

"Are you sure you want to do this?"

"Don't you think I should...I mean, he did molest me."
"He must be an old man by now. How old was the picture?"
"He didn't look that old, maybe sixty-five."
"What are you going to say?"

Amber rocked back and forth. Ted stared at her. She'd had one breakdown, the first month of their marriage. She'd gotten drunk, and the night ended with him on the couch, and her barricaded in their bedroom. She'd been on St. John's Wort ever since.

"I don't know," she said. "I just want to find him."

#####

It took a month to find Largo. He lived in Ireland now. She had no plan, so she allowed herself to be sidetracked by the holidays and Ted's family. Christmas was like a net, drawing in a village of cousins from all cardinal points of Washington, Idaho, and Oregon. She got a call from Grace for Christmas, which was better than any gift. She told Grace, the only human who'd been there, about Largo. "Do what you need to do," Grace told her. That was all the encouragement she needed to follow the lead to the end, which meant traveling to Ireland.

Amber lay awake at night imagining Largo in a dark cell, in solitary confinement. She played out the encounter: he fell to his knees at the sight of her, frail and contrite, and she slapped the shit out of him; he wailed, writhing in unnatural pain. "I'm sorry...forgive me...please!" She needed to forgive him, she knew. In the dream, she held out, prolonging his suffering. But in the light of day, she wondered if she was being realistic about his remorse.

Ted lay on his side, his back a formidable wall. Rage cycled through her. She breathed in the darkness of their bedroom, aware at once of an ocean of hate gurgling in her chest. *Leave him...he's the same as Largo.* Amber got out of bed. She went to the couch and sat awake with Reggie on her lap, until sunrise.

It was a Saturday. The sun peeked through a brownish thundercloud as Amber and Ted sped down I-5 to the travel agent. They knew a friend of a friend, and the prospect of going to Ireland to hunt down the man who'd ruined her life was growing like a wave. Ted guided them down the exit, and soon they sat face-to-face with a plump man in a snap-on tie and a wispy comb-over. He was just back from lunch; a sandwich in his right hand, he typed with one finger, a dab of mayonnaise in the corner of his mouth. Ted held her hand. Amber smiled at him absently, already a million miles away. She found herself hating the plump man, wanting to fling his sandwich against the wall, for taking her pain so lightly. She leaned forward on her toes and clicked her gum loudly.

Ted stared at her when the man quoted them a price. It was the logistics that doomed her closure. "We can't afford that," Ted announced. Amber exhaled, sinking back into her chair.

Ted stared at her...stalled at the sudden gravity. "Maybe we can save up," he offered. Amber went out to the car and lit a cigarette. Ted followed her, lingering by the back bumper. "What are you going to do?"

She didn't answer. It began to drizzle. Christmas was over, and New Year's was going to be a party at Melba's house. She'd just divorced her husband and Ted helped her move into a new place in Marysville.

Amber ended up staying at home. *They don't want you there.* She watched the ball drop on Times Square, the TV glowing across the room with all the lights out. The street outside was surprisingly busy, as she grumbled about how Ted had bought Melba a new TV. They could afford Melba's TV, but they couldn't afford to go to Ireland, to confront the man who'd made her life a living hell.

#####

It was an overcast day in June, typical, and Amber woke early to the sound of mockingbirds battling at sunrise. Ted snored next to her. She promised herself a nap later, as she trudged to the kitchen, then to the bathroom, as the coffee machine began to pop and purr. The mockingbirds followed her to the front of the house; strangely, one struck the kitchen window and lay frozen on the walkway. The kitty clock tail on the wall swished back and forth. Amber sat at the kitchen table. Ted's alarm would go off in three minutes. Reggie, her calico tom, jumped on her lap. "Who's my little putty tat?" she asked, using the voice she was certain cats understood. The image of the mockingbird, still, lifeless, was unnerving, not because of death, but because it invaded her routine. She made a mental note to clean it up so Reggie wouldn't make a mess. She kissed Reggie on top of his head. He protested when she rose. Amber went to the sink to take St. John's Wort. The dead bird was gone. Her hands pressed against the sill, her eyes searching when Ted came in and sat down. She stared at him.

"What?" he asked, scratching his backside.

"Nothing! I can't believe those birds didn't wake you." Amber brought Ted coffee. She laid out boxes of Cap'n Crunch and Sugar Frosted Flakes. She slapped his hand when Ted drank from the gallon of milk. They ate in silence until Reggie jumped up on the table as he did every morning.

"Did you fix my work pants?" Ted asked, rising.

"Time to go on a diet," she said.

After he left, Amber napped in her recliner until Reggie woke her at 10:12 a.m. When she returned from the bathroom the phone rang. Amber recognized the area code, but not the number. Mom called from Las Vegas when she stayed at her friends' house.

An official baritone barked into the receiver, "Good Morning. Is this Amber Rentano?"

"Yes."

"This is Sheriff Jones, calling from the Clark County Coroner's office in Las Vegas. We have Marie Rentano."

"Okay...?"

"She's dead."

Her mind was suddenly a glaring white screen. Amber held the phone away, she wanted to fling it, this sick joke.

The faraway voice continued, "We found her alone. It looks like suicide."

Amber collapsed against the wall. It wasn't surprising. She'd always imagined being composed, even relieved when the news came. But the thought of a Mom-less world had a plunging effect. "What happened?"

"It looks like she was house-sitting. We found a gun."

The Sheriff continued to talk, describing the scene: she was alone, she had been drinking, she shot herself, and she'd been there for over a week. Amber listened but the words did not settle until she called Grace later that day.

Amber hung up the phone and let Reggie out the back door. She went to the bathroom and started the water in the tub. She lay in the bath, staring into the depthless ceiling until the water grew cold. A solid mass of grief weighed her down as if her childhood was compressed between her stomach and her heart. Mom's face whirled above her, mingling with the steam. *She was all alone. Why did she do it?*

The days grew around her and she could think of nothing but why Mom took her life. Amber had never of thought of ending it that way, but for Mom, there didn't seem to be much to live for. Her children didn't want anything to do with her. She was threatening to be a part of their lives again. The decades of alcohol abuse left her in intermittent states of delirium. Amber wished she hadn't refused her the last time she showed up on her doorstep. Mom hadn't had a permanent residence in years. She lived off the generosity of others. She was homeless.

For the next few weeks, Amber kept to herself. Would anyone miss her if she died suddenly? It was just a thought, but a thought that occupied her in a way that few things had, to that point. She was nearly forty, no job, few friends, a husband who didn't appreciate her. Would she be missed? Certainly not by her family. Ted often said, "I'm the only family you have." She hated that he might be right.

When the ashes arrived, Amber put the urn on the mantle. She was the only one who wanted them. She'd seen it done on an episode of *The Munsters* when she was little. She placed flowers around it the first week; withered stems and petals magically appeared on the carpet throughout the house. She wondered if Mom was trying to tell her something about her death. She found out later that Mom was found with nothing but a bottle of Vodka and a .38. She'd been there for days, forgotten, not missed. Amber imagined herself found by the police, in some stranger's home, many miles away.

*What do you have to live for?*

Amber wasn't ready to surrender. The apartment seemed hers now with Mom's ashes on the mantle, and Ted spending so much time at Melba's. She could feel Mom in the room, a feeling that overshadowed the sense that Ted was cheating on her. The evidence of their marriage appeared to be shifting on a daily basis, and she needed to get out.

The flier took an afternoon to prepare. She knew how to clean a home. There was a cork board at the Grocery Outlet advertising small jobs. Amber pinned the flier next to the other housekeeping advertisements. Within a week she'd made three appointments to clean. She was a housekeeper. She made her own money; for the first time in years, she felt like she was pulling her own weight.

#####

It was a long, busy week: two rush jobs for neighbors who had family in town, three jobs for a local realtor, and a job for a new client, a widower who was too wrecked to do his own laundry.

Friday, sore and ready to hibernate, Amber sat on the floor in front of the TV with her Xbox controls firmly in her grip, when Paul called.

They hadn't talked in nearly a year. She knew that he moved to the Bay Area, near San Francisco. He worked in a group home with autistic adults and children. She knew he still drank a lot and did drugs, but had gotten back on his feet, after living in his truck in San Diego. It took her five rings to get to the phone, hoping for a wrong number.

It was a man's voice. Even so, she heard remnants of the teasing tone, and playful jabbing. The purpose of his call came as his voice grew serious and plaintive. "We're having a family reunion." The words she was hoping to hear came at the end of the conversation. "You've got to come, Amber. It won't be a reunion without you." He pleaded with her for another thirty minutes.

"I don't know. We're broke," she said, milking him for more time. At which point Paul recounted the special bond she held with each of them, one by one—Steve, Bryan, himself and especially Grace. He shared the hope that with Mom's death they could all start anew. and put the family back together.

"I'll pay for you and Ted to come. Now you don't have a reason."

Amber was stunned and bitter at the tardiness of this sudden show of love. *Where were you when I needed you?*

Paul signed off with a declaration. "I love you. Book a flight and send me the bill. I can't wait to see you. I'm so sorry I missed your wedding."

She surprised herself when she replied, "I love you too." She hung up the phone and sat on the carpet glowing. *I'm going to see my family.*

A streak of sunlight spilled across the living room floor. The rest of the house was dark and quiet as most of the sky had become overcast. She lay on her bed thinking and softly crying, tears of overwhelming joy and loss. Mom wouldn't be there to see all of her children together. Ted found her in bed when he came home from work. She was so excited she had forgotten to make dinner. Ted said he understood but barely hid his annoyance that her family was rushing back into their lives after so many absent years. They got take out Chinese food. She picked at her meal, already casting forth a commitment to lose weight, to walk off the plane a new person, a lovable person, someone who'd shed her pain. *A martyr*, she thought. She slept on the couch that night, tossing and turning, afraid of keeping Ted awake.

The tickets arrived. Paul was good as his word. She had her doubts; she hadn't heard from him since the call that rippled further away with each passing day. *It won't be a reunion without you.* Ted spent just as much time at Melba's house. "You go...you're the one they want to see," Ted offered as if it were a gift. It was the first time he'd encouraged her to visit them. She was suspicious. He'd bragged that he had the loving family, while hers despised her. Amber imagined Ted on Melba's couch, talking about her...thinking it was Melba talking through him.

"You're going!" Amber declared, as if their marriage depended on it.

With the trip a week away she met Ted at the front door. She'd just watched an episode of *Family Feud.* "I want a baby, Ted."

Ted stared at her on his way to the kitchen for a beer. "Are you crazy? We can't afford a baby." He nursed his beer bottle as they sat in their recliners watching *The Simpsons.* She brooded, a bubbling sea between them. "Why now?" he finally asked.

"It's my body clock," she said, not knowing why now. "I just want a baby, that's all. Can't you at least give me that?"

Ted spent that night at Melba's house. Amber drank Ted's last three beers and slept on the couch, ready for him to sneak in the door. *He's not coming back. You're going to be alone.* Ted didn't come home until Sunday night. Amber put the roast she'd made Saturday on the table, cold, moored in a pool of congealed fat. She pouted by the sink waiting for him to say something. He carved pieces from the cold roast, no side dish, or salad. *He hates you.* She stormed into the bedroom and slammed the door.

She called Grace. "Ted won't give me a baby." Grace spoke sparingly, agreeing too much, offering nothing. When they hung up, she felt more alone then before. Back in the kitchen, Amber banged the roast pan while the TV blared. She stormed into the living room, turned down the volume and stormed back to the kitchen. Ted just stared at her. She took a shower, hoping it would calm her. She wanted a baby, but was it right at her age? Back in the living room, she turned to him, but he was already snoring. Amber sat on the couch and stared at this man-boy who taken her away from hell in San Diego. A force was building between them, disturbing the delicate balance of daily routine that bound them together. She wondered if her family had something to do with it.

That Wednesday she met Denny at the supermarket. He was working on the refrigerator in the dairy section. There was something sad and vulnerable about him, down on all fours, tools scattered around him. He was so absorbed in his work that he didn't notice her reach over him for a pint of yogurt. When he finally looked up, he was so courteous. They hit it off. She felt available, being so distant from Ted. She found out that Denny's wife had recently passed, that he was estranged from his son and that he was living alone in the three-bedroom house—the home where he'd raised his kids and watched his wife die of cancer. She recognized a hole in his life, space she imagined she could fill. She offered her services. He gave her his phone number and she called. Within a month she was cleaning his house twice a week, doing his laundry and even making frozen meals for him. She told herself it wasn't cheating because they weren't having sex.

Each evening Ted's dinner was ready as usual. She counted the days until the reunion. When Ted was at work or Melba's, she made her phone calls—catching up with Paul, making hotel reservations, and long discussions with Grace about Mom. So much was happening so quickly. Her family would be there for her again. Ted could flounder in her undertow, as far as she was concerned.

# 22

The house on Branberry Road in Rush, New York lay in a verdant valley below the Lake Eerie Canals, far from Rochester and the dangers of the city. It was built in 1867. A creek ran between their property and a neighbor on the west side, a distant neighbor was screened by tall evergreens on the east side, while the north facing back yard stretched into a thick forest wilderness. They'd been in such a hurry to move. After a day in their new home they realized why the asking price was so cheap. The slat walls were mushy, the plumbing moaned dolefully, and the electricity was intermittent—they kept a generator on the back porch. Quarters would be tight until they renovated. The boys, including Ben, packed into one little room, while Mimi got her own room. Mimi loved her new room, while Ben was inconsolable. He found refuge on the porch, and soon found space to read and study on the plank steps by the gravel driveway. The two upstairs bedrooms lay off a short hallway, but a miniature door at the end of the hall opened into an attic the size of the entire downstairs. The attic held the dream of future expansion.

The boys thrived in the backyard woods, in a fantasy existence that confined their horrid past into soft folds of fresh memories. Unleashed at last, they stumbled and explored, with boundless energy and wonder.

The first year was a novelty of newness: the experience and glory of all the seasons, of their new church, Ron's blossoming career at Kodak, Mimi on the track team, Ben making the skating team, both thriving in middle school. Grace hadn't figured out schooling for John, the oldest boy. Thomas refused to potty train and Michael, her baby, smiled constantly. Yet, after a very cramped year it was impossible to ignore the need for space. There were master craftsmen in Ron's church band who could do it all, but they wanted to learn themselves, and invited them over for carpentry, drywalling and plumbing demonstrations. They blocked off one room at a time, and set a long term plan for adding rooms and a deck.

Over the first winter they used old newspapers to stem the flow of icy wind from the lakes. There was a constant draft from large cracks in the plaster walls. They bundled up and kept the old wood stove going day and night. Meanwhile, Grace picked up her art again, and spent most of her days in the kitchen sketching still lives.  The kitchen was the center of the house, the last in the plan for construction, and the hub of her world. Once again, she found a friend, Marcy, in church who had a daughter who could babysit. Marcy, like most of her friends in the East, had no idea about her past. They were all so insulated, Grace thought. She shared measured tidbits during quiet moments together, and was relieved when summer came along with an invitation from Terri. She'd moved to Florida to get away from her husband, Tim, who'd fallen prey to the bottle.

"I can't go. I've got two babies and the house is falling apart. We've only got three months to finish the master bed and bath before next winter hits."  They talked for hours, and when she hung up Grace realized how much she missed the beach and the sun.

Each day was a blur of activity; her past receded with each month on the east coast.  When Amber called to give the news of

Mom's suicide, Grace felt...relieved...and sad. It was a fitting end for an alcoholic who'd embraced the 60's party culture, traveled the country, leap-frogging from one trucker's cab to the next. Mom had devolved into a homeless wanderer, and now, another lonely suicide. The sadness in Amber's voice seemed permanent now. It tore at Grace to hear her talk about Mom, dodging the fact that Mom abetted her abuse. Grace felt no pity for the woman who offered her girls for sex. Grace had heavier concerns.

Rex called with the news that Kimo had died of AIDS. Grace was frozen with fear, until she got tested at a clinic in Rochester. Marcy helped watch the kids, while Ron was at band practice at the church. She kept it secret, the test, and when the results came she breathed a sigh of relief. Marcy was her best friend, so after the results came in, she shared a few stories of her Venice days. She'd also gotten a call from Paul, in Berkeley now. She'd heard stories from both Steve and Bryan, about how he'd been drummed out of the Navy for drugs, how he'd become a daily drinker, how he'd kicked meth, gotten his B.A. and moved to the Bay Area to start a new life. He called on a break from a shift at his job as a counselor in a group home. He was so upbeat, she wondered if he'd been using again. When they talked about Mom, his voice leveled off. "I barely knew her." he said.

Grace was surprised at how sad his reaction made her. "I know. She did you a favor by abandoning you boys."

"I'm sorry you had it so bad," he said. When they hung up she held Michael for the rest of the evening, feeling blessed.

#####

Grace realized she was pacing. Breakfast dishes were in the sink, Michael was collecting pebbles in the driveway, the other kids were at school, and Ron was at work. Just off the phone with Paul, she could see him, a dark soul, still searching for himself at forty. He had his head above water, but everyone wondered how long he could stay sober. He'd bought them all tickets for the reunion in San Diego. She'd spent the week grinding through the details of their return to California: packing seven bags, visits to the pediatrician, telling stories of the Magnolia, Highland Park and Venice days, dredging up emotions she thought were expired.

Amber called incessantly to complain about her marriage and her status in the family.

"No one calls. The boys still hate me. Dad calls me Marie half the time. Ted is sleeping with his sister, Melba."

"Hold on! What did you just say?" Grace sat at the kitchen table, absently watching Michael sort pebbles on the floor.

"What?" Amber said.

"Ted is sleeping with who?"

"Oh. Melba, his sister. He doesn't think I know, but I can put two and two together."

Grace wiped her hands on her apron and took the phone off speaker. "How do you know?"

"Well...he parties with her every Friday. When he comes home, he smells like her. He doesn't even hide it."

Grace jumped off her stool. This was exactly why she didn't miss her family. She had enough drama with two teenagers in the house.

"What should I do?" Amber asked.

"I don't know. That's none of my business."

"Don't you care?"

"Amber...I care. But what can I do about it? Talk with him."

This was the point in their conversations that always ended with Grace holding a dead phone line. As she moved to place the phone on its cradle Amber surprised her. "Do you think I should leave him?" she asked.

"If that's what you want. Do you still love him?"

Once again, Grace expected the phone to go dead. "Let's talk about it at the reunion," Amber finally said.

The details of her siblings' lives competed for attention in her head. The dynamic had not changed since the days on Magnolia Street. She resented the invasion into her new life. *I am not that person anymore.* Grace did something she hadn't done in years. She found the bottle of wine she'd been saving for Thanksgiving, uncorked it and poured herself a glass. She sat at the kitchen table and drank glass after glass until she'd finished half the bottle. She marveled at the dense quiet of the old house, and how cozy it was now with the new insulation.

It was the Thursday before the reunion. The boys were at baseball practice with Ron. Mimi and Ben were at friends' houses, and Michael had a play date with the family down the road. Dinner percolated in a crock pot on the counter. She pushed the cork back in the bottle, put it in the fridge and started a bath. She laughed at herself, standing naked, dancing in front of the mirror. In the bath she stared up at the ceiling, following the cracks where they'd done a rushed job on the plaster. Her life was full. She couldn't imagine sharing it with Amber or her brothers; maybe Paul, he seemed to be getting his life together. The wave that began with Mom's death was building toward a reconnection. Slightly drunk, she turned on the hot water spout, warmed by the distance between her families, and the heat swirling around her thighs and over her breasts. She closed her eyes and did something she hadn't the space or time to do in many a day.

#####


It had been rainy and overcast in Buffalo when they left, but when they exited the plane in San Diego the sun made them blink, as if they'd just emerged from a bunker. Everyone at the airport was so polite and helpful. It wasn't until Grace reminded Ron to tip the bellman at the hotel that she realized she was a tourist. They had a suite at the Best Western Lodge off I-8. After settling Mimi and Ben in an adjoining room, and the boys in the front room, Grace took a shower and spent the rest of the day planning a trip to Sea World. Ron had never taken time off: she wanted to make the most of it—their first family vacation.

The next morning she felt sick to her stomach. "Nerves," Ron said while they dressed. "When's the last time you saw your whole family together?"

They spent the day at Mission Bay, wading into the man-made bay, picnicking, swinging and sliding at the playground. The boys made sand castles while Mimi read and drew with Grace on the grass. Ben disappeared for an hour until Ron found him loitering around at the entrance to the yacht club.

The next day they drove to Steve's house after a late breakfast at the hotel restaurant. The house was in a cul-de-sac, cookie cutter boxes with a thin path between them. The family that left the house on Magnolia Street in shambles had morphed into a semi-respectable group. Bryan had two girls, Steve, divorced, had a son, and Grace had her flock. As they pulled up front Grace saw Amber smoking at the curb. Ted waited for her on the porch.

#####


Amber recognized Ron at the wheel of a Dodge minivan. The van appeared empty: a flurry of motion behind the tinted windows dispelled that notion. Grace jumped out of the passenger side and hugged her. "Amber...I'm so glad to see you!" She slid back the side door. Five pairs of eyes stared back at Amber. She forced a smile, ready for another cigarette after the flight from Tacoma.

"Where are you staying?" Grace asked as she handed Amber a paper bag with photo albums.

"We're at the Fashion Valley Inn. We haven't checked in yet." Amber handed the bag to Ted and pointed at the house. Ron came around and shook Ted's hand. They walked together to the porch.

Amber took out a cigarette and lit it. Grace frowned. "Amber...can you smoke over there please?" she said, pointing to a space at the end of the driveway. Amber rolled her eyes, took a deep drag, walked over to the curb and sat down. She stared toward the house, back at the van, children tumbling onto the sidewalk, Grace guiding them. She watched Grace intently as she herded her flock inside.

Alone, Amber shook her head. *Some things never change.*

The house was already bustling. Bryan, his wife Betsy and Steve were talking loudly in the kitchen. Ron and Ted chatted by the cooler in the dining room. Straight toward the back of the house, Bryan and Steve's kids bounced on couches in the den, a tiny room separated from the backyard by a sliding glass door. A nervous Labradoodle pranced around them. Grace settled the boys on the couch with their cousins, while Mimi and Ben shadowed her.

Dad rose from a chair at the dining room table to greet her. "My oldest," he exclaimed with a wine tumbler in his hand. Grace thought he looked like an old mariner in a skull cap and dungarees.

"Hi, Dad," she said, hugging him lightly.

"Where's Amber?" Steve asked.

"She's outside smoking," Grace said.

Steve opened the front door. "Amber," he yelled. "What are you doing out there all alone?"

Amber stood up and smoothed her skirt. Her toe ached—her sandals were too tight. She wanted Paul to drive up just then. At the door Steve gave her a big hug. She loved that about him. He might never call, but he seemed to be able to leave their past behind. Amber avoided the den, too many kids. She settled next to Dad at the table. "Are you still smoking?" he asked sternly. Amber watched him watch the children play in the other room.

Grace was in the kitchen with a wine glass in her hand. She was talking with Betsy, edging toward the table. She pulled the bag with the albums up on the table. She opened one. "See...doesn't she look just like Mom?" Grace said, pointing to a picture of Mom on her wedding day. They both stared at Amber.

Amber rose and joined them. Mom stared back at her. She nodded, screwed up her mouth and quickly turned the page. "Everyone always says that. I don't see it," she said.

315

"Your mother was a beautiful woman," Dad chimed in.

"Aw, Dad," Amber said, punching him in the arm.

"Watch it. You're getting too strong," he said.

Amber and Dad sat down side-by-side, turning pages, switching albums, turning pages. All seemed to be forgiven for the moment. He put his finger on a photo of the family, out on the grass at Magnolia Street. "Remember this one? Here you are. We just got back from your Grandma Dupree's. You were only three." He smiled as his finger traced the page.

Amber was struck by how tiny she was. They were sitting on the porch steps in front of the house, where she remembered catching skippers on the lawn with Paul and Grace. It was the same place, but she couldn't recall her Dad there.

Grace took the Christmas family portrait from the bag. She showed it to Betsy.

"Bring that here," Dad said.

Steve and Bryan joined them in the dining room. They stood behind Amber and Grace. "I remember that," Dad said dolefully. He looked up at Grace and Amber. "I regret not fighting for you girls...my only regret." Grace and Amber shifted. They turned the page in unison.

The doorbell broke the tension. "Paul!" Amber said, rushing for the door.

Grace closed the album; she went to the den, glancing back at Dad, beckoning her children to go see their uncle Paul. Amber opened the front door. She grabbed Paul's hand and pulled him inside. He stiffened at her touch, then composed himself. She figured he was stoned. She hugged him with the dual purpose of smelling his shirt. She whispered in his ear, "Are you stoned?"

Paul smiled and gave her a quick hug. He was clean shaven, his hair pulled back in a pony tail. He wore a buttoned down shirt, loafers and khakis. She'd never seen him so put together.

"Paul...you look great!" Grace said coming forward. She hugged him, stepping aside to showcase her boys, pointing to each. "This is John, Thomas, and Michael." Michael hid behind her skirt, while John and Thomas offered their thin hands. Amber fidgeted next to Paul. Now that Grace and Paul were there, she wanted the kids to go back to the den. She wanted Grace and Paul all to herself, just the way it used to be. She followed Grace and Paul into the dining room. Grace showed Paul the family portrait. "You were so little...see?"

"Who's that baby?" Paul teased, pointing to Amber in the photo.

Amber squeezed his arm. "You were the baby, remember?" she said.

The kids in the den were starting make a ruckus. "Hey," Grace said. "Let's get a family picture."

Bryan called everyone into the dining room, where Grace lined up the kids. The din peaked and subsided: a family reunited by death, packed into a picture frame—sarcasm, sidebar and finally, silence. They could sustain the closeness for only so long, until, with a collective sigh of relief, they broke apart, charged and famished.

After a buffet of Filipino fare provided by Betsy, the kids went out to the back yard—a small patch of grass off an equally small patch of concrete patio. In the center of the yard an age-old peach tree with a thick trunk and sturdy boughs stretched to the sky. Paul walked furtively to the patio and spread exploding Chinese sand fireworks across the picnic table. He motioned for the kids to partake, and soon they danced around the little tree lobbing explosives, squealing and shrieking at every pop.

The adults sat on the patio watching, except for Paul who kept the children plied with fireworks, occasionally lobbing a handful against the wall when calm threatened to invade the chaos. Grace held hands with Ron, chatting with Ted about the burgeoning tech market in Seattle.

Amber and Steve sat smoking in the shadows at the eastern corner of the house, their plastic chairs a yard apart. They sat silently, blowing smoke over the heads of the shrieking and dancing children. One of Bryan's girls feigned a charge toward them, pulled back when she saw Amber's upturned face. She retreated, tossing a single explosive against the fence. Amber jumped up, her purse fell off her lap, she stomped to the peach tree and shook it. The children scattered, as if a scarecrow had come to life. Grace and Ron stared at Amber. The children sprinted around the corner of the house toward the front lawn. The abrupt calm was uncomfortable. Amber stood alone clutching the trunk. Ron got up, kissed Grace on the cheek, and went to join the children in the front yard. Grace glanced at Steve who also rose and went into the house. Grace walked to Amber's side. "It's beautiful isn't it?" she said.

Amber jutted her chin and stared at Grace. The clinging hadn't changed over the years. It started in Highland Park, Grace knew. "What is beautiful?" Amber asked, letting go of the tree. Grace looked up through the boughs. Amber stepped back and saw the tree for the first time.

Grace pointed to a flower in blossom at the top. "See how the blossoms open to the sunlight." She pointed to another. "And how the petals on this one have fallen away. A peach will grow from that one."

Amber touched a mottled bud on a bottom bough, stunted by external forces. "What happened to this one?" Amber asked.

"Sometimes that happens," Grace said with a sigh. "Not all the blossoms turn to fruit." She caressed the blackened bud. "It's not personal," she added.

Amber stared from the bud, to Grace, and back again, clutching her purse to her chest. A strange expression hardened on her face. She stepped away and lit a cigarette. She was suspended in an age and time, adrift from the rest of the family. Grace put her arm across Amber's shoulder, suddenly wanting to cry. Amber slid away, back to the chair in the shadows. She sat and smoked in silence. Grace strained a smile. It wasn't a time to talk of heavy things. They both knew the reunion would change nothing.

Grace went inside the house. Amber sat smoking as the sun dipped, staring at the tree, knowing she was missing something, but completely lost to what that could be. When she went back into the house Paul gave her a big hug, and just as quickly, she forgot about the disturbing little peach tree.

# 23

Back in Washington, Amber experienced withdrawals, coming down from the stimulant of blood family. While there, a great weight had been lifted; she no longer felt abandoned, but their abrupt absence cast her into the doldrums, eyes alight for the slightest breeze to fill her sails. Ted had lied. Her family did want to be around her. Paul already purchased tickets to visit. Her life was on an upswing, the first that she could remember. She felt like a new person. Her past was lighter with the promise of even greater connection.

She put the pent-up energy to good use. The garage was a project she'd put off, waiting for the day she and Ted could do it together. She surrendered to the truth, that that day would never come. Certain items no longer deserved to take up space. Images from the reunion infiltrated her usual routines, making them seem archaic and obsolete. As she filled bag after garbage bag with cracked Tupperware, broken frames, unmatched socks and Tom's collection of 80's porn, she thought of getting a real job, one that paid benefits and a steady paycheck. Life as a maid was not a career. She wanted a bank account of her own. Grace had her own bank account. She didn't bring it up to Ted.

Amber would keep one of her clients though. Denny needed her. At least he told her so. "You light up my day," he'd say. It made her squirm when he said it the first time. *He's flirting with me.* She was secretly delighted. She was the only one in his life. She looked forward to working at his house and continued to do so three days a week.

Amber still had illusions of being a mother, like Grace. One Sunday dinner at her mother-in-law's, she cornered Melba. "I want to babysit the kids." Ted's niece and nephew were five and seven. On that particularly hot day—under a massive poplar tree, a shade cooler under a tarp they'd strewn from the trunk to the chimney— she made a show of treating the children as her own, barking commands and warnings, thinking in her own harping way that she was being a parent. "Eat all your vegetables. No ice cream until you bring your dishes to the sink. Stop hitting your sister." Her voice rang out under the undulating tarp throughout the day. She caught a few of the exchanged looks between Ted and his family. Melba agreed to let her babysit.

She babysat for two weeks. She was shocked when Melba abruptly stopped asking.

"There is just something 'off' about her," Melba told Ted. "They can't breathe without her yelling at them."

Amber recoiled, bitter and hurt by the painfully familiar feelings. *Everyone thinks you're crazy...you aren't fit to have a child.* She turned on Ted. "What did you tell Melba? She won't let me babysit!" It was their worst fight ever. It lasted two days. Amber resumed her routines, the ones she'd abandoned after the reunion. Ted seemed unfazed by the acrimony, which hurt the most, not caring enough to be bothered. She doubled her efforts at finding a job. She needed a safety valve and she found it in Paul. At the end of the worst week of her marriage, she called him.

"I'm getting a divorce." She had no intention of getting a divorce, but she knew it would get Paul's attention.

"Amber. Don't be hasty."

His tone was a slap in the face. She heard, *I'm not going to save you this time.* It was the *last* thing she wanted to hear. "Don't worry. I don't need you," she spat.

It was the beginning of yet another impasse in their relationship. She'd never apologized in the past. It always ended in a siege, and she always outlasted him. But this time was different. She called back within the hour and apologized. "I am sorry I was mean to you. Ted and his family are treating me like shit."

"It's alright," he said. "I'll always love you."

#####

The reunion was a distant memory with the holiday season looming. Amber looked forward to season's greetings from her entire family, images of cards lined up on the mantle next to Mom's urn warmed her during the frigid Seattle fall. Denny promised a special gift and a bonus. Her secret savings account was growing.

It was the end of a busy week of shopping and cleaning. She returned from Denny's house glowing from physical labor and holiday spirit. The second she set her purse down Ted asked her for rent money. She lashed out, "Why do you spend so much time with Melba?" It shut him right up. They fought every Friday now. It ended typically: he stormed out the door and didn't show up until Sunday evening, after the FOX TV lineup.

It was a routine, as relevant as her calls to her family, or Reggie jumping up on the table during breakfast. She called her family on the nights they fought, rotating between Grace and Paul. She even called Dad on occasion. He felt closer after the reunion. Although she knew Dad preferred to be called on weekends, she figured he should take her calls. He owed her that much.

One particular Saturday Dad was especially out of sorts. He'd never been warm and fuzzy, definitely the tough love type.

"If you must know," he started, grumpier than usual, "I have Parkinson's."

Amber didn't know what Parkinson's was, so her silence was an uncomfortable cue for him. "It's terminal. Look it up."

Amber found out from Grace that Dad, in fact, had a type of Parkinson's that would allow him to function, with the right treatment. Amber offered to care for him. It could be good for both of them, she thought. He refused the help. As a consolation, he let her visit.

Amber packed her things for an extended stay: boxes of her favorite snacks, another box of toiletries, her Xbox, and a pad of paper with all the boys' and Grace's phone numbers. She thought of bringing her computer but decided at the last minute that she wanted to give her Dad all her attention. Ted looked askance at the stack of boxes by the trunk of her Tercel, as he pulled up after a day's work. "I thought you hated your Dad," he said, carrying a six-pack to the refrigerator.

On her way out she was so excited that she forgot they were fighting. Her suitcase in her hand, she kissed him on the top of his head as she pushed by his recliner. "I'll call you when I get there." Amber could feel his eyes on her back as she shut the door. She giggled to herself backing out of the driveway. *Serves him right*, she thought.

Pulling up Dad's gravel driveway eight hours later, Amber was exhausted. She'd called from a gas station in Salem, and Dad was his usual crotchety self. Amber bought a six-pack of Pepsi and Red Vines for the last leg. It didn't matter how grumpy he was, she could sweeten him up, baby him even. After their time together, he would regret abandoning her, would wish she'd been his little girl, all along. She would never *tell* anyone, but that was how she felt, even if she was past forty.

Dad lived in a rustic two-story log house tucked within a forest of firs and pines. It looked vacant as she pulled up the shale driveway. The lights were off at twilight, the sky was ashen pink as the sun dipped below the treetops. Amber got out of the car energized. She made a beeline up the wooden steps and rapped on the sliding glass door.

"Come in. It's open." Dad was in his recliner watching *Seinfeld*. "Come on over here and give me a kiss," he smiled, as she rushed across the room.

"Oh, Dad." Amber kissed him on top of his head, her face screwed up when she realized she'd just done the exact same thing leaving home. He went back to his show, gesturing toward the stairs and the guest room.

Amber put her things away in the guest room downstairs. The room hadn't been dusted since the last visitor, probably three months. She cleared a space in the closet, hung up her things and joined Dad back in the living room.

It started so well. That night she made him pork chops, rice, and frozen green beans, just the way he liked. She made him coffee afterward, not knowing that he *never* drank coffee after dinner. How would she know? She put a blanket on him while they watched *Seinfeld*, kept ice in his water glass and turned the volume down during the commercials. He didn't have to lift a finger. She tried to help him use the bathroom, but he pushed her away. "I'm not an invalid!" She figured he was grumpy because of the Parkinson's.

She was so proud of herself by the end of the night, she called Paul. "He'll be back on his feet in no time."

Paul thanked her for visiting him. "You're the best one for the job," he said.

In the next few days, she received calls at the house, from Steve, Bryan, and Grace. They all thanked her for staying with Dad, and she was so excited to serve the family in just that way. She had the caring disposition and patience of a nurse, she thought. The second night of her stay things began to turn. They were so alike, which thrilled her, as they watched TV after dinner, both with their owl glasses, she in her chair, he in his recliner. She couldn't hold her tongue; she was so excited to be with her Dad, after so many years apart. "Look at us, Dad, we're like twins, with our glasses." She was risking conversation during his show, she knew.

"Why don't you shut your trap for once? I'm trying to watch my show."

Amber's jaw dropped. "I was just..."

"You always talk back...always did. You're just like your mother."

Amber bristled. The room exploded in shades of red; she leaped off the couch, banging her stub toe on the coffee table. "How can you say that?" she cried. She stormed down the stairs sobbing. Dad turned up the TV.

*He hates you. He never wanted you to come. Everyone hates you. You are just like Mom.*

The cruel outburst plummeted Amber over the edge. The house was quiet now. It was her third cigarette since she called Grace. She told the entire story of how she was ready to move in with him, even though she was still married. She would have seen him through his recovery. She told Grace about the attack. "I did nothing wrong!" she yelled into the phone, holding a pillow over her head so he couldn't hear her.

Grace listened quietly until Amber paused for a breath. "Amber, Dad has always treated us girls differently. We don't count as much as the boys. We can't expect anything from him. Stop trying."

Amber started up again, unwilling to be mollified. "But, I am not Mom..."

"Amber...I've got to go. Just go home. That's what he wants."

"But..."

Amber stepped out of the downstairs exit, onto the welcome mat leading to the shale driveway. The cool, fresh air soothed her. *This would be a perfect place to share with someone,* she thought. She stared up at the stars, scattered like dandruff on black sheets. The moaning of pine tree limbs fed her darkest thoughts. *What's the use? You are Mom.* Amber trudged back into the house, replacing the plastic yard chair in the same ruts she'd found it. Dad was stuck in his ways. He was not going to change.

The next morning she got up early. It was still dark. She crept like a mouse, foregoing her ritual shower. She loaded up the car in the dark, scaring a deer drinking from a pickle bucket—set there for just that purpose. Amber mused at the care of the arrangement: deer, old man, water bucket, the aloofness of both, intersecting at the bucket at the tree.

In a last fit of hope, not wanting to burn her bridges, she retraced her steps, making sure the house was as she found it. She even wiped the spiders away from the bottom of the toilet and regretted the presumption; maybe the spiders were the indoor deer, for him. She smoked a last cigarette in the cool morning breeze, listening to the trees crackle to life. The rising sun and the creaking house told her it was time to go. She put the yard chair back, got into her car, rolled down the window, waited and listened. When she was sure he was up, Amber revved the engine two extra times, put it in gear and peeled off down the driveway.

#####

Paul was coming—the first family to visit her in Washington. It was time to leave for the airport. Amber slapped the steering wheel. The Tercel wouldn't start. She sat in the driveway waiting for Ted to come around the house with the jumper cables. She resented that she needed him, although when they'd gotten married that was exactly what she liked about him. Her foot tapped along with the windshield wipers. She was going to be late picking Paul up at Seattle Tacoma Airport. Amber honked the horn. Ted trudged through the sopping weeds dangling jumping cables over his shoulder. *He looks like a big wet dog,* she thought. Amber got out to watch him. They'd been together thirteen years, sex for five and only a few words in the last twelve months. She looked the other way and shivered when he bent over the hood, revealing his hairy butt crack. She reached impulsively to pull down his shirt, balked, as he looked around at her.

"You put the red one on the live post and the…" She'd never been any good at taking instructions. She needed to watch. The counselor once told her that she had a disability, that she was a kinesthetic learner.

"Come on! I'll learn later, just get it started," she yelled. She knew Ted was cheating on her. He came home early that morning. He smelled like Melba. *Melba*, she winced. *Who could love anyone named after toast?*

"Start it up," Ted grumbled. Amber held the wheel with both hands and pumped the gas. It turned over on the second try. She honked the horn twice, once to thank him, the second, longer honk, to let him know she knew. The window fogged up as she sat there, letting the battery charge, staring at his dull shape lumbering to her side window. Amber's heart skipped, it looked like he was coming to kiss her goodbye. He bent down and tapped the window. She rolled down the window, tentative, licking her lips, the space between them suddenly clear. "Don't forget, I'm staying at Mom's tonight."

Amber banged her elbow putting up the window. "Fuck you," she muttered, barely missing the trash can, backing out of the driveway.

Interstate 5 was clear sailing, so Paul barely had to wait. Amber watched him gather his backpack. *He's still handsome*, she thought. Amber jumped out as he stepped off the curb. She had it all planned: she hugged him, took his bag, put it in the back seat and opened the door for him. "Is that all you brought?"

"Yup," he said, kissing her on the cheek. He settled hard into the passenger seat.

"Are you stoned again?" she asked. He was always stoned, she could tell by his squinty eyes.

"Yup," he smiled.

They rode in silence until the onramp to Interstate 5. She was surprised as she always was at how quickly they reverted to the old ways. "We're going to the Jimi Hendrix exhibit," she said. Paul nodded. He always took a while to warm up.

"How's Ted?" he asked.

Amber smirked and switched lanes. "I'll tell you later."

Amber started to giggle. It didn't take much. Paul was there. It was so easy. "That's nasty!" he said, pinching his face and opening the window. "What'd you have for breakfast, a shit burrito?" It didn't matter that they'd lived most of their lives apart, or that they'd fought like cats for half of their time together. Like gravity, they always settled into the same comfortable grooves. Paul rolled up the window, staring, silent, with a smile on his face.

"Oh my God!" Amber screamed. "What was that? You're fogging up the windows." They giggled for the next few miles, until the inside of the Tercel cleared. "Are you hungry," she asked between breaths. "Let's get burgers down by the Needle."

The sun came out on the rain dusted plaza. In the shadow of the Needle, Paul brushed a puddle off the picnic bench for her. It was a weekday, a smattering of families, couples in parkas, tourists and vagrants meandered across the cobbled square.

"It's beautiful here," Paul said, scoping out the Needle, and the new museum, the Jimi Hendrix Experience, off in the distance.

"I like it better than San Diego," she said. When their order came Amber let him pay. "I'm cleaning houses now. Ted makes me pay half the rent."

Paul looked at her sideways, chewing down an oversized bite.

"We don't have a lot of money. He keeps getting laid off at the plant. No seniority."

Paul swallowed, taking a long drink of his ice tea. He started to say something but Amber interrupted. "How long has it been?" she asked.

"Three months," he said, without looking at her.

"Wow...that's great. Is this the longest you've been sober?"

"Yup," he said, taking another bite.

"I don't drink much either," she said. "Because of Mom."

Paul stared up at the Needle. "Lucky you," he said.

"Not really. We had to live with her. She was a drunk."

Paul turned to face the bay. He acted as if he were appreciating the towering buildings flowing along the port. He looked up suddenly, taking her by surprise. "I'm sorry."

She knew, but she wanted him to say it. She wanted him to spell it out, the difference in their lives, the obvious inequities, now that he was a college graduate, independent, making it on his own in the Bay Area.

"For everything. The abuse. How I treated you when you moved in. It was weird having you there. You weren't the same Amber."

Amber sighed. "What did you expect? I was molested since I was seven." She edged closer until their hips touched. "We were both fucked up teenagers, right? Look at us now!" Amber put her head on his shoulder. It smelled like onions and mustard. She had no husband waiting for her at home and had no life to speak of, beyond this new thing called family. Paul put his arm around her, the long reflection of the Needle on the concrete. Seagulls danced in the air overhead, begging for fries. She was happy, happier than she could remember.

Later, they made their own experience in the Jimi Hendrix museum. They went from exhibit to exhibit giggling breathlessly, farting, room after room, stomachs aching from laughter and sour onions. Foot traffic was light; they found themselves alone, staring at a life-size Jimi Hendrix in his original garb. His blank stare was captured mid-solo, staring into a void. Wearing headphones, they were ushered by the self-guided tour through a maze of memorabilia set behind Plexiglas. They rushed out into the fresh afternoon air, drained and delirious in one another's company.

On the way home, Amber warned Paul, "Don't expect much from Ted. He's in his own world these days." She was too embarrassed to admit to Paul that her marriage was over. She'd become a good housewife; Paul might see her marriage as another failure and she couldn't stand to see the look on his face when she finally told him.

That night Paul went to bed early. She walked past his door several times on the way to the bathroom, wondering what he could be doing all alone, with the light on. Finally, Mom's urn in her arms, she knocked. He opened the door and they sat on the pullout bed she'd made for him. She spied a book and journal open on the pillow.

"So that's it," he said, as he ran his fingers over the vase. "What are you going to do with the ashes?"

"I don't know...keep them. What is there to do with them, but keep them?"

He handed the vase back to her, grimacing. "It just seems weird to have them laying around. I'd throw them in the ocean."

Amber put the urn on the bureau, returning to the mattress to sit by Paul. They both stared at it in silence. It felt good to be an adult, free of the tension that held them when they were teenagers. She itched for a cigarette but knew if she left the room he'd go to sleep, and that would be the end of this moment.

"Dad was really grumpy last time I visited," she finally said with a pinched face.

Paul shrugged. "Dad's always been grumpy, remember?"

"Doesn't he miss his kids?"

"I doubt it. He's a loner. He's got a girlfriend."

Amber bounced on the bed, laughing in disbelief. "A girlfriend?"

"Yeah. Ruth. She's the nice old lady on the property next door. I've met her a few times. She's tough, to put up with Dad."

"I should call her," she said, pondering a new avenue to Dad. Paul lay on his back.

"I'm getting tired," he finally said after a long silence.

"Paul," Amber said.

"Yes?"

"You should come up for Thanksgiving." The words came out of her mouth, without pretense. The thought of spending Thanksgiving alone made her want to cry.

"We'll see," he said.

When she let him off at the airport the next day, he handed her his business card with Ruth's number on the back.

Amber wanted to talk with Ruth, about Dad. She wanted to know what she'd got from his side of the family, looking so much like Mom. Amber felt empty again on the drive home. Her life energy seemed to drain with every mile closer to the house. The mist in her head thickened with each ensuing second of solitude. She didn't expect Ted to be home, and was grateful to have the house all to herself. Back in her recliner, she dialed Ruth's number.

It took a while for Ruth to answer the phone. Amber was about to hang up when Ruth's gravely voice filled the line.

"Oh, hello," Ruth said, sounding annoyed, until Amber introduced herself.

After a few moments of polite banter, Amber rushed headlong into the reason for the call. "Ruth, do you think I'm like my Dad?" she asked.

Ruth paused for a moment. Amber could hear her breathing on the line. When Ruth responded it was hushed. "I'll tell you one thing you and your father have in common, you worry too much. Your father worries about you constantly."

"Really? I thought he hated me. He's so grumpy," Amber said.

"You remind him of your mother. He can't help himself. You need to be patient."

"So he doesn't hate me?" Amber asked.

"No. Amber…"

Amber waited, but the words never came. She heard Dad's muffled voice in the background. Amber had forgotten the time. Dad was there in the room with Ruth; it was time for their daily routine of cocktails and crossword. Amber blurted a goodbye and hung up the phone. She'd call back later that evening. Ruth, she knew, stayed up late and Dad would be back in his man cave.

# 24

The house on Branberry Road in Rush, New York, was the embodiment of their hard work and love. It had taken ten years, but they finished the remodel themselves. The new master bedroom had French doors that led out to a yellow pine balcony, overlooking the backyard and the forest beyond. Grace loved how the sunrise filled the room in the morning with a buttery glow, and how the drapes fluttered in the wind, carrying the piney, loamy smells of the backyard to her.

She awoke for the last several months to a house full of boys. The taut strings of Mimi in Sweden—her faraway little girl, well on her way to womanhood, and a life apart—pulled at her heart. Mimi wasn't coming home, she knew—internship, then off to Robert Morris University, and who knows, marriage, babies... *I would be a wonderful grandmother,* she thought. For now, Grace's arms were bare.

She walked out onto the balcony. Off in the distance, she spied a blurry figure huddled behind a great sycamore trunk, motionless. Grace put on her glasses and went to the rail. Michael was crouched in the grass, flies buzzing around him in the soft morning sun. His hair had grown out, and Grace was delighted at how much he'd grown in the last year, bounding through the trees with his big brothers. The three boys could survive in the woods behind their house, living off the land. A botanist friend from church spent weekends with them in the outback. They'd be gone for hours, hunting, fishing and searching out edible and medicinal plants, plants to build, plants for tools. The collection of crudely crafted tools and weapons under the back porch was a cache the boys bragged would save them in the approaching apocalypse of Y2K.

Grace waved to Michael. He stared at her—motionless. She wanted desperately for him to stir; there was something eerie in his stillness. He stared back at her, as if she were watching him from behind a two-way window. The area around him was as it should be: seedlings bobbing in the breeze, birds darting in and out of branches, shadows wavering. Then she saw it, a massive buck, pawing the ground, jerking its antlers as it caught a scent, erect and challenging in a small meadow twenty yards East of Michael. Grace jumped. The deer in the area were somewhat domesticated, but became instinctual, hyper feral, during mating season. Mating season, the scent, Michael, all at once she screamed and flailed her arms. "Go away...Get out of here!" She was in her nightgown and slippers still, sprinting through the house, out the kitchen door, down the steps through the damp grass toward the buck. On a slope of new grass, she lost her footing and landed on her back, staring up at the brooding clouds.

The buck would smell her now, and the twisted thought of being mounted shot through her like an arrow. Grace righted herself and continued to stumble to where she imagined Michael to be. Grace paused next to a snag but continued to flail and scream as loud as she could. The hope, to appear larger than she felt. She couldn't see the buck yet. With adrenaline heightened senses, she scanned the underbrush for a line of vision. The buck might bolt if it saw her. Her chest heaved as she paused between two large cedars. "Michael...where are you?" she yelled. To her immediate right, a wispy figure rose out of the brush, shaking. His face was pale, tears glistened on his cheeks. In a timeless rush of motion, the buck leaped into a bright patch of daylight exhaling plumes of steam from its dilated nostrils. Only fifteen yards away now, it seemed frozen in an intermediate state of mate, fight or flight. Grace screamed, stamping her foot and waving for Michael to come to her. As Michael crawled to her—achingly slow—Grace feigned a charge at the agitated buck. Shielded, Michael sprinted toward the house. Grace shifted around the cedar trunk. Michael was on the porch now, the buck had its sights on her. The buck shook its great antlers, stamping, eyes like black yolks. Grace knew that to run would make her an even greater target. She bounced up and down, strangely aware of her large, sagging breasts waving every which way, and how ridiculous it was that the buck could possibly see her—a barren, middle-aged woman, in her nighty—as either a mate or a threat. It seemed to draw just that conclusion as it gave one last snort, turned, and pranced toward the thick woods at the rear of the property.

Michael was on the porch bouncing on his toes. Grace strode briskly through the yard and up the steps before the buck could change its mind.

On the porch, she could see Michael had been crying. "I thought the deer was going to kill you," he cried. As she held him her feet began to ache. She realized she'd lost her slippers and that she was bleeding. Still, she held Michael, aching with the knowledge that time and life would take him, and she wished she could stamp her feet and scream to keep life from taking her last baby.

#####

Y2K had everyone running for the hills. The hardware store was making a killing. The basement became a shelter overnight. They'd yet to put in the new fluorescent lights. It was so dark down there, Grace couldn't tell if her eyes had adjusted, so dark that when she closed and opened them again she couldn't see her hand. The pull cord to light the bare bulb was in the middle of the room. She forged ahead on faith until it touched her cheek. The dim light was hardly better than a flashlight. The basement was their storage dump: boxes of discarded toys, outgrown and seasonal clothing, and excess building materials. She remembered the purpose of her subterranean trip as the plink plink plink of the cistern drew her focus to the plywood she'd stacked to cover the opening.

Y2K was two months off: the prophecy of the end of technology, the return to a rudimentary lifestyle, the dawning of the second dark age, the terror of wholesale chaos loomed. The cistern could provide enough water to last three months. Relieved that the cover was untouched from her last visit, she pulled the cord and edged her way back to the stairwell.

Spurred by the innate need for light, she bounded up the steps, stubbing her toe on the last step. Grace sat down at the kitchen table and started poring over the estimate to repair the cistern. $1,500.00, a bill they couldn't afford. They were still paying off the neighbor for the fence Ben destroyed on a bender. They'd driven around town with duck tape woven over the side window, twine holding together the front fender. They finally saved enough to get it fixed, but now a bill for a thousand dollars for Mimi's lodging in Sweden stared up at her.

Grace slid off the stool and lifted the crock pot lid. The pork loin simmered, Ron's favorite. As she replaced the lid she heard a thud on the porch near the kitchen door. It sounded like the bundled wood their neighbor dropped off every Fall, but that was months away. At a persistent rap, she rushed to the door. When she opened it, Ben was on his back like a turtle, staring up at their hulking teenage neighbor Rolf. Grace always liked the name because it reminded her of Venice, and Aunt Mary's Saint Bernard. Rolf was just as lumbering and loyal.

"He was over at the creek drinking wine coolers, Mrs. Marcos," Rolf stammered. He panted with his hands in his front pockets, "I thought you'd like to know." Ben rolled over to get up, his progress impeded by Rolf's size fourteen in the middle of his back. Grace put her hand to her mouth to stifle a giggle.

Ben hit a rough patch at sixteen; it was an ongoing drama, stealing out after dark, coming home drunk, obnoxious tantrums, and a litany of excuses to justify the tailspin.

"Thank you, Rolf," she said behind her hand.

At that moment Ron pulled into the driveway. "Get in the house," Grace commanded. Rolf took his foot off Ben, smiled and loped on down the street. "What's this?" Ron asked with his briefcase under his arm, each hand carrying a two-liter container of water. Ben looked away as he brushed himself off. He burped loudly as they all walked into the kitchen.

"Get up to your room. I want to talk with your father."

Alone, Grace turned to Ron. "Rolf found him down at the creek getting drunk."

Ron stacked the water in the pantry along with the other containers. He stood with his back to Grace, taking stock of their doomsday collection.

Turning back to her he said, "I think we're going to be all right."

Grace stirred the simmering loin. "I haven't heard from Mimi today...oh, let me tell you what happened to Michael!"

Ron reached over her shoulder and stuffed a piece of pork in his mouth. Grace closed the lid, playfully elbowed him in the ribs. They sat down at the kitchen table. Grace looked up at the clock. It was getting late. *I should call John and Thomas in*, she thought. "A horny buck pinned Michael down in the woods. It scared the daylights out of me. I had to scare it off."

"Is it mating season already?" Ron said, taking out his Bible.

"What do you want to do about Ben?"

"What can we do? He's almost an adult."

The stairs creaked. They both listened. Heavy footsteps shook the ceiling. "He'll be off to college in eight months," Ron said. "Are we going to the meeting tonight?"

Grace went to the kitchen window and looked out. She pulled her hair into a bun. Her feet ached from the morning's barefoot plummet into the woods. Grace sighed. "Everyone'll be there...seems like the Christian thing to do, just in case it turns out to be as bad as they say." Ron nodded, replacing the bookmark in his Bible.

Later that evening Grace and Ron walked into the meeting hall at the church. She could still smell the roses she'd put together for the wedding last Sunday. She walked by a trash can and found the source. The bouquets she'd painstakingly created to match the wedding dresses were tossed, along with half-eaten wedding cake and plastic wine glasses. The cloying scent permeated the hall. *I could use a glass of wine right now*, she thought. She made a mental note to have someone dump the trash cans after the meeting. She was only the florist, but she'd been a member of the church nearly a decade. She could get someone to do it.

They sat in the front row of fifty chairs neatly lined five deep. It wasn't a large hall, just large enough for after-service pastries, and the occasional casual wedding. Ron went to the microphone in front and tapped it. He'd been the sound man for the last few months, a rotating duty. As the chairs filled up the room buzzed with excitement and tension. Grace was relieved when Ron sat back down next to her. "I wonder if this is what it was like when Noah built the Ark?" Ron bent in close to ask. "Without the animal dung, of course." Grace held his hand and smiled, thinking of a punishment for Ben. Ron was right, there wasn't much they could do at this point.

Pastor Pat tapped the microphone. Conversations settled to a low buzz.

"Let's start with a prayer...Our father..."

Grace looked around the room for Marcy. Marcy was her best friend. She'd been there at the wedding on Sunday, helping the bride, working the kitchen, scooting about as she always did, filling in gaps. Marcy was the one who explained to her what bipolar was. She'd never suspected that Ben could be sick. She thought he was just obnoxious. Marcy set her on a course of discovery, and she was still parsing Ben's behavior into moments of youth and moments of bipolar flare-up. She wilted at the simpler explanation—she was a bad mother. Pastor Pat's sonorous voice lulled her. She put her head on Ron's shoulder. Someone behind them cleared their throat. Pastor Pat took the microphone off the stand, began pacing the front of the room, something he rarely did. To this point, he'd been an observer and a temperate believer of Y2K. He didn't own a computer or a cell phone. He seems nervous, Grace thought. She understood the source of his jitters when suddenly from the back of the room a curmudgeonly voice boomed, "Is the church going to provide an emergency shelter when the Y2K hits?"

Pastor Pat scanned the audience for a friendly face. He settled on Grace. Grace's eyes fluttered. She was daydreaming—the house with Ben at college, quiet and serene.

At first, she thought Pastor Pat was looking at Ron, so she took her head off his shoulder. Pastor Pat stepped forward and handed her the mike. "Our Director of Programs will speak on that." Grace's jaw dropped. It was a flashback to last Sunday when Pastor Pat handed her the mike to make a toast to the newlyweds. Then, she'd been tipsy on two glasses of Pinot. Now, the mike weighed a hundred pounds, as Pastor Pat smiled weakly and slid stage right. The crowd was frighteningly silent; a rushing sound filled Grace's ears. It was one thing to handle a friendly, forgiving crowd at a wedding reception, quite another to mollify fear-spiked parishioners nearing the end of humanity.

Grace turned to face the crowd of her peers. *They love me,* she assured herself.

"The first thing I'd like to say is that *we are in this together.*" She held the mike away for a moment to steady herself. Her palms were slippery. She took a deep breath, relieved to see Marcy standing by the entrance, smiling and waving, giving her a thumbs up.

"We're going to have a steering committee to address all concerns regarding Y2K. There will be a sign-up by the kitchen door after the meeting for anyone who'd like to be on the committee."

Grace looked at Ron. His eyebrows were raised. Grace gave the mike back to Pastor Pat. He gave her a short hug. Grace jittered the rest of the meeting. Pastor Pat rushed into one of his passions, the new youth ministry program. As the meeting hit the hour mark, Grace signaled Marcy to join her. They put a sign-up table by the kitchen. She wouldn't head the steering committee; Marcy would handle that, as she always did.

Later, as parishioners crowded the sign-up table Pastor Pat came up behind her. Ron was taking down the sound equipment. Pastor Pat's wife Barbara and his teenage children lingered near the kitchen door. "Thank you," he whispered out of earshot. Grace peered up at him and winked. Pastor Pat had become a dear friend and mentor for both her and Ron.

That night as they lay in bed, Grace stared at the full moon, filling up a pane in the French doors, galvanizing the deck outside. Mimi saw the same moon, on a different day, nevertheless, the same moon. She experienced Mimi's absence, a pressure on her breast, the strain in her arms. She drifted into a dream of washing tiny Mimi's hair with Johnson's baby shampoo, in the kitchen sink in Venice.

#####

Amber was coming to visit. It was a surprise, sprung from a thousand miles away after Y2K's anticlimactic fizz. They had enough extra supplies to last them a month. Grace hoped Amber still liked peanut butter. A case took up a shelf in the pantry and she needed the space. Amber was set to arrive in Buffalo that evening. Grace didn't want to get too excited, yet, it *was* exciting to share their home with her baby sister again. Now that Ben was off to college at Northwestern, on a full academic scholarship (they were still surprised that he'd been accepted), Grace settled into a calm routine, only to find that John and Thomas were beginning to percolate with puberty. Michael was still her baby, sweet, innocent and affectionate.

On the drive to the Buffalo Niagara Airport Grace braced herself with a set of rules for Amber. It felt like she was preparing for a natural disaster. The memories of Amber throwing up in Ron's car on I-5, 5150'ed in front of their neighbors in Venice, and the surly teenager who'd nearly ruined her wedding blew embers in her stomach all the way to the airport. Armed with a set of rules that she knew she couldn't enforce, she rolled her shoulders as she pulled up to the curb at passenger pick-up.

Amber dropped her cigarette and plunged into the front seat. Grace bent to kiss her on the cheek, but Amber was busy blowing her last drag out the window, her suitcase a lonely vessel on the curb. Grace pulled on the parking brake as Amber jumped out and got her suitcase. A traffic cop motioned Grace to move on. Amber couldn't get the Volvo rear door open; Grace reached over the back seat to unlock the door, and finally, Amber settled into the front seat beaming, with her owl glasses steamed up. "Seatbelt," Grace said, switching lanes to get on the freeway, without signaling. *I always signal*, she thought. *I'm already a mess and she's only been here five minutes.*

Amber tapped her foot. "Do you have lunch ready? I'm starved," she said to the windshield. Amber tapped both feet now.

Grace felt the familiar heartburn. "Are you nervous?" she asked, looking down at Amber's feet.

"No. Why do you ask?" Amber replied, defensively.

"Your feet are tapping," Grace said dryly as she maneuvered around a semi truck.

Amber's smile sagged. She looked out the window, smoothed her dress, snorted, began to tap again, caught herself, and squeezed her hands between her thighs.

"How's Ron?" she asked.

"Ron got a new job...thanks for asking. He likes it," Grace replied.

"That's good. You know I caught Ted with his sister having sex."

Grace applied the brake. It was as if she could see an accident up ahead, and was tensing for the impact. "I...what?"

"Remember when I told you he was cheating? Well...I caught him in his truck with her. They were in her driveway, with the windows all fogged up. I thought *our* family was fucked up," she snorted.

Grace reached to turn the radio on, thought better of it.

"I kicked him out," Amber continued.

"How are you going to pay your bills?"

"I've been cleaning houses. Dad helped me get an apartment. He says he'll loan me money if I go back to school. Is 7% interest good?"

"Our Dad...helping you?"

"I think he feels guilty."

"You're probably right," Grace replied, a dull pain hardening between her eyes.

When she pulled into the driveway Grace kept an eye out for the boys. Michael was at Rolf's house playing video games. John and Thomas were supposed to bring down the air mattress from the attic, and clean the upstairs bathroom. She set the brake and stared at Amber. *My Amber*, she thought...*drifting again*. A strained, mechanical smile spread across Amber's face. Grace looked up at the house with its fresh paint, smoke curling up from the wood stove, clouds captured in the upstairs window panes. It was always the same between them. Grace felt herself reacting to Amber, and Amber reacting to her as if the past twenty-five years had been a Sunday afternoon nap. She sighed wistfully.

Michael broke her reverie. He bounded up the driveway with the lumbering Rolf in tow. "Mommy! We found a beaver!" Grace and Amber stared at Michael, sopping wet from waist to toe. His hands were caked in alluvial mud, his hair a nest of curls, leaves, and twigs. "It's in Rolf's backyard. We cornered it under the shed...come see!" Rolf panted next to him, nodding.

"Michael. This is your Aunt Amber. Say hello."

Michael lunged into Amber's arms. Her arms flailed as he wrapped her in an embrace. She stepped back when he released her, with two choclatey handprints on her back. Amber smirked at Michael, and grinned at Rolf. Grace looked at them. "Michael, go inside and clean up. Rolf, can you take Amber's things in? She's had a long trip." Rolf tripped over himself moving around the car. He wrenched the rear door open and carried Amber's suitcase to the bottom of the stairs, as Amber and Grace settled at the kitchen table. Amber stared at him, curling a lock of her hair, wishing she'd worn her contacts. Grace brought out some coffee cake from the last Y2K meeting. She cut thick slices for Amber and her. "Want some coffee?" she asked.

Amber turned her cheek, "No thank you. Do you have any diet Pepsi?" she asked.

"No," Grace said, as Michael hopped off the last step into the kitchen. He was tall for his age. A creme colored mutt followed at his heels.

Grace wondered how Amber would react to Michael; he was extremely affectionate and was obviously her baby. Her answer came when Michael flowed across the room to Amber, who with her owl glasses and knee-length dress could pass for a librarian. She smiled until Michael was an arm's length away, when suddenly he wrapped his arms around her, giving her a wet kiss on the cheek. That was Michael, Grace thought, most people enjoyed his lack of inhibition and even found it refreshing.

Outraged, Amber shoved him as she leaped out of her chair. Michael flew back, confused. "What's his problem?" Amber yelled. "Is he retarded or something?" She slid to the other side of the table, wiping her face with the hem of her dress.

Grace's jaw dropped. *What planet did she come from?* she thought.

"Come here, Michael," she said, stepping forward, hugging him. She looked askance at Amber, who'd settled back in her chair, fishing through her faux leather purse for a cigarette and matches.

Nonplussed, she acted as if she'd been attacked. "You should get him under control. Not everyone likes to be touched like that."

Grace whispered into Michael's ear. "Why don't you go out back and pick some of those flowers you found near the creek. We'll put them on the table for dinner," she asked, warming him with her smile. Michael bounded past Amber, out onto the porch, paused to measure Amber, before plunging off the steps into the yard.

Grace was dismayed. They couldn't be further apart, although she knew *why* Amber acted the way she did. Distance and introspection provided her plenty of reasons for Amber's stunted growth. She knew from the pediatrician that there were myriad syndromes and diagnoses for children who'd experienced trauma in their formative years. Ben had an attachment disorder, and Michael's many delays could be attributed to his mother's alcohol abuse and father's physical abuse. Amber, she'd surmised, no doubt suffered from Mom's alcoholism and early sexual abuse. From that well, she drew a measure of compassion. It was part of her spiritual practice. Even so, her children would always come ahead of her past, and Amber would always be her past. These feelings boiled inside Grace as Amber got up and went outside.

#####

Amber sat on the cinderblock wall by the driveway smoking. She looked down at the Folger's can. Grace, she guessed, had put it there for her. She laughed, gazing after Michael, whose voice resounded off the trees, singing a gospel tune.

*You really fucked that up.*

Amber shrugged at the Folger's can and walked up the driveway. When she passed the screen door she peeked in to see what Grace was doing.

*She doesn't give a shit about you, why should you bother?*

Amber took a drag and dropped her smoldering cigarette on the driveway. She had an inkling, ignored it and blew smoke toward the screen door. A thickness in her chest moored her to the wall. She cringed at the thought of spending time with Michael outside. He is retarded, she thought. Then again, Grace was mad at her, and surely hated spending time with her. Amber sat on the wall and checked her voice messages. *Nothing from Ted, figures.*

Amber flipped her phone shut. She stared at the screen door. She suddenly realized that Grace was alone, the sun was dipping and Ron would be home soon. She had Grace all to herself. She pinched herself for her lack of foresight. She strode into the kitchen offering Grace—who was at the sink washing potatoes—a grand conciliatory smile. "Sorry for yelling at Michael."

Grace responded in kind. "I know. He's so sensitive about being different. He really is a sweetheart once you get to know him. All the kids love him." She dried her hands on her apron. "Come on, help me peel these potatoes." Amber pulled up a stool. Grace placed the strainer of potatoes on the table, along with two graters and a cookie sheet. She came around behind Amber and gave her a big hug. Amber took it, growing stiff when it went on too long, shrugging her shoulders and chuckling until Grace settled next to her.

"I eat potatoes all the time at home. Ted likes them baked, but I like them mashed," Amber said as if she were sharing a most intimate detail.

Grace smiled, wondering how Michael was getting along. Amber took out a pack of gum from her purse, offering Grace a stick. "I don't chew gum," Grace said. Grace was through three potatoes when Amber finished her first. Grace paused. "Can I show you a faster way to do that?" Amber stuck out her lip, offered the peeler, without a word. "Peel away from yourself onto the pan." Grace showed her, expertly flipping peels into a little pile.

"I don't do it like that because it hurts my wrist," Amber said, looking toward the porch expectantly.

Grace followed her gaze. A shadow crossed the porch. "Michael! Is that you?"

"Yes, Mom."

Within minutes there was a pile of peels, and a bowl full of bare chiseled potatoes. Grace was delighted and encouraged that they'd spent nearly an hour together without fighting, exchanging memories of their separate times in Venice, amid islands of silence and fluttering potato peels. They were both astonished to learn that they both knew Herbie. Amber came clean about offering Grace the baby she'd aborted. Grace knew the baby was Herbie's but wouldn't let on. Amber only described him as her boyfriend, but Grace knew better. Herbie did nothing for free.

Grace was at the sink filling up a pot with water and Amber wiped off the table, when they looked up at the same time. Cigarette smoke lingered by the screen door. Grace ran to the screen door and looked out, unsure whether the neighbor was barbecuing. She spied Michael holding a cigarette to his mouth. He had a pack of matches in his free hand. Grace glared back at Amber and rushed out the door, fuming. "Michael, put that down!" she yelled. "Where did you get that?"

Michael's shoulders dropped, as did the cigarette. "I found it in the driveway," he whimpered. Grace stared back into the kitchen. Amber was no longer at the table.

"Amber!"

No answer.

"Go brush your teeth," Grace ordered. "And don't ever let me catch you smoking again."

Grace picked up the cigarette like she might a dud firecracker. She stormed into the house, periscope vision, feeling betrayed. Amber slipped down the steps from upstairs, wiping her hands on her skirt. She smirked as she stepped onto the planked floor.

"What?"

Grace held up the cigarette. The air hardened between them. "You left a cigarette in the driveway. Michael found your matches! He was smoking!"

"No, I didn't. He took them out of my purse."

Grace took a step back, pinching the butt, astonished at the blatant lie.

"Amber...I was with you the entire time."

"He stole my matches and cigarettes. Why aren't you getting mad at him?" She chomped on her gum now, shaking her head.

Grace held the cigarette out. "Why don't you just admit it. You're lying."

"You never believe me...you never did." Amber stormed toward the door, seized up, rushed to the bottom of the stairs, glaring at Grace as she stomped up to the bathroom.

#####

She squeezed her palms against the mirror. The Amber staring back at her looked so old. *Why did you come here? You know she hates you. You're just like Mom...just like her!* Amber always expected to see the little girl with the pigtails and bangs, the girl in the brownies skirt, with bags under her eyes and the faraway stare. She squinted at the mirror. *You fucked up again.* Even a thousand miles from home, the bathroom was her sanctuary. *What are you going to do?*

Ted was at Melba's now, she knew. They were talking about her, she knew. She'd shattered his driver side window as Melba and he fondled each other. After that he'd moved in with her, abandoning the last semblance of their marriage. A cold dark apartment waited for her and her alone.

Amber opened Grace's medicine cabinet. *She won't miss a few pills. Do it. That'll teach her.* Amber spied a row of prescription bottles on the top shelf. She pulled one down and squinted at it. They were large chalky pills. She couldn't read the label, other than Grace's name. *Do it. She hates you.* Amber took a deep breath. The thickness in her chest cleared at the thought of leaving this world. *I could do it anytime*, she thought. Ted was gone. Denny was feeding Reggie. Her cat. What would happen to Reggie?

Amber put the bottle back on the shelf. *Still,* she thought, *Grace shouldn't have yelled at me. I'm her sister, not some orphan she's let in.* She slammed the medicine cabinet and sat on the toilet. The house was strangely quiet. *This home, the pretty fixtures, family photos on the walls, love, so much love, going away from me, to them...*

*Because you are broken. You are broken.*

Amber pounded on her knees until the pink flesh burned and her thighs ached. She heard her name. She jumped to her feet, pulling her dress down to her knees. "Amber. Come down here." The words were offered up, soft and imploring.

Amber blew her nose, tightened her waist tie, checked her face one last time. She rechecked the prescription bottles, made sure all the labels pointed out. She wore a victorious smile as she descended the stairs as coyly as a prom date. Michael was at the sink doing dishes. Grace waited for her in the living room. She sat in a crescent chair near a basket filled with colorful throws and blankets. She was wringing her hands, barefoot, as plump and motherly as Amber ever remembered her being. "Come sit down," Grace insisted.

Amber dragged her foot off the last step, glanced at Michael, and scanned the living room. She settled onto a settee next to an upright piano. Grace moved to the edge of her seat. "I don't want to fight," she said, opening her hands.

Amber stared at her absently.

"If you are going to be a guest in my house there are certain rules," Grace said.

Amber sighed.

"If you are going to smoke, you need to pick up after yourself." Grace stared at Amber, waiting for a response. When none came, she continued.

"You need to remember that my kids come first."

Amber squeezed her hands between her legs, staring at her lost big toe.

A scalding silence lingered, cooled and thickened until Grace got up to turn down the boiling potatoes, and Amber escaped again to the upstairs bathroom. They'd reached a dead end. They always reached a dead end. What lay beyond it was too much for Amber to bear, and their past was lost to Grace in the folds of her new life. She'd moved on.

The next day, Grace drove Amber back to the airport. Grace wanted a gesture, to see that everything was tidy between them. She'd done all she could for Amber. She kissed her on the cheek. Amber stood slack-faced at the passenger door, cars lurching and yielding around them. Grace's last image was of Amber lighting a cigarette, staring over the hood—knowing Grace was looking at her through the windshield—in a ponderous pose.

# 25

Amber decided to become a Medical Assistant. She'd never had a career, and Matson University promised to help her get her GED and certification. It was expensive, but they guaranteed graduation. Dad gave her the loan and bought her a Chrysler Fifth Avenue with a hundred thousand miles on it. She felt young in it, like she had a sugar daddy, tooling around town in antiquated luxury. The first day of classes, she walked into the classroom and chose a seat in the middle of the room. It wasn't like elementary school where she'd been a broken child, or high school where she'd been the outcast; she was a middle-aged divorcee with enough life behind her to go around. She watched her classmates file in and found herself surrounded by young men. She was titillated by their youthful bluster until one called her Mom during an icebreaker.

Amber adjusted her owl glasses and pulled her skirt over her knees. The instructor droned on. She couldn't understand a word he was saying. Some things never changed. She tilted her head to the right, where the boy with the eyeliner sat. He was so cute, with dark stripes in his hair, and a white strip down the middle, like Reggie, her cat. She'd had a burrito for lunch. She rummaged through her purse for a stick of gum. She held the pack up to him but he seemed more interested in his cuticles. She dropped the pack into her purse. Paul told her that ninety percent of getting through college was showing up. He'd done it drunk, he said. Amber watched the instructor, as he scanned the class. She smiled lightly as their eyes met. Matson University accepted her without transcripts. She came with her checkbook out. She matriculated in one day. They said she could graduate in a year if she took a full load.

It was the year of being an unfettered woman. There was no boyfriend or husband holding her back. No father to judge her every move. Her new apartment was hers and hers alone. She left Ted to clean out the old apartment since it was in his name. It was a year of doing things *her* way. She found within the first few months that she'd been doing things *her* way all along. Soon, she settled back into familiar routines, ones that had kept her sane for decades.

Two months into her last semester, she was pulling a C average. She rarely opened her books anymore. Amber traced the fresh price sticker at the upper corner of the glossy text. The instructor took roll. They told her she could sell the books back at the bookstore for half-price. She glanced over at the boy with the black eyeliner. He was nodding off. Reggie, her cat, was getting old. She might have to put him down. The timing was right though; she would get a job as a Medical Assistant after she graduated and couldn't stay home to nurse him.

The instructor wrote on the dry-erase board. Amber wondered if the markers were the same as the ones she used to sniff in high school art class. She still couldn't believe she used to get a buzz off of them, stealing whole cartons, stumbling from class to class. And now she was about to graduate from college.

The girl behind her tapped her on the shoulder. "May I borrow a piece of paper please."

They were so polite, the kids, never prepared, wanting their mommy to help them along. Amber tore a piece of paper from her binder. She began a fantastic doodle down the margin of her binder. The instructor turned on the DVD player, dimmed the lights, and started the DVD. *If I'd have known that school was this easy, I'd have gone a long time ago,* she thought.

Amber graduated that winter. The gown rental cost sixty dollars. The certificate came in the mail two weeks later. Dad called to congratulate her, adding that he wanted the first payment of her loan in a month. The clock was ticking.

After three applications without a response, she panicked and applied for a job at the Salvation Army. It was Denny's idea. That way she'd still have time to clean his house. Grace was delighted when she got the job. "Do you get a discount?" she asked, sounding like the teenager Amber remembered. The truth was, Amber didn't feel qualified to be a Medical Assistant. But, she did feel qualified to sift through other people's clothes at the Salvation Army. There was something right about taking the abandoned personal threads of people's lives, people just like her, washing them and rebirthing them into new homes. She liked working the aisles the best. Intake was grueling: pile upon pile of plastic bags and children's toys, coffee makers and dish racks. The sheer magnitude of human discard was unfathomable. She liked the aisles, under the frosty fluorescent glow, straightening the shirts and pants, fixing prices, watching customers percolate on a trail for bargains. Up and down the aisles she went, enjoying the moments of solitude between rushes.

Her coworkers were a completely different story. She hated that they talked about the customers behind their backs. They giggled when Alice the bag lady came in to peruse the paperbacks against the back wall, or shook their heads at the Mexican families that brought their kids in to play in the toy bin. Amber only liked Betty, the Filipino lady who worked the register. She brought Betty a cappuccino from Starbuck's every morning, placed it on the glass case by the register on her way to punch in. Betty called her Ambar, which made Amber smile, every time. She'd catch Betty watching her when it was slow, and Amber wondered if Betty couldn't have children, like her. Then one day, as they ate lunch on crates by the back door, sharing lumpia and the spaghetti she'd brought, Betty showed her a picture of her granddaughter in the Philippines. "She's my sunshine," Betty revealed in a tender moment that Amber couldn't quite relate to. She only knew that Betty and her daughter didn't talk and that *she* was Betty's work daughter.

Amber began working overtime to make rent. Denny said he would give her a raise if she worked an extra day, but she didn't want to be dependent on a man again so soon after Ted. When the manager's daughter was hired, eighteen and right out of high school, she knew her days were numbered. The new girl joined her coworkers, sneering at Amber when she came in. "Where's *my* coffee?"

The manager called Amber in for her review. She was owed a big paycheck, for all the overtime she'd been pulling. He was strangely formal. He asked her to sit, a first. Amber didn't cry when they handed her the final paycheck. She sat there biting her tongue, burning a hole in the apologetic manager. "There's nothing I can do, Amber," he said. There were a million reasons to cry over the years—getting fired wasn't one of them. Now, she refused to even drive by the Salvation Army. Her only regret was that she was no longer Betty's work daughter.

#####

It was another stormy Seattle day. Seagulls huddled in the dirt lot next door. Amber sat on her couch tapping away on her laptop. Her back ached from the three hours she'd spent writing and rewriting her resume. It felt like she was lying. The staff at the help center swore by their resumes. "We have a ninety percent success rate," they boasted. "You'll have a job by spring break."

The mail icon showed two new emails. She navigated to her inbox and found two "likes" for her last Facebook posting:

"Looking for a job." Nothing from Paul or Grace. She looked down her list of FRIENDS. She wanted to throw her laptop against the wall. Out of a hundred friends, only two people had the courtesy to respond? Amber frowned at her profile photo. It was a selfie she'd taken in the bathroom—too dark and solitary. She was dejected by week upon week of rejection. She'd been at it for three months: sent out five resumes, ten letters of introduction, applied at every doctor's office in Snohomish County. She decided to change things up. She uploaded a Bitstrip and posted: "There's more to the story," with the words coming out of the avatar's mouth. *Someone will respond to that,* she thought.

Amber got up and stretched. She walked past Reggie's empty basket. It cost two hundred dollars to put him down, added to the $20,000 she owed Dad, who still refused to accept her divorce. "It's not like he beat you," Dad said. He financed her renaissance, in spite of his steadfast belief that she would go back to Ted. When she forged ahead with her plan he became surly. Now she rarely answered her phone. The one day she picked up, he spelled it out for her. "You need to start paying me back. Get a job...any job." That was when her toe started bothering her again. She iced it and kept off it for a few days.

Amber returned to the couch. Denny responded to her Bitstrip with a smiley face. *It's about time...* She bent to scratch her leg, smiling at the cushion where she expected Reggie to be watching. She curled her feet under her and pulled a throw over her shoulders. No other comments on her page. Amber went to the refrigerator for a diet Pepsi and lit a cigarette. *If it wasn't for Denny, I'd be alone*, she thought.

As she sat at the kitchen table Amber was suddenly transported to Venice Beach, the Doors concert Grace had taken her to for her birthday. Her face darkened. Grace was so different then, unsure of herself. *She's so full of herself now. Too busy for me.* Amber banished the thought as the doorbell rang. She knew who it was. He was the only one who rang the doorbell. She let

Denny in, went to her bedroom to fetch a sweater and socks, leaving Denny to stand in the open door.

"Let's go to that Mexican place on Main Street," he yelled after her.

"You always get gas when we go there," she teased as they headed out to his truck. Amber shook her head when she saw Denny's Shar-pei in the passenger seat. It'd already bitten her once. She glared at him as he unlocked the passenger side. "Can you put him in the back, please?"

#####

Life in Seattle was over. Dad decided that she should move closer to family. Sure, she could have objected, but she owed him so much money that now he called the shots. She knew in her heart and ached to admit it that she'd failed as a Medical Assistant and that Matson University was a sham. "You got ripped off, honey," Dad said bluntly, disregarding all the work she'd put in to make him proud.

Amber shuffled through the apartment, the home she created for herself and no one else. It was *her* space and the prospect of giving it up deflated her with every step. She walked from the kitchen to the bathroom, the living room and back to the kitchen, a three-point, five-step triangle—pausing by the counter when she realized she'd forgotten what she was looking for. She found the packing tape on the sill in the living room. When she opened the curtain her Chrysler Fifth Avenue—a gentleman's car, her dad liked to call it—stared at her with those heavy-lidded headlights. It was happening so fast. Paul would be there within the hour. The boxes of her life were stacked against the wall by the door. Amber stared back into the empty living room. It seemed so small now, barely enough space to bear her pain, this last year. She whimpered softly at the image of her: a forgotten woman, banished by love, scorned by an ungrateful family, betrayed by the world that wouldn't have her. The image sucked her into the middle of the room. Self-pity is a bitter companion. There, looking up at the plastic chandelier, she noticed for the first time how dirty the ceiling was. *It's too late to clean*, she thought, trudging into the kitchen for yet another diet Pepsi. The fridge was empty, except for a box of Arm and Hammer, and the three remaining diet Pepsis she saved for the road. Still hard to swallow, waking up alone, cooking for one, finding only *her* hair, *her* stains, *her* dust, *her*. Amber taped one side of the last box—*her* spices. She lifted a cylinder of cardamom, it was a good five years old. Back then she decided to spice things up and make curry one summer day. Ted took one bite and spit it back on the plate. He could eat for two but that night he couldn't keep down a spoonful of change. Amber dropped the cylinder into the box and sighed. She stacked the box by the door. Her life: twelve boxes, a bed set, a recliner, the TV, a rack of clothes, a suitcase, her computer, and her Xbox. She went to the window.

It was past noon. She listened for the sound of the U-haul in the parking lot. Paul had moved to Berkeley. After she caught him cheating, Ted had yelled in a fit of anger, "Why don't you go live with Paul in Berkeley. See if he'll put up with you." The seed was planted.

The last thing Dad said was, "Your brother is going to move you down to Berkeley. He's got a job lined up for you." No discussion.

Amber jumped at the rumble of a truck in the parking lot. She flung the door open. Paul materialized on the welcome mat, looking as adult, sober and focused as she'd ever seen him. "Hi, Amber," he grinned, already moving past her.

Amber teetered on the threshold. She grabbed Paul's shoulder and kissed him on the cheek. It wasn't his fault. She forced a smile and adjusted her owl glasses. She was glad they talked on the phone. Paul didn't want to chat. It was going to be a long day. "I'll start loading while you clean," he said.

Amber stepped to the side as he grabbed two boxes and
headed back to the truck. She had no idea where she would sleep
tonight. It had been years since she hadn't known something so
important. Now, she was going to Berkeley and it felt like she'd
been sold. She failed as a wife, as a medical assistant, and now she
put herself in family hands once again. Amber shrugged and set
about cleaning the bathroom.

#####

Berkeley was the smallest country she'd ever seen, a world
apart from rural Washington. Everyone had an opinion, worldly,
confident opinions about things she never knew existed. The speed
of everyday life shook her into an alternate reality the first week.
She got a ticket running a yellow light her first day. She got
another ticket for parking on the street on a street cleaning day, and
yet another for exceeding the two-hour parking limit on her block.
The homeless people read novels and only accepted paper money.
After explaining to a patrol officer that she hadn't time to change
her plates, she took a day off to handle it. The DMV was a
congealed slice of the melting pot America touted, and on which
Berkeley prided itself. She'd grown accustomed to white bread.
The lady at the counter laughed when she asked if she could keep
her Washington license plates. "What's the matter, honey,
homesick?"
Amber liked her new roommate Jay and fantasized about
hooking up with him. Dependable Denny called every night at
seven, rain or shine. It didn't take long to arrange her life into tidy,
nearly manageable compartments. She even went a month without
a ticket. She settled onto a path of two poles, work and home, up
Highway 80 to Richmond and back. She loved the solitude of her
room, but found herself a little too comfortable with alone time.
She missed Reggie. She made the best of it by getting on Facebook
two, three times a day, and playing Xbox for hours.

Paul had gotten her a job at the non-profit he worked for as a director. She worked in a group home, direct care for adults with disabilities. Sunday was her day off. She called Grace every Sunday night because she knew she would be kinder on a church day. She woke up early, drank two Pepsis and played Xbox. Her back was always sore from a week of nudging Delma, her "client", in and out of the car, in and out of the bath, in and out of bed, in and out of moods. It was a tiring and thankless job, but Amber liked it. "Delma is a hoot," she'd tell Paul. Her name tag read "Amber Moleson, Direct Care Provider" in gold letters. She wore it with pride.

Paul was constantly on the move so she didn't call him on a scheduled day. When they did talk she couldn't keep him on the phone. He always had someplace to be. "Paul, my roommate hit on me again. What should I do?" That got his attention. He always had advice, some useful. She left messages, two or three times a week. She never answered her cell when he called, preferring to save his voice on the return message. It was always the same. "Sorry I missed your call. Let's get together this weekend." And they would. He was so predictable.

Relaxed in her new home and city, Amber got drunk for the first time in a year. She'd spent Friday night at the hospital with Delma, who'd decided to eat a roll of pennies. They pumped Delma's stomach, but kept her at the hospital because her blood pressure plummeted. Amber drank coffee from a machine, and gave the waiting room nurse the evil eye when he refused to give her a pillow and blanket. It was a sleepless night. So, Saturday night Amber bought a bottle of wine at 7-Eleven and watched *Simpson's* reruns on Fox. When she woke up Sunday morning her tongue was a thick sandpaper slug. There was a message on her cell. "Don't call me anymore." It was from Ted. Images of the previous evening were like a grey mass of clay. There was nothing to recall, no explanation for his message. She was tempted to call him back, but thought better of it. She got online instead, searching for Darryl, her old high school boyfriend. At least that's what she called him. The search was fruitless so she loaded her Facebook page. There was nothing to say. Too hungover to upload another Bitstrip, she resorted to clicking "likes", which made her feel even more alone. She edited her personal info to "lives in Berkeley CA." Amber turned the lights off and listened for Jay to come home. The ceiling looked like it was breathing, and her bed felt like it was floating. The house was silent when she awoke in the middle of the night. Outside, the street looked frozen and deserted as she peered through the curtains.

A few days later she started a ten-hour shift at the group home. Her odometer clicked several thousand miles since she moved to Berkeley. The Foundation paid her mileage, but it wouldn't pay for the wear and tear she put on the Fifth Avenue.

Amber strained the seat belt across Delma's prodigious belly. It was rainy out, the asphalt coal-black, as seagulls squawked overhead on their way to the bay. They needed to pick up some laxative for Delma. Walgreens was less than a mile away, but Amber knew better than to march Delma down the sidewalk, in public, without backup. She'd learned her lesson, Delma plopping down at an intersection refusing to budge. It took three patrol officers to escort her to the sidewalk.

Amber held up a pack of Red Vines in her left hand. She kept an eye on Delma, who could move like a cobra when she saw something she wanted. "Now Delma, you can have a piece when we get there. You need to have a BM today or your mother's going to give you an enema." Delma screwed up her face and reached for the Red Vines. Amber tucked the Red Vines down between the driver's seat and the door. Delma undid her seat belt and smiled at Amber. "Delma, behave!" she warned.

Back from Walgreens, the group home was the quietest house in the cul-de-sac. It could change at any moment. She'd lost Delma a few times already. Delma had a knack for breaking into neighbors' kitchens for a quick snack.

It had been a successful outing. Amber handed Delma a Red Vine. She got out and walked around to the passenger side door. Delma winked at her.

"Come on," Amber commanded.

Delma leaned forward while Amber grabbed her hands. Amber winced at the puddle on her seat. "Delma!"

Inside, she helped Delma change. Eight hours into her shift she was bored to tears. She called Paul with Delma next to her on the couch watching Dr. Phil.

"I made spaghetti. Are you coming for dinner?" she asked him.

"Sure, will Jay be there?"

Amber resented the question. "His girlfriend is over. They stay in his room when she's there." When they hung up she went to the fridge for a diet Pepsi. It was her third of the day. Her heart pounded from the caffeine and she didn't want to go home after last night. She'd slept with Jay. Paul would find out. She knew it was a bad idea. *What's it any of his business? I'm a grown woman.* Surely Jay's girlfriend wouldn't start anything with Paul there.

On the way home, she called the house to see if Jay was there. It rang and rang.

Later, out of the shower, she went into the fridge for another Pepsi. There was a bright crack under Jay's door and his stereo was on, so she guessed he was home. She rearranged some condiments on her shelf in the refrigerator, vaguely aware that her robe had fallen open. The tile creaked at the entrance to the kitchen. A smile crossed her face. He would be watching. Paul wouldn't be there for another hour. She stuck her butt out. They'd already done it once, so it didn't matter. Amber turned around, her breasts moist from the hot shower. Jay's lips parted as he looked back toward his bedroom. He was so close now, an arm's length away. She could already feel his strong hands on her breasts. Amber stepped to him. Her heart stopped as his girlfriend peeked over Jay's shoulder. Amber yanked the tie on her robe and dashed to her room. On the other side of the door, she listened to the rising voices in the kitchen. She locked the door and smiled as she slipped into a cotton shift, put on makeup, and put two barrettes in her hair. *I can pass for twenty-five*, she thought as she went out to the kitchen. She walked past his door wanting to hear what *she* had to say. They weren't invited for dinner, so she didn't have to be nice.

Amber took the spaghetti pot out of the fridge, placed in on the front burner and put the gas on medium. She remembered seeing a half full bottle of red wine on Jay's shelf. She listened closely. *They're probably having sex*, she thought, as she took the bottle out and poured herself a glass. She went to the sink, filled the bottle with water to replace what she drank; satisfied that the level was right, she returned it to Jay's shelf.

Amber had been in Berkeley for three months. Denny wanted her to move in with him. It felt good to be wanted. *I've worked too hard to live on my own to give it up so soon,* she thought. It was a new life, she was a new woman, caring for the needy and treading water with a smile on her face. The past was like an old black and white film she pulled out when she had company. "I was molested, but I am stronger because of it," she told Paul, straight-faced, with a steely smile. "I love my life."

That night, over dinner, she was especially talkative. Paul wouldn't guess that she'd started drinking before he arrived. After dinner she had another glass of wine while Paul washed the spaghetti pot. Jay and his girlfriend never came out of his room. When Paul was in the bathroom she went to the front room and looked out the window for Jay's car. She cursed him walking back to her room. As she and Paul watched *Seinfeld* she told him she had sex with Jay. He just shook his head. The look of disappointment stung more than words.

Amber wished Jay would come home so they could get it over with while Paul was still there. Paul would see for himself why she had to move.

#####

The new place was in a large apartment building in Oakland, near 580. City life was a whitewater rapid compared to the sleepy creek of Marysville, Washington. So many people packed into a city block. She found the place herself on Craig's list. She invited Paul to come with her to meet her prospective roommate. He still brooded over her sleeping with Jay, and she wanted him to think she still needed him.

It was warm and unusually sunny for Autumn in the Bay Area. Paul commented on the plentiful parking as they walked up the tree-lined street. Maple leaves overflowed the sidewalk and gutter as they approached the building. They moved past a line of garbage cans overflowing next to the driveway. I-580 hummed in the background. On the second floor sundry smells met them: cabbage, curry, burnt hair, and Tide. They knocked and a husky forty-year-old answered the door. His t-shirt was too tight, and his thick hands were desperately in need of a good scrubbing. Amber watched Paul eye the contents of the tiny communal living room. Nubian art filled the walls, statuettes of lithe male and female archetypes repeated throughout the three bedroom apartment. "I'm renting it for my brother. I'll be a roommate," he said.

Amber's room was in the back. They stood in the doorway, curious at the sight of workout equipment and partially filled moving boxes spilled about the room. Amber frowned at Paul. "Will it be ready by the end of the month?" she asked.

The roommate waved her off. "Of course. It'll be ready before that if you want." He began to tell them about his famous entertainer brother when a young Asian female, a student perhaps, peeked her head out the door across from Amber's. She looked frightened until she saw Paul and Amber. She smiled shyly, squeezing between them, avoiding eye contact with the roommate —a detail Paul shared with Amber out at the curb.

"Did you already pay the deposit?" he asked.

Amber nodded. "At least I won't be alone," she assured him.

After the first month, Amber began to complain that her roommate was hitting on her and the student. "He's relentless." Paul came over on weekends to make a show of being a protective brother. When another month passed he asked how she solved the problem.

"Oh, that...he slept with me. Now he only bothers me when he's horny!" She shrugged but looked the other way. "He's driving our roommate insane. She can't afford to move."

Amber went a few weeks without mentioning her roommate, until she called one Friday night crying. "I've got to get out of here. He hit me." Paul came over, angry, but the roommate wasn't there. They went to his house where she spent the night on the couch. She thanked him over and over for being a good brother, meaning every word of it, yet in her mind, she couldn't help thinking he was somehow responsible for her problem. *He forced you to move away from Jay.*

The next morning Amber called the roommate and told him she was leaving. She spoke with her back to Paul as she explained that she'd found a place closer to work.

Paul was disappointed once again that she had to move. She could feel his broiling frustration, and was past caring. She'd lived in the Bay Area ten months and was looking for her third place. She liked her job, but she couldn't afford the new deposit, so she had to borrow it from Paul.

In a moment of weakness, Amber called Ted to see if he was ready to apologize. It was no use. Denny called her that night. They talked for hours. She told him a crafted version of events, leaving out the sex.

Her next apartment was the last in the Bay Area. Paul found a woman, new in sobriety, who had a room to rent in her house in San Leandro. It started so well. Amber told Paul that she made a new friend. It was a three-bedroom house. Amber had her own bathroom. They shared everything else. After a month Amber complained to Paul that her roommate's son was pestering her. "He knocks on my door late at night. I think he's high."

After two months the roommate filed a restraining order against Amber. Paul attended the court date as a character witness and the order was dropped. The damage was done. Amber continued to talk with Denny every night. In spite of her fraying life, she bragged about how she'd made it in the Bay Area all by herself. But Denny had been listening to her for years. He heard another story.

One day he called Paul. "Amber needs someone to take care of her. I need her here with me. You'll never have to worry about her again."

That Sunday over brunch Paul laid out the plan to Amber. His lack of faith in her was insulting. He'd already made up his mind. Amid the ferns and dark polished benches at a downtown café in Berkeley, Paul revealed that he and Denny had been talking. "Denny will take care of you. It's too crazy in the city...too many wolves."

Amber sat in silence, suspicious, watching his eyes dart around the room. *He's trying to get rid of me. Just like Dad and Grace.*

It was during the morning breakfast rush. Amber couldn't think straight with all the chatter and foreign languages, with UC Berkeley three blocks away. She shook her head and went to the café bathroom. She stared into the scratched mirror at the bags under her eyes, seeing her history, floating. She felt like crying, at her failure, at the betrayal, at her inability to see why they thought she should go back to Washington.

Back in her seat, Paul spilled the beans. "It wasn't my idea. Denny said he needs you." Amber stared absently at a nearby ficus. She wasn't going to show how much it hurt. She conceded that Denny was a physical wreck, and had been since his wife died. He needed her more than Delma needed her. Still, Paul *was* trying to get rid of her. "Well?" Paul waited, drinking too much coffee.

"It has been hard for me," she sighed. "I'm not going because I have to. I made it this long on my own." She waited for Paul to extend the sentence, but he just sat there sipping his coffee. They fidgeted in silence for the next few minutes, barely meeting eyes. He was slipping away again. Finally, when the waitress put the check on the table, she felt like she had no choice, that they'd already set the plan in motion.

"All right. If he needs me."

That was how Amber made it back to Washington; it was the last time she saw Paul in person. The experiment of living near family, began as a test to gauge her ability to survive on her own. She'd passed the test, in her eyes, although she knew Paul would say otherwise.

As she settled into domestic life with Denny back in Washington, his needs and life became her obsession. The year in the Bay Area was soon thrown on the heap along with the other failures: her marriage, her family, her career, her motherhood. Soon she led a familiar, plodding life of servitude with a partner who held her in a vice. From then on she maintained a festering animosity toward Paul. He'd given her away, just like all the rest. *Nobody wants you!* The words filled her thoughts, a cascading mantra that weighed on her every breath.

# 26

Grace knew well of Amber's time in the Bay Area. They spoke weekly. That is, until Amber cut her off. Amber didn't want advice. Grace believed that there was a freckle of truth in the details she shared: Ted's adultery, Paul's betrayal, and her roommates' transgressions. The stories appeared credible. Ted did cheat on her. Paul did agree to move her back to Washington State. Her roommates did have sex with her. In aggregate they spelled a pattern: Amber didn't know how to get along with others. She was a victim. She was still the broken little girl Grace left behind. At least that was what Grace thought.

Now that Amber was back in Washington, her tone changed. Grace thought she sounded defeated. There had always been a defiant edge to her whining, now Amber sounded dull and medicated. "Are you taking medication?" she asked.

"No."

"There's nothing wrong if you are," Grace responded, when it felt like she was losing her again. "If you see a therapist they might be able to get you a prescription."

"I don't need a therapist!" Amber bleated into the phone. Grace knew better than to push her on the subject. "Do you still love me?" Amber asked at the end of their "make-up" call.

Grace had her own challenges. Ron wasn't getting any job offers after getting laid off yet again. Mimi was back at school in Rochester; she was knee deep in school work and all her spare time went to her boyfriend. The boys were growing at an amazing clip, playing sports—except for Michael, who still preferred to hang around the house with his mother. The anchor in their lives was the church. Grace could walk through the halls of the little school in the basement to see her handiwork. Murals of Jesus, flocked by children of all ages, Noah's Ark, and Moses on the Mount were some of her best work. It was when working on that mountain that she realized that she'd made it to the top. From living under the pier in Venice Beach to being a valuable member of a loving, supportive community, with a family she could have only dreamed of, a home they'd built together, a husband who adored her, children who were growing and blossoming into fine adults. Sure they'd struggled, most families did, but the abundance in her life could not be listed on paper—it was the result of making wise choices, working hard, and most of all, faith.

One Saturday evening she drove home from Marcy's with an art book she'd found at the thrift store. They'd spent the afternoon shopping in Rochester and she couldn't wait to settle down on the settee with a cup of tea and her new book. Marcy, always the encouraging friend, said she should go back to school and get her art degree. "You're just as talented as any of those people. They all started somewhere."

When Grace walked in the front door Ron was waiting at the kitchen table. A bouquet of flowers sat on the drainboard. His back was straight on the old stool, his face smooth and expectant, reminding her of the day he proposed twenty years ago. "Happy Anniversary!" he said, standing with open arms.

She heard Michael giggle, and in a sudden rush from the living room, he and Mimi, Ben, John, and Thomas came out of their hiding places. "Surprise!"

"What's this?" Grace cried, looking from face to face, beaming. She hugged Mimi first, going on down the line, until Michael held her, as she cried into his curls. "All my babies home. What's the occasion?"

Ben stepped forward, looking dapper and five years older with a goatee. "It's the anniversary of our move to Rochester," he said.

"It's been seventeen years," Mimi said.

Grace smiled. "Close enough. My babies are home." She met eyes with Ron, loving him so deeply for all they'd been through. "We've come a long way, haven't we?"

Mimi stepped forward and hugged her parents. "School's closed for the holidays so we thought it would be a good time to get together. It may be our last chance for a while."

"I didn't cook anything..." Grace started.

Ron handed Grace her coat. "We're taking you out. No cooking tonight."

At the Chinese restaurant, they sat at a great round table with a Lazy Susan in the center. Grace hadn't missed the fact that John and Thomas both had to stoop to enter the restaurant. At her request, the waitress lit the votive candles on the table, although it was still light out. They bowed their heads and gave thanks, each adding a personal prayer of gratitude. After the meal, with piles of dishes, licked clean by the boys, they read their fortune cookies. They teased Ben when his read: You will find love in many places. For the first time in years, the Marcos family rode home together squeezed into the minivan, cozy and sated. "Seventeen years," Grace said, half to herself, as they pulled up the driveway.

At the kitchen table with the lights down low, Ben snoring on the settee, Grace sipped wine and marked an entry in her journal.

*Looking back, these last seventeen years, I couldn't imagine this! Michael is doing well in school, my baby growing up. John is*

*becoming a man, kind, loyal. Thomas is SO creative and talented.
My Mimi, she's become a woman. (grandchildren?) And Ben, we
couldn't ask for anything more. He's at Northwestern, doing the
best he can. Ron is my anchor. And our community. We are loved.
What would we do without Pastor Pat? Thank you, Lord.*

Grace closed her journal and stepped out onto the deck. The
moon was high and a freezing gust from the North made her
shiver. She inhaled the pure night air, and held her hands to the sky,
cupping the moon, smiling, stretching on the tips of her toes. It had
been a good day and a good life.

#####

It was Friday at the doctor's office. Michael had an ear
infection. Grace looked around the waiting room, face pinched,
hands folded in her lap. Michael leaned his head on her shoulder,
aware of the other people looking at them. He was as affectionate
as a child, holding her hand, seeking eye contact. The nurse behind
the sliding glass window smiled perfunctorily, not sure what to
make of the oversized boy. Grace returned her furtive glances with
sharp maternal pride.

She kissed Michael on the top of his head, then her cell
erupted. She looked around the room. "Sorry," she said to no one
in particular.

It was Ron.

"What is it? I'm at the Doctor's office."

"Grace...are you sitting?"

"Yes. Ron...what's going on?" she asked, impatiently.

"Pastor Pat is dead."

"Wha...no...what are you talking about? That's not funny."

"He died this morning...heart attack."

"No."

"Yes. I'll call you later. I love you."

Grace stared at a painting near the nurse's station. She hadn't noticed it, an obscure Norman Rockwell piece. Michael stared at her. "Mommy, what is it?"

Grace's mouth twisted. She took Michael's hand. "Nothing, sweetie. I'll tell you later."

Grace stared at the painting, all her pain flowing into the flat, lifeless composition. The man in the painting, a paternal archetype, was reading the Bible to his children at bedtime. Pastor Pat was the real-life father of their community, their people, his flock.

The picture sucked at her. Children and mothers slipped by on their way to see the doctor. Grace saw none of them. When their name was called Michael nudged her. She didn't realize she had been crying until they sat in the examination room, and Michael brushed her face with his mitten. *Pastor Pat. What are we going to do without you? Stop crying,* she told herself...*keep it together until you get home.* The little room felt three sizes too small. Michael kept looking at her, worry etched on his face.

When the doctor finished the examination, smiling at Michael, declaring that his infection was nearly past, they rushed to the car in a driving rain. Grace guided the minivan through the slushy black snow, hyper-aware of her hands gripping the wheel. So tight, she thought she would twist the steel. By the time they reached the house, she could do nothing but fall onto her bed and cry. The phone rang insistently, but she couldn't muster the strength to rise. It felt like a curtain had fallen on her life, their life, and she could only see an unremitting darkness around her.

Ron came home early. He lay down beside her. His chest rose and fell, gently at first, so much the rock. But soon his body quivered and his chest heaved. She found herself soothing him, with her hands across his face and hair. The phone kept ringing the entire time. Finally, Michael came to their bedroom door. He rarely answered the phone. John and Thomas were still at school. "It's Marcy. She says it's an emergency." He waited in the doorway, persistent. "What's wrong, Mommy?"

370

Grace and Ron pulled themselves out of bed. "Pastor Pat passed away this morning."

Michael's eyes widened. He felt things others didn't. "I had a feeling," he said sadly, dropping his head.

#####

They had no time to mourn. The phone wouldn't stop ringing. She wished she hadn't taken that first call from Marcy after Pastor Pat died. He was the center of the community, and the community was their center. The void created by his passing pulled everyone into a spiral. Grace and Ron were positioned to fill in as best they could. Grace called a meeting at the hall. Ron kept the celebration team prepared, practicing twice a week. At the meeting the members of their tight spiritual family got up one by one to tell a story about Pat. Each and every member shared an intimate connection. It seemed like they'd taken the great man for granted. Grace lingered, making herself available to lend an ear and kind word until the last family left. Pastor Pat was always the last one to leave such events. As she turned off the lights, walking back to the car with a tray of Christmas cookies in her hands, she could hear his voice, something he said when they were alone. *We are so blessed to be here together...*

A month after his death, the church still lacked a shepherd. Grace spent her days consoling, visiting and heading prayer studies at the church. They hadn't found a new pastor, and many of their members were leaving for other communities. An angry rumbling could be heard now at the end of services, when Ron, as the associate pastor, led them in song and prayer. Who could replace Pastor Pat?

At home Grace and Ron found themselves confronting the most simple daily events with irritation, lashing out, blaming, something they'd never done when Pat was alive. Their lives were in a wringer, twisted into a tight unrecognizable knot. The feeling as they lay down at night was that their life was over. Ron fell into a depression. He used up his sick days filling in at the church. His boss informed him one day to clean out his desk. Downsizing was what they called it.

As time passed Grace daydreamed of California and the family she left behind. Terri had moved to Florida, so she'd traveled South every Summer to visit. Kimo died of AIDS. She missed his funeral and sent her love to Rex, who went into an alcoholic spiral at the loss of his soul mate. She read and read and read, holding at bay the rising gloom that threatened to consume her. The one bookshelf they'd brought from Venice had multiplied into four, with an expanding variety of fiction, children's books, spiritual best sellers and art books. They read together in evenings as they always had, but now Ron only read the Bible. He became increasingly sullen as the months passed without employment. The economy had tanked, they said, but the word was that a recovery was on the horizon.

By the winter thaw, Ron began to sleep in, when the rest of the house was up. Grace, helpless in bringing him out of his malaise, immersed herself in her books. Her new passion was comparative religions. Grace studied Buddhism, Judaism and the poetry of Rumi. She embraced alternative teachings on the history of Jesus, considered blasphemous by some in her community. Ron was mired in the loss of their previous life, while she sought light, any light. She had always loved his stability, his consistency. They'd been on the East Coast for most of their married life, but it seemed to be unraveling.

One day at the onset of spring, when the backyard blossomed into a sensuous quilt of color, Grace stood in front of the mirror, staring at a middle-aged mother she barely knew. Like the infant buds, birds, and squirrels full of new energy, she felt herself rising out of herself. Beyond a year of gloom, an end spilled away, while a new beginning sprang from the shadows. That was the scene that greeted her, alone in the house, combing her hair, following the lines of her face.

Ron was at a neighbor's house laying some tile and the kids
were at a friend's birthday party. It took some doing to get him out
of his funk. The work did him good. He always came home
glowing after physical labor.

Sunlight came in through the French doors, and the shadows
webbed out on the worn wooden floor. She ran her hands over her
broadened hips, a brush through her increasingly grey hair. She
peered at the bookcase on the wall leading to the master bath. The
portrait of her family warmed her heart, they'd grown so much
together. The boys tested their burgeoning independence in starts
and stops. Mimi and Ben were on their way. The phone rang, but
she brushed it off, as she was apt to do these days. The church had
gotten a new pastor, and the remaining members complained of his
austere demeanor. No one could fill Pastor Pat's shoes. There was
nothing at the church to keep them. Grace savored the silence of a
childless house, too raw to go out just yet.

#####

Grace kept an apple carton on the floor by the kitchen door
for the bills. The carton caught the overflow of late notices spilling
off the secretary desk. The secretary had been a "find" at a garage
sale when money was coming in. The mortgage payment, credit
cards, even a line of credit for the buildout were maxed and due.
The house they'd built was worth little more than the purchase
price, what with the housing crisis. Grace got in the habit of
throwing her jacket over the carton when she arrived home. She
began to bake and cook as a way to ameliorate the sense of doom.
She worked her way through her Betty Crocker cookbook, marking
notes in the margins: meals that pleased Ron and the boys, meals
to avoid, until the book was tattered and bloated. She kept it on the
island, in full view, so she could refer to it, when she felt
overwhelmed or inspired. She laughed at its girth and how much
she was saving on therapy.

One day Ron came downstairs and settled on a bench near the island, deep in thought. Grace moved the cookbook over to the counter and sat next to him, cupping a fresh mug of tea. She knew he'd been on the phone with his brother. She was pleased that he'd reached out to his family, relieving the pressure for her to be his everything.

"Lance wants us to move to Vegas."

Grace raised her eyebrows. She stood up and put her teacup in the sink. They'd had many ideas over the last six months. California was an option. Ron still had connections there. "Really," she said, with her back to the sink, arms folded.

Ron nodded, searching for the right words to proceed.

In the last few weeks it was as if they'd been running a three-legged race, and separated short of the finish line. "What's left here?" Ron said.

Grace turned and ran her hand along the wood counter. They'd chosen the Maple together, her favorite part of the kitchen. "I don't know. I like Lance. Can we leave? We still owe on the house."

"We'll sell it."

Grace tried to imagine an existence beyond the town of Rush, their comfort zone, away from the homestead they'd built with grit and faith. She jerked her hand away from the counter. "We can never come back," she said, surprising herself. "If Pastor Pat hadn't died..."

Ron rose from the stool. Out on the porch, a squirrel shot across the rail, over the herb pots he'd made for her. Grace turned and faced him. Her chest was heaving. She slapped her sides. "How can we leave?" she cried, "We built this home! What else do we have? It *is* us." She stared into his eyes. Pain, like a stinging fog, thickened between them. Yet...Grace reached for him reflexively, instinctively, after decades together. Ron laid his head on her breast. The kids were at school. Grace wrapped his head in her arms. She could feel his breath, hot and moist. He held her waist as if he were drowning. The room was so still, the dripping faucet marking the silence, as they swayed gently in the sun-swept kitchen. She broke the spell with the simplest of segues. "It's sunny all the time in Vegas."

##### #####

It was the worst year of her life. Grace was shipwrecked, drifting in a lifeboat, day upon day, with nothing to look at but the stagnant desert. Grace prayed for change—an artist, who couldn't see colors. The music and laughter were left behind in Rush: in the walls, the community center, at the grave of Pastor Pat. She told Amber, after a month of staring out the front window at the drug dealers and underage prostitutes parading up and down their block, that she felt like a refugee. Amber seemed to lighten at the image of her big sister being brought to her knees. Grace decided not to share anything of value with her, for fear that she'd put it on Facebook, or with Paul, who didn't know they'd moved. Lance had saved them. He let them live at the house for free. Now she understood why. Many of the houses on the block were boarded up.

She began homeschooling the boys again, unwilling to send them to the closest school. "It'll only be until I find work...probably a year," Ron said.

Grace spent her spare time online playing SIMS. She meticulously created the family she had in Rush, right down to the plants, and the dog. Her pining reached new heights when Ron found a job, two jobs really, selling credit card machines door to door, and doing maintenance at a retirement community. He was gone from six in the morning until nine at night. Talk of finding a real home animated their meals and brief moments together.

Toward the end of their first year in Las Vegas Grace decided to visit Dad. She couldn't explain to Ron why she wanted to trek across two states to visit a man who showed no inclination toward her. *Maybe I'm being needy,* she thought, as she packed supplies for the trip. She borrowed Lance's van, and headed out with her three boys on a pink-skied August morning.

After a grueling eleven-hour drive, a portent of the visit presented itself at a McDonald's in Medford, where she locked the keys in the van. A policeman opened the door with a slim jim, and they were on their way. As she drove up Dad's gravel driveway she was already feeling like it was a mistake to invade his space—he'd become semi-reclusive since moving to Oregon. Amber warned her, "He's an old grump. Don't overstay your welcome."

Grace pulled the van close to the double garage, figuring it would be good to unload right into the downstairs entry. Dad walked out on the upper deck looking older and smaller than she remembered. He moved stiffly, with a perpetual scowl. After a brief, welcoming wave, he asked her to move the van to the edge of the driveway. "That way I still have a path to feed the deer." As the boys jogged up the steps Grace could see his face change. He withdrew into the house. Inside, they all lined up for their grandfather. "What are you feeding these boys?" he joked, scrutinizing them through his bifocals. She settled on the couch facing him, Michael by her side. John and Thomas ventured out into the forest to hunt for wood. In spite of her exhaustion, she was excited to connect with Dad. The TV was on, *Seinfeld* at six o'clock every weekday. Dad turned down the volume but kept looking back at the screen. Grace looked around the living room. There were pictures of Steve and Bryan's kids, the boys' prom pictures, and nicknacks from when they lived in San Diego. There was even a portrait of Ruth, his lady friend. There was a wedding photo of Amber and Ted on the end table. She wondered if Amber told him about the divorce. She was delighted to see the photo she sent of her family three Christmases ago. Grace held the framed photo on her lap so Michael could see it. She was shocked at how much weight she'd gained in Las Vegas. She placed it back on the table and stared at Dad.

"Dad?"

"Yes," he said, dozing in his recliner.

"What are we having for dinner?" she asked.

"I thought you could cook something." he replied.

Grace got up and went to his refrigerator. It was stark, to say the least, a few condiments and a jar of pickles. Michael twisted his face when he looked over her shoulder at the barren white shelves. The freezer was no better, a pack of Jimmy Dean sausage and a sad looking bag of frozen peas. When they came back into the living room Dad had his wallet in his lap. "Here. Go to the store and pick us up some hamburgers and buns. The boys like hamburgers, right?"

He held two twenties out to her. "Take the boys with you. I don't want them getting into trouble while you're gone."

Grace herded the boys back into the van. "I'm sorry your grandpa is acting so grumpy. He's tired, that's all."

When they returned, Dad laid out his rifles on the back porch nestled against the side of the mountain. Grace kept the kitchen door open to listen while she prepared dinner. Dad showed the boys how to load the 22 caliber. He set up cans against the hillside and showed them each how to aim. Grace listened closely as he commanded the boys' attention. She'd never heard her father so at ease, teaching, guiding and encouraging. The burgers were broiling in the oven and there was a break between gunshots. She ventured onto the back deck, wondering what it would be like to shoot a rifle. "Can I try?" she asked as he reloaded.

"No. Girls belong in the kitchen. This is men's work."

The boys stared at their mother, and back at their grandpa. She noticed their confusion. "What about Annie Oakley?" Grace asked.

"She wasn't real. That's just a tall tale. Women can't shoot." He was so sure of himself.

He turned his back on her.

Grace forced a smile and surrendered to the kitchen.

When the meal was ready, she served them, her boys, and Dad sitting at the head of the table. He told stories of his time in Korea and Vietnam, never asking once about their move to Las

Vegas. She noticed his owl glasses. "Amber has a pair just like that."

"I got mine first," he said, apparently sore at the comparison.

Grace watched Dad throughout the meal, his gestures, the way he laughed at his own jokes, how he took it personally when the boys yawned as the meal stretched past sunset.

After dinner Dad became sullen. He sat in his recliner flipping through the channels. He wouldn't look her in the eye. The boys were fidgety, couldn't sit still. After a while, Dad started to grumble. "Why don't you boys go outside for a bit. Go blow off some steam."

All alone now Grace welcomed the time with her Dad. "Dad?"

"What?"

"Is it true that you met Mom at a church dance?"

He stopped switching channels and turned to her. "Who told you that?"

"Mom."

"Your mother was a liar. But, she was right about that. It was at All Souls in Pasadena."

"What did you like about her?" Grace asked.

Dad put the mute on. "She was pretty...very pretty," he smiled.

"Did she drink back then?"

His face changed suddenly, like a green flash darkness spilled over him.

"Your mother changed after she had the kids. She was a good mother once." His eyes misted over. Grace leaned forward, feeling like she'd trod over a track of time that had been cemented over. "Amber reminds me of your mother. Too much sometimes."

Grace went to the window overlooking the driveway. The boys were stacking firewood near two tall firs.

Dad turned up the volume.

As she sat down again, the energy to continue was not there. It had been a long drive. She could see he was already receding, as Amber said he would.

When the boys came in they tumbled across the threshold jostling loudly as boys do. Thomas knocked a stool over at the kitchen counter and lunged forward to grab it, sending Michael across the floor in a heap. Grace tensed. Dad shot to his feet as if he'd been assaulted. He rushed into the kitchen with his hands raised.

"What the hell is going on here? Don't you boys have any respect?" he yelled.

Grace came up beside him. "Dad. They're just boys. We'll clean it up."

Dad waved her off. "You bring your boys up here and they treat it like a playground. No respect. They aren't welcome if they can't behave."

Grace put her hand over her mouth. The boys were frozen. Dad stomped back to his recliner. He ignored them the rest of the evening. Grace and the boys remained downstairs in the guest room while he watched TV. Her boys were rambunctious, she knew, but they didn't deserve to be hushed away in the basement. Nobody did. Grace wasn't sure what she wanted from Dad. Her life had taken a detour in Las Vegas and the future was in God's hands, as she saw it. Their relationship had always been an open wound. It had become gangrenous with the passage of time. The next morning she guided the van down the long driveway, vowing never to return.

#####

The light came back into Grace's life when they moved to Henderson, just up the freeway. It happened when they finally sold their house in Rush, and were able to rent a three-bedroom home. It was on the West side of the valley where newer subdivisions were manicured and shiny new churches rose out of empty sandlots. Grace discovered a florist in the mall and began to see colors again, brighter and deeper than before. She entered the cramped storefront on her way to the market; the little florist was wall-to-wall orchids, wisteria, birds of paradise, camellias, and a vast variety of local flora whose names she couldn't wait to learn. She touched the petals, examining the delicate folds and striations, as if coming out of a state of suspension, seeing spring with new eyes.

The boys' education had guided their search. The neighborhood was equidistant from a high school, a middle school and an elementary school—which serviced students with special needs. Michael loved his new school. Grace sat in his class the first week to observe. She was impressed with the teacher and equally relieved to get her days back. The boys were too big to homeschool.

The new house took on the charm of their old home in Rush. Ron planted a garden in the backyard, inspired by the year-round sunlight, and Grace went thrift shopping to furnish the house. They'd left so much behind in Rush. Her heart still ached at the memory of their last garage sale, and all the things she'd given away. They'd purged, thinking they wouldn't want the items that reminded them of Rush and Pastor Pat. But now, she found herself missing her loom, the old fireplace set, the settee and crescent chair, even the herb pots Ron made her.

Grace met her neighbors at garage sales around Henderson, gleaning their castoffs, starting over anew. The new house was large enough for the boys. Each one had their own room. Grace and Ron attended a few services at local churches but hadn't settled on any one. Life edged forward again and she wanted to celebrate.

It would be the Marcoses' first Christmas together in two years. Mimi and Ben were technically adults now, she thought, so she purchased double the alcohol, a bottle each of white and red wine. With dark times behind them, it was fitting to bring the family back together, she thought as she laid settings on their new dining room table. She created a centerpiece and sent pictures to all her friends on Facebook. Mimi arrived from New York with a new boyfriend. Ben flying in from school in Ohio, was alternately hyper and reserved. She wondered if he was taking his medication. John, Thomas, and Michael wrestled in the backyard until Thomas got upset and stormed up to his room. Ron played his guitar and his new keyboard. An hour into the evening the variant personalities of her children melded together once again. Grace and Ron sat on the couch watching *The Princess Bride*, while their children coalesced around the kitchen table arguing over the better social media site, MySpace or Facebook.

Later as she lay in bed, Grace realized that she'd lost her babies, and that they were in their own stratosphere, touching down briefly, and just as quickly slipping back to their motherless worlds. Mimi and Ben still kept in touch. Grace was torn by their calls, vacillating between a yearning to give advice and the yoga of holding her tongue. Ben was becoming manic. He'd call non-stop for a week, and then not at all for months. Mimi found it a challenge to maintain a long distance relationship. Both Mimi and Ben missed her constant doting, although they wouldn't admit it.

John and Thomas were teenagers now. They both towered over her. She no longer went into their rooms. She bought them deodorant in bulk. John played football, excelling not because of talent but of his preternatural aggression. Thomas made a lifestyle of drifting along the surface, trying new things when he was encouraged, attaching himself to nothing. Grace worried about him. Thomas was caught with pot at school, a tiny amount, and she couldn't rightly put her foot down, having "lived the life" on Venice Beach. *It's not the same*, she told herself. Thomas was suspended and showed a passive defiance that presaged a rough road ahead.

After their first year in Henderson, John was in ROTC and Michael thrived in his special needs class. Thomas acted out more and more, resisting their parenting with increased force. Grace was afraid in her own home. One day, while working a shift at the florist in the mall, she got a call. "He's down at the station. He was caught breaking into a vehicle at the mall." She picked Thomas up, hoping that he'd be "scared straight" by the experience of being behind bars.

When they returned home Thomas went straight up to his room. They'd talked in the car, Grace trying to be even-keeled, trying to pull details out of him, like pulling a splinter out with salad tongs. He was sixteen now, well over six feet, thin and gangly and full of energy he couldn't control. She felt for him. The conversation was one-sided, eventually digressing to a single question.

"Why would you do such a thing?"

"I don't know!" he yelled.

Ron didn't come home until after sundown. Grace told him what happened as he changed. She'd kept two dinners warm in the oven. She wanted Ron and Thomas to eat together. Maybe he could get something out of him. She set their plates on the kitchen table and called Thomas down. When they were settled she took a shower, reassured with Ron in the house.

When she walked into the kitchen with a towel around her head Ron was on the couch, working on his laptop. Thomas was back in his room. "Well?" There was an edge to her voice; she didn't know how to handle the situation and hoped Ron had put his foot down.

"He didn't say anything."

"Do you think we should do something?" she asked.

"What can we do?"

"I don't know." She admitted. She needed him to say something, announce their failure maybe—she thought he must be thinking it.

"He's not a baby. We've given him everything," he said, glancing up from the screen.

They both looked up at Michael, reaching in the fridge. "Michael, don't drink milk, remember? It upsets your stomach."

"Yes, Momma."

Grace smiled at her youngest. *I will always have Michael*, she thought. She watched as he turned to leave the kitchen, but was blocked by Thomas, gloomy, his face an insolent mask. Thomas glared at her. Grace's heart stopped, as he stormed through the kitchen. She jumped up and raced after him. Ron followed at a measured distance. "Where do you think you're going, Thomas?" she asked.

"None of your business."

"You're on house arrest. If you go out, they'll arrest you and put you in jail."

She held his arm. He jerked it away from her. Ron stepped up next to Grace. She could feel his heat. "I'm not going to let you ruin your life," she cried.

Michael came down the stairs and sat on a step watching. He held Rufus the cat, whispering in his ear.

Thomas pulled the door open. "You can't keep me here," he blurted, knocking her arm away.

Grace recoiled. It wasn't the first time one of her boys was physical with her. Even Ben had confronted her, in his own way. But the boys were so large and uncontrollable. Grace felt a cry rising from her breast. She could see him falling away...

"Don't go!" she said with as much love as she could, without sounding as frightened as she felt.

Thomas turned to face her, rising to his full height. His arms rose as well. Focused on her, he forgot about Ron.

As Thomas moved toward Grace, Ron stepped between them. Thomas stumbled back a step. His face changed from anger to fury. He punched Ron on the cheek. They both stood there, in the eye of the storm, until Thomas lunged for Grace. Ron deflected Thomas's momentum, guiding his lanky frame to the entryway wall. Grace leaped out of the way, searching the room, for what, she had no clue. "Thomas!" she screamed. "Stop!" Her mind was a burning bush. She finally ran for the phone, as Ron restrained Thomas.

Grace ran back into the entryway. "I called 911," she stammered. Thomas was fighting Ron's hold, his face distorted and red. Ron shook his head, as their eyes met. Grace began to cry. She'd never seen Ron look sadder than that day. They'd built a home out of love and service. They'd raised their five children to be responsible, respectful community members. The thought of calling the police on one of their own was incomprehensible. They were now in unfamiliar territory.

Thomas spent another night in a cell. The responding officers asked if they wanted to file charges. It was a turning point. Thomas showed no remorse, so they filed assault charges. A court date was set. For Grace, the house was never a home again from that moment on. The judge agreed that Thomas, being a minor, could have the conviction expunged if he completed community service.

#####

Six months later, the house felt like a way station. Thomas spent most of his time at friends' houses, couch surfing, and who knows what. He was a no-show for community service, and a bench warrant hung over his head. He came home mostly when they weren't there. Grace would find signs of him throughout the house: a missing phone charger, empty cereal boxes, the TV on SportsCenter, the upstairs bathroom humid and the shower curtain fresh with droplets. She was constantly reminded of her failure, the family photos in the entryway, the hole on the wall—rough with spackle—where he'd kicked it after returning from lock up.

The house was too big for them now. John went to boot camp after graduation. They signed the papers releasing him at seventeen. Michael was in high school, spending most of his time in the after-school program. He was so good with the younger kids. It broke her heart that their neighbors wouldn't let their children play with him, being so tall, and socially delayed. In Rush, Grace would have spent the extra time at church, painting murals and teaching Sunday school. In Henderson, Las Vegas, that void had never been filled. She found her painting supplies one day and immersed herself in her lost passion. Her perspective was seasoned by the years of raising children, a spring of emotions flowing from her brush.

When Paul came for Christmas she gave him the first piece she'd finished in years, a still-life tomato she was especially proud of. He was visibly touched by the gift, asking for tissue paper to wrap it for his flight home. The visit was the highlight of a dark year. She hadn't been in touch with Dad, Bryan or Steve. Paul reached out more frequently with years of sobriety under his belt. She cherished their moments together. For the first time, he was interested in hearing her story, her recollection of how their family fell apart. They realized that they'd both been abused. "I always knew something happened to you," she said. When it came to Amber, they were both lost.

"Why does she have to be so difficult?" Paul asked.

"She had it the worst," Grace said, revealing Amber's secret for the first time to any of the boys.

"Why doesn't she get help?" Paul asked.

"She doesn't think she has a problem," Grace said. "She blames everyone else...even me."

The next morning Paul and Grace hugged at the airport, not knowing when they would see one another again. The parting was bittersweet. They'd shared so much, and had so much in common: art, writing, their rise out of a tortured past. Grace held him by the curb until a traffic guard whistled them apart. "You're welcome anytime," she said. And for the first time, she meant it.

#####

That spring, Grace found out that they had to move again. Ron got a new job with a printing company in Boulder, Colorado.

She was relieved. There was nothing left for them in Las Vegas with John in bootcamp and Thomas on the run.

Grace got on the phone as soon as she heard the news, promising Mimi and Ben to send their new address as soon as they arrived. Building up to the day of the move Grace saw less and less of Thomas. Her heart ached for him. She could barely face him, for his choices, but clung to the image of him as a soft-cheeked toddler, clutching her hair. She continued to find evidence of his visits. An iPod was missing and she wondered if it was his way of saying goodbye. One morning he walked in the front door and sat in Ron's chair across from her on the couch.

"When are we moving?" he asked, straight-faced.

Grace was crushed. "We...are moving. You are not coming with us."

Thomas leaned back, staring at the ceiling as if a great deluge would spill from the sky and clean away his ugliness.

Grace went into her room and cried. She knew she had to say goodbye. He was eighteen and they were no longer responsible. It was an aching relief. When she returned to the living room to finish packing, he was gone. As his mother, she knew he would still call, not changing the reality that her home would never again be his.

# 27

Amber was on top, cleaved and clawing his face. It was dark, she couldn't see that she was middle age, overweight in her opinion, but "just right," he said. It was dark; that was the way she wanted it because she couldn't stand to look at him, or herself.

Afterward, stark and nude in the lamplight, red lines were etched on his face. "I don't know what happened," she said in the way of an apology. But, she wasn't sorry. Over the last five years, she could only do *it* when she was angry. Denny wasn't into sex, at his age, but she wanted it because...well...she wanted it. It happened every time now, the anger, the confusion, as if she'd had a seizure. It took a day to recover. Arms aching, joints burning, as if she'd gone over the falls in a barrel. The act was wholly hers for the first time in her life. She'd be on top looking down, seeing faces she'd buried, boiling feelings, building, building...until she'd stop short, and be rear-ended by the years. Amber was tired of being Amber.

Denny was not the solution. His business wasn't booming as he predicted. She'd slipped into the grooves of his life, making him a "better man", as he liked to put it. She was back to being a maid and a caretaker.

"Can you pick me up some Pine-Sol on your way home?" she asked, setting a pop tart on a saucer in front of him. She held up one finger—indicating the number of tarts he was allotted. His diabetes was critical. He hit the table two times with his fist when she turned her back.

"Can you pick me up from the doctor's office?" he retorted. Amber turned on him.

"That wasn't until Friday." She was still in her nightgown. There was no use in getting ready until he left.

"I changed it," he grinned, stuffing the entire tart into his mouth. He wiped the crumbs on his jacket sleeve.

"Why do you do that?" she asked, dismayed. "You aren't getting another one."

Denny pulled a granola bar from his pocket, stuffed the whole thing in his mouth when she went to the fridge. Amber turned around and put her pop tarts on the table. She refolded her napkin and glanced at her shadow on the wall, aware of it for the first time. She sat down as Denny got up. "Pine-Sol," she said, following his progress out into the entryway. She hated that she couldn't see the front door from the kitchen. The house was too big, but he insisted that they have a "proper" home, not considering that she had to clean it.

Amber took a big bite of tart, listening for the front door to close. Instead, she heard Denny's boots squeak on the tile, and suddenly he was standing over her, as big as a cloud. He took her face in his bloated hands, hands that could tear sheet metal, and kissed her nose. "That's my girl," he said.

Amber batted his hands away. "Stop it!" You know I hate that." She stared up at him, mouth full of apple pop tart, disgusted, not at the band-aid that was now seeping, where she'd scratched him, but at herself, for needing him.

Amber lounged in the living room watching *Jerry Springer.* When the commercial came on she lowered the volume and stared at a picture of her and Denny at his son Billy's wedding. The young couple were having problems now. She closed her eyes,

388

harkening back to the day Denny drove down to Berkeley to pick
her up and take her north I-5 into the sunset. They'd gotten a room
at a Best Western Inn in Portland, and made love, even with his
bad knee and bad hips. She made love to him as hard as she could,
to make him remember, a memory that would last to their wedding
day. She cried afterward, thinking of how she'd never see Paul
again. Thinking of how she was starting over again in Washington,
becoming a wife again, having circled back around. She
remembered the rest of the drive, that sinking feeling of déjà vu,
and how when Denny looked over at her with his bloated face and
hopeful victorious blue eyes, how much they both needed each
other, not out of love or romance, but of necessity. Now as she
opened her eyes, the show was back on; a scuffle broke out on
stage, and Jerry Springer was stuck in the middle once again.

When the rain stopped Amber went to Smart and Final for
Pine-Sol. She knew Denny would forget. Up and down the aisles
she trudged, lolling in the candy section, the vast space brimming
with Halloween decorations, rifled through collapsible lanterns,
and green crepe paper witches. She daydreamed of what she might
dress up as, if she were somehow, old enough. She stood there
deciding between bags of mini Baby Ruths and mini Snickers
when she felt a hand on her shoulder. When she turned Betty was
beaming with her arms wide. Amber hugged her tighter than she'd
ever held Denny. By Betty's side was her granddaughter, Makaela.
The girl was dressed in a pretty pink dress, with a bow in her hair.
It reminded Amber of how Grandma D dressed her even though
she was too old for such things. Amber shook hands with
Makaela, feeling a little replaced. "Why don't you come out tricker
treating with us?" Makaela asked. Amber threw both bags of candy
into her cart. Denny would have to hand them out, or eat them
himself, to hell with his diabetes.

Amber spent the rest of the day making her costume,
washing her face twice when her make-up cast her as a prostitute,
rather than the princess she was going for. When Denny came

home, she stayed in the bathroom, yelling, "You're going to have to hand out the candy, I'm going out."

He stomped around the kitchen impatient at having to wait to confront her. When she walked into the kitchen in costume he laughed out loud, slapping his knees. "You look like Betty Davis in *What Ever Happened to Baby Jane.*" Amber stomped back into the bathroom, leaving him to make his own dinner. She stared into the mirror, satisfied with how closely she resembled Snow White, even with her owl glasses. She looked up and down the street as she got into her Fifth Avenue, satisfied that she'd beaten the first wave of children.

Amber pulled up to the curb at Betty's apartment as the sun winked below the horizon. It was a perfect night for ghouls, Amber thought as she rang the bell. She remembered how wonderful Betty's apartment smelled when she'd given her a ride home from work.

Betty and Makaela came down, and to her chagrin, Betty had on her work clothes. "Oh, you dressed up," Betty said, without giving her a hug. Makaela was made up like Cinderella, her dress a little too tight, Amber thought. They made their way through the neighborhood, with Betty between them. As darkness filled the spaces around the houses Amber felt increasingly uncomfortable in her dress. Betty talked about work and how well Makaela was doing in school. Amber stared at the passing families, kids holding hands with their moms and dads, begging to eat their candy. She found herself reaching for Betty's hand as the evening went on; repulsed by the impulse, she held Makaela's hand instead, although she didn't care for her. When they returned to the apartment Amber was drained. It was as if she'd spent her life outrunning a wave, and now it threatened to consume her. As they moved up the walk she wanted desperately for Betty to invite her in. Not for any other reason than to just *be* with her. At the door, Betty turned to her. "Thank you, Amber. I hope you find what you're looking for."

It was the strangest comment she'd ever heard. Amber rushed to her car, just sat there, headlights lighting up her face, smoking and cursing under her breath. The old Fifth Avenue smelled like cheap perfume and leather. *You look like a whore.* She sat there until the street was quiet, watching the moths batter the street lamp. At home she took a shower, and slipped back into her nightgown, noticing Denny's blood on the front. He was in bed snoring. The entirely too large house was cold, and she felt empty inside. Amber decided to sleep on the couch. The street light streaming in cast her roiling silhouette on the wall behind the couch. *That's how I feel,* she thought, as she drew the blanket over her head.

#####

It had been building for some time. *Why are you here?* It started with Denny's family reunion, or maybe when she moved in with him after failing in the Bay Area, or when Largo molested her, better yet, when Mom wouldn't believe her when she told her that Largo was fucking her. It had to be prior to Highland Park, maybe in Magnolia, when she lost her big toe on Steve's bike, but mostly, she concluded, finally after years of struggling, that she was born that way.

It was a level of self-acceptance that often precedes a leap forward. For Amber, it was a turning point on her forty-ninth birthday. Grace called to wish her a happy birthday and recommended therapy for the hundredth time. "I am what I am, can't you accept that?" she'd wailed. That set off another interminable monologue that stretched on for a good twenty minutes. Grace responded as she always did, she hung up.

"I want to work," she told Denny the next day. Denny's jaw tightened and his chest rose as if it pained him to imagine her out of the house, seeing him in public.

"We'll see," he said, pouring syrup on his pancakes. She'd stopped hounding him about his diabetes.

Amber went about her housework with added vigor, finally tackling the high cupboards in the kitchen. She loved the smell of Pine-Sol, reveling in a sense of completion as she sat back and drank her third Pepsi of the day. She made a mental list of the jobs she wanted to try. The door was open so the cupboards would dry, and the wind flowing in hinted of spring.

The next evening, a legal pad in hand, standing over a casserole she'd burnt on purpose, she persisted. "I want to get a job." Denny put his hands flat on the kitchen table. He threw his head back, and stared up at the ceiling as if he noticed a leak. Amber carved out the middle of the casserole and plopped it on his plate. "Did you hear me?"

"I'm thinking," he said, focused on a flycatcher circling the overhead light. After a few bites he opened up. "Why do you want to work? I pay the bills. That's the arrangement."

"I'm bored. All I do is clean and cook."

Denny shoveled casserole into his mouth, staring at the magnets on the refrigerator. A string of cheese dripped from his chin. Amber reached her napkin to capture it, but he pulled away.

"Aren't you happy?" he asked.

She shrugged. It was a question she'd never been asked. There were moments of peace. *Happy?* Amber got another Pepsi from the fridge. "I'm just bored."

She watched his face. He only had three expressions: worry, pain, and satisfaction. All variances stemmed from these three. Denny froze when he was worried. He was as stubborn as a two-year-old. Amber got a glass from the cupboard. It still smelled like Pine-Sol and she wondered if he noticed.

Denny dropped his head. Amber couldn't tell if his eyes were closed. He got like that when he wasn't getting his way. After all their time together she still didn't know him, if he was going to blow up or cry.

"Even part-time. I just don't want to be home all day," she said.

Denny raised his face. He exhaled loudly. "Fine. You can answer phones at the office," he said, surprising her. Amber felt a sudden surge of affection for him. It was a tiny gesture, she knew, but at least he was trying.

She got out of her seat, put her arms around his neck, her breasts firm against his back. She kissed the back of his neck and sat back down. "When do I start?"

"Let's not rush into this. I have to tell Billy, and you still need to be trained." Billy was his partner and son. Amber didn't care for Billy.

"How hard can it be?" Amber said, putting her plate in the sink.

"Have you ever been a receptionist?"

"I answered phones at the Salvation Army," she lied, sensing that he was going to rescind his offer.

Denny pushed his plate away. "I'm tired. Can we talk about it tomorrow?"

After the dinner dishes were cleaned and put away Amber wiped down the counter. Denny was in his office down the hall near the guest room. He'd been in there since leaving the table; she could hear him on the phone, and it didn't sound like a pleasant conversation. She paused in the kitchen doorway to eavesdrop.

Denny's voice rose and fell between long silences, like the person on the other end was making a case. "I know. But she really wants this. I can't do anything about it."

Amber looked back into the kitchen, too bright suddenly for her mood. She turned off the light and stared out the night-filled window over the sink.

"She'll last a week and quit, I guarantee," she heard Denny say.

Amber waited for Denny in the hallway. "Who was that?" she asked, taking off her apron.

"Oh...no one...work stuff," he said, brushing past her, looking like he'd been caught cheating.

#####

The morning of her first day Amber wore an Anne Taylor
skirt she'd gotten at the Salvation Army. It was olive green, and
she liked the way it matched her eggshell stockings. She felt
fashionable sitting at the desk facing the door. Denny's office was
a suite in the mini-mall near the I-5 onramp. There was steady foot
traffic by the front window, but no one stopped on their way to
shop at Ralph's. Denny's refrigeration maintenance business was
built on referrals from happy customers, or the work Billy brought
in when he was out in the field.

Denny wrote a script for her. "Keep it simple. Don't try to
have a conversation with everyone who calls...just the essentials."
They practiced, with him in the back room, calling up like a new
customer. It only took a few practice runs. She read the script
exactly the way he wanted.

He stood over her when she received her first call. It was a
telemarketer trying to sell them internet service. He gave her a
thumbs up when she read the script, a thumbs down when she went
off it. "We already have internet...thank you very much." She was
so proud of herself for going off script and handling the call.

"Stay on the script," Denny said on his way out the door.

By the end of her first day, Amber had found the games on
Denny's office computer. There really weren't enough calls to keep
her busy. She played pinball and solitaire at first, but as the week
went on, with few calls to occupy her, she immersed herself in
SIMS. She made a new character, a single working woman, with a
cat, a dog, three plants, and a goldfish. After her second week, she
was so wrapped up with her new SIMS life that she began to resent
the intrusive calls. *I can be bored at home*, she thought.

When she complained, Denny gave her extra work. "Okay.
Maybe you're ready to do the mail."

Denny showed Amber how to open the mail, sorting net-
thirties from pay-on-receipt. He gave her another script, one that
she could use to call vendors, to extend their due dates. At the end
of the day, she'd show Denny her paper cuts, so proud of the stacks
of bills in the wire boxes on her desk. It lasted another week. Soon,

she was back on SIMS, pondering the possibility of her avatar adopting a child. Everything was going so well. When she returned home she still had time to make dinner, and keep up with the housework. Denny worked late. She felt she earned the time alone, and indulged herself with Xbox. When Denny came home she told him about her day, proud that she was contributing to the family business.

On Saturday, three months into her job, she went to the Salvation Army to get a new outfit. She wanted to show off how well she was doing. Betty was there at the register as usual, happy to see her, but not too happy. "I'm working as a bookkeeper," she said, walking tall to the women's section. Amber smiled at the manager's daughter, who was in the furniture section, keeping a love seat warm. On the way home, she picked up steaks at Ralph's. Walking by the suite, she peered in at her darkened desk. Pride bolstered her as she walked to the car, thinking the sky was the limit. Denny was in a horrible mood when she got home. The steaks weren't cooked enough, the potatoes were too mushy, and how was it that after living together for six years, she didn't know that he was allergic to mushrooms. Instead of going to his office, as he did every evening after dinner, he settled on the couch in the living room. Amber did the dishes, hurrying, spurred by his silence. As she settled down next to him, she dreaded the inevitable confrontation.

"I can't have you working at the office anymore."

Amber's mouth dropped open. It was as if she'd been slapped. She took a deep breath to steady herself, thinking if she said the right words, he would see the wrong in his. She didn't want to sound weak, after being so strong for so many weeks. "What is it exactly that you mean?"

Denny grabbed the armrest. "I mean, I don't need you at the office anymore, that's all...work is slow."

Amber's face twisted as she thought of Billy, complaining to Denny. He'd never liked her...always the momma's boy. "I've been doing so well..."

She hated how weak it sounded, so plaintive. "You need me," she blurted. "You said so."

"I—"

"Did I do something wrong? Billy's behind this, isn't he?"

She stood over him now, pointing interrogatively. "He told you to fire me, didn't he?"

"He didn't tell—"

Amber stormed into the kitchen, her eyes wild, searching. Denny stayed on the couch. She rushed down the hall, pausing at his office as if the source of this betrayal would reveal itself. She fled to the bathroom, and stayed there until he knocked. Her anger was too great to indulge him.

She had no idea how long she'd been in there when she finally heard him snoring. She was still fuming. She went out on the kitchen porch, smoked and called Paul.

"Denny controls me...he won't let me work...I don't think I can live with him."

"Amber...don't be hasty. Calm down and make a plan."

"Make a plan?" she yelled. "He controls my money, my every single move. I can't even go to the movies without asking him."

"Calm down. I'm not saying you shouldn't leave...I'm just saying, consider what would happen *if* you left."

Amber stared at the phone. *He just doesn't want to be bothered with me again.*

"Don't worry. I'll stop bothering you! I don't need your advice. Why can't you just listen?"

"Amber—"

"I'm done talking already. You make me so mad." Amber hung up distraught and alone. She had a headache and was having trouble breathing. The bedroom light turned on suddenly, freezing her like a possum. She crept through the kitchen door, went to the couch, pretending to be asleep. She sensed Denny in the doorway, but didn't want to give him the satisfaction of making up. She wanted *him* to lose sleep over this. She fell into a fitful sleep, full of nightmares about past roommates, and of Paul drifting away.

# 28

Louisville, Colorado, a gentrified coal town that survived labor wars, now bragged a listing in the top one hundred places to live in the United States. They'd been there two years, but only recently had she felt that she could exhale. Ron's job took him out of town most days, and she'd finally cleared out the shed on the back patio—the non-essentials they'd lugged from Las Vegas to Louisville. She'd found she could only work in spurts: the emotional toil of fingering old photos—faces evoking sadness and joy, a melange of feelings, the inescapable peaks and valleys of raising a family.

Grace walked through the bookstore on Main Street with Michael. A kind woman behind the counter, she knew from church, chatted with Michael. Sally, whose great uncle was killed fighting for miners' rights, was jolly and warm. The town had accepted them, a mixed race family from New York, via Las Vegas. Grace leafed through a coffee table book of Colorado flora, published by her friend Marcy, a photographer. She moved to Louisville a year ahead of Grace. They knew one another from Rush. It was Marcy who invited her to their church. Grace could depend on Marcy; she was a sister for over ten years. They'd

separated and come back together, maintaining the connection
through Facebook, until they settled again a mere 15 miles apart.

The book was Marcy's latest masterpiece. Grace felt a warm
current rise in her chest as she absorbed the floral colors, running
her hand across the pages, recalling each flower's scent. *I should
do something like this*, she thought. Grace glanced out the fogged
up window. Everything seemed to settle in Louisville during the
season. Not just the snow, but the people. Grace gazed down the
snow covered avenue. Christmas lights were already up on Main
Street. An icy rain threatened to turn powdery, making cars creep
like icebergs, and townspeople tap their steps. Michael finished his
conversation with Sally and pushed up against Grace. She closed
the book, linking his arm in hers, appreciating the company, with
Ron out of town, Mimi in D.C., John in Afghanistan, Ben in San
Diego, and Thomas floundering in Vegas.

"You'll always be here, won't you, Michael?" she said
earnestly, smiling up at him. They waved good bye to Sally.

"See you on Sunday," Sally said.

They edged along the sidewalk, dark clouds forming
overhead. "Bring in your bike when we get home," she told
Michael. "It's going to snow tonight."

It was the worst storm they'd had in over a decade. It lasted
for two days, burying the house in six feet of snow. Ron couldn't
get a flight home. He was stranded in Los Angeles, but they
Skyped; she could see the lines of worry around his eyes, so clear
on the screen as she pulled the comforter over her. The stultifying
quiet outside at rush hour unsettled her. She spent the solitary days
reading. She'd never had so much time to read, and to think.

When the sun came out the house began to plink and drip
with the rhythm of melting snow. Grace came directly home after
driving Michael to his pizza job. She turned up the thermostat
wanting more warmth than layers could provide. She was restless
with two months of winter still ahead. She walked through the
house, rejecting the TV, the stereo, the short stack of library books
on the kitchen table, her knitting—which she'd taken up to share

one of Marcy's passions—past Michael's bedroom door, to her bedroom. The house was deathly quiet, suspended. Grace was restless, reminiscent of her younger days in Venice.

Back then, Mom and Amber had just moved to Reseda. She was fresh out of the hospital, healing from the beating of her life. It was when she first started painting, spending time at Terri's. Terri let her use her paints, and she set up an easel in the corner of her bedroom. Terri, married, divorced, and now lived in Florida, the single mother of a single mother. In a time before computers and cell phones, she'd spent days in Terri's room, her soul spilling out onto canvas after canvas, until Terri gave her a shelf in the garage where her finished paintings collected in the dark.

Grace lingered at her bedroom window, watching a snowdrift sparkle in the afternoon sun. *What I wouldn't give to have those paintings now*, she mused. A glint from the shed window caught her attention, spurring her to dress. She trudged out to the shed, the sun's welcome glare making her sweat under the layers. She found her art supplies and canvases wrapped in plastic near the children's old board games. She'd been meaning to bring them out, but until now, she'd shunned the impulse.

It took two trips to bring her paint box, easel and canvases to the bedroom. One of her paintings hung on the wall, a sunflower she'd completed in Rush ahead of their sudden departure. Grace moved the chest of drawers to create space in the corner for her easel. A sudden thought pulled her to the kitchen. She had promised to make Michael cookies. She walked to the freezer, reaching for a tube of Toll House cookie dough. She paused. The cool air masked her face as she smiled at the orange and red paint on her hands. She placed the cookie dough on the counter and rushed back into the bedroom, to the blank canvas in the corner.

Grace spent the next three hours entangled in a creative flurry. Colors flowed from her brush onto the nebulous canvas, giving birth to a latent self she'd exiled to build a family. The dawning awareness that she'd caged a vital part of herself, a soul appendage, when she rushed into her life, became clear as the hours passed. She told herself while cleaning up that it wasn't the piece that was important, but that she had done it. She had been so perfectly centered, at peace for the first time since leaving Rush.

For the next few days, until the weather cleared and Ron came home, she painted—at times upon waking, after shopping or after dinner, staying up late (so out of character for her), teetering on obsession, making up for lost time. The murals, the dabbling were not enough over the years. Grace felt like she'd caught a wave that'd been building her entire life, a daunting wave that held her, although she'd just become aware of its existence. She was rising to its crest with a new view of herself.

Grace began to exhibit her paintings around the house. She had time to dream, hands free of the duties of motherhood. "I like that one," Michael said, at a portrait of Mimi. "That's me!" he exclaimed at a portrait of himself. Grace dreamt of becoming a great artist, a respected painter, producing beauty from the labor of her heart. Where she'd shelved such dreams in the past, they now accompanied her daily life, demanding the spotlight.

One day Marcy came to visit. Marcy spoke her mind, harshly on occasion, which made her a precious ally. Grace trusted her opinion. "Those are nice," she said, which made Grace recoil. "I think you could be an amazing artist if you got some training." Grace smiled politely, suddenly feeling a million miles away. Marcy tempered her comment, always aware of how blunt she could be. "CU Boulder has an Art Masters Program. A friend of mine is a professor in the department."

Grace smirked and went into the kitchen to start some water for tea. It was preposterous to think she could sit through an art class, let alone an art program. She loved painting in her bedroom, the light, the solitude, her creative incubator. When she returned to the living room with two steaming mugs, Marcy stood by the mantle with her arms crossed. Grace sat down on the couch and waited.

Marcy dropped her arms. "Why do you always do that?"

"What's that, Marcy?" Grace asked.

"You dispel yourself. Here you have all the talent in the world, but you aren't willing to develop it. I was serious when I said you could be amazing."

Grace lingered over her mug. The steam warmed her cheeks.

"I wasn't trying to be rude," Grace said.

Marcy sat down next to her. It reminded Grace of the time in Rush when Marcy pushed her to confront Pastor Pat, to allow her to paint a mural in the school basement.

Marcy sipped her tea, staring at her expectantly.

"It's not that easy to show my work to strangers. It's very personal," Grace said.

A minute passed in silence—to the point of discomfort. Grace's world was shifting under her feet. Timing and opportunity synced up in the momentary void. The church bell from across the street broke the stillness.

"I'll help you apply to the program," Marcy said.

"I'll think about it," Grace said, putting her arm around Marcy's shoulders. She kissed her cheek, knowing she'd already made a decision.

At dinner that night, Grace shared the idea of going to college with Ron. She'd predicted that he would bring up the money issue. To her surprise he just nodded, and said, "I think that is a good idea."

The truth was, all those days dreaming about becoming an artist had planted a seed. The transformation had begun. She sang that night doing the dishes. *Every journey begins with a first step— something Pastor Pat always said.*

#####

Grace loved the smell of wet clay. It was a biblical element. Pottery class was her favorite, one of the electives for her Bachelor of Arts program. Her classmates were all Mimi's age. They spoke in hushed tones around her, she noticed, until the middle of the semester, when they began to treat her like a long lost fairy godmother, bringing her treats and offering to help her clean up after class. Grace was tempted to indulge in their smoke sessions on breaks, and finally joined them, recalling her high school days and why she nearly flunked out.

The program was a blur after the first year. She knew they were going into debt for her dream, but she also knew that she had to complete this part of her life. Ron had always been solid—fine with who he was, his faith, his music. Grace felt like she was just beginning to live, after years of sacrifice. It was exhilarating and daunting. Family life was a dream she'd awoken from, whose remnants lay about her in photos and in the beckoning interludes with her satellite children. She had no regrets, in fact with Michael still at home, she knew she was blessed with a new beginning, the chance at a second life.

The transformation took four years. During that time Grace barely talked with Amber. Paul checked in regularly. Dad was in decline, but he'd built a wall around himself that she gladly respected. She indulged herself in new things that made her stretch as a human being. She worked in the campus library, and the coffee shop where she was invited to show her work. She felt even closer to Ron for sacrificing his time with her. She was away from the house from dawn to dusk.

After four years Grace walked across the stage with the rest of her classmates. Mimi, her husband, Dan, and her infant daughter, Emma, along with Ben, Michael and Ron, were in the audience to witness her graduation. John was in Afghanistan, and Thomas was still treading water in Las Vegas. It was a clear blue day in June, summer just rising, as the sun spilled over the audience. She couldn't have imagined the joy she now felt, the day she pulled her supplies out of the shed, and filled that first blank canvas. The graduation ceremony marked an arrival, a ripening of her soul. As she skipped across the stage, she sensed a tipping from one life to the next. When her name was called she paused, wanting the moment to last.

That night as she and Ron lay in bed, as they had for the last thirty years, images of her life paraded through her mind: Magnolia Street, Highland Park, Venice Beach, Rochester, Rush, Vegas, and now Louisville, the pain and misery, the friends and family loved and lost. Every memory seemed so distant, yet a line connected each, placing value on even the most cruel moments.

The bedroom window was open and she could hear the neighbor playing piano, a light melody wending about the swaying curtains. Ron was warm and solid next to her. Mimi, Dan and Emma slept in the living room. Emma was the spitting image of Mimi when she was that age, Grace thought, making a mental note to take Emma's photo in the morning so she could paint a portrait. Grace's life was picking up speed again. The momentum promised a newness she'd yearned for. Ron shifted next to her as the music ceased. It had been a glorious day. From an obscure place, she wondered how her parents knew to name her Grace, after arriving at this point of receiving so much. Grace fell asleep thinking of Amber, the one person in the world she knew who could use a little blessing.

# 29

Billy was in her space, replacing her. Amber went to the thermostat for the fourth time since they went to sleep. The first time, she'd felt her way along the wall, absorbing the texture through her fingertips; but still couldn't get to the living room without the hall light. That was Billy's room now. She slapped the switch angrily, hoping it would wake him on the couch. Denny had said, "You can sleep in the office if you want." She knew what that meant. *It's over.*

Amber set the thermostat at ninety degrees. *That'll burn him out.* She pulled her robe tightly around her. All her anger focused on the dark lump on the couch. *What a loser. How could Denny let him take over my house like this?* Amber went to the office. Denny snored soundly in the other room. *Our room!* She thought of going in there, putting a pillow over his head, a preemptive strike before he could kick her out. *I built this home!*

She stood in the bedroom doorway. Denny liked his night light bright. She needed darkness to sleep. It had always been a point of departure in their relationship. *Does he know how much he's hurting me?* Amber took her glasses off and cleaned them on her nightgown. She walked back into the office. At the desk, pushed the power button, stared at the grey screen, feeling grey, and certainly betrayed, as icons materialized. She clicked her way to her Facebook page. *I've got to change that profile photo,* she thought for the hundredth time. She scanned down the page for likes and comments. Nothing from Paul, Grace, her family, nothing. Her cousin Linda commented on one of her posts. "Are you sad?" it said. Amber clicked to de-friend Linda. After doing so, she created a post.

*Why does everyone think that you have to have family around to be happy?*

She de-friended Betty because she never called. She de-friended Marisol, her friend from San Diego because she was married now and had three children. Lastly, she de-friended Paul and Grace. They never responded to her posts.

*I am alone.*

#####

Amber rubbed her lower back with one hand, guided the mouse with the other. She'd been at it all night flowing between SIMS and her Facebook page. The glowing hint of sunrise found her talking out loud to herself. *If that's what he wants...* She got up and scratched. No one had responded to her post yet—it had been three hours. She looked at her watch, 6 AM. Amber wanted her old life in San Diego back. Times were the best in hindsight. She had been young and desirable, and hibernation was unspeakable under the uplifting blue skies. Back in San Diego she'd flittered in the slightest breeze. Now, unwelcome in her own home, it was as if the raw truth of her life, every horror, every slight, hung off her like skins. She couldn't stand herself like this. The house was an unmoored barge floating further from the dock. Soon, there would be no escape, she'd be stuck with the father and son, bobbing in limbo toward an unreachable horizon.

Amber went into the kitchen and turned on the coffee machine. She intended to make a racket, to wake Billy, but thought better of it. Couch springs drew her attention to the front room where a sight made her jump. Billy was leaned across the back of the couch staring at her. He was motionless and smiling as if he'd fallen asleep like that. He looked so smug, so victorious; the couch was his, the expression stated, and the rest of the house would follow. Amber stared at him, sagging with each second between them. She rushed into the office and picked up the phone. Denny sawed away in the master bedroom. *Doesn't he know what he's doing to me?*

She couldn't call Paul. He'd abandoned her. She couldn't call Grace, she betrayed her. Was there anyone? Ruth! Dad's girlfriend. Her chest heaved as she dialed the number.

"Ruth?"

"Amber."

Amber cried, "I can't stand it living here. Denny controls me. His son moved in." Amber hiccuped into the phone. It was hard to breathe. Ruth sighed on the other end. After a painful silence she finally responded.

"Dear, I'm sorry he's treating you that way."

Anger welled up in Amber, replacing the hopelessness that prompted the call. There was something strange and new in Ruth's tone. It had been a dependable source of maternal calm and sagacity.

Now she heard pity, detached and distant. "Amber, stop thinking of yourself. Your father needs you. Call him."

Amber started again. "Denny's going to kick me out...I just know it. Billy lives with us now."

"I have to go now, dear. Call your father… He needs you..."

Amber did call Dad. She drove down to Oregon the next day. She stopped at Denny's for a grand slam, gas in Eugene, and made it after dark. Dad was waiting on the second floor balcony overlooking the gravel driveway. She rushed up the steps and gave him a big hug, holding him until she felt him pull away—a mag light in one hand and the remote in the other. "What took you so long? I'm going to bed," he said, as he turned around and hobbled to his room. Her mood began to soften as she lay in the guest room downstairs. It was her room when she was there. In her nightgown, she went through her pre-sleep routine: Noxema, a thorough flossing, a quick game of *Mario* on her cell phone and her clothes laid out on the antique chair by the window. Her problems were many miles away to the North. Surprisingly, the family photos Dad displayed on the antique bureau on the wall facing the bed evoked nothing from her, no familial longing, none of the former pull that plagued Amber her entire life. They were dusty and faded, and void of emotional charge. Amber stared at them searchingly. She saw faces of people she knew of but never really knew. The room seemed suddenly tight and airless, a lone bed bordered by four walls and the window, a black slate. Amber shunned the darkness within her. She wanted to be strong for Dad. She surrendered to a much needed sleep with the faces staring down at her.

It was her shortest visit, and the last time she would see him. Amber woke up early to make Dad eggs and bacon and had his coffee on the counter; the plate perfectly placed on the island, with fork on the left and a knife and spoon paired on the right, just like she used to do on Mount Everett Street in San Diego. She greeted him—still in his pajamas—wringing her hands, adjusting her eyeglasses, tense but smiling brightly.

"What are you so happy about?" he glared, shuffling by her on his worn path to the kitchen. She couldn't hold it back any longer.

Amber caved. "You are so mean. Enjoy your breakfast!" she cried and ran downstairs sobbing. She'd already packed. Her eyes blurry and swollen, she peeled out with finality. He would never get his money back. They were even, as far as she was concerned. Amber chain-smoked up Highway 5, crying at the rest stops when she couldn't keep it together, leapfrogging from outrage to contempt, self-hatred feeding her in a loop back to outrage.

When she got home no one was there. The house smelled of sweat and stale beer. The comforter Ruth had made her was lying on the floor at the foot of the couch. There was no sign of Billy's things, which had occupied the corner by the TV. In the kitchen, she was met by an overflowing sink and a countertop covered with take-out Chinese and pizza boxes.

She went to her room now, the office, and found Billy's things. The desk with the computer was shoved into a corner. It looked like he'd cleared out his storage space. *I can't deal with this now,* she thought, and got on SIMS. She released her anger onto her SIMS family: divorced her husband, kicked the kids out, sent the dog to the shelter and purposely failed to water the crying plants. Amber posted updates on her Facebook page, adding another Bitstrip, with a dancing avatar and a speaker tag, *drama, drama, drama.* She leaned back in the office chair and smoked, breaking the first rule they'd made together, a smoke-free house. When Denny and Billy returned from work she got up and locked the door. They slammed cabinet doors and murmured in the kitchen. Amber was certain they were planning to leave. When the house went quiet she crept out to find Billy on the couch once again and Denny sawing away in their bed, peaceful and oblivious. She grabbed a bowl of cereal and a pack of Red Vines. She made a makeshift bed on the floor of the office and binge watched *The Simpsons* on Netflix. She never slept in the bedroom again.

# 30

Grace had a lot to be thankful for. A healthy grandchild, a son who'd made it through his first tour in Afghanistan safely, family who loved and depended on her, and her growing notoriety in the local art scene. Her show at the Denver Museum of Contemporary Art was recognized as the Best Contemporary-Realist Show in "Best of Boulder", in the Entertainment and Arts section of the local paper. Three years after graduation, she was offered a teaching position in the art department at Front Range Community College, where she taught painting three days a week. She rented an art studio off Main Street, and had monthly exhibits in support of new young artists. She even volunteered time at the Children's Museum on weekends, demonstrating painting techniques. Grace was excited to show Paul her current exhibit at the Louisville Center for the Arts. He was flying into Denver for Thanksgiving.

She worked in the kitchen preparing the feast. His flight landed in a few hours. Over the years she settled on a traditional menu: a twenty-pound turkey, her own stuffing recipe, asparagus, rice, candied yams, and homemade cranberry sauce and pumpkin pie. The turkey was already roasting, all the dishes were prepped and ready for the oven. Grace rolled the dough for pie crust while Michael lingered at the counter. He'd just been laid off at Papa John's and was a little down. "We have a lot to be grateful for, Michael. Don't look so down. Your Uncle Paul will be here soon."

"I know, Mom. Is Dad going to be here?"

"He's flying in this evening. He's picking Paul up at the airport."

"Will Uncle Paul remember me?"

"Sure he will. We sent him the family portrait last Christmas."

Grace rolled the dough flat and flipped it onto the pie tin. She deftly manipulated the dough with her thumbs and fingertips, filling the tin evenly around the edges. "Why don't you go take a shower?"

"I took one yesterday," he said.

"Really, Michael, yesterday?" she said, looking askance, but laughing on the inside. Michael reached over the counter to pluck a piece of dough from her hair. Grace wiped her hands on her apron, smiling at him, amazed at how adult he looked.

Grace put the pies in the oven, hoping that their flights were on time. She took a shower, carefully picking out a seasonal dress, her newest purchase from the thrift boutique on Main Street. She FaceTimed Emma in D.C. Emma was in preschool now, with three months of art displayed in her room. Emma walked around her gallery with Mimi's cell phone, acting like a docent for her grandmother. All the while, Grace kept her eye on the clock. The pies needed checking, and Ron and Paul would arrive soon.

They came in looking tired, but instantly invigorated by the sumptuous smells wafting from the kitchen. The front room was the de facto guest room. Grace showed Paul where he could put his things, a single sports bag, and took him on a tour of the house. She watched his face change when he spotted the family portrait she'd taken from Mom's closet the day they left Magnolia Street. "You were so cute," she said, pointing out his bow tie and Christmas sweater.

She was delighted that he noticed a few of the things she'd brought from Rush—the crucifix, the quilt Grandma D made for her wedding and *The Art of Happiness* by the Dali Lama. "That's a great book," he said. "I've got a copy back home." She showed him *Living Buddha, Living Christ* by Thich Nhat Hanh. He took it off the shelf and placed it on the table near his bag. "I'll look at that later," he said.

Grace was nervous, yet grateful to have Paul at Thanksgiving. Over the most difficult years in Rush and Las Vegas, he was the only one of her brothers to visit. They had much in common: art, a spiritual practice, and similar temperament. They'd both evolved beyond their blood family, and thrived. After a quick tour, they moved into the kitchen. "Have you spoken with Amber?" he asked.

Grace took the lid off the turkey, basted it, turning back to Paul with a shrug. "You would think Amber and I would be close after what we went through, but, sadly, that's not the case." Grace leaned across the counter on her elbows, facing her little brother. "She won't talk to me."

"Me neither," he added. "She's pissed at me for helping her move in with Denny. She thinks I abandoned her."

Grace straightened up. "All you did was help her move, right?"

"Well, I didn't want to keep saving her ass. She kept sleeping with her roommates."

Grace watched Paul's face grow dark. "I just didn't want to deal with it... It was like having a teenage daughter. Does that make me a bad person?" he asked.

Grace went to the coffee machine. She pointed to the pot. Paul nodded. Grace poured him a cup. She handed him the mug across the counter. They both recoiled into their own thoughts for a moment. Amber had that effect. It was impossible to maintain the perfect distance, while still loving her. Paul watched as Grace placed the yams in the oven. She settled on a stool at the counter, wiping her hands on a dish towel.

"It doesn't make you bad to do what's right for you. She isn't your daughter. If anyone is responsible, it's Dad."

The truth and weight of her words evaporated in anticipation of the Thanksgiving feast. The turkey spat in the oven. Water was running, Ron in the shower on the other side of the pantry wall. Grace wanted to tell Paul to move on. He should be proud of how far he'd come. She wanted him to see the grace in his life, how he'd been given a second chance after a rough start. "You pulled yourself up. We both did," she said. "Amber could never do that."

Michael walked into the kitchen, sleepy after a nap. He towered above both of them, with a boyish smile and bright dark eyes. He flowed to Paul and gave him a hug. "Hi, Uncle," he said with a broad smile. It was impossible to be serious with Michael around.

At the table, when it was time to say grace, Paul joined in. Grace felt a pull in her chest to see her little brother praying, across from her. Ron cut the turkey, and a guest knocked on the front door. It was one of her students who couldn't fly home for the holidays. He sat down at the table looking like he hadn't eaten in a week. He talked about what a great art teacher Grace was. He stole longing glances at Grace between bites, making her and Ron exchange looks.

Afterward, they lounged on the living room floor and easy chairs near Paul's air mattress. Grace brought out two family albums. "That's you, me and Amber on the porch in Magnolia," she said, pointing to a glossy, unfocused Polaroid. Amber was just out of diapers, with her mouth open...in mid-sentence.

"Why are you so dressed up?" Paul asked.

"Mom dressed us up for her parties." Grace paused, tentative, even after all the years, still stitching together the story, always struck by each surfacing detail. "You were too young to remember. When Dad left, Mom went crazy. She used to have parties. She dressed Amber and me up...she made us do things..."

Paul recoiled. "You were so young, and Amber," he said, incredulous.

"See that photo?" Grace said, pointing to a shot of herself in a mini-skirt and boots. "I was thirteen there. I wasn't a virgin."

Grace looked around the room. Ron, Michael and their guest were in the kitchen. She was glad they were alone. She stared at Paul's face. She could see no sympathy, nor any compassion, for that matter, just a blank stare, as if what she was saying was too much to bear.

After a moment he sighed loudly. "Dad always told us that Mom was a whore, that we should just forget about her, and you and Amber." He stood up. "Grace...I'm so sorry." Paul hugged her. It was a tardy gesture, she knew, but it was the only acknowledgment she'd ever received for those years. The room, its tight memories, book-lined walls, and the old family portrait held them in a murky shell.

"Thank you for saying so..."

It was getting late, and Ron was preparing to settle for the night. "It was great talking with you, Paul," Grace said.

"Me too," he said, giving her another hug.

The next day Grace drove Paul to the airport. She'd never told anyone in the family about what happened to her and Amber. At the curb she turned to him. "What I said stays between us, okay?"

Paul looked out the passenger window. He seemed to avoid her gaze. "We already knew," he said finally. "Just not the details. Steve told me. All I remember is that you took care of us." He was staring into her eyes now.

Grace pulled to the curb. "Thank you."

Paul squeezed her hand this time. It was as if a deal had been struck, formalized by contact. He grabbed his bag and headed toward the terminal. Grace watched him fade into the flow of foot traffic heading to the gates. Heading out of the airport and back toward the highway, Grace felt another layer of her past slough off. It was all out in the open—her life galvanized by shared memory: the abuse, the betrayal, the abandonment—at the hands of Mom and Dad.

Back in Louisville, she had a light-hearted life. She pulled into the driveway, turned off the engine and stared through the windshield. Sunlight washed over the frost-laden front yard, sparkling like earthbound stars. Grace thought of Emma, that she would grow up knowing a grandmother who was warm and caring, who was a success, wise and deep. She thought of Ron: he'd walked with her hand-in-hand, from homelessness to celebrated success. She thought of her boys, who'd become men under her guidance. Grace stepped out of the car wary of the icy driveway. She lurched onto the porch, strangely aware of a pressure in her palm as if a child had taken it. She squeezed her hand, chuckling at the strangeness of it. She walked through the front door, and head to the kitchen for a cup of tea.

#####

Amber could no longer see out of the windshield. The Fifth Avenue floated on an angry cloud. She peered out the side window, gauging her speed by the passing trees, and signs close enough to touch. The driver of the car behind her laid on the horn. "What the fuck do you want me to do?" she yelled at the dash. Amber stuck her arm out the window to signal the tailing car to pass. Steam stung her eyes, as she hurriedly rolled the window back up. The engine was barely responding, flat-lining in her hands. She put the gear shift in neutral, coasting down the off-ramp. She didn't recognize the stop. She was past Portland but hadn't hit Salem, she knew that much. A gust of wind cleared a line of vision, enough to see a gas station up ahead. Not a Chevron, or a Shell, but a local edifice, the last in a line of businesses, predating automobiles. The pumps were abandoned, a deathly thin teenager manned the cash register. A late model car hovered on jacks in the open garage. Amber steered the Fifth Avenue toward an open stall. A scarecrow with shoulder length white hair peered out from under the hood, strode to the opening, and waved her forward into the empty stall.

Amber waited with the window up until he sauntered over. "Looks like you've got some engine trouble," he said, with something between a smirk and pity on his face.

"Can you fix it? I need to make it to my Dad's in Grants Pass."

"Well, let's just look and see."

Amber went to the side of the garage while the mechanic worked on the Fifth Avenue. Her heart was still racing and she wished she hadn't drunk the three Pepsis on the way there. She held her cell phone with both hands, shaking. *I can't call Denny*, she thought. They'd all but broken up that morning. She was fleeing on impulse. She walked to the side of the old stone building where weeds had broken through neglected asphalt.

"Dad."

"Amber. Where are you?"

"My car broke down. The mechanic is working on it now. I'm sorry."

"It's not your fault. That Fifth Avenue is getting old."

Amber couldn't believe how old he sounded. It pricked her heart to imagine him dying alone. *One last job to do.* She was the only one in the family who could do it. If only he'd let her. "I might have to spend the night here, but I'm going to need money to pay the mechanic, and for a motel."

There was silence on the other end. Amber felt in her dress pocket for her cigarettes and lighter.

"Let me talk to the mechanic," he said, sounding agitated.

Amber walked back to the shop. The mechanic had the radiator off. She handed him her cell phone. Amber stood there as a smile spread across the mechanic's face. When he handed her phone back he said, "Looks like you got a sugar daddy."

Amber squinted at him. "He's my Dad," she stammered.

Amber carried the phone back to the overgrown side of the garage.

"Amber...it's all taken care of. There's a motel down the street from the gas station. Go there. The car will be ready in the morning."

Amber nodded. There was nothing left to say. He hadn't asked for her help but she knew he needed it. She wanted to cry. He came to her rescue. She couldn't depend on Denny, but Dad was there for her.

"Thanks, Dad." She wanted to tell him how much it meant to her, to massage the moment into a healthy relationship. Maybe they could finally talk about what happened. She was leveled by his next words.

"You don't need to come, Amber."

"But I'm—"

"I don't feel well. I'd be too grumpy."

"Let me take care of you." She really wanted to tell him that she couldn't go back, that she and Denny were finished. That he'd chosen Billy over her and she no longer had a home to go back to. "Dad, I really—"

"Goodbye, Amber." And then he hung up.

"I—"

The world stopped spinning. Amber stood there, so alone that even the trees seemed to taunt her solitude. It didn't matter if they kept the Fifth Avenue now. She started walking down the frontage road, kicking gravel, picking up speed toward the motel. She didn't want to fall apart out in the open where a stranger would undoubtedly come to her aid and she'd have to either lie or worse yet, tell them the truth. The mechanic called after her. She didn't hear him. The sinking feeling she'd weathered her entire life, since Grace had left, and Paul let her go, was gone. There was nowhere else to fall.

Amber spent the night in the motel room spiraling over the same old ground. The peach hued wallpaper with the leaping horse print seemed to get closer and closer as the night grew longer. She chain-smoked in her dress, lying on the bed with her shoes on. She heard a knock on the door around midnight, turned off the lamp and sat on the toilet, smoking, and listening. It was the night before Thanksgiving Day, and some family a few doors down was up with a crying baby. The shifting gears of eighteen wheelers on I-5 drew memories of Dad pulling up in that new truck back in Highland Park—taking Paul and Steve and Bryan away. At dawn's creeping glow she was seething. She knew what she was going to do. She didn't need anyone to do it. The next morning she drove back to the house.

The too-large house was empty again. Evidence of her former life, a troll doll, her cat clock, a photo of Reggie, failed to shake her resolve. Denny and Billy were at his family's. She wasn't invited, she was supposed to be at Dad's. The kitchen was as she left it.

*They'll be sorry. Serves them right. Serves them all right.*

Denny kept his pistol in a box in the closet of the master bedroom. Amber took the box down and stared at the pistol in her hands.

Amber walked to the couch, facing the front door. She leaned back on the couch, knowing that was how he would find her. She was tired, so sick and tired. She put the muzzle in her mouth and pulled the trigger. It was Thanksgiving Day.


#####


The news spread from sibling to sibling. They kept their grief to themselves in an unspoken pact whereby none of them need take responsibility for her choice. Dad received the news of her death without a hint of emotion. He continued to ask how she was doing, as if it never happened.

None of her blood family came forward to claim her belongings. Denny told Steve that she didn't have anything. Steve got the death certificate from the county so they could cremate Amber's body. Denny cried tears that he'd seemingly saved for just that moment. Paul was numb when he heard the news. He quit his teaching job a year later, unsure why he was no longer able to put his heart into his work. Grace was angry at first, taking on an additional class at Front Range Community College. Her days were filled with teaching, and she barely had enough time to paint. Later, she would admit that Amber's death changed her life, that it started an avalanche that would sweep her off the top of the mountain.


#####


The boardwalk was packed but the pier was strangely uninhabited for a weekend. Grace and Paul stood at the rail watching the sun peak out from behind an orange-black bank of clouds. They'd made a date after hearing of Amber's suicide. Venice was as beautiful as she remembered. The emotional tar they trudged through to get there was rewarded with a pristine day. Grace took a sabbatical: canceling classes at the museum, spending days on the phone with Paul, talking with Steve and Bryan for the first time in years. There was no funeral. It was January now, Amber's birthday month. The wind whipped the waves into a foamy mush. There were a few hardcore surfers on longboards bobbing on the horizon.

"I wish we'd done this sooner," Grace said, looking at Paul. He looked older now, although she'd just seen him at Thanksgiving. He shrugged. "You mean, *with* Amber," he said dropping his eyes.

"I've said it a thousand times, but it still doesn't seem to help," Grace started.

"What's that?" Paul asked.

"Amber didn't have a chance. She had absolutely nothing going for her."

"Don't you think it was a choice? We all have a choice," he said.

Grace didn't answer. She pulled a freezer bag from her pocket. It was half full of grey dust, Amber's ashes. "Let's do it together," she said, looking up into his face. "Maybe it'll bring closure." Grace didn't believe it, but it might for him. They both took a corner and let the bag tip. The dust caught the wind and rose toward the boardwalk. Paul groaned.

Grace threw the bag into the salty breeze. She didn't feel any different. They both watched as the bag fluttered, suspended briefly by a current, until it descended in grades, hiccuping on the fickle wind, disappearing into the shadows of the Santa Monica Pier.

#####

The snow had long since melted. It was graduation day at Front Range Community College Grace stood in her cap and gown, dizzy from the bottle of wine she'd drunk the previous night. She was still surprised that they'd asked her to give the commencement speech. Marcy helped her practice in front of the mirror. A bottle of wine later she'd had a meltdown, when all she could think about was Amber. The dais was filled now with her fastidious colleagues, with perfect postures and nervous smiles. A sea of black and white penguins with fresh faces, ready to take on the world, wiggled and chattered across the lawn. Grace clutched her notes like an ancient scroll, already feeling out of place and damp from the early Summer heat. Marcy sat in the first of the non-graduate rows beaming up at her, hair still wet from the shower she took at Grace's that morning. *She never had a chance.* The words kept repeating in her head. Each time she willed them into the shadows, they returned with greater force. Grace unrolled the scroll to scan her notes. It was nearly time. The Chair of the Art

Department crossed the stage, activating a current in the front row of students, rippling outward to the farthest rows.

In the brief pause, Grace rose on a barely perceptible signal and embraced the Dean at the podium. It was the pinnacle of her career in the visual arts. It was an unlikely but profound honor. She stood behind the podium and adjusted the microphone "Good afternoon, graduates," she began. A polite applause rose and fell like shore break.

"Amber..." Grace caught Marcy's eye and looked away. "...finds its origin in ancient trees and can be said to be the blood of trees. It is never alive, but seeps and is petrified, and over time, becomes precious, long after its living host has crumbled back to its roots." Grace clutched the scroll in her hand. Her lips lingered, inches from the microphone. A murmur swept through the crowd. She continued. "Amber does not change once it hardens. Thousands of years pass, and no matter its journey, Amber stays the same, a hardened artifact of its beginning." Tears filled Grace's eyes. She coughed and continued. "As you go forward into your lives some of you will find life unbearable and seemingly immutable. In those moments, remember that you are not your past. You are not petrified. You will always have the choice to be what you truly are. There is a benevolent spirit that lies within all of us. Seek it, and you will find yourself."

Grace didn't remember coming down from the podium. Marcy told her later that the Dean helped her off the dais, that she had taken her home and spent the night beside her. Grace remembered none of it. In fact, when she resigned from her position in the Art Department, surrendered her lease on the art studio and left her volunteer positions, essentially abandoning the career that defined her, they thought she'd lost her mind.

# Epilogue

She walks into the largest greenhouse she's ever seen. The atrium is wall-to-wall house plants, and as she makes her way to the nave, there is aisle upon aisle of racks with every kind of plant and flower stretching as far as the eye can see. Every sense is stimulated as she breathes in the myriad fragrances, takes a vase from a wood plank work table and retrieves blossom after blossom, as she works her way toward the rear atrium.

Grace is in heaven. She can't believe she gets paid to create art from nature's bounty. She stops in front of a canister of Magnolia blossoms. She glances up at the sound of fluttering wings. Another sparrow nesting in the rafters. *They love it just like I do*, she thinks. She moves across the Terra Cotta floor, a feature that shook her the first time she stepped foot into the expansive space. Grace peers down the aisle as far as her eyes can see. Her long white hair whirls about her shoulders, caressed by the overhead fans.

Emma is coming today. She is moving to Boulder to go to college. Grace walks down the aisle, stopping to examine a poinsettia, continues on and finds an exotic bloom that makes her gasp. When she has gathered a simple collection of flowers, Grace makes her way to the workstation near her office. It is early. Her co-workers have yet to arrive for the day's labor. It will be another long day: creating floral arrangements for a vast network of customers and vendors. *A labor of love*, she thinks, shuffling to a chair in the office.

Emma arrives carrying a tattered denim backpack and a daisy in her hair. They embrace and Grace mentions for the hundredth time how much Emma looks like Mimi, her mother. Emma is going to live with Michael in an apartment off-campus. Michael will always need a roommate. Grace gives Emma a tour of the facility which lasts until the workstations are buzzing with workers. Grace watches Emma's reaction in silence. She will never tire of the beauty of her life.

At the exit, Emma reminds Grace that she is coming for dinner that evening. Grace sees Emma's earrings for the first time, amber buds capturing the sun, and is inescapably imbued with the salty air of the Pacific Ocean.

Manufactured by Amazon.ca
Acheson, AB

11564747R00245